USA TODAY BESTSELLING AUTHOR OF *SUNSHINE BEACH*

WENDY WAX

> "[Wax] writes with breezy wit and
> keen insight into family relations."
> —*The Atlanta Journal-Constitution*

One Good Thing

A NOVEL

PRAISE FOR THE NOVELS OF WENDY WAX

"[A] sparkling, deeply satisfying tale."
—Karen White, *New York Times* bestselling author

"Wax offers her trademark form of fiction, the beach read with substance."
—*Booklist*

"Wax really knows how to make a cast of characters come alive . . . [She] infuses each chapter with enough drama, laughter, family angst, and friendship to keep readers greedily turning pages until the end."
—*RT Book Reviews*

"This season's perfect beach read!"
—Single Titles

"A tribute to the transformative power of female friendship . . . Reading Wendy Wax is like discovering a witty, wise, and wonderful new friend."
—Claire Cook, *New York Times* bestselling author of *Must Love Dogs* and *Time Flies*

"If you're a sucker for plucky women who rise to the occasion, this is for you."
—*USA Today*

"Just the right amount of suspense and drama for a beach read."
—*Publishers Weekly*

"[A] loving tribute to friendship and the power of the female spirit."
—*Las Vegas Review-Journal*

"Beautifully written and constructed by an author who evidently knows what she is doing . . . One fantastic read."
—Book Binge

"[A] lovely story that recognizes the power of the female spirit, while being fun, emotional, and a little romantic." —Fresh Fiction

"Funny, heartbreaking, romantic, and so much more . . . Just delightful!"
—The Best Reviews

"Wax's Florida titles . . . are terrific for lovers of women's fiction and family drama, especially if you enjoy a touch of suspense and romance."
—*Library Journal Express*

ONE GOOD THING

WENDY WAX

BERKLEY
NEW YORK

BERKLEY
An imprint of Penguin Random House LLC
375 Hudson Street, New York, New York 10014

Copyright © 2017 by Wendy Wax
"Readers Guide" copyright © 2017 by Penguin Random House LLC

Library of Congress Cataloging-in-Publication Data

Names: Wax, Wendy, author.
Title: One good thing / Wendy Wax.
Description: First Edition. | New York : Berkley, 2017.
Identifiers: LCCN 2016048899 (print) | LCCN 2016056299 (ebook) | ISBN
9780451488619 (paperback) | ISBN 9780451488626 (ebook)
Subjects: LCSH: Female friendship—Fiction. | BISAC: FICTION / Contemporary
Women. | FICTION / Romance / Contemporary. | FICTION / Humorous.
Classification: LCC PS3623.A893 O54 2017 (print) | LCC PS3623.A893 (ebook) |
DDC 813/.6—dc23
LC record available at https://lccn.loc.gov/2016048899

First Edition: April 2017

Printed in the United States of America
1   3   5   7   9   10   8   6   4   2

Cover art: *Close up of mojito* © by Anton Eine/EyeEm/Getty Images;
Tropical leaf pattern © by Kseniav/Shutterstock Images
Cover design by Rita Frangie
Book design by Kristin del Rosario

ACKNOWLEDGMENTS

E. L. Doctorow famously said, "Writing a novel is like driving a car at night. You can only see as far as your headlights, but you can make the whole trip that way."

Given the truth of this observation, I'd like to once again thank intrepid critique partners and extremely good friends Karen White and Susan Crandall for being in the car with me and for giving new meaning to the term "road trip."

Thanks also go to agent Stephanie Rostan for her continued efforts on my behalf and to the team at Berkley for all they do to bring my books into the world.

Most importantly, thank *you* for choosing this book and for getting in the car. I hope you enjoy the ride.

Prologue

Midlife crises come in all shapes and sizes. They can manifest in the form of a shiny red sports car, a distant mountain peak demanding to be scaled, a new head of hair, or a plastic bottle of little blue pills. Bertrand Baynard's starred an exotic dancer named Delilah with whom he fell in love, fathered a child, and ran away.

His wife, Bitsy, discovered this late one January afternoon when their private banker called to confirm that Bertie had transferred the last of their holdings to an offshore account in the Cayman Islands. And to let her know that the mortgage Bertie had taken out on their Palm Beach estate was seriously in arrears. Which was when she realized that Bertie was not actually in Aruba fishing as he'd claimed, but on his way to a shiny new life that did not include her.

Stunned and silent, she wandered the huge house and its lush grounds trying not to remember that it was Bertie who'd fallen in love with the aging Palladian villa and then overseen every detail of its three-year restoration. At night she lay awake in the bed they'd shared, staring up into the high shadowed ceiling, her cheeks and pillow damp with tears. *Bertie.* Whom Nicole Grant of Heart Inc. had found for her. Whom she had married and loved. And who had genuinely seemed to love her back, was gone. And he'd taken her money with him.

As a child, Bitsy had been slightly embarrassed by the size of her fortune and the fact that neither she nor her parents had had a hand in making it. In her teens she'd felt twinges of guilt that there were so many who had so little when she had so much. But while she had been an earnestly philanthropic adult, the millions she'd donated had been but droplets from the Amazonian-size river of money on which she'd floated. That river had lubricated all wheels, opened any door she'd chosen to walk through. Like a soft focus lens, it had tempered the adjectives used to describe her. Turned her horsey face "long," her too narrow nose "aristocratic," her scrawny body "fashionably slim."

She'd been so certain of Bertie's affection that she'd refused to let him sign the prenup he'd suggested. In their decade and a half of marriage, he had validated her faith in him and had even protected their financial reservoir from Malcolm Dyer's Ponzi scheme. When others had lost everything, her fortune had remained intact, free-flowing, and bottomless. She had never imagined that it could dry up or disappear. Or that the very person who had safeguarded it might simply walk away with it.

The sun was painfully bright and the sky a too cheery blue as she watched her possessions inventoried, tagged, and carried away by the auction company. She kept her chin up, her face carefully blank, and her eyes dry as the Lalique chandelier that had belonged to her grandmother and the Louis IX chairs that had been her mother's were loaded into the van.

It took two days to empty the house. When it was done, she felt the hollow ache of loss; a cessation of who she'd always been. Despite her philanthropy, her attempts to see herself as more than just a rich woman, it had always been her money that defined her.

Who was she without it? Where would she go? How would she live? She had an Ivy League education, a million volunteer hours, and no actual work experience. She knew how to throw a party, how to hire good help, how to make conversation, how to have a good time. She did not know how to be poor. And she had a sinking feeling she was not going to be good at it.

One

"Are we there yet?" Madeline Singer turned from a mango-streaked sky to look at the man beside her.

"Almost." William Hightower's eyes were dark, his tone mischievous, as he drove the Jeep south on US 1, which snaked through the Florida Keys and separated the Florida Bay from the Atlantic Ocean.

In her former life it had been Maddie's children, strapped into the backseat of her minivan, who'd asked if they were "there" yet. Somehow, and she still wasn't sure how, her life had rearranged itself. One minute she'd been a suburban housewife and mother facing the end of a quarter-century marriage and the world as she'd known it. The next she'd landed on Fantasy Island, aka Mermaid Point, a small private island in Islamorada that belonged to the recently rehabbed rock icon known as "William the Wild."

"That is so not an answer."

Will took one hand off the wheel to mime the zipping of his lips. Just shy of the 7 Mile Bridge, he took a right onto a sand-strewn road that led toward the bay. She laughed when she realized where they were. Another turn and the Jeep jounced across a rutted parking lot filled with cars. Music and light seeped out of a thatched-roof building built atop a series of docks.

"Bless you," she said as he parked facing the Keys Fisheries Market and Marina. "How did you know I needed a stone crab fix?"

"The entire population of the Florida Keys and everyone on Mermaid Point know about your addiction. I'm thinking there should be a seven-step program to help you get over it." Although Lifetime had sent Maddie, Avery Lawford, Nicole Grant, and the crew of their renovation-turned-reality TV show *Do Over* to turn Will's private island into a B and B, he'd managed to turn it into a sober living facility.

"I have no interest in getting over stone crabs. And it's not my fault the season's so short." Though she'd had an occasional stone crab claw in her lifetime, it wasn't until she'd come to the Keys and tasted her first that had been pulled from one of Will's own traps that she'd understood what the fuss was about.

A low building hugged the dock that stretched out into the bay, but Will led her up a narrow set of stairs to a large square of a room packed with people. The atmosphere was roadhouse honky-tonk. The material of choice was wood. A life-size tarpon hung on one wall. Another fish she could not identify dangled from a wooden rafter that spanned the pitched thatch ceiling. In keeping with the fish theme, people were packed in like sardines. The lucky ones sat at high tops; others hovered, drinks in hand, chatting while they waited for a table or chairs to open up.

They stood for a moment in the narrow entrance. To the left, mounds of stone crab claws sat in bins of ice while a young man precracked shells and filled cardboard baskets a dozen at a time.

To the right, a lone guitar player perched on a stool, his bearded face grizzled, his fingers gnarled yet agile on the strings. A bar ran along the wall beyond him. The signage was belligerently instructive. One read simply, *Claws and Straws.* Another listed rules for stone crab claw ordering and eating that ended with, *No kids. No TV. No butter. No exceptions.*

"Hey, Will." The musician nodded at Will then smiled at Maddie as they passed. Eyes noted and followed their progress, but no one yelled or aimed a phone at them. "Looks like a mostly local crowd," he said quietly. "I doubt anyone will bother us."

Maddie didn't ask how he knew this, but her shoulders began to relax. She had never aspired to being the center of attention and had already experienced far more than her fifteen minutes of fame.

A skyscraper of a man leaning on the bar shook Will's hand. "Good to see you, man."

"Likewise." Will placed an order for a dozen claws and a Coke. "Wine, Maddie?"

"Thanks." She still marveled at his strength; the way he'd come out of rehab two years ago then reclaimed his life and rejoined the world. Their gazes got tangled up in each other's and she had to force herself to look away. At sixty-two, William Hightower was, as her daughter, Kyra, had pointed out more than once, "hot as hell." The black hair that brushed his broad shoulders was threaded with gray, but his features were still sharp and angled. His dark eyes missed little. Exactly why he was in a relationship with her—well, she'd promised she would stop asking herself this question—but even roughhewn fish-themed honky-tonks had shiny surfaces.

He found a half-empty table in a corner and asked the couple if they could join them. The man, a retired New York policeman, nodded amiably and introduced himself as Jake. His wife, Ingrid, stuttered hello in almost exactly the same way Maddie had when she'd first arrived on Mermaid Point and discovered it belonged to the Southern rocker whose poster had once hung on her bedroom wall. Only Maddie's stutters had been captured by a *Do Over* cameraman and broadcast to a television audience.

Will talked fishing with Jake for a few minutes then shifted slightly so that his back was to their tablemates. Maddie sipped her wine and did her best not to notice the number of women who watched Will as he went to retrieve their order. He returned with a container of claws, which he placed between them. Despite the precracking, a certain amount of effort and skill was required to get every last centimeter of crab. The process was messy but worth it. Maddie wiggled the joints, extracted a good-size bite, dipped it in the mustard sauce, and placed it in her mouth. She closed her eyes in unfeigned ecstasy. "God, that's good." She finished the claw then reached for another, making quick work of each one and celebrating whenever she pried free a large, intact piece. The claws gave up their sweet meat under their determined assault. Will was a far more experienced claw cracker and eater. The mound of shells grew. She looked up to find him watching her in amusement. "What?"

"It's nice to see a woman who isn't afraid to have an appetite."

She met his eyes as heat spread across her cheeks. William Hightower had brought out all kinds of things in her that would have been downright shocking if she hadn't been so busy enjoying them.

"You up for another dozen?"

She considered the offer as she inserted a tiny fork into a crevice to get the last bit of crabmeat. "I'd say yes except then I might not have room for key lime pie."

"Now that would be a tragedy." He watched her set down the fork and lick her fingers. His eyes darkened the way they did when he was taking off her clothes, pulling her into bed. He handed her a wet nap. "You have about two seconds to wipe that sauce off your mouth. Or I'm likely to kiss it off."

This time the heat spread a lot farther than Maddie's cheeks. Ingrid whimpered then looked Maddie up and down, clearly searching for some explanation of what William Hightower saw in her. Maddie, who understood her confusion, took the wet nap and dabbed at the corners of her mouth. She and Will said their good-byes and carried their trash to the container. Moments later they were out on the docks. The music and noise fell away. Boats bobbed gently at their moorings. Light glittered on the dark surface of the water. They ordered a piece of pie to share and carried it outside to a favorite picnic table overlooking the water. She leaned on the dock railing to look down at the spotlit water. The dark shapes of fish moved beneath the surface.

They sat side by side and dawdled over the pie—an everyday activity heightened by his nearness and made perfect by the soft breeze off the water, the occasional splash of a fish, the soft clank of lines against a mast.

"They're sending us out on a bigger tour to help support the album."

"Oh."

When they'd met, he'd been virtually hiding out on Mermaid Point, his career in tatters, unable to make music. Then he'd written "Free Fall," put together a band, and begun playing local gigs. His old record label had come calling. They'd thrown enough money at him to fund the sober living facility he'd named in honor of the younger brother who'd lost his life to the same excesses that had almost claimed Will.

"They were happy with the response in the small venues we played and seem to feel we can draw bigger crowds."

She heard the hesitation in his voice, saw the uncertainty

on his face. She had her own misgivings, which she was trying her best not to telegraph. She was happy for his success and wished him more, but as much as she enjoyed being with him, she couldn't imagine their relationship surviving the Rock God status Will was on his way to reclaiming. "Don't you want to go?"

"Part of me is thrilled. Part of me doesn't want to have anything to do with it." His smile was crooked. His tone was rueful. "I know what it's like on the road. And it doesn't bear any similarity to real life."

"I've seen articles about performers who travel with personal trainers and chefs and, you know, whatever they need," she said. "It could be different this time around."

"Yeah. I have the file you've been amassing," he said lightly. "I know it must be possible. For some."

"You can do anything you set your mind to, Will. You've proved that already." She looked down at the shadowy fish, the pie crumbs on the plate. Once he was back at the top, evenings like this would be a memory. "Not everyone gets a second chance like this."

"No," he said softly. "They don't. I'm lucky to be alive. Alive and making music? That's a total miracle and way more than I deserve. But . . ."

"But what?"

"But we're looking at three to four months of nonstop travel and performing. I'd like . . . I'd like you to come with me. You know, for the whole tour. I trust myself." He swallowed and met her eyes. "But I trust myself more when I'm with you."

She saw what the admission cost him. He'd gotten sober and stayed that way through sheer dint of will and what might have been millions of laps in the swimming pool. But addictions didn't disappear; they were overcome and fought off forever.

Maddie dropped her eyes to the empty plate, the taste of key lime tart on her tongue. The mother in her, the nurturer/caregiver wanted to say yes, wanted to be there for him. But she'd spent most of her life being there for others. For her husband. For her children. More recently for her grandson and the women who'd become her closest friends. She'd learned a lot of things about herself when her husband lost everything, including his job and himself, to Malcolm Dyer's Ponzi scheme. She'd become far stronger than she'd ever imagined. What she had never learned to do was to put herself first.

"I don't see how I can be gone that long." She'd been here for two weeks and knew she had to get back to Bella Flora, the castle-like beachfront home that was all she, Avery, and Nikki had left after their losses to Malcolm Dyer and which now belonged to Maddie's daughter, Kyra. The network they'd quit so publicly on Mermaid Point was suing them for breach of contract and claiming that the name *Do Over* did not belong to them. "We have the lawsuit to deal with and Kyra is trying to edit the special on the Sunshine Hotel together so it can be sold. And Nikki's twins are due next month. I promised I'd be there to help. She and Joe are moving into his new cottage at the Sunshine Hotel soon."

"I get it," Will said. "Four months on the road is a lot to ask."

She looked into Will's eyes and wished once again that she could see herself the way he seemed to see her. But at midnight this New Year's Eve, she had made a resolution. She had promised herself that she would learn to be more than an appendage. That she would live her own life and not just live to support others'.

She reached for his hand and squeezed it. "I love being with you, Will. And I'm happy to come visit you here or on the road as often as possible. I want you in my life." She swallowed and almost whispered, "But I can't let you *be* my life. I'm fifty-two years old and I think it's time I finally figure out who I am and what I want to be when I grow up."

Will nodded but said nothing. It took every ounce of will-power Maddie possessed not to change her mind or her answer. It seemed that growing up could be painful no matter when you chose to do it.

Two

Nicole Grant no longer recognized herself. Her body had ballooned into a blimp-size storage facility for the two babies that floated inside it, fighting for elbow room. Her skin stretched tight across the massive protrusion that had once been her stomach. Her breasts were the size and consistency of overinflated basketballs, her face red and splotchy and dotted with pimples. Her auburn hair hung dull and lifeless while the brain it encased had taken to misfiring and short-circuiting without warning or apology.

And then there were her moods, which had stabilized during the middle months of her pregnancy, but which now swung this way and that like a metronome sprung from its housing. With a groan of effort, she attempted to roll onto her side. She was half-way there when a muscled arm reached out to pull her up against a rock-hard abdomen. That abdomen belonged to Special Agent Joe Giraldi. Whose gold medal sperm had found and fertilized the eggs she'd believed were way beyond their expiration date. His large hand curled protectively against her stomach as he placed a kiss on the top of her head. "Are you okay?"

"I'd be better if I could actually turn over on my own. Or think. Or stop peeing every two minutes," she murmured. "Seeing my feet would be nice."

"It won't be long now," he said, his hand lightly stroking her stomach, his tone meant to reassure.

But then Joe had none of the fears or doubts that stalked her. She was eight months pregnant. If nothing went wrong, she would be the thing she'd given up on long ago and failed at so spectacularly as far as her younger brother was concerned. She would be a mother.

As if in response to the thought, a soccer-strength kick landed beneath Joe's hand. A second came swift and sure from the side. "They're fighters." His breath was warm against her ear. She could feel him smiling.

"They're girls," she reminded him.

"All the more reason for them to know how to fight," he said. "Like their mother."

"Do you have to see the bright side of everything?"

"Can't help it," he replied easily. "I can't think how things could be better."

"That's because you aren't carrying them around in your stomach. And they're not sitting on your bladder."

"True." But he smiled as he said it.

Being married might be better, she thought but did not say. Because she had refused him one too many times and he'd taken the offer off the table with no sign of renegotiation.

Today they would drive up to Pass-a-Grille, a trip that would have only taken about four and a half hours if she didn't need so many potty breaks. There they would move into the two-bedroom cottage Joe had purchased at the Sunshine Hotel, which she, Madeline and Kyra Singer, and Avery Lawford had recently renovated for what they'd hoped would be their own version of *Do Over*.

Joe slid out of bed naked and gorgeous. Not for the first time she wished that men carried the babies. That it was their skin that stretched to the breaking point and then sagged. She pulled on her robe as she struggled to sit up. She saw him bite back a smile as he reached out a hand to help her to her feet.

"It's not funny."

He headed to the kitchen while she padded into the bathroom to wash her face and brush her teeth. And, of course, to pee. When she got to the kitchen, her juice and prenatal vitamins awaited her. She downed the juice and the horse-size pills looking enviously at the cup of fresh-brewed coffee in Joe's hand. She wasn't a caffeine addict like Avery and had typically preferred a morning run to a morning coffee, but there was something about knowing you couldn't have a thing that made you want it desperately. She sighed and barely resisted cozying up to him in order to steal a sniff of the dark roast.

"How long do you need to get ready?"

"Not long." In truth she had no idea if this was true or not. Her sense of time and timing had decamped along with her brain cells. She'd spent the last two days dithering over what to take and what to leave behind. Often she got lost mid-thought or mid-task. She looked around Joe's living room, at the spot where the Christmas tree had stood. At the dining room table where his large Italian family had gathered for large pasta-filled meals. His parents were excited about their new grandbabies; his Nonna Sofia had looked smug, as if it had in fact been her fertility curse that was responsible for Nikki's pregnancy. Everyone had fed her and pampered her. Only Joe's sister, Maria, had watched her carefully as if trying to understand how her brother had chosen Nikki and whether or not something should have been done about it.

She'd felt her guard slipping on occasion, imagining how it would feel to be a part of a large, loving, involved family like his. Her own childhood had been spent in poverty, and when her father had died, her mother had worked multiple jobs to keep a roof over their heads. Nicole had "mothered" her brother, Malcolm, while their mother worked. Thereby creating a conscienceless human being who currently resided in a correctional facility for the criminally greedy.

"Nikki?" Joe said, taking her by the shoulders and turning her gently toward the bedroom. "Why don't you go finish packing? I'll start loading the cars."

"I think we should have just towed the Jag," he said an hour later when both cars were ready. He'd wanted to leave the Jag in his garage, but she'd refused. The '74 XKE had been her first splurge when Heart, Inc., had become successful, one of the few things she hadn't sold when she was bankrupted by her brother's Ponzi scheme. It had become a symbol for all that she'd achieved and who she'd managed to become. She'd vowed they'd have to pry the keys out of her cold, dead fingers. More than that, she needed to keep it for when things went south and she lost everything, including Joe and the life he envisioned for all of them.

"Seriously, Nikki. I'd feel better if we drove together." He opened the door of the shiny new SUV and waited for her to get situated.

"I'm not an invalid. I'm capable of driving." In truth, the SUV he'd insisted on buying had so many buttons and features, it could have launched a lunar probe and could undoubtedly have driven itself. "We're caravanning. It's not like I'm taking off to climb Kilimanjaro on my own."

She saw the set of his jaw war with the flicker of amusement in his dark eyes. As an FBI agent, he'd sworn to protect and defend. The day he'd found out she was pregnant, which was far later than it should have been, his protective instincts had warped into overdrive. "I really think we should have planned to move directly into the cottage," he said. "We could have furnished it ahead of time so it would be ready for us."

"We can stay at Bella Flora as long as we like and take our time furnishing and moving in," Nikki said for what might have been the hundredth time. "There's no rush." Kyra had made it clear they were always welcome. It was as close to a home as Nikki had at the moment.

"You're thirty-two weeks, Nik. Most twin pregnancies don't go past thirty-five or thirty-six." Mercifully, he didn't add that at forty-seven, she was unlikely to go even that long. Joe had read her copy of *What to Expect When You're Expecting* cover to cover as if it were a training manual, which she guessed it was. "We should at least furnish the nursery."

She busied herself rearranging the things on the passenger seat. She was afraid that furnishing a nursery would tempt fate, that it would somehow trigger the ultimate karmic payback for all her failings. Because deep down she didn't see how this could all work out. Not the babies. Not Joe's love. Not having a real family of her own. These were things that she'd only seen from afar, things that other people had and that she did not deserve.

Once Nikki had had her brain, her body, and a seemingly unlimited supply of ambition and persistence. She'd parlayed them into a career as an A-list matchmaker and dating guru with offices on both coasts. She'd excelled at assessing personal attributes and attraction. She'd brought people together, brokered their relationships, and paved their way to the altar. A belief in "Happily Ever After" had not been part of the job description. And she had never imagined that those words could ever apply to her.

. . .

Avery Lawford dropped the screwdriver into its slot in the worn leather tool belt that had belonged to her father. As she stepped back to look at the cabinet door she'd just rehung, she drew the scent of freshly sawn wood into her lungs then tilted her head to better hear the whir of the electric saw slicing through a two-by-four. Others might meditate, strike a happy baby pose on their yoga mat, or pour a stiff drink. Avery had grown up on her father's construction sites. For her, the aromas and sounds of construction were automatic stress busters. Sometimes when Chase Hardin was nearby, those scents and sounds qualified as foreplay.

"You okay?" Chase turned off the saw and set it aside then removed his goggles. His bright blue eyes narrowed.

"Um-hmm." She brushed a stray blond curl out of her eyes and had to crane her neck to meet his gaze. In her mind she might be tall and lanky, but in reality she was short and curvy, with a bust that was too large for the rest of her. That bust combined with Kewpie doll features caused strangers to automatically deduct IQ points and talk *reeeeaaaal slowwwwllly*.

"I know that look," he said, taking a step toward her.

"You're a smart man."

Interest flared in his eyes. "Hmmm. A compliment. That can only mean . . ." He closed the distance between them and slid his arms around her waist. His hands cupped her bottom. "If *Do Over* doesn't get figured out, I think we should move forward with the construction-scented perfume and cologne line."

She tried to push the words *Do Over* out of her mind so that she could focus on the way he was nuzzling her. His lips nibbling her earlobe. The press of his body against hers.

But if construction scents were a turn-on, thinking about the remodeling-turned-reality TV show that seemed to be slipping through their fingers and could cost them what little they had was the anti-aphrodisiac. So was the slam of the front door and the heavy footsteps that thudded through the hall and toward the kitchen, where she and Chase had been lowering cabinets to accommodate his father's wheelchair.

Jason, Chase's youngest son, stomped into the kitchen. At sixteen he was even taller and broader than his father. Over the last months his open face had closed, his once sunny personality had turned increasingly dark and unpredictable. He snorted when they pulled apart, his expression making it clear that he thought them far too ancient to be caught in lip-lock.

"Where have you been?" Chase asked quietly, keeping one arm around her.

"Practice."

Chase said nothing, but he'd gone still.

"Where else would I be?" Jason taunted. "Isn't that where I always am?"

Jason and his older brother, Josh, had been in love with baseball practically from birth, or so family lore went. Jason had made varsity as a freshman and was now Hamden High School's most efficient closer. Josh, a senior and first baseman, had been awarded a full ride to Clemson next fall.

"There was a time when I would have said yes," Chase replied through tight lips. "But Coach Jenkins called. He wanted to see if you were feeling better. Given that you haven't been at practice all week. A scout from Clemson was there today to watch you."

Jason's jaw clenched. His look said, "So what are you going to do about it?"

Avery put a cautioning hand on Chase's arm. The blowups between father and son had become more frequent and explosive. Chase seethed with tension. "Whether you continue playing or not is up to you," he finally said. "But you're a member of a team and it's wrong to let your coach and teammates down. If you want to quit, quit. Don't go to college." He shrugged as if it didn't matter to him one bit. She might have bought it if it weren't for the quivering of his muscles. His jaw had gone hard and his eyes had darkened to navy. "You have enough experience to work construction pretty much anywhere. But as long as you're under my roof, you will be civil and you will keep your commitments."

"And if I don't want to live under your stupid roof anymore?" The challenge came out in a rush of anger. Jason's chin shot up. His hands fisted at his sides.

"Chase . . ." She grasped his arm more tightly.

He shook her off.

"Chase. Please!"

"He's my son," he snapped. "I'll deal with him."

"Yeah, just like you deal with everything," Jason taunted. "Just like you know what's best for everybody all the frickin' time."

She took Chase's arm again and this time she held on to it as she watched the hurt and anger suffuse his face. She wanted to take him in her arms and comfort him almost as much as she wanted to shake the two of them. But she knew from experience that this might only make things worse. She stood, feeling helpless, unable to help, unable to leave.

"Who died and put you in charge?" Jason sneered out his fury.

"Your mother," Chase said, slowly spearing his son with his eyes. "And this is the first time I've been glad she's not here to see how the baby she loved so dearly is turning out."

Three

As far as Kyra Singer was concerned, being a grown-up was nowhere near as easy as her mother had always made it look. At twenty-seven, she was the single mother of three-year-old Dustin and the creator and producer of *Do Over*, which the network had hijacked and then refused to let them quit. She was also the current owner of Bella Flora, the 1920s Mediterranean-revival-style mansion Dustin's movie star father had bought for them and which she had put at risk.

At the moment, Bella Flora's formal dining room was doing double duty as a video-editing suite. Her crystal chandelier, each glass drop of which her mother had painstakingly cleaned by hand, spread shards of light over the piles of notes, the dual monitors, and the keyboards. Troy Matthews, former network cameraman and ongoing pain in the ass, sat beside her, his fingers nimble on the keys, as he attempted to cue up an edit point.

"Kyra?"

"Hmm?"

"I said I think we should insert the purple cow shot here. Or maybe the one with the polka-dotted palm tree if you like that better."

"No, I don't like either of those. They're too . . ." Disagreement was quick and automatic. Registering what had been said took longer. "What did you just say?"

"Just checking. I thought you might be sleeping with your eyes open."

She opened her mouth to argue again, but Troy was right. She hadn't been listening. Or watching. Or thinking. Her brain had been fully occupied playing out potential worst-case scenarios, of which there were many.

The most troubling was the network's lawsuit, designed to force them back to work on the insulting and unflattering reality TV version of what they'd intended as a remodeling show. And the hard money loan she'd taken out against Bella Flora to finance their attempt to produce their own series.

At the moment their only real hope of income was finishing and selling the documentary of their renovation of the midcentury Sunshine Hotel featuring the reopened investigation into a mysterious death and disappearance that had taken place there. Or having every single cottage at the Sunshine sold at top dollar. But being under this much pressure didn't make for a whole lot of clear or creative thinking. How her mother had kept them all afloat when their father had lost everything including his job to Malcolm Dyer's Ponzi scheme, she did not know.

"Personally, I don't know if we should include this bit." The scene was of Daniel and Dustin playing catch on the beach in front of the Sunshine Hotel.

"You're the one who's been preaching that we need the money shots to build and hold on to an audience. Feel free to cut it out." At three, her son was a carbon copy of his famous father. But while Daniel Deranian had built an audience intentionally, their son had had no choice and was as familiar with paparazzi as most three-year-olds were with *Sesame Street.*

"Yeah, well, I'm getting kind of tired of looking at his face." Troy paused on a close-up of Daniel and began to examine it. Daniel's dark curly hair, golden skin, and whiskey-colored bedroom eyes were instantly recognizable and more than a mere mortal woman could resist, as she had reason to know. If Troy was looking for a bad side, he was out of luck.

"I think perfection is overrated," Troy said. "The guy's in his forties and he doesn't even have a frickin' wrinkle?" His fingers flew over the keyboard. "Where's the reality in that?"

"He's got good genes," she snapped, stung. Genes he'd passed on to Dustin, who was his only biological son.

"Now, his wife, well, you expect female movie stars to stay beautiful." He pulled up a barrage of photos of Tonja Kay. Vindictive, foul-mouthed, and angelically beautiful Tonja Kay. "But you want to see guys look like real guys."

"Are you saying Daniel isn't masculine enough?"

"Well, he is kind of a pretty boy." Troy smirked.

"I think we'd be a lot better off getting this video put together than discussing Daniel's face. Or his masculinity." Her voice rose. "Which FYI—is not in question."

"Whatever you say."

She watched his hands move over the controls, watched the frames of video go by. Watched him find the edit point and add just the right beat of transition before the next shot. Even his competence grated. He'd appeared last summer claiming he'd been fired from the network for giving her an advance copy of *Do Over* season two, which Nikki had used to hook Palm Beach matron Bitsy Baynard as a sponsor. He'd said that he'd been accused of aiding and abetting the "enemy" after they'd quit the network. He was currently sharing the pool house with her father and seemed in no hurry to leave.

Troy stopped shuttling between shots. Slowly, he turned to face her. "It's going to be okay," he said. "The attorneys will figure it out." His features had gone strangely soft. She barely recognized his voice without its usual mocking sarcasm. "And if we get this special where it needs to be, I'm sure we can sell it."

She blinked, but the trademark smirk and sarcasm were absent. It was like seeing Jim Carrey without the stretched-out face. Or the night sky devoid of stars. She wasn't buying it. "Wow. What was that? Are you searching for your feminine side? Or doing an impression of Pollyanna?"

He shrugged and looked away. "I just don't want you caving under the pressure, that's all. There are a lot of moving parts right now. Producing and selling a series isn't exactly a walk in the park."

"Thanks for the advice," she managed through gritted teeth. "I'll be sure and let you know when I need you to spout some more clichés."

"Suit yourself," he said with a careless shrug. His eyes were once again taunting. And his normal shit-eating grin was back in place.

• • •

Maddie drove over the final span of the Sunshine Skyway, which soared high above Tampa Bay, and took the Pinellas Bayway west to St. Petersburg Beach, where she was deposited directly in front of the massive Don CeSar Hotel. There she headed south into the Historic District of Pass-a-Grille, passing the hedges that hid the Sunshine Hotel from view and ultimately turning onto the aptly named Gulf Way. Drawing in a deep breath of salt-tinged air, she watched a formation of seagulls sweep out of a puffy white cloud, saw the sea oats sway lightly in the breeze. Islamorada was beautiful and her time on Mermaid Point with Will was exciting, but this stretch led to *home*. The blocks were short and the avenues, which stretched from the bay to the Gulf, were barely longer. She took her time passing the crossovers and dunes on her right and the hodgepodge of mom-and-pop hotels and newly renovated homes on her left.

At the southernmost tip stood Bella Flora. Built at the same time as the Don CeSar, it had the same fresh-from-a-bakery-box look with pale pink walls and white icing trim framing banks of arched windows. Bell towers topped a multi-angled barrel tile roof and jutted up into the bright blue sky. She'd barely pulled into the brick driveway when the front door flew open and Dustin came bounding across the loggia, down the front steps, and through the garden to reach her.

"Geema!" he shouted happily as he threw himself in her arms and buried his face in her neck. She held his sturdy body tight and spun him around.

"I see the mutual admiration society is in session," Kyra said, coming to join the group hug. "We missed you. Bella Flora's pretty fabulous, but even she's not the same without you."

"And I missed both of you!" Maddie said, giving them each a last heartfelt squeeze. "You'll have to fill me in."

"What I can carry, Geema?" Dustin asked.

Maddie opened the rear sliding door of the minivan, retrieved an overnight and makeup bag, and placed them carefully in his arms. "These are very important," she said solemnly as Dustin puffed up with pride. "And there may even be a present in there for you."

Together they carried her things inside. Her ex-husband stood in the high-ceilinged foyer, his expression far too eager. "Why don't you let Dustin and I carry your bags upstairs?" Steve asked.

"Thank you," Maddie said, keeping her voice and expression friendly but neutral. When she'd vowed to "get her own life," she'd vowed to stop trying to "get one" for Steve, too. But after two children and more than a quarter century of marriage, this was easier said than done.

She linked her arm through Kyra's as they headed for the kitchen. Late afternoon sun slanted in through the windows that overlooked the pool and the pass, where the Gulf of Mexico bled into the bay. The Spanish tile floor, reclaimed wood countertops, and soft green glass-fronted cabinets that Deirdre Morgan had chosen welcomed and comforted. "I heard from Nikki while I was on the road. She and Joe should be here before sunset and Avery's on her way from Tampa. Is there anything here for dinner or should we run to the store?"

"Let's leave the store for tomorrow," Kyra said. "I've got plenty of snacks and I'm pretty sure there's red and white wine. And maybe we can send the guys out for pizza while we catch up."

"Sounds good. Sunset's not far off. It's not quite as warm as the Keys, but if we bundle up a bit, it should be perfect."

"I'm in," Kyra said. "It'll be nice to have everybody together. It's been kind of quiet here."

"How's your dad been doing?" Maddie asked as she helped herself to a glass of water.

"Well, he did pass the real estate exam. And John Franklin suggested that he hang his license with him."

"And?"

"I don't know. He said he'd consider it, but he still seems kind of stuck." Steve had fallen apart when he'd lost everything, including his job, to Malcolm Dyer's Ponzi scheme. Their marriage hadn't ended because he'd lost everything, but because he'd never forgiven her for carrying on when he couldn't.

"Well, maybe we need to push a little harder to get him unstuck," Maddie said before she could stop herself. "No, strike that. This is his life. He needs to figure it out for himself."

"I don't know, Mom. I don't think he's all that motivated. And I don't think he knows how to live on his own."

Maddie kept her mouth carefully closed. Steve Singer was no

longer her husband. What he did with his life was not her responsibility or even her business.

A tap of the horn announced Avery's arrival and there were hugs all around. Avery had opened both bottles of wine and filled a large bowl with Cheez Doodles by the time Joe and Nikki arrived. Joe looked calm and collected as always. Nikki not so much.

"Wow, look at you!" Avery said, taking in Nikki's huge stomach.

"Please don't. I try not to," Nikki replied.

"I think you look beautiful," Maddie said, slipping an arm around Nikki's shoulders as Joe sent her a grateful smile. "And so do those babies. May I?" She reached a hand out toward Nikki's stomach.

"Have at it. I think they're as tired of sitting in that car as I am." She stretched and yawned.

"I'll grab our things," Joe said. "Do you want to lie down?"

"No, thanks." Nikki yawned again.

"We'll get her a seat outside for sunset. Are you up for going out with the guys for pizza?" Maddie asked Joe.

"Sounds like a plan," Joe said easily, but he looked closely at Nikki as if to assure himself she was really okay.

Nikki yawned again and rotated her head on her neck, clearly trying to work out some kinks.

"I can't believe you drove," Avery said. "Doesn't your stomach get in the way?"

"Yeah, well, I wish you all had been there to talk her out of it," Joe said. "I have hostage negotiation training, and I'm powerless to convince her of anything." His tone was light but Maddie could see the concern in his eyes.

"Well, fortunately, you both made it. And no one looks the worse for wear," Maddie said.

"So you never practiced on a woman pumped full of pregnancy hormones?" Avery asked.

Nikki snorted and helped herself to a handful of Cheez Doodles.

"Nope," Joe said. "But I think I'm going to suggest they add it to the curriculum at Quantico." He smiled and pinched a Cheez Doodle. "I've faced a lot of challenges on the job, but I'd sleep a little better at night if I knew the FBI had the ability to talk a pregnant woman into laying down her weapon. You know, just in case the need ever arose."

Four

It was just past six P.M. and the winter sun hung low over the Gulf of Mexico. The beach was quiet, the swish of the tide soft as a whisper. A lone fisherman stood on the jetty.

Avery sat on the rear loggia with Maddie, Nikki, and Kyra, watching the sky pinken. Bella Flora hunkered protectively behind them, her thick walls swathed in shadow.

"So?" Maddie said.

"So what?" Kyra asked.

"So, anyone have a good thing they want to share?" It had been Maddie, whose picture belonged in the dictionary next to the definition of "mother," who'd come up with sharing "one good thing" at sunset back when all of their lives had been decimated by Malcolm Dyer's Ponzi scheme and they were first trying to nurse Bella Flora back to life. Then, coming up with one good thing had been almost as challenging as rebuilding the house that was their lone remaining asset along with their lives.

The mother who had abandoned Avery to become an interior

designer to the stars had been a part of that rebuilding. Deirdre Morgan's touch could be felt in every inch of Bella Flora. She'd returned determined to repair her relationship with her daughter and had begged Maddie to teach her how to be a mother. Deirdre had died on Mermaid Point, just when Avery had finally begun to accept her.

She thought about the strain between Chase and his son and wished she'd taken mothering lessons herself. Her eyes moved to Nikki's stomach as the woman shifted uncomfortably in her seat.

"I gorged on stone crab claws last night at the Keys Fisheries," Maddie offered when no one spoke. "And Will and the band are being sent on a major tour to support their album." Maddie's smile remained bright, but there was far more enthusiasm behind the first statement than the second. She turned to her daughter. "Kyra?"

"Okay," Kyra began tentatively. "The special on the Sunshine Hotel is looking pretty good." From Kyra this was high praise. "And Troy seems to think we can sell it even with the lawsuit going on." Her smile did not dim but her tone said she doubted it.

Maddie's gaze turned to Avery.

"Chase and I finished adapting the kitchen for his dad's wheelchair. Jeff's always been so active, he's having a hard time adjusting. We're hoping that helping him become more self-sufficient at home will help."

Nikki shifted in her seat again. She grasped the arms of the chair and attempted to pull her body into another position. "Okay, so I can't help noticing that everybody's 'one good thing' is sounding a lot more like good news/bad news."

"So now *you're* the 'good enough' police?" Avery asked.

"No, I'm just saying it would be nice to hear one good thing that doesn't require a qualifier."

"Well, why don't *you* give it a go," Avery said.

Clutching her protruding stomach so that it moved with her,

Nikki made another attempt to reposition herself in the chair. "That is not gonna happen. I can't sleep, I can barely walk or hold on to a thought for more than ten seconds. And sitting totally sucks. I can't imagine ever being comfortable again." Nikki's sigh was closer to a groan. "And as you've probably noticed, I can't seem to stop whining about it."

"But soon you'll have two daughters to show for it," Maddie, their resident glass-is-half-full proponent, pointed out.

"Right," Nikki said without an ounce of conviction. Beads of perspiration dotted her upper lip despite the dropping temperatures. Her eyes fixed on Avery's wineglass. "And at the moment I'd kill for even a sip of alcohol."

Avery stopped chewing her Cheez Doodle. She would have washed it down with wine but decided it would be better—and probably safer—not to wave her glass in front of Nikki.

"Joe seems wonderfully patient and very loving," Maddie added, still focused on the bright side. "I understand his family is coming for the birth."

Nikki nodded miserably. Even in the dark, Avery could see the tears glistening in her eyes. "They're taking rooms next door." She nodded vaguely toward the Cottage Inn, which sat to the east of Bella Flora. Her lips twisted in a rictus of a smile as a lone tear slid down her cheek.

Nikki's phone rang.

"Do you need to take that?" Maddie asked quietly.

Nikki sniffed and squinted at her screen. "It's Bitsy Baynard. I'll call her back tomorrow."

"Well, be nice to her," Avery said. "She put money into the Sunshine Hotel renovation and *Do Over* and at the moment she has nothing to show for it."

Car doors slammed. Male voices sounded in the kitchen. There was the scrape of a chair and Dustin's piping voice. The back door opened and Joe stuck out his head. "There's pizza for anyone who wants it." His unerring gaze located Nikki in the gathering darkness. "I brought you a thick-crust meat lovers topped with sardines and anchovies."

Nikki swiped the last of the tears away. "Thanks. I'll be in in a minute." She began to lever her bulk into position. "Or as soon as I can get out of this chair," she muttered.

"Anchovies and sardines?" Avery made a gagging sound.

"Ha! Just wait until you get pregnant," Nikki said, pausing and planting her feet for final liftoff. "I can't wait to see your face when you have to go cold turkey on the Cheez Doodles."

"A—I'm not getting pregnant," Avery shot back. Not after witnessing the kind of havoc a teenager could wreak. "And B— I think I've mentioned this before—a life without Cheez Doodles is simply not worth living. That won't be happening."

"I'm going to make sure they're not overfeeding Dustin," Kyra said, getting up and extending a hand to pull Nikki to her feet. "And I sincerely hope there's something a little less gag inducing available. Though I do remember chowing down on more than a few peanut butter and pickle sandwiches when I was pregnant with Dustin."

Avery and Maddie stood and began gathering the empty wine bottle and glasses. Avery picked up the Cheez Doodles and hugged them to her chest.

"Are you okay?" Maddie asked quietly, her eyes searching Avery's face.

"Yes."

Maddie remained silent. Waiting. A knowing and sympathetic look on her face.

"It's just that Jeff is so horribly unhappy with his situation. And Jason is—I don't know what's going on with him. He used to be so sweet and eager to please and all he wanted to do was play baseball. Now he's skipping practice and trampling every possible rule. It's kind of like World War Three in the Hardin household at the moment."

"And?" The question was gentle. As was the expression on Maddie's face. She was the mother all children deserved but rarely got.

"I'm not equipped to handle any of it. And when I try, Chase won't allow it."

"Do you need to get back to Tampa?"

If it had been anyone besides Maddie asking, Avery might have lied. She shook her head.

"Good," Maddie said. "Stay. You can bunk with me. It's been far too long since we've had a proper pajama party."

. . .

Nikki struggled out of bed on Saturday morning with eyes gritty from lack of sleep. By all rights, the amount of tears she'd been shedding lately—often for no apparent reason—should have kept them lubricated, but it didn't seem to work that way. Though she couldn't have said why, the bigger her stomach got, the more pathetic and needy she became. Instead of rejoicing that the babies were "viable" and seemingly healthy, she continued to worry that something somehow was going to go wrong. Every morning as she dragged her ungainly body out of bed more exhausted than when she'd gotten into it, she vowed to do better. To focus on the positive, to appreciate Joe and her impending motherhood. Every day she failed.

Bella Flora was oddly empty when she made her way downstairs and into the kitchen. Everyone but Joe had gone off and left her without a word. Even Maddie had deserted her. And who could blame her? Nikki had become someone even Nikki didn't want to be around.

"Why don't we go out for lunch?" Joe said after she'd stared first at the coffeepot and then dejectedly out the kitchen window for an embarrassingly long time. "You know, get dressed up a bit? Maybe go downtown and sit outside at one of the new restaurants. Or tour the Dali Museum?"

She shook her head glumly. She'd pulled on a pair of ratty running tights—the only ones whose elastic waist hadn't stretched out too far to hold them in place beneath her massive stomach—and topped it with one of Joe's long-sleeved FBI T-shirts that she'd claimed months ago. It strained across the vastness of her middle and hung unevenly across her upper thighs. Its Rorschach of food stains bore silent witness to her gluttonous appetite. The auburn hair she used to color and maintain religiously had been woven into a clumsy French braid, and her bloated and blotchy face was devoid of the makeup she'd always donned like armor and once wouldn't have left the house without.

In contrast Joe wore a freshly pressed button-down shirt, sleeves rolled to the elbow to reveal lightly tanned and muscled forearms. It was neatly tucked into a pair of khaki shorts that hugged the slim hips she currently envied. She'd had hips once. And a waist, too. His thick dark hair was still damp from the shower.

"I'm just going to take a walk on the beach." She hated the pathetic tone she heard in her voice but was powerless to stop it.

Avery would have rolled her eyes. Maddie would have said something soothing. Joe said only, "I'll come with you."

When she nodded, got up, and walked toward the French door, he added, "Wouldn't you like to change first?"

"To walk on the beach?" Not too long ago, she would have only shown him her dressed and made-up best side. She'd rarely even gone for a run without makeup and designer Lycra. But she couldn't remember the last time she'd run and couldn't imagine ever having the strength to run again. The idea of walking back upstairs and confronting herself in a mirror was far too painful.

The sun was out and with her extra bulk providing furnace-like warmth, she didn't bother with a sweatshirt or jacket. Or shoes for that matter.

"Don't you want to at least bring a pair of flip-flops?"

Reluctant to see her sorry self reflected in Joe's sunglasses or, worse, in his eyes, Nikki did not turn around. She tromped down the sandy path past the jetty and onto the beach, where she lifted her face to the weak winter sun. At the water's edge the cold damp sand sucked at her feet.

Joe caught up with her. Rather than scold or criticize, he slipped an arm around her shoulders and matched his steps to hers.

"I don't understand how you put up with me. I can't even stand me right now."

"Don't worry about it, Nik. If I was carrying the load you are, I have no doubt I'd be just as prickly. My mother told me that when she was pregnant with me, she packed her bags and threatened to leave my father regularly." He squeezed her shoulder. "Are you sure you don't want to shower and, um, dress? It might make you feel better. Then we could go to a movie or out for lunch."

"No. I . . . I just want to walk." She kept her chin up and focused on putting one foot in front of another, careful not to lean too heavily on him. "But you can go back if you want." She thought about Joe's mother and father—they'd been together so long, it was hard to imagine either had ever been seriously un-happy with the other. They were due in next week. *Because she could go into labor at any time.* A tingle of fear snaked up her spine. It didn't matter how many times the doctor told her that every-thing looked fine; the fear of something going wrong hung on her like a sodden blanket she couldn't shake off. And then there was the fact that Joe professed to love her, refused to get angry with her, but no longer wished to marry her.

They passed the Paradise Grille, where music played and people sat at the picnic tables with their burgers and fries. She breathed the scent of fried potatoes that carried on the breeze and felt a too familiar stirring of hunger. The image of a hamburger planted itself in her head and refused to go away. They continued onward and the movement, the sand squishing between her toes, the soft breeze on her face combined with Joe's solid presence, caused her shoulders to relax. Her mood began to lighten.

The Don CeSar grew larger, its bell towers and cupolas more defined as they approached. A text dinged in on Joe's phone and he pulled it out of his pocket. She felt a slight burr of irritation as he removed his arm so that he could text an answer.

"What is it?"

"Nothing. Just my parents' flight information."

Her stomach rolled at the thought of their imminent arrival. They'd never been less than warm and gracious to Nikki. She knew how much the birth of Joe's children meant to them. She also knew she was not what they'd envisioned for their son.

"Nonna Sofia is coming with them." He pocketed his phone. "Why don't we stop at the Sunshine Hotel and take a look at our unit—maybe figure out what we need."

She missed a step. She'd hoped to put off dealing with furnishing the apartment a little longer, though she couldn't have said exactly why.

"We can have lunch there first."

"Oh, but . . ." She could hardly argue that she didn't want to be seen in her current state when he'd given her every opportunity to make herself presentable. And what logical reason could there be for refusing to set foot in the place he'd bought for them? "I could probably eat a little something."

His lips twitched at that, but he wisely said nothing. Together they walked up the beach and between the dunes that had hidden the once-moldering midcentury hotel from view.

Nikki tossed her braid over her shoulder, clamped down on her regret at leaving the house looking like shit, and vowed that this one time she would be grateful if no one looked past her mountainous stomach.

Another text dinged into Joe's phone. He texted back. She wondered at the odd smile of satisfaction that flitted across his face, but her nose had picked up the scent of burgers on a grille. She followed that scent—and Joe—through the opening in the low pink wall and across the Sunshine Hotel and Beach Club's brand-new pool deck.

"Why don't we eat up on the rooftop?"

At the moment she didn't care where they ate as long as large quantities of red meat were involved. With a nod of agreement, she headed for the staircase and was too intent on keeping her balance and getting to the food to protest when Joe came up by her side and slid an arm around her waist as if she weren't capable of walking up a flight of stairs or holding on to a railing.

Midway up, she began to huff a bit, but forced herself to keep going. Joe's arm tightened at her back when she swayed slightly. *Focus!* Her eyes strayed to the Plexiglas shield beneath the tubular railing and she swayed again. *Almost there.*

"What did you say?"

"Just wondering what kind of burger to have." She took one more step. Then another. The single flight was beginning to feel like Everest. The breeze stirred the hair that had come out of its braid. She swiped it out of her eyes, appalled. Was she really wheezing midway up a flight of stairs? What had happened to the woman who used to run three miles without giving it a thought and then spent the rest of the day stripping floors?

"Don't push yourself, Nikki. Let's just stop for a minute and—"

"Don't be silly!" she snapped. Before he could respond or she could think better of it, she bounded up the last four steps in something that may have resembled a run.

Through sheer force of will, she reached the top. But instead of victoriously planting her flag at the summit, she doubled over, gasping for breath. Which was when she realized that right before she'd closed her eyes and begun gulping air into her lungs, she'd seen a large group of people. A group that included all the current residents of Bella Flora, Realtor John Franklin, his wife Renée, and her sister Annelise as well as Joe's parents and grandmother. Chase and Jeff Hardin were there, too, along with interior designer Ray Flamingo, who'd replaced Deirdre after her death and whose talent had helped transform the Sunshine Hotel. Two video cameras were filming Nikki's every move. And if her oxygen-deprived brain hadn't been imagining it, they were all holding bunches of pink balloons. And all of them, including Joe's Nonna Sofia, had shouted, "Surprise!"

Five

If not for the iron band of Joe's arm at her back, Nikki would have been somersaulting down the stairs she'd barely managed to climb. As it was, she raised her head, still trying to drag air into her lungs and make sense of what she was seeing. Kyra and Troy were still shooting—she knew enough to recognize they were zooming in for close-ups of her bloated, makeup-free face. Everyone else had fallen silent.

Despite fervent prayers, the assembled group was real. This might be a nightmare, but it definitely wasn't a dream. Joe's arm shifted slightly, urging her forward.

Dustin stepped closer and handed her a pink balloon. Maddie stepped up behind him and hugged Nikki tightly. "Welcome to your baby shower!"

Ray Flamingo, who had traded his signature sherbet-hued linen shirts for a winter white sweater and pants, said, "We definitely surprised her."

"Yeah, great job," Avery said. "I was afraid she was going to have a heart attack."

"I'm surprised we didn't shock her into labor," Kyra said, lowering her camera.

Joe's mother, Gabriella, gave Nikki an enthusiastic hug. Of average height with a short saucy cap of salt-and-pepper hair, she had warm brown eyes that glimmered with humor and full lips that, even in repose, tilted upward. Joseph Senior was trim and athletic and possessed a full head of thick white hair. The chiseled nose and chin he'd bequeathed to Joe were still strong and determined.

"I hope the surprise is a good one," Gabriella said.

"Of course it is." Nikki found her voice. "I just wish your son had tried a little harder to convince me to dress and put on makeup."

Joe laughed. "I did consider slinging you over my shoulder, carrying you back upstairs, and dressing you myself. But it didn't seem right to resort to brute force. I'm pretty sure there must be some law against cosmetic coercion?"

"I don't think even you could be slinging her over your shoulder at the moment," Avery said.

"Nor would it be good for the bambine," Nonna Sofia said, her piercing black eyes aimed at Nikki's stomach. Her olive-tinged skin was surprisingly unwrinkled for a woman of ninety. A white streak zigzagged through her still dark hair like a lightning bolt. Barely over four feet, she carried herself with an air of command and had a reputation for dabbling in ancient Italian curses. The jury was out on whether she had, in fact, aimed a fertility spell Nikki's way. "Come, sit down. Get off your feet." She motioned Nikki and Joe to their seats at the center of a long rectangular table covered in a pale pink tablecloth and dotted with flowers no doubt plucked from Renée Franklin's garden and arranged in babybootie-shaped ceramic planters.

Renée and her sister, Annelise, owned the Sunshine Hotel

and Beach Club, which Maddie, Avery, Nikki, and crew had recently renovated for what they'd hoped would be a kinder, gentler version of *Do Over*.

There was talk and laughter as everyone took a seat. Waiters brought big platters of cheeseburgers fresh off the grill and placed bowls of salad and French fries within easy reach. Nikki sighed happily. "The perfect meal," she said as she popped a fry into her mouth.

"Enjoy," Maddie said. "After dessert you two can open the presents." She nodded to a nearby table piled high with gifts of all sizes, their common denominator being their pink wrapping paper and bows.

As she tucked into the meal, Nikki's dark mood lifted. In that moment the affection that surrounded and flowed over her and the babies jostling inside her could not be mistaken or misunderstood. She was pleasantly full when the cake, which was covered in pink fondant icing, was wheeled over.

"I would have put the girls' names on the cake if we actually knew what their names were going to be," Maddie teased as she cut a large piece, set it in front of Nikki, and watched her dig in.

"I have a sinking feeling they're going to come home from the hospital as Baby Girl Number One and Baby Girl Number Two," Joe said in mock horror.

"Instagram filters are popular for babies right now," Kyra said. "Maybe you should name the twins Lux and Reyes."

Nikki finished her piece of cake then cast an inquisitive eye toward Joe's.

"Okay, I take it that's a no on the Instagram names. Why don't you tell us your top contenders so we can vote? It could be a secret ballot—just to provide helpful input," Kyra suggested.

But there were no top contenders. Nikki had been afraid to choose names due to the nebulous "just in case" that she'd been unable to shake. "I saw an article recently that suggested waiting until they come home and you see their personalities," she said.

"I saw that article, too," Kyra said. "But I'm pretty sure they were talking about puppies."

There was laughter.

"Maybe waiting's not such a bad thing," Avery chimed in. "Yesterday Nikki spent two hours trying to decide between orange and apple juice. Do you get your brain cells back after you give birth?"

"Not immediately," Renée said. "But part of that's due to sleep deprivation."

"Great," Nikki said as she polished off the rest of Joe's cake. "I feel so much more confident now."

"They're going to have their names for a very long time. It's best to choose with care," Nonna Sofia said. "I personally think Sofia is a very beautiful name."

"It is, Mama," Gabriella said. "But Nicole may want to name the babies after her own grandmother or mother."

For the briefest moment Nikki allowed herself to imagine how much her mother would have loved not only this shower, but seeing her only grandchildren. It might have been an antidote to her son's criminal behavior. The food she'd just consumed turned leaden in her stomach. Her only living family member resided in jail. The only time she'd seen him since helping Joe put him there, he'd threatened both of them and tried to use her yet again.

"I'm sure you'll figure out just the right names," Renée said kindly as the table was cleared. She and Maddie carried the gifts over and piled them near Nikki and Joe. "This is from us," she said, handing Nikki a brightly wrapped clothing box.

Inside were two adorable tiny bathing suits. "So they can learn to swim before they walk like I did," Annelise said.

The box also held two tiny terrycloth cover-ups, two pairs of tiny pink flip-flops, and two infant-size Sunshine Hotel and Beach Club sweatshirts.

"Oh, those are adorable!" Maddie said.

Nikki stared down at the tiny leg openings and mock ballerina skirts. Her heart clenched as she held a pair of the flip-flops in one palm. Surely no feet could be that small.

"Wanna stetshirt!" Dustin said.

"I'm glad to hear that," John Franklin said. "We just happen to have one here in your size." He handed the folded sweatshirt to Dustin, who wasted no time putting it on.

Kyra turned the camera on Dustin as he beamed and shouted, "Tank too!"

"Open ours." Maddie nodded to Steve, who slid a large wrapped box across the deck to Nikki and Joe. She managed to rip off most of the paper. Joe tilted the box so they could see the picture on it.

"Trollher!" Dustin shouted and he was right. The box contained a double version of the jogging stroller that Dustin still liked to cruise the beach in.

"This is for you, too." Maddie handed her an envelope. The handwritten coupon inside promised unlimited babysitting.

"We are your village," Kyra added. "Don't forget it."

Steve Singer handed her an envelope. His card read, *I promise NOT to wash your baby clothes in any way at any time.*

"Yea, and who knows," Kyra added helpfully. "Maybe the girls will be able to share that Chanel suit Dad shrunk one day."

There was laughter.

"That was my lucky suit that you destroyed, you know. My very first designer piece." One of the few she hadn't been forced to sell off when Malcolm had bankrupted her.

Nonna Sofia looked at them with piercing eyes. "I think we make our own luck," she said. "But it's good to have protection." She handed Nikki a small box that held two tiny pearl necklaces with delicate gold crosses dangling from them. "And if you'd like to use them, I brought my daughters' christening gowns. All of my grandchildren and great-grandchildren have been baptized in them."

"Thank you," Nikki said, her eyes once again blurring with tears.

"We're so pleased to be here with you and Joe. We're happy to babysit anytime, too. And we look forward to extending our family through you." Gabriella smiled. Nikki noticed that she did not say becoming a *part* of their family, only extending it. "You'll see our gift soon. This is from Maria and Dom. She said to say it's for both of you."

Nikki opened the gift from Joe's sister and brother-in-law while Joe looked on. He whistled as she pulled out a black silk negligée cut low and slit on both sides. Nikki couldn't imagine fitting any part of herself into this. Nikki felt her face go warm. She thought Joe might be blushing, too. The note said, *Trust me. One day you'll actually want him to take this off you.*

"I have something for you, too." Joe handed her a jewelry-size box and Nikki's heart began to pound. This was it. The thing she'd refused repeatedly and now realized how much she wanted. She ripped off the paper with fumbling fingers and watched him out of the corner of her eye so that she wouldn't miss the moment he dropped to one knee. He simply continued to sit there as she extracted the pale blue Tiffany box. She held her breath as she opened it.

"Oh." She was careful not to allow a hint of disappointment at her first sight of the gold charm bracelet and the two heart-shaped charms that dangled from it. "It's beautiful."

He smiled. His eyes twinkled briefly, so briefly she thought she must have imagined it. "I wanted you to have this. I figure we can engrave their names later."

She swallowed, holding on to her smile.

"Here," Avery said. "This is from us." The box contained two tiny pink hardhats and two onesies decorated with tool belts and pearls. "We thought maybe they could wear them home from the hospital."

Nikki felt her smile slip. Once again she felt that vague fissure of fear at tempting fate by envisioning the babies coming home from the hospital without trauma or delay.

"Thank you." Tears began to fall. "I can't tell you how much this means to me."

"To both of us," Joe added. He handed her a Kleenex.

"Wait, there's one more gift." Ray Flamingo stood and handed her a pink ribbon, its end hung over the railing. "This is from me and Avery and Chase and Jeff. Well, actually everybody had a hand in it."

"I don't understand." She looked to Joe, expecting to see the same confusion she felt, but he was smiling.

"It leads to something really special." Joe offered her his hand and gently pulled her to her feet then waited patiently while she straightened.

She tugged gently on the ribbon. "Is it bigger than a bread box?"

"Definitely," Joe said.

"Come on," Ray said. "You need to follow it to the gift."

Everyone was grinning. Apparently she was the only one not in the know. With Joe's arm to steady her, they went down the stairs. In a chattering group they huddled around her as she followed the pink ribbon past the pool and dining room and down the concrete path that bisected the property. They wound past brightly painted one- and two-bedroom cottages, which were in fact unfinished shells waiting for owners. The ribbon slid between Nikki's fingers as they cut between the Happy Crab and the Salty Seahorse to the two-bedroom cottage Joe had purchased for the four of them. It had been his concession to her wanting to stay near the women who had become her closest friends as they figured out what to do about *Do Over*. Although they were contemporaries, Maddie was the closest thing to a mother figure Nikki had. The pink ribbon was wrapped around the doorknob.

Nikki looked at Joe. He smiled the smile that turned her knees to mush and her heart to . . . "I know you already own this. So why the ribbon?"

He shrugged as if he had no idea.

"Try the knob," Avery prompted.

The door was unlocked. Nikki pushed it open. With everyone watching her, she stepped into a fully furnished and decorated home. Ten days ago it had been completely empty.

"What happened?" she asked as she took in the quartz countertops, double sink, and clean lined cabinets. Though the kitchen itself was small, the brand-new appliances were full-size and high-end. Joe Giraldi would be able to cook here.

They pressed inside, filling the living area, which now sported a cozy sectional surrounding an amoeba-shaped cocktail table. On the opposite wall a large-screen television hung over a shelving unit that contained a desk. A table and four chairs had been centered beneath the window. Restored terrazzo floors gleamed beneath a multihued area rug.

The master bedroom contained a queen bed with a padded headboard flanked by simple but elegant nightstands. The closet could never be called big or walk-in, but it had been built out to take advantage of every available inch. The master bath was also small, but beautifully appointed. A French door led out to the walled garden, which included a stone fountain, two chaises, and a profusion of greenery that snaked up the wall and fell back in a spill of flowers. It was a private oasis.

The second bath was more utilitarian with only one sink and a bathtub/shower combo appliquéd with hot pink flowers. The white wood cabinets were stocked with baby products—everything from powder to shampoo.

"And now the pièce de résistance." Ray took her hand and led her into the second bedroom, which was a completely outfitted nursery. Those who could fit followed. The rest watched from the small hallway.

"I can't believe this," Nikki said, barely able to get the words past the emotion that clogged her throat.

Kyra pointed to the two oval cribs painted in a whitewash finish. "They're called Gentle Waves and they convert into toddler and youth beds," Kyra said. "I love the rounded edges."

A changing table in the same finish had a quilted fuchsia pad. Newborn diapers, wipes, and items Nikki had never seen before and had no idea what to do with filled its shelves. A low dresser painted in abstract blocks of pink, white, and black sat beneath a framed mirror and free-floating shelves. The closet had been fitted with rods, cubbies, and shelves, and a wardrobe of tiny outfits had been hung and stored inside it. The walls were hand-painted pink and white stripes. A cushioned glider and ottoman covered in a bold floral pattern sat in one corner.

"What's that?" Nikki pointed to a tall, almost egg-shaped thing next to the changing table.

"That's a Diaper Genie," Maddie said. "No muss, no odor. Wish they'd been around when Kyra and Andrew were born."

"It's apparently the Cadillac of diaper pails," Joe said almost proudly.

"But where . . . how?" She had been dreading making these choices, afraid of tempting fate, and the whole time this had been happening. "I don't understand."

"We just wanted to make sure you and Joe had everything you needed," Maddie said. "This is from all of us." She opened her arms to include the people packed into every inch of the cottage.

Joe's parents and grandmother. The Franklins and Annelise. The Hardins. Maddie, Avery, and Kyra. Even Steve Singer and Troy beamed back at her.

"Ray selected the furniture and ran the design choices by Joe," Maddie explained. "Chase and Avery and Jeff built out the kitchen and bathrooms and so on. But we all helped."

"I haven't checked with Guinness, but I think this may be the pinkest place on earth," Avery observed.

"If it isn't, I'll have to try harder," Ray Flamingo said.

"It's beautiful," Nikki croaked. She couldn't quite find her voice, but for the first time she was able to picture herself here with Joe and their babies. She tried to swallow them back, but the tears came of their own accord. An ocean of them gushed down her cheeks. She made no move to stem their tide. She didn't have the words to name the emotions that flowed through her. Her hand caressed the pink polka-dotted baby blanket in the nearest crib, ran over the whitewashed birch of its beautifully curved frame. Through the blur of tears she tried to focus on the mobiles hanging above the cribs. Each had a combination of stuffed sea creatures interspersed with stuffed pink tools dangling over it. Each was a unique work of art.

"A friend of mine made those," Ray said. "I told him we needed something special, something mesmerizing enough to keep the girls occupied."

"I helped-ed Ray to hang-ed the bomeels," Dustin said proudly.

"You did a great job." Nikki smiled down at him. "Everything is perfect. I could never have imagined anything half so fabulous." She smiled and sniffed, trying to stem the flow of tears. "Thank you all so much."

Joe's arm slipped around the place her waist had once been. For the first time she didn't bemoan its loss.

A knock sounded on the front door.

Given that they were packed in so tightly, Chase, who was closest, opened it. It was one of the waitresses. "Sorry to interrupt," she said. "But there's a woman here asking for Nicole."

"Who is it?" Nikki asked as everyone pressed out of the way as best they could.

"She said her name is Bitsy Baynard."

"Bitsy's here?" Nikki asked. "Was she invited to the shower?"

"No," Maddie said. "The season's in full swing in Palm Beach, so I assumed she wouldn't be able to make it. I didn't want to put her on the spot."

"Hmmm," Nikki said. "I wonder why she's here."

"She didn't say," the girl said. "But she has a great big pile of luggage. And she wants to know which cottage belongs to her."

Six

The Sunshine Hotel was not the Ritz. Or the Pierre. Or any one of the five-star hotels at which Bitsy normally stayed. She had sponsored its renovation and what was supposed to have been a new season of *Do Over*, as a favor to Nikki and Maddie, and because being on a first-name basis with William Hightower and attending a comeback concert deserved payback.

At the time, $250,000 hadn't exactly been pocket change, but it hadn't been a significant amount, either. Certainly not an amount she had ever imagined missing or needing. Women born into the kind of money Bitsy had been born into simply did not end up without funds. And they most certainly didn't end up homeless.

Except it seemed they did.

She stood on the concrete walkway not far from the hotel's main building with Bertie's ancient and ill-tempered French bulldog in her arms. She and Sherlock had never particularly warmed to each other. He had been Bertie's since puppyhood, and the day Bertie moved in with her, Sherlock had taken one look at Bitsy and lifted his leg on her Aubusson carpet. But they had things in common now. Both of them were older than Bertie's current girlfriend, and both of them had been left behind.

"Gog!" Dustin said, racing ahead of the group of women who rounded the corner and coming toward her. She watched Nikki, Avery, Maddie, and Kyra's faces as they approached and was relieved to see only surprise. It seemed the news of Bertie's desertion and theft hadn't reached them, but then Palm Beach and St. Pete Beach were worlds—not just two hundred miles—apart.

"Bitsy! What a nice surprise!" Nikki stepped forward with her arms outstretched. Between Nikki's stomach, which was immense, and Sherlock, who still clung to Bitsy, they managed little more than an air kiss.

"If we'd known you were coming to town, I would have made sure you got an invitation to Nikki's surprise shower," Maddie said.

"'Surprise' being the operative word," Nikki said. "I wasn't exactly dressed or prepared." She took in the mound of luggage, which held the very last of Bitsy's possessions.

Bitsy knew all about being caught unprepared. She smiled. "I'm sorry I missed it. I didn't know for sure whether I was coming." Or going, for that matter.

"It's great of you to stop by. Where are you headed?" Kyra asked.

This was a good question. One she wished she knew the answer to. "Oh, you know, wherever the road takes me." She attempted a casual shrug, but her shoulders were so tight, she wasn't sure whether they moved or not.

"How nice." Nikki looked around. "Is Bertie with you?"

"No." She hoped her response hadn't sounded as curt as it felt.

"He's away on business." That, of course, would be *monkey* business. She'd always been grateful to Nikki for bringing her and Bertie together. Now she wondered if her contract with Heart, Inc. had contained a satisfaction clause. Maybe she was due a refund?

All of their eyes dropped to her luggage. "You look equipped for a world tour," Avery said.

If only. A trip around the world would have been the perfect cover as well as a chance to lick her wounds and get her head back on straight, but she'd barely had enough money to make it here in the Land Rover that their former cook had used to run errands. "I just needed to get away on my own for a bit. I thought maybe I'd stay here for a while to unwind and have some 'girl time.'"

There was a shocked silence. Hoping to head off further questions, she went on the offensive. "When I was here for the grand opening, it was my understanding that a finished-out two-bedroom went for around two hundred thousand, maybe more depending on upgrades. Since I contributed two hundred and fifty thousand, which I haven't been paid back, I thought I'd just go ahead and take the unit." So that even if she'd been forced to lower her standards, she would not, in fact, be homeless.

Sherlock whimpered in her arms and she set him down. He splayed his back legs and buried his chin between his front paws, exhausted and dejected. She fought off the urge to do the same.

"The only two-bedroom besides Joe and Nikki's that's finished out is the model," Avery replied. "The Franklin Realty people are using it to sell from."

"I'll take it."

"But . . ." Avery protested.

"How long would it take you to finish out my unit?" Bitsy asked.

"I don't know. You never mentioned wanting one," Avery said. "Our agreement was that you would front the money and we'd pay you back with interest."

"Well, I suppose I could take the money if you prefer, but . . ." But what could she possibly buy for that even on this coast?

"We don't actually have the money," Nikki admitted. "The units that will be completed first are group time-shares that need to be available the weeks they're spoken for."

Bitsy remained silent. It was important not to appear desperate. But she needed a roof over her head, even a small temporary one. She tried not to blanch as the recollection of her home growing ever smaller in the Land Rover's rearview mirror rose in her mind. It had been empty and padlocked. The bank's For Sale sign posted on the gates.

"You know the Sunshine Hotel and Beach Club belongs to Renée and Annelise," Maddie said. "The Beach Club is operational, but it takes time to get enough time-share owners to pay for a finished cottage. Everything's moved far more slowly than expected."

"I understand," Bitsy said pleasantly. "And I don't mind staying in the model until you finish my unit. If the Franklins need to show it, I'm okay with that." She smiled carefully, keeping her tone light. "Now. Is there a bellman?"

"Afraid not," Avery said. "Things are pretty casual here."

Maddie shot her a look. "But we do have some extra muscle stashed at Joe and Nikki's place. Kyra, can you go ask the guys to come help?"

When the men arrived, everyone chattered and acted as if nothing out of the ordinary had happened, but Joe looked at Bitsy and her possessions far more closely than she would have liked, and she caught Avery and Chase with their heads together and their eyes on her. Her suitcases, which bulged with things she'd probably never have reason to wear again, filled the model's second bedroom and spilled out into the tiny living area, which could give a phone booth a run for its money.

"Why don't you come have drinks and dinner with us?" Maddie

asked at the cottage door. "You can come straight down Pass-a-Grille Way." Maddie didn't give her the chance to refuse. "Good. We'll expect you at six. You'll want to bring a sweater or jacket. The temperature drops when the sun goes down."

Bitsy stood in the tiny doorway of her new home and watched them leave. Sherlock nudged her leg with his nose and let out an anguished snuffle as if he couldn't quite believe the fate that had befallen them. "No shit, Sherlock," she said as she closed the cottage door. "Bertie has a hell of a lot to answer for. But at least we have a roof over our heads."

• • •

"You don't mind if I stay on for a while?" Avery hugged Jeff good-bye and waited while Chase helped his dad into the passenger seat, folded his wheelchair, and placed it in the trunk.

"Naw. I'd stay, too, except Dad's pretty tuckered out and I know he hated having to be carried up and down the roof deck stairs, even if he won't admit it. We really need to find a way to add an elevator." He turned to face her. "And I hate to leave the boys alone too long." His shoulders slumped. Avery knew that by "boys," he meant Jason, who'd started rebelling and acting out within what seemed like minutes of turning sixteen.

"What about what the psychologist said? Do you think it's a delayed reaction to losing his mother? Or the pressure of having all those college baseball scouts watching and judging him?" she asked. "Maybe an intervention would—"

"Don't," he said quietly. "Just don't."

"But I hate seeing you carrying all this alone," she said. "I wish you'd let me help."

He sighed. "It's just the way it is. He's my responsibility. You don't need to worry about it." He leaned down to kiss her, and the resignation and misery that laced his words were even more painful than his anger. Whether he snapped or sighed, the result was the same, she reflected as she watched Chase and his father leave; the door was firmly shut and she was left standing outside.

"I'll be back at Bella Flora in time for sunset," Nikki called out as Joe helped her into the SUV, where his parents and grandmother were already seated. She and Joe were moving into their unit at the Sunshine Hotel in the morning, something Nikki didn't look at all excited about.

Steve and Troy loaded Dustin into Troy's car for a trip to the playground and then to Gigi's Italian Restaurant for pizza.

"You know, it would take about ten seconds to Google Bitsy and find out what's going on," Avery said as she climbed into the backseat of the minivan and waited for Kyra to fire it up.

"No," Maddie said.

"Obviously, something's happened," Kyra agreed as she circled the block then turned south toward Bella Flora.

"And if she wanted us to know what it was, she'd tell us," Maddie countered.

"But even if something did happen between them, why would she be the one who left?" Avery couldn't help asking. "I mean, it's all her money, right? And why take the cottage when the Don CeSar, which is clearly more her style, is practically next door?"

"Again, not our business," Maddie insisted.

This might be true, but thinking about Bitsy's problems and possible motivations was a lot less stressful than examining her own. "Well, I don't see how we can just pretend she happened to show up with a mountain of luggage and a depressed bulldog," Avery countered. "And I don't appreciate being steamrolled."

"Bitsy's been a good friend to us. It's time to return the favor," Maddie said.

"I know she and Nikki have a history and she has been helpful, but Avery's right. We are being steamrolled," Kyra said as she cut across to Gulf Way and bits of beach began to flash by.

"Handing over a unit is a big deal, given that none of us have been paid back. And we should ask for Renée and Annelise's permission. I think we have every right to know what's going on."

"I'm not saying we can't ask. I just think it's wrong to *force* information out of a friend before she's ready." Maddie's tone was reflective.

"So we're going to pretend like nothing's happened?" Avery asked. "Frankly, I don't think I'm that good an actress."

"You're not," Kyra agreed. "And I've got the video to prove it."

Maddie smiled. "I didn't say we have to pretend nothing's happened."

"No?" Avery said.

"No. I said I don't believe in *forcing* things. That doesn't mean there's anything wrong with making someone so comfortable they *want* to share what's bothering them."

"We don't have a lot of time to gain her confidence and make her comfortable enough to share," Avery pointed out. "We can't leave her in that model indefinitely, and we definitely can't afford to build out a unit for her in the top-of-the-line finishes she's going to expect, especially not now. Maybe once more units have sold and we see what happens with the network."

"Oh, I don't think it will take all that long," Maddie said as they passed Eighth Avenue, which served as Pass-a-Grille's main street.

"No?" Kyra asked.

"Nope," Maddie said with confidence.

"And how do you intend to make her that comfortable quickly?" Avery asked.

"I'm going to put her at ease the old-fashioned way," Maddie replied.

"Which is?" Kyra asked.

"Otherwise known as plying her with alcohol," Avery said wryly.

Maddie shrugged good-naturedly.

"What makes you think that's going to work?" Kyra asked as they neared the southern tip of Pass-a-Grille.

"Well, when Will's record label flew Bitsy, Nikki, and me up to Will's concert in North Carolina, we discovered that alcohol is Bitsy's sodium pentathol—her truth serum. She doesn't get sloppy or anything, but it pretty much eliminates her filter."

"Well, we need to find out what's going on and why she's here," Kyra said to Maddie. "How many drinks do you think it will take?"

"That's the part I'm not sure about," Maddie admitted. "But Nikki won't be drinking, so she can play bartender. Her number one job will be making sure that Bitsy's glass is always full."

"I guess that could work," Avery said. "Besides, she's wound so tightly that getting a little tipsy and sharing whatever's going on is bound to make her feel better. It's practically therapy."

"True, but we're going to have to drink with her," Kyra said as she pulled the minivan into Bella Flora's bricked drive. "Otherwise she'll get suspicious."

"I'm prepared to have a few drinks for a good cause," Avery said. "We'll spend a couple hours and let Bitsy get things off her chest. We're not talking *The Lost Weekend* or anything. How much alcohol could Bitsy Baynard possibly consume?"

Seven

As it turned out, Bitsy Baynard could consume quite a lot of alcohol as she was only too willing to demonstrate. She and Sherlock arrived shortly before sunset looking haggard. Bitsy's long face was blotchy, her eyes were red, and her straight blond hair had been pulled back into a low ponytail. She wore jeans and a brand-new Sunshine Hotel sweatshirt. The massive diamond engagement ring that she'd always worn paired with a diamond-studded band had been replaced by a plain gold wedding band.

"I hope you don't mind that I brought Sherlock," Bitsy said. "He's really always been more Bertrand's dog than mine." Her voice broke slightly on her husband's name. "But he's in a completely new environment, and I didn't have the heart to leave him behind."

"No problem. Where did you say Bertie is?" Maddie asked as casually as she could.

"Oh, overseas on business," Bitsy said vaguely. "I'm not completely sure where all he's going."

"Come on back. Nikki's whipping us up some piña coladas and Avery's putting together the hors d'oeuvres." Maddie led her down the central hallway to the Casbah Lounge with its leaded windows, Moorish tiles, and red leather banquettes. "Not fancy ones, of course, but since Avery's in charge, you can count on an abundance of fake cheese products."

Avery smiled hello. A large bowl of Cheez Doodles and a plate of celery stuffed with pimiento cheese sat on the bar. "Don't listen to anything they tell you. I don't only eat things made with cheese, I just happen to prefer them." Avery began to arrange plates and bowls on a large tray. "Tonight we've got bagel bites, miniature hot dogs wrapped in pastry, the last of the Ted Peters smoked fish spread, which is absolute perfection on crackers with just a drop or two of Tabasco."

"Sounds like a feast," Bitsy said, taking a seat at the bar.

Sherlock snuffled and settled on the floor next to Bitsy's stool. Nikki pulsed the blender.

"It does seem kind of cruel to make someone who can't drink be the bartender," Bitsy observed.

"Not a problem," Nikki said. "Honestly, the last thing on my mind at the moment is alcohol. Well, maybe not the very last. It comes somewhere after sex. But nowhere near sleeping through the night, not having to pee every five minutes, and being able to wear clothes instead of tents. And . . . sorry. Didn't mean to get all whiny. I just feel like I've been pregnant forever. And I don't own a single article of clothing that doesn't have a food stain right here." She pointed to the front of her maternity blouse just above the mound of her stomach, which did in fact sport an extremely large and prominent spot.

"It won't be long now," Maddie said. "And everything's going well."

"Yes, so far." Nikki knocked on the bar for luck. "It's just that until the babies are born and okay, it's kind of impossible not to worry. And I'm not particularly good at being pregnant, except for the gaining weight part. I never glowed or anything—not even for five minutes. I had morning sickness for what felt like forever and then I got huge and . . ." She seemed to catch herself. "Sorry. I *am* good at blender drinks, and piña coladas are one of my specialties." She poured a generous glass and handed it to Bitsy. "Here. Try this."

"I hate to drink alone," Bitsy said.

Without asking, Nikki poured glasses for Maddie, Avery, and Kyra.

"To friendship!" Bitsy raised her glass and waited for them to raise theirs.

"Friendship!" They clinked glasses. Bitsy had downed her entire glass before the rest of them had taken more than a few tentative sips. She reached for a Cheez Doodle and then another. If she was dismayed by the lack of caviar or expensive wine or champagne, she gave no sign.

"Shall we head out back and enjoy the show?" Avery suggested.

"Sure. What can I take?" Bitsy stood. Sherlock got to his feet.

Between them they carried the tray of snacks, their now empty glasses, and two pitchers of piña coladas out to the loggia and settled around the wrought iron table. Over the Gulf, the sun glowed a golden red. Streaks of color shone between the clouds. When everyone had a full glass, Maddie hefted hers. "To sunset and to having Bitsy here."

They clinked glasses and drank.

"What a gorgeous view," Bitsy said, staring out over the jetty and the Gulf. "I'm more used to sunrises over the Atlantic, but this is really nice."

"It does make you see things a little differently," Maddie

said. "When you confront Mother Nature and experience something so much larger than yourself."

"You might want to get your thoughts in order," Avery warned Bitsy. "Maddie makes us come up with one good thing that happened during the day or that we're grateful for at sunset," Avery said.

"I don't *make* them do it," Maddie protested.

"She does. And when we first met and discovered what horrendous shape Bella Flora was in—this house was all we had left—things were pretty grim. Finding anything good was a challenge," Nikki said.

"Sometimes it was impossible," Avery said.

"Amen to that," Nikki added.

"So Mom started the 'one good thing' tradition."

"And then she *strongly encouraged* us to participate," Nikki said.

"It's just an exercise in finding the positive," Maddie said. "There's no judgment as to how good the one good thing has to be."

"Yeah, she doesn't like to be called the 'good enough' police," Avery said. "But if the shoe fits . . ."

"She does have a habit of seeing the glass as half full," Nikki added. "Even when you're convinced it's more of a dribble glass."

"Hey!" Maddie protested.

"That was a compliment," Nikki said. "In fact, I'm co-opting your positive attitude for my good thing tonight. I'm not sure where we'd all be without it."

"Compliment accepted then." Maddie took a sip of her piña colada and turned her attention to the sky, which was most definitely a gift *and* a very good thing.

They munched and drank while the sunset played out. As instructed, Nikki kept Bitsy's glass full. But each time, Bitsy insisted that she refill their glasses, too.

"At the moment you guys are my one good thing," Bitsy said, raising what Maddie thought was her third piña colada in toast. Or was it the fourth? "But there are three of you. Do you count as one good thing or three? And are you allowed to repeat a good thing or do they have to be new?"

"I've asked those very questions myself," Nikki said. "The rules are kind of fluid."

"Speaking of fluid, these piña coladas are really excellent." Bitsy drained her glass and once again waited for Nikki to refill theirs. "So I'm going with Nikki and her blending skills as my good thing tonight." She downed the drink.

Maddie watched the enthusiasm—and desperation—with which Bitsy drank. She drank her own down. Kyra and Avery did the same. "Sometimes things get rough. Being able to talk about it can help," Maddie prompted as Nikki leaned forward to refill Bitsy's glass and then Kyra's.

"Damn straight. I propose a toast to the best piña coladas I've ever tasted." Bitsy held the glass aloft then tilted it to her lips, drank it down in quick gulps, then slammed it down empty as if doing shots. "Are you all with me?"

"To Nikki's blending skills!" Maddie, Avery, and Kyra said then did the same.

"Can that count for all of us tonight?" Avery asked.

"Is that a trick question?" Maddie asked. Her thoughts had begun to slow and blur.

"I don't think so," Avery said slowly.

It occurred to Maddie that she'd lost track of how many piña coladas she'd had but didn't want to say anything that might inhibit Bitsy, who definitely seemed to be loosening up. The sun puddled into the water in a final shimmer of color then slid beneath the surface. The temperature dropped a bit more, but no one complained. She felt warmed from the inside out.

Male voices sounded inside. A text dinged in on Kyra's phone.

Kyra squinted down at it. "Dad says Dustin fell asleep in the car. He's putting him to bed before he and Troy head out for a drink."

"That's so nice," Bitsy said. "I've been wondering why your ex-husband is living here. I mean, isn't it kind of awkward? Especially when Will visits?"

Maddie blinked at the directness of the question then had to remind herself that she'd wanted Bitsy to speak freely. "Divorce can be difficult and awkward," Maddie said, trying to marshal her thoughts. "Shh . . . suh . . . sometimes you just have to find what works best in a given shituation." Maddie froze. Had she just said, "shit-uation"?

Nikki smiled. "I think 'shit-uation' is an absolutely brilliant word, useful in lots of shituations!"

"It is!" Avery crowed. "Almost as good as suckage and sucka-licious!" She laughed. "We came up with those at a sunset in August," she explained to Bitsy. "By God, we're not only conjugating existing words, we're creating our own language."

"Very impressive." Bitsy's words were crisp and clear and un-accompanied by extra letters or syllables. "I don't think I could ever live with my ex-husband."

Nikki raised an eyebrow at Maddie.

"Assuming I ever had one," Bitsy amended before Maddie could form a follow-up question. Bitsy held her empty glass up and waited for Nikki to fill it. "Speaking of husbands, I've been wondering why you're not marrying Joe. He's hot as all get-out."

Nikki's eyes narrowed.

"Of course, so is William Hightower," Bitsy continued happily. "And Daniel Deranian is no slouch in the looks or charisma department. The Singer women have a *lot* going on." Bitsy turned her sharp, clear gaze on Avery. "And Chase? Phew." She fanned her face with one rock-steady hand. "When a man is good to his parents, well, that's a total turn-on, isn't it?"

Avery opened her mouth, but nothing came out. Nikki sent Maddie a nudge of a look, but Maddie's thoughts were moving far too slowly to contribute.

"I used to think Bertie was hot," Bitsy said. "But he's proven a bit disappointing." She sighed. "I seem to be the only one here who is not with someone hot. Well, me and Sherlock, poor thing."

Maddie shook her head in an attempt to clear it. This was her cue to . . . what?

"Where did you say Bertie was?" Nikki asked.

"Away." Bitsy waved a hand vaguely. Then she yawned. Her eyes fluttered shut briefly before she jerked them open.

She wasn't the only one starting to fade. Maddie could barely keep her own eyes open. Kyra rubbed her temples and took a deep breath. Bitsy slumped in her chair, her head bobbed a few times, then her chin went to her chest.

"Sorry . . . can't . . ." Avery closed her eyes and laid her forehead on her hands, which were folded on the table.

"Maddie?" Nikki's voice seemed to be coming from a great distance.

There were footsteps and then Joe's voice. "Nik? Just wanted to let you know I was . . . what happened?"

Maddie considered answering. She also considered opening her eyes. Both were beyond her.

"I think I'm going to need some help getting everybody inside." Nikki's voice floated somewhere nearby.

"What happened?" Joe asked again.

"We were trying to find out why Bitsy's really here." Nikki's voice was little more than a whisper.

"Did you consider asking her?" Joe again.

"Very funny," Nikki said. "And by the way, have I mentioned how much it sucks to be the only sober person all the time? It's downright suckalicious."

Maddie's eyes were not responding to her command to open,

and she seemed to be swaying slightly, but her lips twitched at the word. "Is a suckalicious shituation," she murmured.

"Maddie was the mastermind." Nikki's voice was followed by the sound of a chair scraping against concrete.

"You weren't supposed to keep filling our glasses, too," Maddie murmured sleepily. "Even if Bisssy doesn't like to sdrinks alone."

Joe snorted. "Sounds like you all need to work a little more on the details of your operations. Not incapacitating the members of your own team is a pretty important consideration."

"Tell me about it," Nikki said. "We totally underestimated Bitsy. All those years of drinking at society fund-raisers while keeping her wits about her have clearly given her some serious evasion skills." Nikki yawned and sighed. "Now we have to get everybody inside and up to bed."

"Do you want me to run Bitsy back to the hotel?" Joe asked quietly.

"No." Maddie heard Nikki struggle to her feet. "Let's let Sherlock tinkle then put him and Bitsy on the couch."

As if in a dream, Maddie heard movement and murmurs, and felt herself moving. Unsure how she'd gotten there, she felt her bed beneath her. Someone gently laid her head on the pillow and pulled the cover up over her.

"Do we find why she's came?" Maddie roused herself to ask.

"No." Nikki's voice floated somewhere above her. "She didn't share a single important piece of information about herself. But she was pretty spot on about the rest of us."

Eight

Kyra's dream was vivid and filled with images of Daniel Deranian. The dark bedroom eyes noticing her on the set of *Halfway Home*. The first time they really saw her. The way they'd worshipped her just before they glazed over the first time they made love.

Hints of morning began to intrude on the memories. Shards of sunlight. The scent of coffee brewing. The whine of a Jet Ski. *No.* She tried to call the dream back but it refused to be summoned. Her eyes were still closed against the reality of the new day when she felt the throbbing in her head. With a groan, she opened her eyes and discovered that the sunlight was far brighter than it should be. She reached for the iPhone on the nightstand even as she registered the fact that Dustin's car bed was empty. She shot up and the throbbing turned to jagged lightning bolts of pain. At three, Dustin knew how to swim, but the pool was just outside and the Gulf and bay just beyond it. If he had wandered out on his own, anything could happen.

Her head spinning, her eyes caked with sleep, she sprinted out of the bedroom and raced down the back stairs, her head pounding with each step. The house was quiet—too quiet for Dustin to be in it. She reached the salon and scanned the back patio for some sign of him then skidded into the kitchen praying that he'd be there. A note on the kitchen table snagged her gaze. A glass of water and two aspirin sat next to it. *Took Dustin to Paradise Grille for something to eat,* the note read. *Take two aspirin. I'd say call me in the morning except it's already going on noon.* It was signed, *Doctor T.*

Relief flooded through her. It was immediately followed by anger that Troy would have taken Dustin without waking or asking her.

Upstairs she opened her mother's bedroom door a notch and saw Maddie and Avery in their beds apparently still sleeping off last night's attempted interrogation/intervention. One or both of them was snoring. Nikki, Joe, and their two cars were gone. Ditto for Bitsy Baynard and her dog.

Anger mixed with the residue of panic still coursing through her, she washed her face, brushed her teeth, and pulled on shorts and a *Do Over* sweatshirt. Shoving her feet into flip-flops, she took the sidewalk that bordered the beach and walked briskly toward the open-air restaurant that had once been a concession stand.

They were sitting side by side at one of the picnic tables that overlooked the Gulf. Dustin was eating with gusto, his legs swinging happily, his sandals dangling far above the ground. His hair was uncombed and he was still wearing pajamas with his beloved Sunshine Hotel sweatshirt pulled over them.

"She lives," Troy said as Kyra slid onto the picnic bench across from them.

"Hi, Mommy!"

"Good morning, little man." He was holding a hamburger in both hands. Ketchup covered most of one cheek. Despite the grid of string crisscrossing the air above the tables, a nearby seagull was eyeing the French fries on his plate.

"We played-ed porn cold!" He said this with joy. "I got two beaned bags in the hold!"

Kyra had yet to figure out why the bean bag toss game set up on the sand beside the Paradise Grille was called corn-hole, but wasn't completely sure she wanted to know. "How long have you been out here?" she asked Troy. "He'll be burnt to a crisp."

"You don't look so good. I'm guessing the aspirin haven't kicked in yet." Troy pulled the sunscreen out of his pocket. "And FYI, I've got it covered." He looked down at his watch. "We've been out here a little over an hour, and we're only out here because some people can't hold their alcohol." His tone and look were taunting. "A simple hello and thank-you would be good."

"I appreciate the gesture, but you could have woken me up."

"I tried-ed," Dustin said. "I couldn't get your eyes open."

"I was in the kitchen when he came down. He was a little concerned about your corpse-like state, so I came up to make sure you were okay." He ruffled Dustin's hair. "I told you she was fine. Just a little lazy this morning."

She speared him with a look, which he ignored.

"Broy let me wear my pajamas!"

"So I see." She wasn't sure why she was so angry with him, but she knew she didn't like the idea of him standing over her bed seeing her at her most vulnerable. Anytime he did something nice, he ruined it with a backhanded slap of some kind. His niceness made her suspicious. They'd been on opposite sides of the fence too long to fall for a flag of truce. He was the Trojan horse who'd taught her to examine each kindness for a trapdoor. Still, the fresh air and sunshine were beginning to banish her initial panic just as the aspirin seemed to be fighting off the worst of her hangover.

"I'm getting a refill. Want a coffee?"

She wanted to say no, but her entire system was now clamoring for caffeine. She patted her shorts pockets but it seemed she'd raced out of Bella Flora without so much as a dollar bill in her pocket. "Thank you," she said primly when he returned with their coffees.

"There. That wasn't so hard, was it?"

"You've got that wrong. Everything you do seems to have some ulterior motive attached."

"So you think I had some sinister reason for taking Dustin out so you could sleep?"

"I didn't say that."

"Didn't you?"

"You don't know anywhere near as much about me as you think."

"Oh, no?"

"No."

"I know you act a lot tougher than you are. I know that you have a weak spot for a certain undeserving movie star that's big enough to drive a semi through. And I know for a fact that if I brought you an order of French toast swimming in syrup with a side of bacon right now, you'd act like you don't want it and then eat every single bite."

"So you know what I like to eat," she said. "I don't think that makes you an expert on me."

"Maybe not." He shrugged and then pulled a copy of *Variety* out from underneath his plate. "But I'm pretty sure how you're going to react to this." He turned the paper so that she could see the front-page photo of Daniel and his wife, Tonja Kay, taken on a red carpet at some awards ceremony. Kyra tried not to appear interested. Tried not to look too closely, to see if he looked happy, to see how close they stood to each other. Daniel Deranian and Tonja Kay were one of Hollywood's golden couples, at the top of the A-list.

"Dandiel!" Dustin said, smiling and placing a finger over his father's face. Kyra was glad that he ignored Daniel's beautiful wife, who had once tried to take Dustin from Kyra in order to add him to their familial entourage. Her eyes moved to the headline, which read, *Deranian to direct and star with wife in family drama.*

She drew a deep, hopefully cleansing breath. "So what's the big deal?" she said, shoving away the hurt of finding this out like the rest of the world. "He's been looking for the right opportunity and vehicle. It was only a matter of time."

"Probably. I guess if you're big enough box office, directorial talent isn't a requirement."

"Daniel has loads of talent," she said, dropping her voice. "Lots of actors move successfully from acting to directing. Lots of them do both." She picked up a fry from Dustin's plate and ate it angrily. "You're just jealous that he's getting this chance when you're stuck shooting video for room and board."

"I'm jealous?" Troy asked. "You should see your face right now. You can't stand that he's going to be working with his *wife*." He emphasized the word cruelly then reached over to wipe Dustin's face and hands as if he were the parent and she wasn't there at all.

She schooled her features. She would not give him the satisfaction of knowing how sucker punched she felt. Not for a million dollars. Not even for the two million she'd need to pay off the loan she'd taken out against Bella Flora.

"Bid catsle?" Dustin looked up at them expectantly.

"We can do that," she said, glad for the distraction. "But first we'll have to go back to the house and get your—"

"Not necessary." Troy held up the mesh bag of Dustin's sand toys.

She wanted to tell him to get lost, wanted to tell him to shove the plastic shovel where the sun didn't shine. But Dustin was already jumping up off the bench and grabbing for Troy's hand. "Les go, Broy!"

She trailed them down the steps to the beach and over to a prime spot near the water, her coffee in hand. Once Dustin was digging happily, Troy came back to stand next to her. "He didn't tell you, did he?" he said in a sympathetic tone that made her want to punch his lights out.

"Daniel doesn't owe me explanations or advance warning of his business decisions," she snapped. "And I don't owe you insights into my thoughts and feelings."

He shook his head and shrugged. "You're really something, you know. I just hope you're only lying to me and not to yourself."

She gritted her teeth and somehow managed to remain silent.

"He's never going to leave his wife for you or anyone else. You do know that, right?"

She turned to face him. His smug, satisfied smile was still missing, which somehow made his sticking his nose into her life all the more infuriating.

"Thank you for your concern," she said as calmly as she could. "But I'm not the imbecile you seem to think I am. And I certainly don't need you protecting me from anyone or anything."

"Got it," he said evenly. "I'd settle for protecting you from yourself."

• • •

Nikki eased out of bed. No, "ease" was far too graceful a word for the scooting, rolling, and hefting it took to sit upright on the edge of the bed with both feet on the floor.

"You okay?" Joe murmured sleepily. He was by nature and occupation a light sleeper.

Though she'd never caught him at it, she suspected he slept with one eye open. The bag he'd insisted she pack for the hospital sat near the bedroom door ready to go, and she was fairly certain he'd already timed the drive to Bayfront Medical Center, which they had toured together and where Dr. Payne would deliver the babies. The thought had her reaching for the nightstand so that she could knock on wood. She pulled back her hand at the last moment. "Yes. Go back to sleep. I didn't mean to wake you."

Another scoot, a push, and a bit of levering and she was finally on her feet. God, when had getting out of bed turned into a workout? She turned to look down at Joe. His eyes were closed and his breathing was once again rhythmic. A sliver of moonlight sliced through the slit in the wood blind and fell across his rugged jaw and one strong cheekbone. The window was partially open and a cool breeze accompanied the wash of the Gulf on and off the shore. Joe didn't feel the cold, and with her increased bulk and her thermostat continually set at "high," she welcomed the crisp air.

After what felt like her hundredth potty break of the night, she found herself in Ray Flamingo's "ode to pink," where she stood attempting to visualize two babies sleeping peacefully in their cribs in the same way that she'd once visualized the ladder on which she'd climbed out of poverty rung by rung. The image was blocked by her fear that something might still go wrong and by the equally pressing fear that even if both girls were somehow, miraculously, born healthy, she would discover that she did, in fact, lack the mothering gene. That she'd have no idea how to soothe them, or care for them, or bring them up to be good people.

The closet door was open, and the tiny pink clothes that hung on tiny pink padded hangers caught her eye. She lifted a pair of footed pajamas from a shelf and held them to her cheek. In that moment she would have given anything to be Maddie, who'd been born to mother, or Kyra, who went about raising Dustin as if it were the most natural thing in the world, or Joe's mother, Gabriella, whose children, grandchildren, and husband practically worshipped at her feet. She wouldn't even have minded being Nonna Sofia, who did not seem to possess a single doubt or fear.

Clutching the pajamas, she dropped into the glider and put her feet up on the ottoman. The mound of her stomach rippled. Little Girl One and Little Girl Two were apparently awake and taking a midnight kickboxing class.

"Shhhh," she said quietly, beginning a slow glide. "I can't promise I'm going to be the mother you deserve, but I promise I'll do my best." The promise echoed in her mind and deep in the recesses of her heart though she wasn't sure whether she was speaking to them or herself.

. . .

"Come on, let's go for a walk." Bitsy dangled the leash in front of Sherlock. He cocked his large head and twitched his bat ears as if considering her idea. But there was no tail wagging or signs of enthusiasm, just a sad little whimper. "We are not going to sit here all day feeling sorry for ourselves," she said sternly. "You're a dog. You're supposed to want to go outside."

He whimpered again and sat back on his haunches.

"I know, I know." She clipped the leash to his collar and headed for the door. Sherlock remained where he was. When the leash grew taut, she pulled gently and he slid across the terrazzo on his bum as she reeled him in. "But we both need to stop wallowing. And I am not going to carry you to the toilet."

Another pathetic whimper. He lay down on his tummy. The folds of skin on his face wrinkled in misery as he rested his muzzle on his front paws.

"I know. It hurts. But we are not going to roll over and play dead."

Sherlock lifted his head. She wasn't certain but she thought he might have rolled his eyes at the obvious dog humor. "Seriously, Sherlock. If I can move on with my life, so can you."

He looked at her with the same pitiful expression she'd seen on her own face this morning in the bathroom mirror.

"Okay, so maybe I'm not really moving on. Maybe I'm squatting in this cottage that doesn't really belong to me and praying that Bertie either dies or comes to his senses." She hoped one of these things would happen before she was forced to admit the truth that Maddie, Nikki, Avery, and Kyra had tried to pry out of her last night. She wasn't going anywhere until she had somewhere to go and enough money with which to get there. In her former life she would have already hired a battalion of private investigators to find Bertie and retrieve her money, and a second battalion of lawyers to prosecute him.

When she'd been rich, she'd rarely thought about money at all. Now she couldn't stop.

She reached down and gathered Sherlock up into her arms tsk-ing as she did so. But she held him tight, pathetically grateful for his company and for the cool, wet nose he nudged against her neck.

The sun was bright, the sky blue, the breeze mild as she carried Sherlock outside and over the concrete path to Thirty-first Street, where she set him on his feet in front of the first nice bush they came to. Not that she actually knew what constituted an acceptable bush for an unhappy dog.

"All right," she said after he'd piddled halfheartedly then looked up at her with those sad, betrayed eyes. "I'm doing the best I can here." But was she? She could still see her great-grandfather Phineus, founder of the Fletcher Timber Company, staring down at her from his gilt-framed portrait as he was carried away for auction. She would be the Fletcher known for losing the last of a great family's fortune.

She tugged on the leash, but Sherlock refused to move. He simply looked up at her, shook his head, and gave a short bark.

"Oh, come on. Have a heart." She felt every bit as wretched as Sherlock. Only she had no one to carry her to the nearest bush or to hold her in their arms. Her life, once so clearly prescribed and finely oiled, had turned into a soap opera with a heavy dose of sitcom. "Oh, God. I'm starring in my own version of *2 Broke Girls*. Only there's only one of me, and it's my husband, not my father, who shoved me into poverty. And I didn't take a horse into exile with me. I took you."

As she carried Sherlock to a second bush and then to the base of a nearby palm tree, the comparisons bombarded her. Most important, Bertie wasn't in prison like the fictional Caroline Channing's Ponzi-perpetrating father, and he never would be. Unless she found a way to earn enough money to hire people to find him and put him there.

As the first tears fell and she clutched Sherlock tighter to her chest, she pictured herself in that sitcom working as a waitress and trying to start a cupcake business. Then she wondered just how many cupcakes putting Bertie behind bars would take.

Nine

Maddie removed the egg soufflé from the oven and carried it to the table, where Steve, Dustin, Kyra, Troy, and Avery sat. Its golden brown top was impressively poufed.

"Magnificent!" Troy said.

"Bravo!" Avery added.

"Thank you! Thank you!" Maddie made a small bow as she retrieved a second soufflé and set it next to the first.

Kyra snapped a photo of both soufflés just before they fell. "I'm posting this to Instagram right now and adding it to the new Facebook and Twitter pages later. But I don't think we're ever going to match the numbers we had on the original *Do Over* social media." She should know; she'd been the one who'd built their presence by chronicling their original renovations of Bella Flora.

"I can't believe the network had the right to take over all of the show's social media the way they did," Avery said. "Or how long it's taking to get any kind of ruling."

A knock sounded on the kitchen door. It opened and Nikki

stuck her head in. "Am I dreaming, or is there egg soufflé for breakfast?"

"It's no dream," Avery said. "Lots of cheesy wonderfulness of the never-fail variety."

"Come on in," Maddie said. "You're just in time and we've got plenty. Is Joe with you?"

"No." Nikki closed the kitchen door behind her and Kyra noted the difficulty with which she moved. "He's on his way to Tampa, but he insisted on dropping me off first."

"Is there something wrong with your car?" Troy asked.

"Not exactly."

They looked at Nikki in question.

She grimaced. "It seems my stomach's too big. And when I move the seat far enough back for it to fit, my feet don't reach the pedals."

Troy and Steve laughed out loud. Avery attempted to hide her stutter of surprise. Kyra made a point of staring down at her camera until the desire to laugh had passed.

"It's probably just as well," Maddie said, displaying no hint of amusement. "You could go into labor at any time. It's probably better not to be behind the wheel of a car when it happens."

"Yeah, well, that's what Joe said," Nikki said stiffly as she maneuvered her bulk into the closest vacant chair. Maddie set a place and poured her a large glass of orange juice. "Sorry," Nikki said. "What did I interrupt?"

"We were just discussing the fact that we're pretty much dead in the water until we get some sort of ruling on the breach of contract and noncompete," Maddie said. "I can't believe any judge will decide we have no right to the title of the show we created or the ability to sell the documentary about the Sunshine Hotel."

"That did it. I think I just lost my appetite," Nikki said. "And as you can see, that rarely happens."

"I wish that were all," Avery said. "But it seems we've lost the paparazzi, too."

"Yeah, even Nigel has given up and gone looking for more interesting game," Maddie said.

Nigel Bracken had been the most persistent of the paparazzi who had once stalked them in hopes of catching Daniel frolicking with his son. When Kyra had managed to bore them into leaving, Daniel and Will had hatched a plan to get them back in an attempt to save *Do Over*.

"They were out in force for the grand reopening of the Sunshine Hotel and Beach Club," Nikki pointed out.

"Yeah, well, that was mid-October and both Daniel and Will were there. This is January and we're on our own. I heard there was an Elvis look-alike sing off in Clearwater. Apparently even imitators of dead celebrities are more interesting than us," Kyra said.

"Stop it," Avery said. "Or you're going to suck all the pleasure out of this egg soufflé."

"Right." Maddie picked up the knife. "Why don't you do the honors, Steve? In celebration of your first official day as a Realtor?"

"Don't mind if I do." Kyra's father accepted the knife and began to cut across the first soufflé.

"Me first, Geedad!" Dustin held up his plastic Superman plate.

"Absolutely." He placed clumps of cheese and egg on Dustin's plate then began to carve out other pieces.

Her mother winced but made no move to take the knife or relieve him of the task.

"I have to admit I never imagined trading finance for real estate." Her father had been a successful investment adviser in Atlanta before he'd lost his clients' money, their money, and his job to Malcolm Dyer's Ponzi scheme. That had been three and a half years ago, and a lot of lying around feeling sorry for himself had followed. Her mother had been left to get them out of the mess and she had. Which was when Kyra had discovered how strong her mother really was.

"Maybe we need to give the paparazzi something to photograph," Avery said. "Anyone want to shoot a seminude selfie or two like Kim Kardashian?"

Nikki snorted. "It would serve them right if I did."

There was laughter, but Kyra didn't join in. Her stomach churned and the loss of the paps was the least of it. Sunshine Beach Club memberships were growing, but they had to sell every one of the Sunshine Hotel cottages as well as the documentary if she was going to have a snowball's chance of paying back the loan she'd taken out against Bella Flora.

"Why don't you give Daniel a call? Maybe he could stop by. Just to wave the flag a bit?" Her father, who had once called Daniel an overrated, overpaid prick of a movie star, said this around a mouthful of soufflé, as if it were no big deal.

Dustin sat up at the mention of his father's name. "Is my Dandiel coming?"

"No," Kyra said. "Right now we're just going to enjoy our breakfast." Assuming she could choke any of it down. "Here. Try some of these." She distracted him with a small bunch of red grapes. Feeling Troy's eyes on her, she forced herself to take a bite of soufflé and even managed to swallow it though it might as well have been cardboard for all the pleasure it gave her. "Now that you're working for Franklin Realty, I hope you'll focus on selling the Sunshine Hotel cottages."

Her father, who was the only other person at the table who knew about the loan, lost some of his smile. "You know I'll do everything I can to find the right buyers for those units," he promised. He was careful not to look at her mother.

"What do we do about Bitsy Baynard?" Avery asked.

"Good question." Nikki was eating with gusto.

"We can't afford to let her steamroll us," Kyra said.

"I agree." Avery sat back in her chair. "Why don't I set up a meeting for her with Ray and me to choose finishes? I'll try to stall for as long as I can before the meeting actually takes place.

We're not starting build-out or anything else until we know what's going on."

"The woman is an heiress to a huge fortune. She can't really want to live at the Sunshine Hotel. Something's obviously wrong in Bitsy's world," Maddie said. "We need to find out what it is."

"Yeah, well, the next time we try to find out what's going on, I suggest we leave out the alcohol," Kyra said.

"Good thinking," Troy said.

"I'll speak to her," Nikki said before Troy could yank their chains about their last failed attempt. "Bitsy and I have a history. Maybe if I can get her alone and ask the right questions, she'll confide in me."

"It's worth a try," Avery said. "Leaving her in the model isn't going to work, either. It's not going to show well overflowing with her things like it is."

They ate on, though not with their original gusto.

"Do you need a ride back?" Maddie asked Nikki when she'd finished.

"I can give her a lift. The Sunshine is only a few blocks away from the office," her father said, clearly proud to have an office to go to. Even if it was located in a small bungalow in an equally small beach town.

"Thanks," Nikki said. "But Gabriella invited me to stop by."

Kyra noticed she didn't exactly look eager to go.

"Well, I've got some errands later," Maddie said when Nikki had carried her plate to the sink and was preparing to leave. "I'll call you when I'm heading out in case you're ready then."

· · ·

The Giraldis' two-bedroom unit at the Cottage Inn was smaller than the one she and Joe had moved into at the Sunshine Hotel. It had not been updated by Avery and Chase or decorated by Ray Flamingo. It did, however, have a large plate glass window that overlooked the pass and Shell Key just beyond it. Its broad front porch was even closer to the water and was furnished with a table and chairs. A wooden swing dangled from the ceiling and stirred gently in the breeze.

Gabriella welcomed her with a hug and led her to the dinette where Nonna Sofia sat sipping tea. Sofia wore black track pants and a neon pink T-shirt. The arms that protruded from the short sleeves were pale but wiry; the hands that held the cup were heavily veined. A coordinating neon pink visor sat atop her head.

"Please sit," Gabriella said. "Would you like a cup of tea and a chocolate croissant?"

Nikki was already stuffed from the egg soufflé, but decided it would be rude to refuse. "Thank you."

"Come, sit next to me," Nonna Sofia said, patting the empty chair. "I promise I won't bite."

Nikki noticed that the gleam in Sofia's eyes contradicted her assurance. Nonetheless she smiled and sat, chiding herself for being nervous as Gabriella placed a croissant on a plate and set it in front of Nicole. "Joe Senior found these at that little bakery near Belle Vista. They're completely irresistible."

Nikki took a bite while Joe's mother poured hot water over the loose tea in the cup's strainer, chatting amiably as she did so. "Your cottage is just lovely. I think Ray is incredibly talented. And we so enjoyed meeting Madeline, Kyra, Avery, and the Hardins. The Franklins, too." Gabriella smiled. "In fact, Renée brought these flowers by yesterday." She motioned to the bright tropical arrangement that sat in the center of the table. "It's nice to know that you and Joe have such a lovely community of people around you."

There had been times when Nikki had felt overwhelmed by Joe's family and how much a part of each other's lives they were. But Gabriella's voice was soothing and her smile was kind. Nikki began to relax. "From what the Franklins have said, the west coast of Florida was largely settled by Midwesterners." Nikki set the tea strainer aside and stirred in milk and sugar. She took another bite of the croissant and felt the perfect combination of pastry and chocolate melt in her mouth. Her eyes closed briefly in ecstasy.

"I wouldn't really read your tea leaves," Nonna Sofia said. "Unless you wanted me to."

Nicole's eyes flew open.

"Mama," Gabriella said. "Don't tease Nicole."

"Who's teasing?" Joe's grandmother said as Nicole lifted the teacup to her lips. "Besides I don't need tea leaves to know that she and Joe should be married before those babies are born."

A bit of croissant stuck in Nikki's throat. Attempting to wash it down, she took a too-large sip of hot tea. Mouth open, she waved her hand frantically, as if that might actually put out the fire in her mouth.

Gabriella shot her mother-in-law a look, then raced to the refrigerator, where she dispensed ice cubes into a glass. Placing it in Nikki's hand, she winced as Nikki tilted the cup to her lips and sucked a cube into her mouth.

"Mama!" Gabriella scolded as she watched Nikki's face. "You promised!"

"Promised what? To keep my thoughts to myself? *Pffft.*" Nonna Sofia flung her hand open, beseeching fingers and all, in obvious dismissal. "Not to ask her why she hasn't married Joe yet? It was one thing when it was just the two of them. But now?" She cast her gaze on Nikki's stomach, as if she could see the babies curled up inside and knew everything about them. "It isn't as if he hasn't asked her many times."

Nikki's tongue had finally begun to numb, but even if it had been in working order, she would not have corrected Sofia's statement. It seemed Joe hadn't told them that he'd finally stopped asking. He'd given her what she'd said she wanted just when the babies were becoming real in her mind and she'd begun to realize that she wanted for them what she'd never had—a solid, extended, loving family tied strongly together.

She was trying to imagine what it might feel like to confide in Gabriella and Sofia when her cell phone rang. Seeing Maddie's number, she answered.

"Nikki?"

"Yes."

"I'm out back with Dustin. Do you want us to drop you at the Sunshine?"

Any thought of sharing confidences evaporated as soon as a means of escape presented itself. "It's Maddie," she said to Gabriella. "I have to go. Thank you so much for the tea."

She found Maddie and Dustin standing on the seawall midway between Bella Flora and the Giraldis' cottage. Both of them were watching a shiny black boat out in the pass.

"Are you all right?" Maddie asked as Nikki joined them.

"Yes," Nikki said. "Just burned my tongue." And fled like the coward that she apparently was.

"Look at that!" Maddie pointed to the boat, which was racing through the pass at breakneck speed.

Nikki looked more closely and saw *Hard Case* painted across the side in big white letters. It was Chase Hardin's boat. But while the driver bore a striking resemblance to Chase, Chase would never be driving like that. Nor would he flaunt a girl in a bikini under their noses. Nikki narrowed her gaze just as the driver turned his head. The driver was one of Chase's sons. The girl, who was pressed against him like a second skin, was very young.

"Is Jason!" Dustin chortled happily. But then Dustin had no idea it was a school day. Or that Jason's father probably had no idea that his younger son had taken his boat without permission. In order to play hooky with a girl who was as close to naked as it was possible to get.

Nikki lifted her phone and snapped several pictures as the boat practically flew over another boat's wake.

"Do you think I should call Avery?" Maddie asked. "I'd feel terrible if something happened and I hadn't said anything."

"I'm not sure," Nikki said around her still tender tongue. "That would make Avery the messenger." And everyone knew that sometimes the bearer of bad news was the one who ended up getting shot.

. . .

Avery paced the marina parking lot in south Tampa late that afternoon waiting for Jason Hardin to show up with his father's boat. She'd spent close to an hour wishing Maddie hadn't told her what she and Nikki had seen, and another debating whether to call Chase and tell him. In the end she'd raced to the small bay-side Hi and Dry where Chase kept the boat, ultimately arriving with no real plan in mind.

The sun was close to setting when the *Hard Case* finally pulled into the marina and nosed up to the dock. Avery had actually prayed that Maddie and Nikki were mistaken, but Jason was at the wheel and the young, dark-haired girl, now bundled up in Jason's baseball team hoodie, was still welded to his side. He tied the boat up swiftly but made no move to spray the boat down. In the fading light, he leaned down and kissed the girl, who giggled seductively.

This was not a first kiss, but one between two people who knew each other's bodies. When she'd arrived, her biggest concern was that Jason had skipped school and another practice on top of taking the boat without permission. But this was something with an even greater potential for disaster. There'd been no hint of a girlfriend or even signs that Jason had been dating. She hoped to hell Chase had already discussed the birds and bees with his son, and that Jason had paid at least some attention.

He was so caught up in feeling the girl up that he didn't notice when Avery stepped out of the shadows and walked onto the dock. When she cleared her throat, he only looked up lazily, not the least bit self-conscious about the public display of affection.

"What are you doing here?" he asked with the insolent tone he often turned on Chase.

"I was going to ask you the same question," she replied.

He didn't look away, but he didn't respond, either.

"If you were planning to keep the fact that you skipped school and took your father's boat without permission a secret, you shouldn't have been showing off so close to Bella Flora. Or were you hoping to get caught?"

"I'm allowed to take the boat out," he said sullenly.

"Not alone. And not when you're supposed to be at school."

"He wasn't alone. He was with me." The girl's tone was belligerent, her eyes glassy.

"So your parents don't care if you skip school and spend the day partying alone with a boy?" Avery asked.

The girl stuck out her chin defiantly, but it was Jason who answered. "Sleeping with my dad doesn't make you my mother." He stepped up onto the dock then leaned down to help the girl out. With his arm around the girl's shoulders, he walked toward Avery with an unpleasant swagger, stopping right in front of her so that he towered over her. "And you have no right to tell me what to do."

She was careful not to fall back. Despite the bluster and intimidation tactics, her heart ached for Chase and Jeff and for the young, eager boy she remembered.

"You're right. I'm not your parent. But I've known your father and grandfather most of my life. You all are as close to family as I've got. I'm an adult who cares about your family and you." She looked up at him because she had no choice, but she remained on the offensive. "I don't care how tall you are. You're behaving like a little shit. And no one, including me, is enjoying watching you piss your opportunities down the toilet." She had no experience with parenting and hoped that using so many potty words did not nullify the importance of what she said.

His blue eyes turned dark and decidedly stormy. "Thanks for the concern. It means so much to me." His words dripped with sarcasm. "Come on, Kylie." He led the girl toward the parking lot.

"Just a minute!" Avery called, striding after him.

He didn't turn until they'd reached the Explorer he shared with his brother. "What the hell do you want?"

Avery raised her chin, held her ground. "I want you to tell your father what you did today. You owe him honesty at the very least."

Jason snorted. "He doesn't give a crap what I do unless it's playing baseball to get some stupid scholarship. And I can't think why I need to tell him what I did today. It would only piss him off." His look turned crafty. "Besides, it's not like you can do anything to me if I don't."

"That's true," she conceded. "But if you don't tell him, I will." She said this with every bit of assurance she could muster. But as she turned to walk away, she hoped like hell she wouldn't have to.

Ten

Maddie was in the minivan on her way to the grocery store when the DJ introduced William Hightower's seminal seventies hit "Mermaid in You." She froze for an instant as the opening strains of the song that had seemed the very definition of love to her teenaged self swirled around her. At the time she'd been busy spinning fantasies about "William the Wild," whose poster hung on her bedroom wall, never imagining those fantasies might one day come true.

She had coral cheekbones and sunkissed hair . . . Skin that shimmered everywhere . . . Maddie sank into the powerful lyrics and haunting melody, even more affected now that she knew how intensely personal the song had been to him and sang along with her favorite line, *I didn't know what love was or what it could do 'til I found the mermaid in you . . .* Lost in the song, she remembered who she was then and shivered at how Will made her feel now.

She tuned back into the DJ's voice as he cued up "Free Fall," the current hit that had fueled Will's unexpected comeback.

"William Hightower's forty-city tour sold out ten minutes after tickets went on sale!" the DJ announced. "But I have it on good authority that Hightower's people are adding more performances. Yours truly will be giving away some of those tickets right here on WLCK, so stay tuned!"

Maddie reached for her cell phone, but once she had it in her hand, she hesitated.

You're too big a wuss to call him. How do you think you're going to hold on to him if you don't even have the nerve to call? It was her subconscious, who'd taken to popping up uninvited, and who was unfailingly negative.

I am not afraid to call Will. She was getting kind of tired of having to defend herself to herself.

You are—you're afraid to call him. Afraid he won't answer. Afraid he will but will sound eager to get off the phone. Afraid he's already looking forward to getting on the road, where there will be lots of younger and better-looking women to choose from.

Am not.

Are too.

Irritated with herself and her relentless subconscious, she shoved the phone in her purse.

I don't blame you for being afraid, her subconscious conceded. *It's been four days since you heard from him.*

We communicate in other ways. He sent me that photo of the redfish he caught. Will is still Will, Maddie countered.

And you're still you.

Maddie wasn't sure when her subconscious had begun copping this attitude, but this was clearly not a compliment.

How long do you really think your relationship is going to last once he's on the road for all those months without you?

He's not a player anymore. He's only doing the tour to make music and for the money to subsidize the sober living facility, she fired back.

So he'll just turn his back on all those women? He won't even be tempted? Her subconscious wasn't buying it. *You should have agreed to go on tour with him. He told you he needed you. He even said he "trusted himself" more with you there.*

She parked the van, slammed the door, and crossed the parking lot. As she pushed the cart through the aisles, the internal debate continued. In the produce section she weighed a bunch of bananas and wondered whether thinking to yourself was as bad as talking to yourself.

She told herself to stop as she threw the grocery bags into the van. Back on Gulf Boulevard, she reminded herself that there were far more important things to worry about at the moment, most notably their lack of funds and their inability to sell the documentary or shoot their own version of *Do Over* until the lawsuit was dismissed or settled.

Her "self" didn't seem to be listening.

"Fine." She picked up her phone and called Will. This time she didn't get a chance to reconsider because he answered on the first ring.

"Hi, there, Maddie-fan. How are things going?"

"Oh, they're going," she said brightly. "I just called to say congratulations! I heard on the radio that your tour sold out in ten minutes."

"It's crazy, isn't it?" Will said.

"Crazy," she said.

Yeah, just fabulous, her subconscious added with a far heavier dose of sarcasm than a subconscious should possess.

"That's what Aaron keeps telling me. We hit the road in March, and I think we play Tampa in early April. But I hope I'll be seeing you before then."

"When do you think you can come up?" She was ashamed of how hard it was to ask.

"I don't know. I'll have to see. They've hired an assistant to handle my schedule and keep me organized. I think Aquarian's afraid that if I have too much free time on my hands, I might get into trouble."

"Well, being organized never hurt anyone that I know of," Maddie said a bit too cheerily. "What's his name?"

"*His* name is Lori Blair—that's Lori with an *i*." There was amusement in his voice. "Or so I was informed when we were introduced."

"Oh." Was it wrong that she was now hoping that Lori was a transvestite or a badly dressed cross-dresser and not an attractive female?

Will laughed. "*She's* a little on the young side. In fact, I'm pretty sure she was still wearing diapers the first time I went on tour."

Maddie did not want to think about just how young that would make Lori with an *i*.

Doesn't matter. There's no such thing as too young, her subconscious assured her.

"But she's surprisingly competent. And fiercely protective," Will said. "She kind of reminds me of you."

"Oh?"

"Yeah."

Why don't you ask him in what ways? her subconscious nudged.

But she couldn't do it. Because she was afraid of hearing him describe the girl. Afraid to know just how young Lori was. Terrified that Aaron had chosen to send a younger, presumably prettier version of Maddie on the road with Will for reasons that were not completely professional. And because, as her subconscious pointed out, *If you'd agreed to go with him, there wouldn't be a Lori.*

"The residents here are all already a little bit in love with her. Even Hudson doesn't seem immune," he said, mentioning his longtime fishing guide and closest friend, who had taught Maddie how to operate a boat.

"That's great," she said as enthusiastically as she could, which was to say with the stiffness of a board. "I look forward to meeting her."

Liar, liar, pants on fire!

"And I look forward to seeing you." His voice grew quieter, more intimate. "All of you."

There, she told her subconscious. *Take that. There's no need to panic.*

"I'll ask Lori to put some time aside," he said without a trace of irony. "She's very big about making sure even personal things are on the schedule."

Ha! Her subconscious sneered. *I don't know about you, but I think it's definitely time to let the panicking commence!*

Maddie sighed. It was bad enough having such a negative, know-it-all subconscious. Did it always have to have the last word?

. . .

"Sorry, Sherlock." Bitsy looked down into the bulldog's forlorn face as he pushed at the bowl that contained actual dog food rather than the sautéed hamburger and grilled steak bits he was used to. "It's this or a granola bar." Which was what she'd been reduced to eating for breakfast and lunch and sometimes even dinner. "You may have noticed we don't have a cook anymore. Or a housekeeper. Or even a house for the housekeeper to keep."

Sherlock snuffled and looked even more pathetic, but Bitsy had been shocked to discover that even the lowest-quality ground round was too expensive for her nonexistent budget. "Hey, it's not like I'm sneaking foie gras and feeding you this." She, too, was now eating food that came in boxes and wrappers, though fortunately not yet in dog food cans. "Eat up. Then we'll go outside for some fresh air."

Though he looked at her accusingly, Sherlock ultimately ate the entire bowl of food then quickly washed it down with fast slurps of water. Bitsy changed into a bathing suit and cover-up, took him outside to do his business, then carried him and the local newspaper to the pool. Slipping his leash under one leg of a chaise, she removed her cover-up and began to apply sunscreen. The sun was warming in the cloudless blue sky, and the rhythmic wash of the water out on the beach was far more calming than her white noise machine had ever been. The people at the pool were not former models or socialites who went after cellulite and varicose veins as if they were enemies of the state. Their bathing suits and cover-ups did not carry the designer labels she was used to or show off hard, sculpted bodies honed in private Pilates classes and at the hands of personal trainers who came daily to one's home gym.

Although the cottages didn't appear to be selling—only the two models and Joe and Nikki's unit were more than empty shells—the beach club, if not thriving, seemed to be attracting members. Four women sat at a card table beneath the overhang playing mah-jongg and chatting while casting an occasional eye at the children diving for pennies or bobbing up and down in the pool. Two teenage girls in bikinis sat on the low wall that bordered the beach and pretended not to watch the nicely mus-cled, bare-chested lifeguard who was perched on a retro stand between the deep and shallow ends of the pool. Voices floated down from the rooftop deck, and out of the corner of her eye she could see several tables of people in the glass-walled dining room as well as a Ping-Pong match taking place in the main lobby. Every once in a while a child would walk inside and come out licking an ice cream sandwich or cone from the soda fountain. Even the seagulls soaring above the string that crisscrossed above the pool and pool deck, looking for a way in, seemed less strident than their Palm Beach counterparts. Sherlock curled up on the concrete next to her chaise and watched the children as if they were a fascinating new species. If she hadn't been so desperately poor and embarrassingly lonely, it would have been downright relaxing.

Bitsy pulled the local newspaper out of her beach bag and turned to the alarmingly slim classified section. Nowhere did she see an ad for a job that required skills in entertaining, charitable fund-raising, lunching, or shopping. The closest listing to Bitsy's skill set was for an activities director at a nursing home that paid the annual sum of thirty thousand dollars. Which she was fairly certain was less than their part-time gardener had made. The other was for a concession stand trainee, which listed a salary that was frighteningly close to zero, but promised free meals.

She was waffling over whether to even circle the two ads when Sherlock gave a small woof. A shadow fell over the paper. She looked up to see Nicole Grant, who had, despite her increased bulk and pronounced waddle, somehow managed to sneak up on her.

"May I join you?"

"Please do." Bitsy motioned to the chaise beside her and waited while Nikki lowered herself down onto the cushion then lifted and levered her legs off the ground. Lying down, her belly was even more pronounced. One hand cupped the bottom of her stomach, the other rested on top of it. "That's quite a load you're carrying."

"You've got that right." Nikki drew in a deep breath of air then expelled it slowly. "You know it's time to give birth when even sitting down makes you short of breath."

They lay side by side for a moment silently watching the jigsaw of clouds rearrange themselves in the sky. "Are you afraid?" Bitsy asked.

"Yes."

"Of giving birth or being a mother?"

"Both." Nikki's eyes remained on the sky as she spoke. "Back when I was wishing I could have a child, I never imagined it happening at this point in my life. And I sure as hell never expected I'd end up having twins."

"Joe seems pretty happy about becoming a father." In fact, Bitsy envied Nikki's support system. She had Joe, who clearly loved her, a set of grandparents and even a great-grandmother for the babies, plus good friends nearby at Bella Flora. Despite her brother's thievery and what it had cost her, Nikki was far richer in the ways that mattered than Bitsy had ever been.

"Yes. And I have no doubt he'll be better at all of it than me. The only person I ever mothered was Malcolm and we all know how that turned out."

"I don't think you can be blamed for Malcolm. Sometimes the people you love just behave badly."

Nikki gave her a sharp look. "Has Bertie done something, Bitsy? I don't mean to pry, but I had the impression it was a good match and that you two really loved each other."

So had Bitsy. She wanted to ask Nikki to explain just how in love they'd looked, wanted desperately to reassure herself that Bertie had not simply been a fortune hunter who'd bided his time until he could make his escape and take her fortune with him. But the loss was far too staggering and the hurt too great to admit.

"We were. I mean, we are." Bitsy grimaced.

She'd become a pariah in the town that had once courted her. Without money, she was beneath their notice though not their contempt. Nikki had also experienced a great fall through no fault of her own. Yet, she had survived it, made real friends, and even found love.

"I hope you know that I'm here for you," Nicole said. "All of us are."

Sherlock raised his head and looked up at her. Bitsy reached out to scratch him lightly behind one ear. He snuffled and looked at her with what she thought might be gratitude. "Thank you," she said to Nikki.

"If you told me what's really going on, we might be able to help," Nikki said gently.

Bitsy sat up and swung her legs over the side of the chaise. "I appreciate that," she said, pulling on her cover-up and releasing Sherlock's leash. "Really, I do." Just not enough to share her sad, humiliating story. "But I think Sherlock needs to go to the bathroom." She tugged on Sherlock's leash but he didn't budge. In fact, he snuffled at her with what sounded like disapproval and refused to move.

For some reason that Bitsy didn't understand, Nikki and the others had not yet done a Google search or run into anyone from Palm Beach eager to share the clichéd soap opera Bitsy's life had become. She was not about to clue them in unless she had to. Reaching down, she gathered Sherlock into her arms. "I'm going to take him over to his favorite tree on Thirty-first," she said inanely, being careful not to meet Nikki's appraising gaze before she turned and walked away. Surely inanity was better than pity. She intended to hang on to the remnants of her pride as long as possible. At the moment, they were all she had left.

Eleven

Nikki was sound asleep on the chaise when she felt a gentle nudge on her shoulder.

With the nightmares that had been waking her in the wee hours of the night absent, she'd been floating peacefully wrapped in a fluffy cloud and had no interest in leaving it. "Not now," she murmured. "Sleeping . . ."

"Yes, I can see that." The voice was Joe's, the words breathed close to her ear. "But you look like you've been out here for a while. Do you want to go inside and lie down?"

"No. In sky. Is nice . . ."

"Okay." A beach towel was laid on top of her. Something scraped across concrete. She tried to turn on her side but something was in the way. Her eyes flickered open, she looked down. That thing was her stomach. "Good Lord."

She heard Joe's chuckle and turned her head to face him. "I dreamed I was floating in a cloud. It was so beautiful. The best thing was that I didn't weigh anything at all." Nikki sighed with real regret. "The only place I feel like that now is in my dreams if I'm lucky enough to sleep for more than five minutes at a time. And in the water."

"I think the Gulf's a little cool, and the pool probably is, too. But I could run a bath for you."

"You'd do that for me?" Her eyes got moist. But then she teared up at Hallmark commercials and pictures of puppies in magazines. Yesterday she'd sobbed uncontrollably when Dustin handed her a weed he'd picked. "I don't know, the cottage feels so far away right now."

"So what would you like?" He bowed like some courtier. "Your wish is my command."

She looked into his dark eyes and for the briefest moment what she wanted was to ask him to marry her. But how humiliating would that be? And what if he really had changed his mind and no longer wanted to get married? What if the occasional distance she felt from him was real and not imagined? "I wouldn't say 'no' to an ice cream sandwich."

He smiled with a reassuring flash of white teeth. "I'd be worried it would ruin your dinner, but I happen to know that's not possible. Be right back."

When he returned, she wasted no time peeling off the wrapper and licking her way across the ice cream edges. Her eyes closed in unfeigned pleasure. "God, I love ice cream sandwiches. I think they're unfairly underrated in the dessert world."

He unwrapped his own and took a large bite.

"How can you do that?"

"You don't get the full flavor when you lick around the edges and eat one chocolate layer at a time," he said. "It's called an ice cream *sandwich* for a reason."

"Ha!" she replied, her tongue coated with ice cream. "It lasts way longer this way. And you get to enjoy each part thoroughly."

"We'll have to agree to disagree on this," he said, taking the final bite of his sandwich. "But I would like to reach some sort of agreement about the girls' names." He looked steadily at her. "I'd really like to name one of them Sofia. It would mean a lot to my grandmother. I was thinking maybe we could each choose one name. I'd pick Sofia and you could choose anything else you like."

"So they could end up having names that are polar opposites? Like Sofia," she said with the Italian accents and lilt that Joe's family used. "And, I don't know, Hildegarde?"

"Well, I'd like to believe you wouldn't be that cruel to our daughter, but basically yes. You know, it's called a compromise. They teach it in hostage negotiation training." Joe's smile didn't quite reach his eyes. "And chances are they're going to be very different from each other anyway given that they're fraternal twins." His tone remained light, but it was clear that this was important to him.

She couldn't meet his eyes. "I'll give it some thought."

"What's going on, Nik?"

"What do you mean?" She directed her gaze just over his left shoulder.

"I know you a lot better than you seem to think I do. It's pretty clear your reluctance to choose names has nothing to do with the names themselves." He reached out, placed a finger under her chin, and turned her face so that her eyes met his. "I'd appreciate it if you'd tell me what the problem is."

This was what came of living with a man for whom reading faces and sweating confessions out of people were simply part of the job. He knew her all right, but that didn't mean she was going to come out and voice her fear that even naming them would tempt fate. She knew it was silly and superstitious, had chided herself for being ridiculous a thousand times, but there it was. When the babies were born and declared healthy, he could name them after any member of his family he wanted—well, maybe not after his Aunt Zanobia, which sounded like the name of a small village in a fairy tale. "Let's just think about it a little longer," she hedged. Then eager to change the subject, she continued, "I spent some time with Bitsy earlier. Something serious has happened between her and Bertie."

"It would take all of five seconds to find out what might have happened," Joe said.

"I assume you're not referring to some sort of FBI investigation."

"No. I was thinking the Internet. Possibly Google. I doubt it would take more than a quick scan of the Palm Beach papers to get the lowdown," he replied. "I'm kind of surprised none of you have done that yet."

"It wasn't completely unanimous," Nikki admitted. "But we decided to wait until Bitsy told us herself." Which Nikki, who'd been the subject of way too much gossip and currently had quite a few issues she didn't want to talk about, was pretty much on board with.

One of Joe's dark eyebrows sketched upward.

She studied his expression. "You already know, don't you?"

"And so should you. She's put you all on the spot. Is there any budget available to build out and give her a two-bedroom?"

"No. Our agreement about what she'd get in return for her 'sponsorship' of the next season of *Do Over* was a little vague," Nikki admitted, remembering just how grateful they'd been when Bitsy had agreed to become a sponsor. "We were in serious need of the capital and were not expecting the network to sue us." She blew a bit of bang out of one eye. "The thing is I really appreciated the people who didn't force me to acknowledge or discuss all the ways my life fell apart when Malcolm committed his fraud. Personally, I think it's a lot easier not to know something than to *pretend* not to know it." She sat up straighter and began to lever her legs off the chaise.

"There's no shortage of sand out there," Joe said with a curt nod toward the beach. "But unless you're an ostrich, sticking your head in it is almost never a good idea."

She suspected her smile was more of a grimace as she got her feet set on the ground. "Speaking of sand, I think I'm ready for that bath now. If the tub were bigger and I were smaller, I might even ask you to join me." It was a clumsy attempt to change the subject and she was relieved when he didn't object, but instead took her hands and helped her to her feet.

"Come on then." Once she was steady, he put an arm around her shoulders and led her toward the cottage. It wasn't far and yet she was winded when they got there. "Are you sure you're feeling okay?" he asked.

"Sure. I just get a little out of breath from carrying around so much extra weight."

"Well, I'm glad you're seeing Dr. Payne this week."

Nikki snorted inelegantly. "God, I wish she'd change her name already. It's a wonder anyone goes to her at all." She kept her tone light and did her best to breathe evenly when he slowed his pace to match hers. As he held the cottage door open for her then carefully helped her into the bath, Nikki knew just how lucky she was to have Joe in her life and his children in her belly. The acknowledgment added fuel to her fear. Happiness, if it came, had always been fleeting, not something she'd ever managed to hold on to. How on earth was she supposed to believe that this time would be different?

• • •

Renée Franklin was fairly certain there weren't too many women her age that enjoyed playing in the dirt as much as she did. At the moment she was kneeling in it, working her trowel beneath the roots of a snake plant that had somehow slithered into a flower bed in which it did not belong. She yanked it out with enthusiasm and set it aside with satisfaction. She believed plants and flowers appreciated order and structure in the same way that children did—they might not give voice to it, but it made their lives more secure, a quality that Renée had especially appreciated given the loss and turbulence that had infused her own childhood.

It was a perfect late January day and ideal for gardening with an abundance of sunshine and temperatures hovering in the sixties. The scent of rain teased at her nostrils, which meant the white and orange birds of paradise she'd added to the bed that she'd created around the mammoth hibiscus would be properly doused in just a few hours. The hibiscus, which her grandmother had planted to commemorate the opening of the Sunshine Hotel and Beach Club back in 1942, sat at the junction of the main walkway that bisected the hotel's guest cottages, directly across from the unit where they'd been living when her father died and her stepmother disappeared. With the help of the garden club, of which she'd been president more times than she could count, she'd taken cuttings from the overgrown bush and planted them in each cottage's walled garden as part of an overall relandscaping.

Her cell phone vibrated in her pants' pocket and she removed one dirt-caked gardening glove to answer.

"Renée?" It was John, with whom she'd fallen in love when she was a girl and he was the handsome lifeguard who'd kissed her behind a nearby cabbage palm. "Have you whipped all those flowers into shape yet?"

"Not quite. There are a few holdouts," she said, still plucking weeds with her remaining gloved hand. Her knees on the rubber pad had gone quite numb and she sat back on her heels.

"Well, I have no doubt you'll have them toeing the line soon enough. Just like I always do."

She rolled her eyes though there was no one but the plants to see it. "No one's buying you as the henpecked husband, dear. You'll have to try a different tack."

He chuckled. "I had a call from a family named Hirsch. They're down from Michigan for the week and want to look at a two-bedroom before they leave on Sunday. I told them they could come see the model."

"But Bitsy Baynard's in it." Renée tossed a handful of weeds onto the nearby path.

"She said she'd vacate if we needed her to, didn't she?"

"Yes, but I'm not sure she meant it."

"I've asked Steve Singer to set up the showing for Saturday. That'll give her a few days to get used to the idea."

"But where on earth is she supposed to put all those things she brought?" Renée asked.

"We have eight empty units. Surely she can stash her excess in one of them."

"I don't know. I'm not sure she'll agree to that," Renée said. From what she'd seen, Bitsy Baynard was used to giving instructions, not taking them.

"Well, no one's going to buy a unit sight unseen," John said reasonably. "And we're all anxious to find buyers for them. So someone will have to find a way not to ask her, but tell her."

Renée stuffed the pile of weeds she'd plucked into a plastic bag. No point letting them end up back where she'd pulled them from. "I'm meeting with Annelise about the upcoming family night, then I'll ask Nicole to give Bitsy a heads-up." The most miraculous part of the renovation of the hotel that Maddie, Avery, Nikki, Kyra, and crew had done was discovering what had happened to their father and Annelise's mother in 1952. Finding closure on that tragedy had brought her sister back from the abyss on which she'd teetered for much of her life.

"Do you think handling the social activities is too much for Annelise?" John asked, as always attuned to her slightest inflection or hesitation.

"Well, I think she could use help but it's such a joy to see her happy and productive." Using their grandmother's notes in the guest logs she'd kept for decades, Annelise had already duplicated several of Nana's most successful entertainments and come up with a few of her own. They'd subcontracted to a local restaurant group to handle the rooftop grille and the inside dining room, and tried to handle whatever problems arose together. Renée had grown up watching her grandparents run the hotel and beach club yet had had no idea how much effort it required.

"Hold on. I need both hands to get up." Slowly she straightened and looked around her with satisfaction. "I'm going to go find Annelise. And I'm thinking Maddie might be the one who should talk with Bitsy about clearing her things out of the unit."

"Good idea," John said.

"Why, thank you, kind sir," Renée replied. "I'm pretty sure not even Bitsy, who's used to having her way, is going to give Maddie a hard time. It would be too much like kicking a puppy. Or telling off Mother Teresa."

Twelve

Kyra and Avery were sitting in the dining room at Bella Flora when Kyra's cell phone rang at precisely 9:02 A.M. that Thursday morning. The call came from Bradley Forsyth of Forsyth, Fallon, and Montmart, entertainment law practitioners, or more precisely Forsyth's secretary. Kyra had no doubt that the clock had started ticking at exactly 9:00 A.M. when Bradley Forsyth had instructed his secretary to place the call. "Mr. Forsyth is returning your call. Can you hold?"

"Yes," Kyra said.

"I hope to hell we're not paying for dialing and holding time," Avery said. Grimacing toward Kyra's phone, she lowered her voice. "We weren't on speakerphone just then, were we?"

"No." Kyra shook her head. "I'll put us on speaker when he comes on the line. And let's try to be clear and concise. They're billing us at $750 per hour."

"Jeez," Avery said. "Do you think it's too late for me to go to law school?"

"I'm thinking we should apply together." Kyra managed a tight smile, but the legal fees were no joke.

Five minutes elapsed before Bradley Forsyth came on the line. Kyra noted the delay even though she suspected a refund would never be issued.

"Hello?" Bradley Forsyth's voice was smooth and unhurried. "Kyra?"

"Yes," she said. "Avery Lawford is with me."

"Hello, Avery," he said jovially. "Nice to speak with you both. I know you've been eager for an update."

"Well, we'd love for you to tell us that you've convinced the network to drop the suit and allow us to walk away free to do the kind of show we originally intended and that they agreed to," Kyra replied.

The attorney laughed. "Sorry." The laughter died to a chuckle when he noticed they hadn't joined in. "I thought you were joking."

"None of this is funny to us," Avery said tersely. "We need to know where things stand and how soon this can be wrapped up."

"Certainly," he said. "Let me see." The sound of rustling papers reached them through the speaker.

Kyra and Avery exchanged glances. Kyra pictured him attempting to speed read the file before answering. She tried not to pay attention to the minutes ticking by. Ten minutes was seventy-five dollars wasted. "Perhaps you could just tell us what it is they really want," she prompted.

"Well, that's easy," he said. "They want what they've wanted from the beginning. They want you back."

"Are they willing to pay us more money and a percentage of profits?" Kyra asked.

"No."

"Are they prepared to drop the reality TV aspect and allow us to do an actual renovation show?" Avery asked.

"Well, no."

"So they're not actually negotiating in any way," Kyra replied, stating the obvious.

"No."

"But isn't that what we're paying you for? To negotiate either an exit or a new contract with more favorable terms and conditions?" she pressed as she and Avery stared at each other across the dining room table.

"I know that's what you wanted," Forsyth conceded. "And we have tried. But they're not interested. Each season has pulled increasingly strong ratings and they like the program just the way it is."

"That's because everything is in their favor and we've been puppets for slave wages." Avery's voice rose.

"Yes, well, to put this in layman's terms, they don't think anything is 'broke' and therefore see no need to 'fix' it."

"Jesus," Avery said under her breath.

Kyra attempted to draw breath into her lungs.

"I can get you out, but you wouldn't be leaving with anything. The noncompete in the contract you signed is very clear and ironclad." The attorney sighed. "We could have been a much bigger help to you *before* you signed this contract."

"We were desperate," Kyra said dully. Which was something of an understatement. They'd been virtually penniless with no assets but their shared ownership of Bella Flora, which had been pummeled by a hurricane shortly after they'd finished renovating her.

"Yes, it's unfortunate, but that's when you need an attorney the most," Forsyth said.

"And when you can least afford one," Avery snapped.

Not, Kyra thought, that they could really afford one now. Certainly not one that had accomplished next to nothing. "Don't you think you should have told us this was hopeless before you took that retainer?"

"Well, you can't really be certain until you try," he said in a reasonable tone that made her want to choke him.

"So we paid you half a million dollars to go fishing?"

"I wouldn't put it like that," the attorney said.

"But you haven't accomplished anything!" Avery said, her face going red.

"That's not entirely correct," Forsyth said. "We now know that we can get you out, but you won't be able to do a renovation program for yourself or anyone else in any televised format. Nor do you have the right to use the title *Do Over.*"

"But that's our title. We came up with it." Kyra drew another breath.

"Unfortunately, it doesn't really matter who came up with it. Not when they can show that your use of the title could adversely impact them and their investment."

"I don't believe this," Avery sputtered.

Kyra's next breath put her perilously close to hyperventilating.

"I know it's disappointing." Forsyth managed to insert a tinge of disappointment into his own voice. "But they clearly own the pilot and the completed seasons. They also have the right to put *Do Over* into reruns for as long as they choose, or recast the entire show."

Kyra took another deep, fruitless breath. The anger clogging her throat made it difficult to speak. "And the documentary we shot of the renovation of the Sunshine Hotel and Beach Club?"

"We can continue to negotiate to try to win you the right to see it aired, but it's kind of shocking how much you managed to sign away."

"About as shocking as you managing to do nothing with all that money we gave you but fish and run the clock." Kyra's heart pounded in her chest. She thought it might be breaking. Or preparing to stop.

"I'm sorry you see it that way. We never guarantee a win, only that we will negotiate in good faith on your behalf."

"I'll give that documentary away for free before I let them have it," Kyra said through gritted teeth. "If we refuse to go back to the show, is there anything they can do to make us?"

"No," the attorney replied. "As I said, we can gain you your freedom, though it will take the remainder of the retainer to do so."

"So, all we get is our freedom?"

"It's not a small thing. And it's hard to put a price on freedom," he began.

"No it's not," Kyra cut him off. "It's costing us exactly five hundred thousand dollars." Which she had borrowed against Bella Flora along with the additional one point five million they'd needed to renovate the Sunshine Hotel and Beach Club. Which they could not recoup unless they sold all the cottages. Which meant it could also cost them Bella Flora. A gruesome fact that she'd kept secret and did not yet have the nerve to tell Maddie, Avery, or Nikki.

• • •

Whoever said idle hands were the devil's workshop knew what they were talking about, Maddie thought as she watched Avery pace the pool deck at Bella Flora and listened to Kyra and Troy argue across the loggia table. So far they'd covered the network, the documentary, and Kyra's conversation with the attorneys the day before.

"All I said was that you shouldn't give up," Troy said to Kyra.

"That's easy for you to say since it's not your program or your money at stake," she fired back. Her voice broke on the word "money."

"What? Afraid your boyfriend will actually expect you to repay his loan?" Troy taunted. "I'm sure there are things he'd take in lieu of cash."

Kyra's face flushed, but anger was only one of the emotions

that flamed her cheeks. Maddie was shocked to see fear and what looked like guilt flare in her daughter's eyes.

"That's enough, Troy," Maddie admonished the cameraman. "More than enough." She nodded to the child-size Bella Flora in which Dustin was playing.

"Oh, it's easy for him to criticize," Kyra said. "He never commits to anything all the way or puts anything important at risk."

Maddie was watching Troy's face when Kyra aimed this last accusation at him and she saw his eyes close briefly as the blow hit. But within seconds he'd gone back on the offensive.

Maddie closed her own eyes, hoping for a reprieve. When she opened them again, the two were still arguing.

Avery stopped pacing long enough to weigh in. "I still can't believe we have no recourse with the network. Or that all that money was wasted. I wouldn't mind suing Forsyth, Fallon, and Montmart for nonperformance."

"Sure, why not? Kyra can just ask the bank of Deranian to front her another million or so," Troy bit out.

"You don't have any idea what you're talking about," Kyra retorted. "As usual."

"Oh, yeah? Well, why don't you enlighten me?" Troy shot back.

Maddie expected Kyra to get in Troy's face, but instead she turned her back on him.

"We'd be a lot better off figuring out our next move instead of arguing," Avery said. "And from what I can see, our next move needs to be figuring out how to get back what Kyra and the rest of us put into the Sunshine renovation and video production."

"Yes," Kyra said. "There's too much at stake to just sit around and hope for the best."

Maddie felt a prickle of discomfort at the tremor in Kyra's voice, but her daughter did not elucidate.

"Well, as far as I can see, our only real path to raising that money is to see the Sunshine cottages sell and the beach club a success," Avery said. "What I don't know is how we help make that happen." She paced out to the seawall then back to the loggia, collapsing in a chair next to Maddie. "Everything's such a mess. Unless units sell, we have no income and nothing to renovate. And I feel so torn about everything. When I'm here, I feel like I should be in Tampa. When I'm in Tampa, I feel like I'm constantly trying to keep Chase and Jason from knocking each other's blocks off. Not that either of them ever listen to me." A shadow passed over her face, but Maddie knew from experience that there was no use trying to pry anything out of Avery. "And watching Jeff become so dependent?" Avery blew a blond bang off her forehead. "I'd give anything to have Deirdre back criticizing my clothing and food choices. She'd know how to handle Jeff and Chase and probably even Jason."

Nikki came outside and sank clumsily into the chair opposite Maddie. Though she and Joe often dined with his family and she slept at the Sunshine cottage with Joe each night—or didn't sleep if the dark smudges under her eyes were any indication—she spent her days at Bella Flora, napping in her old room and dragging herself ever more tentatively from seat to seat.

"Would you like something to drink?" Maddie asked her now.

Nikki shook her head.

Maddie chose to take this as a yes. When she returned with a tall glass of juice, Nikki was watching Dustin with a faraway look in her eye. "Here. Drink up," Maddie said quietly.

"But then I'll have to pee again. I've been to the bathroom about sixty times so far today."

"That seems unlikely," Avery said.

"No seriously, I've been counting." Nikki held up her phone so Maddie could see the times noted on her screen.

"When do you see the doctor next?" Maddie asked.

"Wednesday afternoon. Joe wanted me to see if I could get in sooner, but honestly, I don't see what difference a day or two would make."

"Dustin pee too!" He hurried over to Maddie and grabbed her hand. "Wanna go batroom, Geema!"

She hurried inside with him and stood in the bathroom doorway while he took care of business. He was beaming happily as he wiggled his pull-up back on. "I'm a big boy, Geema!"

"Yes, you are." He stepped up on the stool and she helped him wash his hands in the sink. He'd taken to potty training with an unexpected enthusiasm. Unlike his Uncle Andrew, whose passage out of diapers had been fraught with anxiety and the occasional pitched battle. But then her grandson had one of the sunniest personalities she'd encountered. If only he'd rub off on the grownups around him, she thought, when they went outside to find Kyra and Troy arguing about what shade of blue the sky was.

"What do you say, Mom?" Kyra challenged. "Would you call it sapphire or robin's egg?"

"I say you've got to be kidding," Nikki said. "I've heard some stupid arguments in my day, but the sky? There are people here who need to get a life."

"Agreed," Maddie said. "We've got way more stuff worth worrying about than that." And no one, including her, likely to broker any kind of agreement at the moment. Her phone rang and she glanced down hoping it would be Will. When she'd called that morning, Lori "with an *i*" had answered and had promised that she would let Will know, but warned that his only window between practice and his afternoon swim would be at 3:15 P.M. At the moment it was 2:45.

Caller ID indicated that it was Steve. "Arguments are us," she answered, attempting to hide her disappointment. Steve said only, "Can you call Bitsy and let her know that we have to have an emergency showing?"

"You're going to have to explain that one," she replied. turning her back on Kyra and Troy, who'd moved from arguing about sky color back to *Do Over* and the attorneys' edict. "I've never really thought of real estate in life-and-death terms."

"Well, this is one of those times. At least if we want a shot at selling the Hirsches a two-bedroom. They've had to cut their vacation short and are heading back to Detroit tonight. I convinced them to stop by to see the unit on their way to the airport."

She was too glad to see Steve so motivated to protest. Plus, as Avery had pointed out, selling the units was their only unobstructed path to recouping the money they'd put into the renovation.

"We only have two hours to get Bitsy and her things out of the model and erase all sign of her presence," Steve said in a rush. "And we have someone else coming tomorrow. She's going to have to be out at least through the weekend. After you break the news to her, can you ask Troy to meet me there to help move her things? And bring whatever cleaning supplies we might need to spruce up the unit?"

"We'll all come," she said, staring at the warring, pacing, sighing crew currently spewing their unhappiness all over Bella Flora. "We all need something positive to do. Even if scrubbing is involved."

• • •

"I thought you were joking when you called this an emergency." Bitsy stood near the path holding Sherlock in her arms as Maddie, Avery, Kyra, Dustin, Troy, and Nikki climbed out of the minivan and began to unload cleaning supplies.

"Afraid not," Maddie said, picking up a box packed with cleaning rags, a feather duster, and an assortment of spray bottles. Kyra carried a mop and bucket, Avery had the vacuum. Dustin wore a large pair of rubber gloves that reached all the way up both arms. "But I did bring a cleaning crew and some muscle with me." She nodded at Troy, who flexed pretty impressive biceps as

Steve's car screeched to a stop behind the van. He jumped out steely eyed and determined as if there were, in fact, a fire or some other disaster to be dealt with. Maddie helped Nikki out of the van. "Remember, you're just here to supervise and keep Bitsy company. No lifting or carrying."

They made their way to the cottage, where Bitsy unlocked the door. They followed her in and came to a stop, frozen in shock. Troy whistled in amazement. Maddie was still trying to make sense of what she was seeing. Bitsy's open suitcases lay everywhere. Articles of clothing had been strewn across the furniture. A negligée hung over one door. Dirty dishes teetered in the sink and covered the small counter. The trash can lid stood open, supported by the mountain of garbage inside it.

"I don't understand," Maddie said. "What happened here?"

Even Steve, who had left many a room looking as if a bomb had gone off in it, appeared shocked. And worried. He glanced down at his watch.

"I kept waiting for maid service," Bitsy explained. "It was bad enough that no one ever came to turn down the bed at night, or bring the room service I ordered. But no one ever came to clean or make the bed, either."

"I don't know who you were calling. There is no room or maid service here," Nikki said as she shoved a heap of clothing to one side so that she could lower herself onto the sofa. "Unless you contract for it on your own, this is a do-it-yourself kind of operation."

"Oh." Genuine shock etched itself onto Bitsy's face.

"In fact, this apartment has a washer and dryer." Maddie opened the bifold door to reveal the shiny apartment-size units. "It's quite convenient."

"Oh, I didn't realize," Bitsy said. "I've never seen them so small. Or sitting on top of each other like that. I thought they had something to do with the air-conditioning."

Kyra opened her mouth but seemed to think better of it.

Sherlock buried his nose in Bitsy's armpit with a small whimper of what sounded like embarrassment. Steve cleared his throat and pointed to his watch. He gave Maddie a pleading look.

"So we're going to move you into the one-bedroom model for the weekend," Maddie explained. "But there's probably only room for about a quarter of this . . . your . . . things. So you need to choose only the items you really need as quickly as possible. We'll store the rest in one of the empty cottages."

"But . . ." Bitsy looked completely lost. Sherlock let out a snuffle.

"Nikki?" Maddie looked to Nicole.

"Right." Nikki began to work her way to her feet. "Why don't I help you make the choices, Bitsy? Then I can help you get settled while this apartment is cleaned."

Nikki huffed and puffed a bit, but she took the still bewildered Bitsy in hand. Inside of thirty minutes everything had been fit back into a suitcase or carryall then placed in a "move" or "store" pile with none of the mimed whip cracking that Ray Flamingo had imposed during the renovation.

Maddie mouthed a thank-you to Nikki as she reached out a hand to help Nikki up from her latest seat at the dinette table. She watched Nikki put an arm around Bitsy's shoulders.

"Come on, we'll go get you settled," Nikki said, falling in behind Steve and Troy and Bitsy's luggage. "Then maybe we can go sit out by the pool. I'll treat you to an ice cream sandwich."

Thirteen

For the first time in recent memory, Daniel Deranian arrived at Bella Flora as himself. Without costume, makeup, wig, or prop, he pulled into the bricked drive in a sleek black convertible with glove leather interior, walked through the garden, up the steps, and onto the front colonnade to ring the doorbell like any everyday movie heartthrob might.

It took Kyra, who pulled open the front door, a moment to register what she was seeing. Dustin needed less than a second to race into his father's arms. "Is my Dandiel!" he shouted as his face split into a smile. "Dandiel comed to see me!"

Daniel scooped up Dustin and swung him around amid shouts of glee. Dustin was used to his father appearing and disappearing without warning and had not begun to question why it worked this way. His excitement was total and unfeigned while she expended a great deal of energy attempting to hide her excitement when he arrived as well as her disappointment when he left.

"I didn't realize you were in town," she said carefully.

"I wasn't. I just flew in. It's been way too long since I had time with the man here." He rubbed noses with Dustin and switched him easily to one hip. "I hope I'm not interrupting anything."

"We were just heading down to the beach, but we can . . ." Kyra began.

Dustin put one hand on each of Daniel's cheeks and leaned toward him so they were face-to-face. "Wanna build a catsel?" he asked hopefully.

"Absolutely. I was hoping you'd ask. I've even got my bathing suit on just in case." He winked at Dustin.

"Me, too!" Dustin crowed.

Their faces, so similar, wore almost identical expressions of joy.

"Great." She stepped away as if a foot or two might help her resist his pull when even being on the same planet made him impossible to ignore. Daniel was the magnet. She was the hapless paperclip unable to keep her distance.

"You two go ahead," she said. "I have some things to take care of."

"No way." Daniel reached for her hand and lifted it to his lips. The tickle of warm breath sent goose bumps shooting up her arm. "Not a chance."

"No way! No shanste!" Dustin imitated his father's pronouncement in a childish timbre that would one day carry Daniel's resonance. The dark eyes, golden skin, and curly hair coupled with the wide smile were all Deranian. No one with two eyes could have ever argued that Dustin was not Daniel's son.

"Let me grab the sunscreen and some cold drinks. Dustin, go get your sand tools together. Your dad can help you." She headed for the kitchen, very glad that no one was there to witness the lightness in her step or the smile that she could feel teasing at her lips.

Their voices carried through the open windows along with the late morning breeze. She caught her smile growing as Dustin instructed Daniel as to which building toys he wanted to bring and why, then described exactly what kind of "catsle" he expected to build. He chattered excitedly all the way down the path past the jetty and chose a spot close, but not too close, to the water's edge on which to build.

When they were seated and Dustin and Daniel had begun to dig into the damp sand, Kyra slid her sunglasses on and watched surreptitiously from behind their dark lenses.

"So you're going to direct," she said when he sat back to eye the moat that Dustin had begun carving around the castle's foundation.

"Yes." Satisfaction laced the word and etched itself on his face. "I finally found and secured the right screenplay. I fell in love with it the moment I started reading it. It's the perfect vehicle."

"That's great. And it looks like the studio wants to make sure to keep you happy." She picked up a handful of wet sand and watched the coquinas left behind burrow their way back into the ground. "They're even letting you and Tonja work together." She tried not to sound bitter as she uttered his wife's name and imagined the headlines.

She noted the tic in Daniel's cheek, and the way he didn't quite meet her eye, as she forced herself to imagine how intimate it would all be. "It won't be easy directing yourself, your cast, and your wife." She left out the adjectives "nasty," "vindictive," and "foul-mouthed," which normally preceded Tonja's name in her mind. Daniel already knew these things about the woman he was married to, cheated on, and refused to leave. Kyra didn't know if his loyalty was to her, their children, or their careers and wasn't sure if Daniel did, either. "Do you think it will go all right?"

He shrugged casually as if the outcome didn't really matter, and she reminded herself for what might be the millionth time, just how good an actor he was. "I guess I'm about to find that out."

Kyra leaned back on her hands and turned her face up to the warmish winter sun while Dustin and his father drizzled dribs of wet sand over the turrets and walls. When Dustin caught him with an unexpected glob of sand, Daniel hefted Dustin up, slung him over his shoulder, and carried him giggling into the Gulf, where he tossed him in the air and occasionally dropped him into the water, much to Dustin's delight.

"Quite a happy little picture, isn't it?" Seemingly materializing out of nowhere, Troy Matthews dropped down on the sand next to Kyra.

"You're talking to the wrong person if you think I'm going to be irritated that Dustin's father wants to spend time with him."

Troy snorted. "I'm sure if you cozy up to him, he'll make room for you on the set. Though I guess that could get a little tricky with his wife and children there and all." He watched her face for a reaction. "Did he happen to mention that he was only allowed to direct if Tonja played opposite him?"

Surprised as he'd obviously hoped, she said nothing.

"Yeah, apparently they figured out that even if he did a shitty job as a director, people would still come to see them on-screen together. And of course, they can trot their kids out for the publicity machine and make it look like they're just one big happy family."

"I'm sure he won't be doing a shitty job," she shot back. "Whatever you choose to think, he's very talented." Once again Troy had forced her to defend Daniel, a fact that only infuriated her further.

"Oh, he's talented all right."

She heard the dry tone, and was even vaguely aware that Troy was still speaking. But her eyes were on Daniel as he emerged from the water, his trunks clinging to his slim hips and lightly muscled thighs. He held Dustin beneath one arm like a squirming football while water sluiced down his chiseled torso, trickled through his chest hair. She didn't even try to look away. It was possible that she sighed.

"His biggest talent is keeping normally intelligent women hanging on long after it makes any sense at all."

"Hmmm?"

"I think that's my cue." Troy stood abruptly. "I can't bear to watch all those IQ points evaporating."

She didn't bother to respond or even get particularly irritated at being called stupid. Between all the golden wet skin, the clinging bathing trunks, and her son's earsplitting smile, there was simply no room in her brain for anything even slightly unpleasant. When father and son got close enough to shake themselves dry like wet animals and spray her in the process, she laughed out loud.

Daniel set Dustin on his feet and wrapped a towel around him as Dustin giggled. When Dustin picked up his shovel and hunkered down in front of the castle, Daniel slid an arm around her shoulders and pulled her close. She stiffened, trying to summon her resistance, and it had nothing to do with the fact that her T-shirt and shorts were now soaked, and everything to do with the fact that he was married and therefore unavailable. She'd vowed not to allow herself to melt every time he showed up. But when he turned her in his arms, the heat of his body was inescapable. His lips on hers were like a match to flame. His kiss caused her to sway against him.

"I'm glad you got rid of him. I can't stand seeing him crush on you."

"No," she murmured against his lips, not at all interested in talking about Troy or anyone else when Daniel's lips were moving so insistently on hers. "I didn't. He doesn't . . ." He kissed her more deeply and held her tight enough that she could feel his body's reaction to hers.

"Oh, yes he does," he breathed. "I know. Because he looks at you exactly the same way I do."

• • •

"I can't possibly weigh that much. I knew I shouldn't have worn shoes. Can I take them off and try again?" Nikki stepped off the scale, toed off the stretched-out flats, which were the only shoes she could cram her feet into anymore, and stepped back on. The bar wavered for a moment before settling.

"Well done. You dropped close to six ounces," Joe said.

Getting weighed was bad. Doing it while Joe was standing next to her was even worse. He turned and pretended to study the print on the wall after she swatted him, but there was no way he'd missed the fact that she now weighed one hundred seventy-five pounds. She was within spitting distance of two hundred.

"Don't worry. You're still in the acceptable weight gain range for twins." Dr. Payne's nurse glanced down at Nikki's chart. "And you're right around thirty-three weeks. You're almost there."

Nikki knew this was meant to reassure her, but she could feel her heart jackhammer at the thought. She drew a deep breath, took her time exhaling it, hoping to slow it down. Excess pounds were not what mattered here—healthy, viable babies were.

Dr. Payne arrived with a warm smile for Joe and Nikki, who now lay on the examining table with her bared stomach aimed up at the ceiling. It bulged slightly with each kick and movement, which were mirrored and amplified on the sonogram screen and accompanied by the staccato whoosh of the babies' rapid heartbeats.

"Tell me how you've been feeling," the doctor said as she moved the wand over Nikki's stomach.

She was preparing to tell her everything was fine when Joe caught her eye.

"Well, I have been kind of short of breath. And I do get a little light-headed." His look clearly said that if she didn't tell all, he would. "And, of course, I have almost no energy. But I figure that's because I'm not really sleeping at night. And I'm carrying a lot of extra weight around. Right?"

Dr. Payne glanced back through her chart, jotted down some more notes. Then she pulled out the blood pressure cuff and re-took Nikki's blood pressure. She frowned.

Now Nikki really couldn't breathe. Her heart galloped like a horse straining toward the finish line. Clearly something was wrong.

"What is it?" Joe asked as Nikki groped for his hand.

"Some of your breathing problems are undoubtedly a result of the babies pushing up on your lungs and the extra weight you're carrying. A certain amount of fatigue and the other symptoms you're experiencing are to be expected."

"But?" Nikki ventured even though she was pretty sure she didn't want to hear what was coming next.

"But I am concerned about your blood pressure. The more babies, the more placenta. With the additional hormones involved, this can lead to high blood pressure. We've been monitoring you carefully and it's more borderline than dangerous, but preeclampsia is something we have to be on the lookout for and we want to be vigilant."

She had a stranglehold on Joe's hand. She was not reassured by how closely he was watching the doctor's face. Nikki braced herself for the two words she'd been dreading from the day she discovered she was pregnant. But the words that came out of Dr. Payne's mouth were not "something's wrong." They were, however, words well worth dreading.

"What did you say?"

"I said I think bed rest is in order here. With plenty of hydration." Dr. Payne smiled kindly. "Because the longer you're able to carry them, the more time the babies have to mature, and the more fully developed their lungs will be. Even a few more weeks can make a positive difference."

"You mean resting as in putting my feet up now and then?" she asked hopefully.

"No, I mean *bed* rest. As in lying in bed and drinking as much liquid as possible."

Nikki shook her head. Being so big and slow sucked. Being

confined to bed? "Oh, no. That's not going to work. I can't possibly—"

"Do you have a 'do' and 'don't' list?" Joe asked before she could finish explaining. "There was a section in the *What to Expect* book, but as I recall, there are different degrees of rest."

Dr. Payne smiled as if at a star pupil. "Yes. I'll ask Margaret to give you our instruction sheet. I would stay horizontal as much as possible. No stairs. Only trips to the bathroom as required. You let others wait on you," she admonished Nikki before turning back to Joe. "Are there people who can help out?"

"I'm here," Joe said. "Plus my family's in town. And I have no doubt Nikki's friends will be glad to pitch in."

"But . . ." Nikki thought about the tiny cottage. It was adorable but far too small to be trapped in twenty-four hours a day, seven days a week. "I'm claustrophobic. I won't be able to bear lying there doing nothing. I'll . . ." She'd go stark raving mad and possibly howl at the moon. If she could escape her bed and the cottage in order to see it. "Isn't there something else we could do? Some pill I could take?"

Joe looked Nikki directly in the eye. "I'm sure we're both willing to do whatever we need to, to help ensure the health of our children. Aren't we, Nik?"

Nikki swallowed. Joe wasn't the one who'd have to lie around all day and night. "Well, of course. It's just that—"

A knock on the exam room door interrupted her train of thought and her objection. Margaret stepped in and handed them each a printed piece on bed rest. Dr. Payne closed the file and stood to leave. "Just call the office if you have any questions or issues." The door closed behind her.

"This is not going to work," Nikki said as she attempted to straighten her clothes and smooth her hair without actually having to confront herself in the mirror.

"Of course it's going to work," Joe said as he opened the examining room door for her then walked her toward the checkout desk. "We'll make it work. Because I didn't hear the word 'optional' come up."

But she couldn't help noticing that once again although he said "we," he would be free to come and go. Free to go to work. Free to take a run if he felt like it. Free to go out and watch the sunset.

"It's just a couple of weeks, Nikki. We'll all wait on you hand and foot. Rent you movies. Download you audio books. Bring you trays in bed. It'll be like a mini spa vacation. I promise you, Maddie and Kyra and Avery will be envious. You have an actual doctor's order to do absolutely nothing. I suggest you figure out how to enjoy it."

. . .

It was two long days before Maddie got to speak with Will. Two days of phone tag and Lori "with an *i*" leaving messages that Will had asked her to call and let her know that he'd be in touch soon. Days in which Maddie's subconscious played kick the can with a vengeance, the can clattering and ricocheting in her skull with each delay and every missed opportunity. All of it pointed to as proof that Will had lost interest and that absence did not make the heart grow fonder.

She was in the minivan on her way to Nikki and Joe's cottage with a slice of egg soufflé and a cup of mixed fruit when her cell phone rang. The number was Will's. She answered, half expecting to hear Lori's carefully chosen words. Instead she heard the warm timbre of Will's voice. She thought she heard a splash in the background.

"Is that really you?" she asked.

"It is. Hud's here, too. He says hello, by the way. We snuck off Mermaid Point just before sunrise. I'm thrilled to be making music again, but I was in deep withdrawal. I hadn't had a fly rod in my hands for close to two weeks."

"Where are you?"

"Out off Roscoe Key." She heard a smile steal into his voice. "Had a couple of gray ghosts ask after you." He referred to the often elusive bonefish prized by flats fishermen.

Maddie smiled in turn, picturing him out in what was, for him, his most natural habitat.

"Of course, I can hardly get Hud to shut up. Apparently no one's ever told him that most fishing guides are men of few words and sometimes mostly grunts."

She laughed. Hudson Power was one of Will's oldest friends.

"He wants to know when you're coming down," Will said. "And I want to know if you've changed your mind about coming on tour. I told Lori I thought I still might be able to talk you into it. She didn't think I needed the distraction, but I disagreed."

She pulled into a spot on Thirty-first and turned off the engine, but she didn't make a move to get out of the van. "I can't tell you how much I'd like to." She missed Will. Time with him would be a great escape from the pressure they were all under and the decisions that had to be made.

"Then say yes. That's all it'll take."

"God, I wish it was that easy."

"It is, Mad. I promise you."

"I just don't see how." She counted the countless reasons off on her fingers. "Nikki's on bed rest. The beach club's doing okay, but the cottages aren't selling, which means no income. And apparently the only thing our attorney's been able to negotiate is our ability to quit *Do Over* and the extremely tiny income it produced." She hated the whine in her voice as she tried to make him understand. "I don't feel like I can just take off. I'd be letting everyone down."

There was a silence and it wasn't the warm, no-words-needed kind of quiet that they'd sometimes shared, especially out on the flats. She pictured Hud peering out through the shallow water, dropping his fly in front of a bonefish and halfheartedly tempting him with it in an effort to give Will the privacy a conversation that had taken an unexpectedly serious turn required.

"You know," Will said finally. "You told me you weren't coming because you wanted to find out who you were, wanted to live your own life instead of living for others. I respected that. I mean it's not what I wanted to hear, but I got it. Only it sounds to me like you're still living for other people and dedicating yourself to dealing with their problems. Everybody's, that is, except mine."

She wanted to protest. Or to cry. Possibly even both. But she had no idea what to say. It was really, really hard to argue with the truth.

Fourteen

Nikki on bed rest was not pretty. And it wasn't just the bloated face, dull moss-colored eyes, and unwashed hair. Bitsy tried not to stare when she arrived with the ice cream sandwich Nikki had requested and found Maddie sitting at her side. The relief on Maddie's face and the speed with which she departed should have been a warning, but it all happened too quickly for Bitsy to react.

"Oh, look, Nik, your favorite!" Maddie said as she leapt to her feet and began gathering her things. "She's about due for another glass of juice, a blood pressure reading, and a potty break. Joe's planning to leave Tampa early to beat the traffic. He should be here right around five o'clock."

"But . . . I thought I was just delivering the ice cream sandwich." Bitsy had volunteered to help when needed and had thought she was just bridging time before scheduled shifts. Not that she had anything she had to do or anywhere she needed to be. Her job hunt so far had proven not only fruitless, but humiliating. Sherlock whimpered in her arms and eyed the door, but she set him down.

"Yes, well, Avery was supposed to be here for the next two hours but there was an issue with Jason and so she had to take Jeff to his doctor's appointment." Maddie spoke so quickly, it was almost impossible to follow. Though she looked distinctly guilty, it was clear that she was leaving. As soon as possible. "I'd stay except Kyra has to be somewhere and she can't take Dustin. So . . ." She leaned over and gave Nikki a quick hug. Before Bitsy could respond, she was gone.

"You know you're a pain in the ass when even Maddie can't stand being with you." Nikki's eyes pooled with tears. "I don't blame her. It's been ten long, excruciating days. I don't even want to be here with me."

Sherlock curled up in the farthest corner, not that "far" existed even in the two-bedroom cottage, which was downright palatial compared to the one-bedroom she and Sherlock were now stuffed into.

She sat down on the chair next to the bed and placed the ice cream sandwich where Nikki could reach it. "Is there a show you'd like to watch?"

"No." Nikki began to unwrap the ice cream.

"A movie?" Bitsy picked up the remote and began to scroll through the On Demand selections, trying not to think of the large-screen TVs that had hung in so many of the rooms of their Palm Beach home, so that Bertie would never be far from a sporting event or a favorite drama.

She paused on everything that looked like it might do.

"Seen it. Seen it." Nikki's responses were quick and merciless.

Bitsy pulled up the TV program selection. "I've heard good things about *Jane the Virgin*. Oh, and look, there's the first two seasons of *Grace and Frankie* with Jane Fonda and Lily Tomlin." She pointed the remote at the television.

"No, I told you. I've seen them. And am able to quote large

sections of dialogue. Well, at least when my brain doesn't crap out on me."

Bitsy lowered the remote. Sherlock, the lucky devil, had begun to snore.

"It's pointless," Nikki said. "I've already binge-watched more TV episodes than I used to know existed." She groaned as she tried to reposition her body. "If I don't go somewhere besides here and the bathroom soon, I'm afraid I'm going to hurt someone." She sighed. "I made it to the kitchen the other day when Avery had to step out to take a call. I thought I'd just put some peanut butter on a piece of bread, but I couldn't."

"You didn't have the strength?"

"No. It wasn't that. Joe must have gotten rid of all the sharp objects."

"You're joking."

Nikki shook her head sorrowfully. "I think it had something to do with me threatening to cut the throat of the next person who told me how lucky I was to get to lie here and do absolutely nothing."

Bitsy's hand went to her neck reflexively. "But he had to know you were joking."

"Maybe. But Joe's a be-prepared kind of guy. I mean, look at that suitcase sitting there taunting me." She pointed to the carry-on that sat next to the bedroom door. "When I know I'm never going to actually get out of here and see true daylight again." Tears seeped out of her eyes and began to slide down her cheeks.

"How about a book? I could read one to you."

"Can't concentrate. Not even when they're audio books. My mind just wanders all over the place—I have no control over it any more than I do my body. Then I don't know where it started wandering. I'd give everything I have just to walk outside and sit by the pool."

"What about a magazine? I could run down to Dolphin Village." The shopping center was only five minutes away. If she drove real slow, she could stretch it to eight. "Then you could just look at the pictures."

Nikki motioned beneath the bed. "There are piles of them down there. Feel free to help yourself. I'm all caught up on how many male superstars are sleeping with their nannies."

"So we'll talk," Bitsy said with a quick glance down at her cell phone. She looked again, shocked to discover she'd been there for only fifteen minutes. Two hours was beginning to sound like a lifetime.

"All right." Nikki sniffed and swiped at her eyes again, but she looked interested for the first time, Bitsy looked at her phone again, in eighteen minutes. "Why don't you tell me where Bertie really is and why you're really here."

Sherlock whimpered in his sleep at the sound of his beloved's name. Bitsy held her whimper in. Nikki unengaged was no picnic. But sharing her story would eat up, what, ten minutes, max? And it wouldn't accomplish or change anything. It would only make Bitsy appear even more pathetic. "I told you. I just needed some me time. And I don't know exactly where Bertie is at the moment."

She shrugged as if it made no difference. Nikki gazed at her in disappointment. Sherlock whimpered again. What followed was an uncomfortably long silence in which Nikki consumed the ice cream sandwich in an oddly choreographed combination of licks, bites, and nibbles.

"Do you want another ice cream sandwich?" Bitsy asked as soon as Nikki had finished.

Nikki seemed to consider this for a moment before shaking her head sadly. "What's the point? It's just more empty calories and only two minutes of pleasure."

"Have you considered trying to look on the bright side?" Bitsy said, stung. She'd give a lot for even one minute of pleasure right now. Something to look forward to would do.

"I can't help it," Nikki complained. "I've lost a lot of brain cells and I don't know if I'm ever getting them back. I lie here all day and all night, but I can't get comfortable enough to actually sleep. And all anyone who's had a child ever tells me is how I should get all the sleep I can right now because I won't be sleeping again for a long time."

Since taking a nap had been her only other suggestion, Bitsy tried to remain quiet. But as she contemplated Nikki's bloated face and body, the hair that needed washing, the obvious fear in her eyes, she felt the sharpest stab of jealousy she'd ever known. She could not feel sorry for this woman who had literally everything when she, Bitsy, had nothing. She wasn't used to tiptoeing around others. Others had always tiptoed around her.

"You know, you could try following Maddie's example and focusing on the positives here. I mean, you have a man who loves you and a large support group of people who would do pretty much anything for you. Including actually listening to you whine about how awful it is to lie in bed while everyone takes care of you. Not everybody's so lucky!"

Nikki blinked in surprise. Her gaze sharpened. It was the first time she'd seen Nikki look like Nikki since she'd been confined to bed. "Says the woman who was born with a silver spoon implanted in her mouth! Nobody's falling for your 'everything's fine, Bertie's just traveling, I need some "me time"' bullshit."

Bitsy froze. The Nicole Grant she knew had always been direct, but she'd never been cruel. Or out of control.

"You want to keep your troubles to yourself? Fine. But that's not going to cut it long term. In case you haven't noticed—and why would you, given your own self-absorption—the units we all sank the last of our money into renovating aren't selling and our brief, if painful, television career seems to be over. We don't have the money to pay you back or even give you a two-bedroom tricked-out apartment. And as empathetic as Maddie is, even she's not going to hand over things we can't afford. You've been given a pass so far. Maddie talked us into waiting for you to share what's going on. But not even Mother Teresa has endless patience. So I suggest you find a way to tell the truth soon. Or you're going to find yourself out of here. And then you can go throw yourself on the mercy of some of your *other* friends."

Bitsy's cheeks flushed hot with hurt and anger. Nikki looked like she was preparing to sling another incendiary bomb her way any moment.

"Got it!" Bitsy jumped to her feet.

"Good!" Nikki nodded her head vehemently as Bitsy grabbed her glass off the TV table and stomped into the kitchenette to refill it. Back in the bedroom, she placed it back on the tray, clicked on the television, sped through the channels until she found an episode of *Modern Family*, then set the remote none too gently back on the table. Sherlock stared up at her in surprise. She bent down to scoop him up. His cold nose snuffled up beneath her ear.

She wanted to storm out of the cottage and the Sunshine Hotel and Beach Club and never come back. But she had nowhere to go and she had promised not to leave Nikki alone. "It's not good for you or the babies to get so worked up," she said drawing a deep breath into her lungs. "I'll be back in to help take your blood pressure once we've both had a chance to calm down," she called over her shoulder. Then she settled on the sofa with Sherlock in her lap and began to count down the ninety-four minutes until Joe Giraldi would arrive.

• • •

"You're going to have to stop driving people away," Joe said when he walked into the bedroom shortly after five P.M. "Bitsy practically mowed me down trying to get out of here."

Nikki sniffed and said nothing, though she did, in fact, feel more than a little remorse.

Joe came and sat on the chair next to the bed. "I know this lying around isn't easy. But it's not some arbitrary punishment that's been foisted on you. There's a compelling reason for this. Two of them." She could hear the anger just beneath the reasonable tone. She turned her head, unable to meet his eyes, like a chastened child. If she could have, she would have jumped out of bed and fled the cottage like Bitsy had. But she was trapped.

Joe fell silent, but his scrutiny remained intense. She felt like that child. Small and miserable. So often now she said and did the wrong thing. No matter how she tried to talk herself down or plan a rational response, the fear she tried so hard to contain bubbled up and mixed with all that seething emotion and she'd fly into a fit before she could gather herself. Once she'd taken a stance, no matter how unfair or ridiculous, her pride wouldn't let her back down. The excess anxiety and emotion were even more exhausting than the surplus pounds she carried. And she knew it wasn't good for the babies.

His reasonable tone and the obvious disappointment on his face only made her feel worse.

"Here." He gently eased her up and rearranged the pillows behind her head then went to refill the glass of water. When he came back, he placed it within reach. He sat on the chair and spoke quietly. "This isn't some life sentence, Nikki. It's been a week and a half. It's unlikely to be more than another three to four weeks—the longer the better. You need to stop dwelling on your discomfort and think about why you're doing this. You're about to have children—our children. It's time to stop acting like a child yourself."

She sniffed, determined not to rail or cry like the child he'd accused her of being. The anger wasn't gone, and neither were the fears she refused to give voice to lest it turn them real, but the adrenaline had dissipated. She took a long sip of water and let his presence calm her. She managed to ask about his day.

For dinner he warmed up two bowls of Gabriella's manicotti. There was a plate of his Nonna Sofia's biscotti for dessert. They nibbled on them during the evening news. With Joe there, the tiny bedroom felt homey and the fear receded.

She was drowsing when he turned off the light and climbed into bed. He fit himself against her back spoon fashion and placed one large hand protectively over her stomach. There was a kick and then another. She felt his quiet expulsion of breath in reaction. His hand caressed her stomach and the babies inside. She pressed back into him, comforted by his touch. Protected by the fortress of his body, she was finally able to fall asleep. It was not a deep or restful sleep, but his presence helped keep the darker thoughts at bay.

. . .

Daylight seeped in through the blinds the next morning.

"You awake?" Joe asked, his voice pitched low behind her.

"Mmm-hmmm." She drew a deep breath. Another. Her eyelids fluttered.

"I'm going to have to go out of town for a few days."

The vestiges of sleep disappeared like the flame snuffed from a candle. Her eyes popped open. "What?"

"I have to go to LA to interview and bring back a witness."

Wide awake now, she worked her way on to her back then on to her other side so that she could face him. "But you said you weren't going anywhere until after. That they wouldn't ask you to and that even if they did, you wouldn't go." Even now she couldn't bring herself to say "after the babies are born." She would not say it until they arrived safely, both of them healthy, and she and Joe were together. "You promised."

"I know," he said. "But I'm the only one who can debrief and hopefully convince this witness to testify. And I'll be back in time no matter what. It's only a four-and-a-half-hour flight."

The panic hit her low and deep. She tried to clamp down on

it, but her emotions were in lockstep with her hormones and they were jerking upward to the top of the roller coaster in preparation for the bloodcurdling drop that would follow. She wanted to scream at him. Wanted to ask whether they would have sent him if he were married and it was his wife who could end up going into labor at any time since twins tended to come early. She struggled to maintain her composure. She managed not to beg him to stay or shout when she asked when he was going.

"This afternoon." He looked her in the eye when he said it. "I spoke to my parents. My mother and Nonna Sofia have offered to take turns spending the night here while I'm gone."

He'd already discussed this with them. He'd told them before he told her. She struggled up onto her elbows. "No. We can't expect your mother or grandmother to sleep on the couch."

"They're fine with it," he said smoothly. "In fact, they offered."

"Bitsy could just check in on me," she said. "I could call her if there was a problem."

"No." He held her gaze. Despite the tick in his cheek, he spoke calmly, resolutely. "First of all, that woman has plenty of issues of her own. And I'm not sure she'd ever set foot in here again based on the way she rushed out. You're not sleeping here alone. It's bad enough that I have to go. I can't spend the whole time worrying about you."

She managed to sit completely upright with her back propped against the pillows. "So this is for your peace of mind. Your convenience."

"Jesus, Nikki. You twist everything into some kind of affront. I just want to make sure you've got someone I trust with you until I get back."

"Well, I'm not staying here with anyone but you," she said. "I'm going to Bella Flora, where I can be with my friends." She barely resisted adding, "You're not the boss of me."

"Nik . . ."

"No, this is my decision, not yours. Especially since you're not going to be here."

"But my family's here. And they've offered to help."

"Well, they're not my family." She looked at him but he did not drop down on one knee or bring up the idea of making her a Giraldi as he'd once been so eager to do. She began to work on swinging her legs over the side of the bed.

"Nikki." He got out of bed and strode to her side. For a moment she hated him for being able to move and bend when she was still trying to get her feet on the floor.

"They'll be right next door and they can come to Bella Flora anytime they want to. It'll be less disruptive for everyone if they don't have to come to the cottage. And at least I'll have people I know around me," Nikki said as her feet pressed into the rug and she scooted toward the side. "People who know the way to the hospital in case you're not back."

"I'll be back in time, Nikki. I promise."

But he'd promised he wasn't going anywhere and now he was. And he'd said he wanted to marry her and now he clearly didn't. It was about time she started relying on herself and the friends who'd proven they could be counted on.

"I'm going to Bella Flora," she said. "I have a whole bedroom there to use anytime I want to."

"But it's upstairs," he pointed out.

"That's just a detail. One I can work out with Kyra and Maddie." She held out her hand, beyond irritated that she needed his help to stand.

"You're not supposed to get up."

"I have to go to the bathroom, damn it." She let him pull her to her feet, but shook off his hand when he tried to escort her. "I can go by myself!"

In the bathroom she took her time peeing then washed her face and brushed her teeth. She even ran a comb through her hair.

When she came out, she'd located her backbone and was determined to use it. "Please get me my suitcase."

"Be reasonable, Nikki."

"I am being perfectly reasonable. Disagreeing with you does not make me unreasonable. Now please get me my suitcase." She considered telling him where he could shove that suitcase but managed to refrain. When it was open on the bed, she began to fill it. Fortunately, the room was so small the dresser was only a few steps away.

"Nikki, this is really not a good idea."

She didn't bother to respond although she did allow him to help her into her clothes. When you were shaped like Humpty Dumpty, getting dressed on your own was pretty much out of the question. She also let him carry her suitcase to the car, but only after threatening to walk to Bella Flora dragging it behind her.

She kept her chin up and her eyes averted for the duration of the drive. As they drew near to Ten Beach Road, she hoped Maddie, Kyra, and Avery, on whom she'd occasionally unleashed her new roller coaster self, would be glad to see her. And if they weren't glad, that they'd at least be willing to take her in.

Fifteen

"Would you like to come to the site with me? I know Chase could use your input." Avery placed a piece of chocolate cake and a glass of milk on the kitchen table in front of Jeff Hardin then cut a smaller slice for herself. She and Jeff shared a lot of things including a penchant for junk food and a virulent sweet tooth. "Then you could ride back with him when I head to Bella Flora."

"Nah." Jeff picked up his fork and pulled the plate closer. "I don't think Chase wants me sticking in my two cents."

"Of course he does," Avery insisted. "When hasn't he wanted your input? You taught him everything he knows."

Jeff took a bite and chewed appreciatively. "Doesn't seem worth the effort it takes to get me anywhere. I've watched you maneuvering this chair into the back of the Mini Cooper, and to tell you the truth, I'm getting tired of being hauled around like a sack of potatoes."

She topped off his milk and took a seat beside him. He was the closest thing to a parent she had left. "I wish my dad was here in any shape, mobile or otherwise. And I promise you neither

Chase nor I feel anything but gratitude that you're available to give input and be a part of our lives." She took a bite of cake as much to hide the emotion rising up inside her as to enjoy the chocolaty sugar rush.

Jeff harrumphed, but ate with a little more gusto. They were consuming their cake and milk in a companionable silence when a screech of tires sounded outside. A car door slammed. She and Jeff exchanged glances as the front door whipped open and Jason stomped his way into the kitchen. The perpetual scowl slipped slightly at the first sight of chocolate cake. Avery reached for the bakery box. "Hungry?" She transferred the slice onto a plate and waved it in his direction. "It's the last one. And I think it's got your name written all over it." When he didn't move, she set it on the table for him then poured him a glass of milk to go with it.

She was careful not to move too quickly, as if he were some small skittish animal that she didn't want to spook and not a hulking boy/man. She bit back a smile at the idea of setting out a trail of chocolate cake crumbs for him to follow the next time they needed him to do something. "You know if your dad or Josh finds it, it'll be gone in ten seconds flat."

Jeff acted as if he wasn't interested in anything but his own cake, but she could feel how carefully he was eating. "Go on and take it, Jace," he said. "Liking chocolate cake is a sign of intelligence, not weakness."

She held up the plate and the glass of milk in a last bid to tempt him. She knew she should have already called him on not telling his father about playing hooky and taking the boat without permission, but that would just call attention to the fact that she hadn't found the courage to tell Chase, either.

When Jason reached for the plate and the milk with a rusty "thanks," she suspected he was as interested in depriving his father as he was in consuming the cake. Or maybe it was just a double win. Jeff made as if to move over, but Jason was already turning and leaving, carrying the cake and milk back to his lair.

"Lord, that boy beats all," Jeff said as the bedroom door closed and the music went on. "He's been thrown off the team for skipping practices and classes. The other day he left school during his lunch hour and never came back. He supposedly gave his car keys back to Chase, but he clearly has an extra set. Left Josh, who he used to worship, stranded there like he probably did just now." He pushed his half-eaten cake away. "It breaks my heart to see the distance building up between those boys. The worse Jason behaves, the harder Josh tries to be perfect. And I can't bear the way Jason and Chase go at each other. One of these times one of them will go too far and . . . well, I try not to think too much about that. They're my flesh and blood."

"I know." Avery put the carton of milk back in the refrigerator then checked to make sure she had the notes and drawings she wanted to go over with Chase. "I wish you'd come."

Jeff was looking down the hallway toward the boys' bedrooms. The throbbing bass of a rap song whose lyrics she did not want to hear reverberated through the house, making the windows rattle.

"I think I'll stay here. You know, just in case the boy decides he wants to talk or needs anything." Jeff had to raise his voice to be heard above the din.

"You're a good man." She leaned over and put her arms around his neck, dropping a kiss on the top of his head. "I'm not sure how long I'll be at Bella Flora, but call me anytime if there's anything you need."

. . .

"Why on earth did you give her that bell?" Kyra asked, resisting the urge to cover her ears so she wouldn't have to hear Nikki's latest summons.

"It's the same bell I always gave you and Andrew when you were sick," her mother pointed out as she turned the burner down on the stove and prepared to go into the salon to see what Nikki needed.

"Yeah, but that was before cell phones and texting. And we were just children."

"Dustin wanna bell, too. And wanna sleep in saron with Nikki." Dustin reached for Kyra's hand and gave it a tug.

"You see?" Kyra said as all three of them stopped what they'd been doing to jump to do Nikki's bidding. "I don't see why you decided to put her bed in there."

"Because she would have been stuck upstairs alone. And we would have been running up and down. Plus, we can hear her from wherever we are. It's better for her to be in the center of things," Maddie said.

"Better for who?" Kyra asked. "It's only been two days and she's lucky no one has stuffed a gag in her mouth yet. She's exhausting."

"Honey, Gabriella and Sofia have been here helping. It's not like it's all on us."

"Yeah, she's quiet as a mouse when they're here, and then as soon as they're gone, I feel like I'm listening to a bell choir," Kyra complained. "We should have made Dad and Troy give her the pool house."

"But she would have been alone. And that's not any larger than their cottage at the Sunshine," Maddie said.

"Don't you think she'd be better off there?"

"Stop it. When Joe gets back, she'll go there. He only expects to be gone four or five days." The bell rang again. "Just stir this for me, will you? Dustin can come with me. We'll be right back."

Kyra stirred the soup. From the sound of things, a trip to the bathroom was in progress.

"I get the door!" Dustin's feet pounded on the hall floor as he raced ahead to the guest bathroom. Almost fifteen minutes had elapsed by the time her mother returned to the kitchen.

"Is she still being nasty and grumpy?" Kyra asked.

"You weren't exactly Little Miss Sunshine while you were pregnant with Dustin," Maddie pointed out. "And she's difficult because she's frightened. Do you remember what that feels like?"

Kyra knew what that felt like all right. Sometimes when she let herself think about their present financial situation and all that they stood to lose if things didn't improve, she had trouble catching her breath.

"And Nikki's been there for us. We need to be there for her." Her mother set the pot of soup on another burner and lowered the vent fan.

"That's what you said about Bitsy. And that's not going well, either. You know we can't afford to give her a two-bedroom. We have to sell every one of those to recoup our money." And they needed to do it soon.

The bell rang again. All three of them went into the salon.

"I wanna sleepover in saron, too," Dustin said again, his eyes on Nikki's tummy. "Can Geedad and Broy bring in my bed?"

"No, little man," Kyra said. "Nikki's only here because she can't climb the stairs right now like you can."

"Is it cuz her tummy's so fat?"

Nikki sighed as Dustin put his hand lightly on her stomach as Maddie had shown him.

"She's not fat, sweetheart," Maddie said. "She's pregnant. Remember I told you she's having twins—two babies are inside her tummy."

"How did dose babies get in?" Dustin leaned his head sideways as if trying to gauge where the entry might be.

"It's magic," Kyra said, ashamed of herself for lying. But she was fairly certain that three was too young for the birds and bees talk. "When you're older, I'll explain how the trick works."

Nikki rolled her eyes.

"You meem when I'm four?"

She could see Nikki trying not to laugh.

"Mom?"

Her mother was laughing. "I'm sorry. It reminds me of the time when Andrew had that sex ed class and came home from middle school wanting to know if he *had* to have sex one day."

"Hex!" Dustin said, trying the word on for size.

"You asked me to explain the whole thing in the car one day while I was driving carpool to Brownies," her mother said, laughing. "I couldn't figure out how to explain without those little girls going home and repeating it to their parents."

"I think I remember that. Didn't Tina try to argue that babies came out of cabbages?"

"Yes," Maddie said. "That whole cabbage patch dolls thing was very confusing."

"I don't know." Nikki shifted in an attempt to get comfortable. "At the moment I kind of wish the whole stork thing was true. That's the sort of delivery a woman could look forward to." Her smile was weak, but her tone had turned dry.

They laughed and the tension was broken at least for a comforting few moments.

. . .

Brave people volunteered, they didn't draw straws. It seemed they were a cowardly bunch. No one wanted to be the one to have to tell Bitsy Baynard that she could not have a two-bedroom.

"But I already told her," Nikki said late that afternoon when Kyra held out the straws. "And I don't think I should have to tell her again."

"A tirade is not an explanation," Maddie said in her sternest "mom" voice. One Nikki couldn't imagine ever emulating. "I think we need to make sure she understands what's possible, what's not, and why."

"I don't know," Nikki said, looking at the straws. "Maybe we should ask Nonna Sofia to tell her. She doesn't mince words." Just yesterday she'd brought over a plate of her world-famous biscotti and then while Nikki was munching on it, she'd taken advantage of the opportunity to lecture Nikki once again on how important it was to make sure the babies were legitimate Giraldis. It was all Nikki could do not to suggest she take that up with her grandson. Instead she'd kept her mouth full of biscotti and her look as innocent as possible.

"It needs to be one of us," Maddie said firmly. "And we don't want to put anyone who can bake like Sofia in harm's way."

"Fine." Nikki drew a straw. "But if I lose, I'm claiming double jeopardy."

Avery drew last. "Shit," she said as they opened their hands and she held up the short straw. "I'll bring up the conversation, but I'm not doing it alone. I expect you all to back me up."

"It's not like I'm going anywhere," Nikki said. "Although being outside for sunset is a huge improvement."

"I hope Joe's going to understand that we counted the number of steps to the loggia and it was two steps less than it takes to get to the bathroom," Maddie said.

"And almost as important," Nikki said. It had been a tough negotiation, but she'd promised to hold her tongue as much as humanly possible in exchange for getting to come outside for their sunset ritual. "Just be careful how much you drink first. We all know now that Bitsy can outdrink all of us combined. You need to keep your wits about you—especially you, Avery—while making sure she gets enough wine to help soften the blow."

Bitsy arrived about thirty minutes before sunset, carrying Sherlock in her arms. The dog perked up at the sight of Dustin and settled happily on the loggia near the playhouse, where Dustin was pretending to build an addition to his child-size Bella Flora.

They drank wine and nibbled on focaccia and crostini courtesy of Gabriella while the sun slipped slowly toward the water. "Mmmm. God, I hope the Giraldis decide to move down here permanently," Avery said after licking the last bits of cheese from her thumb. "These are delicious. And I saw that pan of homemade lasagna in the refrigerator. Are you sure Joe doesn't have any brothers?"

"We'll be sure to let Chase know you're ready to sell him out for someone who excels at cooking with cheese," Nikki said drily.

"Hey, it's not only men whose stomachs lead to their hearts. And at the moment I'm not sure Chase would even notice if I traded him in." She stuffed another crostini into her mouth and hoped like hell Maddie wasn't about to pick up on her aside about Chase. She raised her wineglass, starting off the sunset ritual. "To great Italian food delivered to the door."

Maddie smiled and raised her glass. "My good thing is having Nikki back in the fold for a while and to having Bitsy and Sherlock *visiting* with us." The emphasis on the word "visiting" was slight but noticeable.

"I'm co-opting that," Kyra said, "since there are no rules about originality. And adding 'to girl power and friendship and beating back the dark forces that are too often aligned against us.'"

Nikki raised her glass of juice. "To friendship. And vanquishing the dark forces." They clinked again. "God, sunset's just not the same with pomegranate juice."

When everyone else had toasted, Bitsy raised her glass and looked steadily at each of them in turn. "To all of you. With thanks for making Sherlock and me feel welcome." She clinked glasses then downed her wine in one long gulp as if she'd somehow divined that bad news was coming. "Everyone isn't as welcoming or as understanding as you all have been." She pounded down another glass. Her eyes shone slightly with what Avery was afraid might be tears. "Am I allowed to have another good thing?" she asked Maddie.

"Of course," Maddie said.

"To not needing men to complete us." Another drink went down. "And to learning how to be alone." Bitsy reached for the wine bottle. Disappointment showed plainly on her face when she realized it was empty.

"Hold that thought." Avery jumped up. "I'm going to grab another bottle."

"And I'm going to put on *Thomas the Tank Engine* for Dustin." Kyra rose, scooping Dustin into her arms.

"Bring Cherlock!" he begged.

Sherlock was already shaking his collar on the way to his feet. He stared up at Bitsy, who nodded. Avery and Kyra raced into the house like some sort of tag team in a relay.

"The opener's on the bar," Kyra directed. "Just grab it and the bottle. You can open it out there. I can't really tell how much softening is going to be necessary. We're just trying to make her comfortable, not knock her out."

Avery had the cork halfway out of the bottle by the time she sank back down at the table. She'd already begun filling Bitsy's glass by the time Kyra slid into her seat a moment later.

"What were we drinking to again?" Bitsy asked.

"I think we were drinking to independence," Maddie prompted.

"To the sisterhood!" Avery added.

"Because let's face it, even the most excellent men can be disappointing on occasion," Nikki said.

"Yeah," Kyra added.

Avery raised her glass and took a healthy sip. "Sometimes they can let you down without even meaning to."

"And sometimes they mean every second of it," Bitsy practically whispered.

"Is there a good thing in there somewhere?" Maddie prodded. "Or something you'd like to add?" She looked directly at Avery.

"Right." Avery took a deep breath and faced Bitsy. "We think it's great that you've come to stay for a while. And your friendship and support have meant a lot to us."

"Thank you." The first clear tear formed in the corner of Bitsy's eye.

"And we'd love to be able to give you exactly what you want," Avery continued.

"I really appreciate that." Another tear, then a third.

"But." Avery swallowed. "Well, the thing is, we can't afford to turn over a two-bedroom to you. We absolutely have to sell every single unit and every possible beach club membership to recoup the money that went to fund the renovation and the lawyers. It took everything we had plus what Kyra borrowed from Daniel."

"But . . ." Bitsy's face began to crumple. "You were on television. You had a series. I assumed . . ." What had been a trickle of tears picked up speed and intensity.

"The best we can do is offer the use of a one-bedroom," Kyra said. "Then pay back the remainder of your sponsorship once the units sell."

They all watched helplessly as the trickle became a downpour. "But the one-bedrooms are so small," Bitsy said through her tears. "I don't see how I can live in one of them."

"That's because the Sunshine cottages aren't designed for full-time living," Nikki said. "They're beach cottages. But I'm sure we could make a one-bedroom available whenever you wanted to vacation here. I mean, I'm sure you've got more exciting places to go?"

Bitsy choked out a sob. "No, I don't." The downpour became a deluge that carved creases of misery into her face. "I don't have anywhere else to go."

Avery blinked, thinking she must have misheard.

"What happened, Bitsy?" Maddie asked quietly. "Can you tell us?"

"Is there someone you'd like us to call?" Nikki asked.

Bitsy shook her head as the tears continued to rain down. "I don't have anybody. I'm completely alone. Except for Sherlock."

"What about Bertie?" Nikki asked.

"He's gone. He ran away. He left me."

They were all too stunned to protest when Nikki levered herself to her feet and walked the length of the table to Bitsy. "Awww, honey. What happened?"

"I thought he loved me. I really did. But he left me. He ran away with a stripper!" Her lips quivered pitifully, her face furrowed in grief and a vain attempt to staunch the tears. "And he took everything I had with him. Everything. Including every cent my parents left me."

Dumbfounded, they watched Bitsy cry. "I'm not just here to visit. I'm here because I have nowhere to live, no money to even try to track him down, and no means of making any." She cried in gasps and shudders. "And I understand what you're saying, but I'm not leaving. I can't. I'm going to live in whatever ridiculously tiny one-bedroom cottage you put me in. Because I don't have any other choice."

Sixteen

Nonna Sofia arrived at Bella Flora looking like an advertisement for beach retirement wearing white capris, a jaunty red and white striped T-shirt, and a pair of navy Keds. Her short dark hair with its lightning bolt white streak was held back by the *I Heart Pass-a-Grille* visor that Joe had picked out for her. Her time on the beach had given her already olive skin an even warmer glow. No one running into her on the beach or in the grocery store would guess that she was in her nineties, that her dark eyes were equipped with x-ray vision that allowed her to see into your innermost recesses, or that she had an encyclopedic knowledge of ancient Italian spells and curses.

Fortunately for Nikki, the weapon Sofia was wielding at the moment was her cooking, more specifically her homemade lasagna. Which could bring you to your knees and make you promise things you might later regret.

"Oh, God. This is so incredible." Nikki was appalled to hear the nearly orgasmic tone in her voice.

Sofia smiled. "*Grazie.* I am glad you like it. Joe told me lasagna is a favorite food of yours." She gave Nikki a penetrating look. "He also tells me that he tried to reach you last night and the night before. I assume this is just a coincidence and that you're not angry with him for having to be away?" The words were quietly spoken but her eyes had turned laser-like. Images of Marlon Brando as the Godfather rose in Nikki's mind. She sincerely hoped Nonna Sofia was not about to make an offer that Nikki could not refuse. "Because that would be a shame, wouldn't it? First you refuse to marry him. Then you insist on being up here rather than in Miami, where Joe works and lives. Then you become angry that he must travel for his job."

The lasagna turned leaden in her stomach. She set the plate on the TV table then took her time downing half a glass of water. In a moment she'd escape, at least temporarily, to the bathroom, her only haven now that she lived in the middle of the salon, which served as Bella Flora's family room. "I'm not sure you're being given the complete story."

"No?" Sofia countered. "Then perhaps you would like to tell it to me."

No, actually, Nikki wouldn't. It was bad enough that Joe had taken her at her word and taken the whole subject of marriage off the table. Having people know it would be beyond humiliating.

"Gabriella tells me that I should leave you both alone. That it's up to you and Joe to work this out. But a woman must be bold in order to get what she wants." The look again, even more piercing. Spock's Vulcan Mind Meld had nothing on Nonna Sofia's x-ray eyes. "You do want my grandson, don't you?"

The dark eyes pinned hers and searched them, leaving nowhere to hide.

"What exactly do you mean by 'want'?" was the best Nikki could manage.

"This is not about semantics," Sofia chided. "Do you want to be his wife or not?"

Nikki wondered for a moment what would happen if she said yes. Would Sofia call her beloved grandson and insist he do "the right thing"? If Joe refused, Nikki would be devastated. And if he agreed?

She tore her gaze from Nonna Sofia's. She had said no one too many times back when she'd assumed she could never give him the children he deserved. When she'd been unable to believe that he really loved her. Did she only want to marry him now because he'd stopped asking? She drew in a breath and let it out slowly. She did not want Joe to marry her because he had to and certainly not to please his grandmother. It would be agony to have to watch his face for the signs of regret or resentment that he might one day feel for being trapped by Nikki's pregnancy and his family's expectations.

She'd watched Bitsy's sunset confession with a deep-rooted horror. She'd known something was wrong between her and Bertie, but she'd never imagined the extent of the nightmare Bitsy was living. Now she couldn't look at Bitsy without pitying her. If it came to choosing the least awful scenario, surely being unhappy trumped being pitied. Didn't it?

She turned her head to meet Sofia's eye. "I'm not sure about anything at the moment." Despite her current anger, she didn't want Joe stuck with her when everything went south as she was still afraid it might. "And I don't think this is the time to make important decisions." She'd need all her brain cells back first.

Nikki began the levering, struggling, and scooting that were now a part of sitting up. It was clear that Nonna Sofia's laser beam eyes had noted every one of the contradictory emotions that flooded Nikki's brain and body. That didn't mean she could force Nikki to do anything she didn't want to. Nikki got both feet on the floor and stood, very glad to be towering over Sofia and careful not to let on that her legs were quivering like Jell-O.

"The only thing I'm absolutely certain about is that I have to go to the bathroom. And that after that, I'd love to have one of your cannolis."

. . .

Kyra inhaled the sharp salt air blowing off the water as she and Maddie pushed Dustin's jogging stroller north over the sidewalk that rimmed Tampa Bay. The day was sunny, the temperature in the low seventies, the sky an exquisite shade of blue. They were on their way to Franklin Realty to pick up the minivan that her father had borrowed for a showing.

Dustin clapped his hands in delight each time a boat sped across the glassy water and called friendly greetings to the fishermen they passed. It was one of those gorgeous winter days when you knew just how lucky you were to be in Florida and felt duty bound to make the most of it.

"If Dad's going to be showing real estate regularly, he's going to need a car." Steve's car had died in Bella Flora's driveway and finally been towed away for scrap. At the moment all three of them were sharing the minivan and occasionally borrowing Nikki and Joe's SUV, when the Giraldis weren't using it.

They lingered at the historic Merry Pier at the eastern end of Eighth Avenue so that Dustin could watch the *Miss Pass-a-Grille* come into port and the Shell Key Shuttle depart. Water slapped lightly against the seawall. Pelicans perched on pilings, keeping a sharp eye out for an afternoon snack.

They passed the small Vina del Mar Bridge, the Pass-a-Grille Women's Club, and next to it, the St. Petersburg Yacht Club at Pass-a-Grille, where Roberto Dante had tied up his houseboat while they worked on the Sunshine Hotel. After that came the mostly large, mostly renovated homes that lined the bay on their right. Across the narrow, two-lane Pass-a-Grille Way, a network of tiny streets and alleys led to the beach.

At Twenty-fifth Street they walked the short block to Franklin Realty, which was housed in a white clapboard bungalow. The trusty beige-gold minivan sat outside.

"John! Neh Nay!" Dustin broke into a smile as Kyra parked the stroller near the front steps then unbuckled her son. He clambered up the steps and across the wooden porch and reached for the doorknob.

"Anees!" Renée Franklin's younger sister, Annelise Handleman, sat at the front desk. Dustin offered her one of his endless supply of sunny smiles and she smiled back, something that never would have happened before their renovation of the Sunshine Hotel and Beach Club brought closure to the childhood tragedy that had derailed her life.

"Dustin!" she replied with an enthusiasm that matched Dustin's. "I'm willing to bet Renée's already headed back to the kitchen to look for a cupcake for you."

"Cutcake!" His smile grew larger.

"Can I take him into the kitchen for a snack?" she asked. "John and Steve are in the conference room, but it's fine to go on in. Oh, and I hope you all will sign up for the Sand Castle Showdown. You can enter as a family or on your own."

Annelise and Dustin headed to the kitchen while Kyra followed Maddie into the next room. It was here that they'd signed the papers to sell Bella Flora to a then-unknown buyer, only finding out later that Daniel had purchased it for her and Dustin. Even thinking about how she'd put their safe haven at risk caused an all too familiar ache of dread.

"Welcome." The ruff of white hair that circled John Franklin's otherwise bald scalp resembled a crown of cotton balls. His bassett hound face lifted in a smile. Her father sat beside him. He, too, was smiling.

"How'd it go?" her mother asked.

"Good," Steve said. "Better than good actually. They want to put in an offer on the house in Belle Vista." His smile carried a hint of confidence that had been missing since he'd lost everything, including his position as a financial advisor, to Malcolm Dyer's Ponzi scheme.

"That's so great, Dad. Congratulations!"

"It is, isn't it?" John beamed. "I think Steve here's going to do well in real estate. And I'm glad to have new blood in the office." John had lived in Pass-a-Grille since God was a boy and had sold and resold much of the real estate in its two-and-a-half-square miles. But he was somewhere in his late eighties and moved more slowly than he had when they'd first met him a little over three years ago. "But we are going to have to put a much more concerted effort into selling the Sunshine cottages and beach club memberships. I know we all counted on recouping our money far more quickly than looks likely. And I can't help worrying about what could happen if Kyra's unable to service her loan."

Kyra stiffened in her seat. Her father, who was the only other person aware of what she'd done, winced. Her mother looked understandably confused. Kyra tried to catch the Realtor's eye. He rightfully assumed that she'd told everyone about the loan she'd taken out against Bella Flora and that he had guaranteed. Because, of course, she should have.

"Daniel's been very generous," Maddie said. "I can't imagine he would ever want to take Bella Flora away from Dustin or Kyra."

John looked at Maddie in surprise.

Kyra shook her head as subtly as she could. Not certain that he'd noticed or understood, she jumped up. "Of course Daniel wouldn't take the house. That wouldn't make any sense at all." This was true, but not an actual admission that the money hadn't come from Daniel as she'd let everyone believe. Unsure how to prevent John from spilling her secret, she blathered on. "I know you're the real estate person, John, but are there ways we could all help? I could amplify whatever you're doing online and through social media. And, I don't know, what if we helped give tours during Annelise's Sand Castle Showdown? Or raffled off a beach club membership or a weekend stay in one of the furnished models?"

Kyra felt her mother's gaze on her and knew she'd telegraphed more of her panic than she'd meant to. She almost wept with relief when John nodded then grasped his cane to steady himself as he stood.

"Yes, Steve and I will have to sit down and come up with a comprehensive marketing plan now that he's available on a full-time basis." John speared Kyra with a look. "There's no question we need to focus our energies on selling the cottages and memberships. And it's even more important to make sure everyone understands exactly what's at risk if we don't."

"Yes. Absolutely," Kyra said though she had no idea where she was going to find the courage to confess what she'd done at this late date. Her smile felt forced as she gathered up Dustin, who was now happily smeared with icing, said good-bye, then loaded the stroller and Dustin into the minivan. As they headed north to pick up groceries and work their way through her mother's carefully laid out list of errands, Kyra ran through possible explanations and best-case/worst-case scenarios in her mind. But no matter how many times she thought it through, she couldn't figure out how she could possibly explain the reality of the situation without sending everyone into an irreversible state of shock.

• • •

Cradling Sherlock in her arms, Bitsy opened the door of the one-bedroom model to Avery and Ray Flamingo at exactly three P.M. Avery wore jeans, a white button-down, and a pair of sneakers. A curly blond bang fell across her forehead and over one bright blue eye, cementing her resemblance to a Kewpie doll. Ray nodded a head of spiky blond hair and was immaculate in billowy winter white pants, a loose pale blue cotton sweater, and a smart pair of oxfords. He looked as if he could have walked the catwalk for Ralph Lauren or posed for a Florida winter vacation campaign.

"Come on in." Sherlock propped his muzzle on Bitsy's arm as she stepped back so they could enter. In this one-bedroom unit, three was definitely a crowd.

"So," Ray Flamingo said.

"So," Avery said uncomfortably.

Bitsy watched their faces as she braced for the coming conversation. But she was remembering the architects and designers that Bertie had retained during the three-year renovation of their Palm Beach estate. How he had loved the entire experience down to the tiniest decisions about finishes and fixtures while she, who had always lived opulently, had simply been happy to see him so happily engaged. When the house was finished, he'd spent another year redoing the grounds and then another six months on the pool house. He'd seemed so attached. And yet he'd had no difficulty leaving their home or her behind.

"So I don't see how Sherlock and I can possibly live comfortably in a space this small."

Bitsy motioned to the corner in which a pile of luggage reached halfway to the ceiling, the small dinette in front of the window, the extremely compact kitchen. A love seat, a chair, and a television on a wheeled stand were the only other furnishings.

"What do you feel is missing?" Avery asked.

"Seriously?" Bitsy looked to see if she was joking. "You mean other than space?"

"Right," Ray said. "Other than that?"

"Well, I'd say storage, but that's really the same thing, isn't it? I have only half of what I brought and even that doesn't fit in here. And realistically how many people could be in here at one time?" She looked at Ray and Avery then into Sherlock's big brown eyes. "There are three of us and one dog and I'd say we're at capacity."

"So you're concerned about entertaining?" Avery asked.

"Well, no, not really. But being able to breathe if someone stopped by would be nice."

"Do you anticipate overnight guests?" Ray asked.

"Well, no. Not really." One would have to have friends for that. The few she had left lived here. If Bertie showed up, she'd carve him into pieces and let him go sleep with the fishes. "There's just not enough room." Certainly not for someone who'd always considered a twenty-thousand-square-foot home cozy and a hotel suite under five thousand square feet not worth bothering with.

"You know it can be incredibly freeing to live in a really tiny space," Avery said with feeling.

"For who?" Bitsy asked. "Squirrels? Hummingbirds?"

"For people," Ray said quite earnestly. "There's a whole tiny house movement going on in this country right now."

She looked at the two of them, but they didn't seem to be joking.

"If it swept through Palm Beach, I missed it," Bitsy said drily. "But perhaps it cut a very tiny swath."

"Yes, well, there are books and television programs about it," Avery said, undeterred. "I watched one show where a family down-sized so that they'd be forced to spend more time together."

"I saw that one," Ray said. "It was a couple with three children and they were looking for five hundred square feet—one hundred square feet per person."

"You're joking." It was not a question.

"Honest." Avery raised one hand as if to make a pledge. "The one-bedroom cottages are about four hundred and fifty square feet. That gives you and Sherlock two hundred square feet each. Plus you could have another small dog or two."

"Or half a person," Bitsy said. Neither of them laughed.

Avery looked at Ray, then back at Bitsy. "I'm sorry, but this is our only real option. The unit's small, but we could maximize the space so that you could use it as a full-time residence."

Ray nodded enthusiastically. "We've talked it over and we have a two-pronged approach."

"I'm not sure two prongs will fit in here," she said.

They smiled, but continued with determined smiles. Ray handed her a pamphlet-size paperback. It was titled *The Life-Changing Magic of Tidying Up*. "It's a bestseller. It's all about the emotional advantages as well as techniques for freeing yourself of unnecessary objects."

She'd already been forced to give up the Palm Beach estate, several vacation homes, and thousands of undeveloped acres, not to mention her whole life. She'd pared and packed her possessions into a pile of suitcases. She was a bag lady whose bags carried designer logos. Surely that was freeing enough? "And prong two?" she asked dully.

"I design the space so that every single inch does double or triple duty," Avery said. "I've already started sketching. When you approve the plan, we start building it out. You, Maddie, Kyra, and me—and maybe Chase if he has time—should be able to handle it. I'm sure I can get Robby to update the plumbing and Chase's electrician to sign off on the electrical. It could be fun."

Clearly their perceptions of what qualified as enjoyment differed greatly. But Bitsy only nodded numbly as she tried to process her shocking new reality.

"Then I come in and make it absolutely gorgeous," Ray said with a smile.

Sherlock raised his head and looked at them in disbelief as they looked at Bitsy, waiting for her answer. She wanted to tell them they were out of their minds. That she couldn't possibly live in what sounded like an excruciatingly small, completely stationary mobile home. But what choice did she have?

Bitsy reached deep into the hollow place inside her for what she hoped was a smile and some modicum of gratitude for what they were attempting to do for her. But there were no words in there. At least none that wouldn't be accompanied by tears. So she remained silent and let Sherlock do the whimpering for her.

Seventeen

Maddie stood in front of the bathroom mirror and tried to make peace with the woman who stared back. She'd never had Nikki's strikingly elegant bone structure or the blond, blue-eyed pertness that Avery claimed caused people to talk down to her. She had once looked like Kyra—long limbed and fresh faced with even features and a mass of dark hair. She still felt that way deep inside, but even a quick, unintentional glimpse in a shiny surface proved that her interior and exterior were no longer in sync.

She raised her chin and forced herself to look. No matter how carefully she tilted her head or narrowed her gaze, a slightly overweight, fifty-two-year-old woman whose roots needed coloring and whose face cried out for Botox and an industrial-strength moisturizer stared back.

She closed her eyes then opened them quickly hoping to see herself as Will professed to. But her wattle neck and blurred jaw were still there. And were those gray hairs in her eyebrows? It was a relief when a knock sounded on the bathroom door.

"Mom?" Kyra called out. "I'm taking Dustin down to the

beach. Nikki's in the foyer bathroom. She's . . . she's been in there a really long time."

"Is she all right?" Maddie whipped open the door. "I didn't hear her ring the bell."

Kyra shrugged apologetically as she pulled the bell from behind her back. "Sorry. I just couldn't take listening to it anymore." She handed the bell to Maddie. "Joe is coming back, isn't he?"

"Of course he is. He's been checking in every day, but there's been some problem with the witness he was supposed to escort back." His return had, in fact, been pushed back twice now. Each time, Nikki, who had always been so independent, became that much more fearful and needy. "Just give me a minute to finish dressing then I'll go down and check on her."

Five minutes later she stood outside the guest bathroom. "Nikki?" she called through the door. "Are you all right?"

A loud sob floated back in answer.

"Nikki?" Worried, she twisted the knob. Finding it unlocked, she pushed the door open. "Nikki are you . . ." She halted. Clad in a full-length robe, her feet in sport socks, Nikki sat on the closed toilet lid sobbing into a tissue. "Oh, God, I thought your water had broken. I thought you'd gone into labor." All the things she'd been expecting to happen when she was least expecting it poured from Maddie's mouth. She'd been acting calm for Nikki's sake, but she held her breath every time Nikki's blood pressure was measured and was constantly worried that something would go wrong. Nikki wasn't the only one desperate for Joe's return. "I thought you'd—"

"I'm never going into labor," Nikki said. "It's just a cruel hoax to make me feel better about getting so huge, isn't it?"

"No, of course not. We've all seen the sonogram. You're having these babies, Nikki. And it's going to happen when it happens whether Joe's back or whether you think you are or aren't ready.

When it's time for them to come out, they'll come. There's no stopping Mother Nature."

Gently, she led Nikki down the central hallway to the salon. There she smoothed the sheets and plumped the pillows then helped Nikki back into bed.

"He's never coming back, I know it. I've scared him away. And, oh God, who could blame him? I look like a beached whale. I can't carry on a conversation. I know the longer they're inside, the better, but I'm scared to death that something's going to go wrong. I want them to come out so I can be sure they're okay." She sobbed as Maddie pulled a sheet up over her. "I just want it all to be over."

"Shhh." She smoothed Nikki's hair. "It's all right. It's normal to feel all those things. But feeling them doesn't make them so. Everything's going to be all right."

Nikki looked up through her tears like a child desperate to believe there was no bogeyman under her bed.

"And you know Joe hasn't run away. He's on assignment, but he's poised to fly back at a moment's notice if he's not already on his way when you go into labor."

Nikki's tears slowed as she sniffled and dabbed at her eyes.

"Really, Nikki. It's okay. We're here for you and Joe will be back soon." Unlike William, whom she hadn't heard from since he'd pointed out that she was not, in fact, living her own life but taking care of and living through others'.

Nikki snuffled. Maddie resisted the urge to join in.

"I think you need to find something besides yourself to focus on." Maddie clicked the television on and handed the remote to Nikki. "Why don't you find a movie we can watch while I get you a few of Sofia's biscotti."

Ten minutes later Nikki was dunking her biscotti into a large glass of milk while Maddie sat on the sofa folding laundry. Both of them sighed as Annette Bening and Michael Douglas kissed in the oval office midway through *The American President*. By the time the laundry was folded and stacked, Nikki had fallen asleep. Careful not to wake her, Maddie delivered the clean clothes to their owners. Placing the last pile on Steve's bed in the pool house, Maddie closed her eyes in frustration. She'd originally begun doing his laundry to prevent him from shrinking anyone else's clothing like he had Nikki's Chanel suit. Somehow she'd never stopped. She was crossing the pool deck when she noticed Steve sitting motionless on a chaise staring out over the water. "Are you okay?" she called.

"Not really."

Maddie walked over and stood looking down at him. "What's wrong?"

He continued to stare out at the water. His voice when he spoke was wooden. "The Belle Vista offer fell through. The buyer couldn't get a mortgage."

"That's too bad. But you said it's a great house. I'm sure someone else will buy it."

"I don't know." His shoulders drooped. He wore the "oh, what's the use" expression he'd adopted when their world had fallen apart and he'd taken up residence on the couch, where his primary relationship had been with the television remote. "Nothing ever seems to go right. At least not for me."

She moved to stand directly in front of him, blocking the view. "You cannot give up because of one little setback. That's just part of doing business."

He didn't argue but he didn't meet her eyes, either. She knew she should simply walk away. He was a grown man and they were no longer married. The best way to help him get his act together was to leave him alone to figure it out. What she said was, "Kyra and Dustin should be back from the beach soon. How about a grilled cheese sandwich for lunch?"

"Thanks." He brightened. "That would be great."

Maddie went into the kitchen, put a large pan on the burner, then began to assemble the bread, butter, and cheese. In the end she used the whole loaf. Once she was cooking, she might as well make enough for everyone.

She put together a tray for Nikki. The rest of them were gathered around the kitchen table eating when Renée Franklin arrived carrying an arrangement of fresh-picked flowers.

"Neh Nay!" Dustin's smiling face was smeared with cheese. His T-shirt was littered with bits of potato chip. "Want krill cheese?" He held up the smooshed remainder of his sandwich.

"Thank you, Dustin." Renée smiled back, but that smile lacked some of its usual wattage. "I've already eaten. I'm going to take these to Nikki. Why don't you come visit us when you're finished?"

He nodded happily and popped a large strawberry into his mouth. After the table had been cleared and the plates loaded into the dishwasher, they trooped out to the salon. Dustin climbed into Kyra's lap and began to suck his thumb and twirl his hair as the conversation flowed around him. Nikki's eyes strayed to him repeatedly. Worry creased her forehead.

"The flowers are beautiful," Maddie said, nodding to the arrangement on Nikki's bedside table.

"They are, aren't they?" Renée agreed. "That's the thing about flowers. Plant them in the right spot, water them, feed them, and chances are, they'll do all right."

"Yes, kind of like children," Maddie said. Her eyes moved from Nikki's face to Renée's, which was also troubled.

"Is everything all right?" Maddie had lost count of how many times she'd asked that same question in the last few hours.

"Well, not everything, no," Renée replied. "The most immediate issue is the upcoming Sand Castle Showdown. Annelise is under the weather and the event's less than two weeks off. Entries aren't at all what we'd hoped."

"Does it matter how many people participate?" The question came from Nikki. It was the first sign of interest she'd shown since she'd been put on bed rest.

"Yes, because it was meant to not only be a fun activity for existing beach club members, but a means of raising awareness about our yearly memberships and also to show off and try to sell the cottages. The original idea of finishing out each unit after enough time shares had been sold to cover the cost of finish out for that unit just hasn't worked. The units are really too small to be permanent residences—unless you're used to living in New York City. And while the grown children and grandchildren of Nana and Pop Pop's original guests were initially enthusiastic, they're nostalgic about the Sunshine Hotel but they don't necessarily want to come here every year."

"What happened to the family that looked at the two-bedroom model Bitsy was in?" Kyra asked her father.

"I think they're still considering it, but so far they're not willing to commit." Steve's voice was tight, his shoulders still slumped. "The units have been for sale since mid-October, and so far, Joe's the only person who bought a unit outright. And he had a specific reason."

Renée reached out to adjust a sunflower. "John has planned a series of open houses and other incentives, but I know he's afraid we won't be able to sell them for enough per unit for any of us to even get our investments back, let alone make any kind of profit. And we don't have the front money to finish them out so that we have a better chance of selling them."

"But the Beach Club's doing okay, isn't it?" Maddie asked. "I mean I see people around the pool and in the dining room. The rooftop deck seems to be popular at sunset."

"It's building," Renée said. "But slowly. The place is nowhere close to supporting itself. The restaurant management group is barely breaking even. And of course, our percentage was supposed to come out of their profit. So far memberships are throwing off just enough to cover utilities, lifeguards, pool maintenance, and other operating expenses, but we're barely squeaking by."

The room had grown quiet. They had all put in virtually everything they had left in order to see the Sunshine Hotel brought back and to shoot the renovation in hopes of creating a version of *Do Over* that they'd assumed would help them take control of their own destinies. Now they couldn't even sell the documentary.

"Thank God we have Bella Flora to live in," Maddie said fervently.

Kyra went so still, she could have given a statue a run for its money. Steve was watching their daughter's face, too, and his own looked just as troubled.

"So how can we help?" Maddie asked.

"I'm not even sure what to ask for at this point," Renée said.

"What you're talking about is a lot of separate issues. God knows that can be overwhelming," Nikki said, clearly referring to herself. Maddie was glad to hear her talking at all.

"Nikki's right," Steve said. "All of these issues are related, but it's probably best to attack them one at a time."

"So maybe we should just focus on the Sand Castle Showdown for now?" Maddie asked, unable to take her eyes off Kyra's face, which had turned a chalky white. "Surely, at the very least we can field a team."

"Dustin wanna build catsle!"

"You are a fine castle builder, Dustin," Renée said warmly.

"Maybe we should make Dustin our captain," Maddie said.

"And maybe we need to set up an on-site sales center for the showdown," Steve suggested.

"That's a great idea," Renée said. "I know we'd hoped to sell the units ourselves, but maybe John can invite other Realtors to participate in the competition and take a look at the units while they're there."

"I can post video of the hotel then and now to help promote entries," Kyra said in a rush as if she'd been holding her breath and was only now letting it out.

"Are you allowed to do that?" Maddie asked as Troy ambled into the salon holding a half-eaten grilled cheese sandwich.

"I don't see why not," Kyra said. "The footage is ours and we're not trying to sell it, air it on television, or market it as a renovation or part of *Do Over*." It seemed her worry had been replaced by anger. "And I'll shoot on the day of the competition and see what I can put together."

"Thank God we're finally shooting something," Troy said. "I'm starting to get rusty."

"There is no 'we' here. I don't think a multi-camera shoot of a sand castle building contest is necessary." Kyra glared at Troy. "And since we're on the subject, I don't know why you're still here when we're not shooting a series, or anything else, and the documentary we can't sell is finished."

"Are you evicting me? Because I don't think our agreement included an eviction clause," Troy replied.

"There is no agreement." Kyra's voice was taut with anger. "We never had an agreement. You turned a favor into something it was never meant to be. There's no good reason for you to hang around. Unless you're spying for the network, or trying to take advantage of us in some way."

Maddie saw Kyra's last salvo land, saw the brief detonation of hurt in Troy's eyes. Dustin was looking between his mother to Troy and back again.

"For a reasonably smart and talented woman, you really can be amazingly . . . unwise," Troy said with a small sorrowful shake of his head. His glance at Dustin made it clear why he'd chosen a synonym for the word "stupid."

"Coming from you, I'll take that as a compliment," Kyra said in an impossibly sweet voice for the same reason.

"Feel free to take it however you want to." Troy matched her tone, but Maddie could see the effort it cost him. "I'll need a day or so to make other arrangements, but I'll get out of your hair if that's what you want. I actually thought I might be of help." He shrugged. "But you can lead a horse to water and all that . . ."

They watched in silence as he turned and left the room.

"Did he just call me a horse's ass?" Kyra asked several long moments later.

"Yes," Nikki said with a rare smile. "I do believe he did."

Eighteen

The Hardins' garage door rumbled up, then down that evening. In the family room, Avery heard the door into the kitchen open and braced for an angry teenaged stomp, which would signal Jason's arrival, or an enthusiastic, nonthreatening footstep, which would mean Josh. But the door had opened and closed with a quiet click, and though she was no longer alone, the vibe in the house remained spectacularly stress-free. She exhaled the breath she'd been holding as Chase entered the room.

"Do you hear that quiet?" he asked in wonder. "I feel like a soldier in a foxhole when the shelling finally stops. There's a slight ringing in my ears, but I can actually breathe and hear myself think."

"Copy that," she said, inhaling another breath.

They shared a conspiratorial smile. Her shoulders relaxed. Her nervous system followed suit, taking it down a notch to a less noticeable jangle.

Chase came forward and leaned down to kiss her cheek. "What are you watching?"

She swiveled around and roused her computer screen. "You-Tube. Tiny house videos." She hit "play." A young woman standing on a postage stamp front porch welcomed them to the tour of her 140-square-foot home.

"Wow, that is tiny."

"Yeah. More than three hundred square feet smaller than the one-bedroom cottages at the Sunshine Hotel. And look how much the builder fit into it."

As they watched, the woman pointed out each feature in the miniature kitchen, including a drop-down cutting board that fit precisely over the top of the gas stove and a miniature dishwasher. In the bathroom she pulled back a shower curtain to reveal a custom-made soaking tub with a detachable showerhead.

"I've been intrigued by the whole tiny house thing for a while," Avery said. "If we utilize some of these design elements into Bitsy's one-bedroom, we could better accommodate her things and also make it feel more spacious. If we make these vacation cottages fun and functional, they'll be more attractive to buyers looking for a full-time residence."

"Good thinking." Chase stepped up behind Avery as the young woman on-screen stepped back to reveal the cleverly disguised storage that had been built into the narrow staircase that led up to the sleeping loft.

"Cool." He leaned closer, resting his hands on Avery's shoulders as the woman demonstrated how even the bottom treads concealed deep drawers. "There's a lot of skill involved in utilizing the space so efficiently." He dropped a kiss on the top of her head. "Plus the more efficient the design, the fewer the materials needed."

"Mmmm." The back of her head pillowed against his abdomen, not a soft spot but a comforting one. Reluctantly she leaned forward to cue up another video. "Look at this." She hit "play" and they watched another tiny home owner slide a cut-down barn door across two room openings. "One sliding door covers the bathroom and the bedroom without taking up more than a couple inches of floor space." She leaned back against him again, enjoying the physical connection, as she pulled up another example. "With enough building-in and tiny space technique, we can create the illusion of space. Which can be more important than the actual square footage."

"I like it," Chase said and Avery realized how long it had been since they had really collaborated.

"The Sunshine cottages won't be portable like a lot of tiny homes are," she said. "And we can't afford to sell them for as little as they tend to go for. But they'll come with club membership, the pool, a gorgeous stretch of beach, and the Gulf of Mexico." She could see the cottages in her mind's eye. "We could make Bitsy's one-bedroom into a model and build out a two-bedroom version as well. I'm betting most buyers would prefer the more efficient versions. I know I would."

He turned the desk chair around and pulled her to her feet. She had to crane her neck and look up to meet his eyes, but tonight she didn't resent the disparity in their heights. Because those eyes were filled with admiration.

"Did you ever read any of Sue Grafton's alphabet mysteries?" she asked. "You know, *A is for Alibi*, *B is for Burglar*, and so on?"

"No."

"I used to inhale them. The main character, Kinsey Millhone, lives in this really compact studio apartment converted from a single-car garage. I remember some of the descriptions of the space—everything tightly fit together like the cabin of a boat. It always sounded so cozy."

"Cozy is good," he murmured, pulling her up against him. "So is tightly fit." He grinned. "And I'm especially partial to compact." He ran his hands down her sides to illustrate, let his hands settle on her buttocks. "I don't remember the last time we had the house to ourselves." His kiss was long and lingering. "I never thought of DIY videos or anything with the word 'tiny' in it as turn-ons before, but . . ." He kissed her again. His hands moved over her backside with more intent.

"Shows what you know," she teased. "Home and Garden programming of almost any kind is total porn for women."

He pulled her tighter so that their bodies melded. "Good to know." His lips quirked up as he leaned back in for a kiss. "I guess it's kind of like when you talk construction to me."

"Square footage," she breathed. "Slope ratio."

His lips found hers. They shared a smile that turned into a bone-melting kiss.

"We might not get the house to ourselves for another millennium," Chase said.

"Oh, is there something special you want to talk about?" She looped her arms around his neck.

"I don't want to talk at all," he whispered as his lips moved to nibble on her ear and his fingers began to unbutton her blouse. "But I'd like to help you get undressed. At the moment you have way too many clothes on for the kind of communication I have in mind."

. . .

Maddie was outside on the loggia watching Dustin "renovate" his replica Bella Flora when Troy finished loading his car and came to say good-bye. Each layer of his shaggy hair shone a different color of blond in the morning sun. His chiseled face was lightly tanned. A wry smile twisted his lips. When he removed his sunglasses, his eyes were missing their usual challenging glint.

"Well, I guess I'll be getting on the road."

"Where are you headed?" Maddie asked.

"I'm not sure. I've had some offers. I may take a little time weighing them."

"Will you be all right . . . financially?"

His eyes lit with surprise, which he quashed quickly. "Oh, I'll be fine. But it's nice of you to ask. In fact, you're one of the nicest people I've ever come across."

Maddie smiled. She'd watched his gentle manner with Dustin, the fact that even when he'd worked for the network, he'd done what he could to protect her grandson and Kyra.

"Your daughter, on the other hand, can be a bit harsh. And her taste in men is seriously flawed." He looked out over the playhouse, beyond the fishing pier to the Gulf beyond.

"We all have our weaknesses. And truly charismatic men can be especially hard to resist," Maddie said, trying not to think how poorly she seemed to be handling her own relationship with the way too charismatic William Hightower. "But if you'd been less confrontational and more forthcoming, Kyra might have been able to see your good qualities. You do have more than a few."

"Forthcoming about what?" he asked as if he had no idea what she was talking about. But when he turned his gaze back to meet hers, his discomfort was plain.

"About your feelings for Kyra."

He put his sunglasses back on. His broad shoulders stiffened. "What makes you think I have feelings for Kyra?"

Although she was ashamed of herself the moment she did it, she rolled her eyes at him. "Are you serious? The only person who doesn't seem to be aware of your feelings for Kyra is Kyra. And that's no one's fault but your own."

He shook his head sadly. "I guess it's a little late to be asking for advice now." He cocked his head. "Unless you happen to have some?"

"I'm really not sure what to offer unless you're prepared to walk in there right now and tell her exactly how you feel about her."

His face reflected his horror at the suggestion.

Men could be such emotional cowards. She thought again of Will and retracted the thought. Emotional cowardice was not only a male prerogative.

"Well, then. If honesty is out, I suggest you say a pleasant good-bye, add a compliment or two, and make sure that if your paths cross again, you avoid picking a fight right off the bat."

"Got it." Troy stepped over to the playhouse and crouched down to Dustin's height. "See you later, pal."

"Have to go, Broy?" Dustin threw his arms around Troy's neck and hugged him tightly. Troy hugged him back. Finally, Troy stood and ruffled Dustin's hair. "You be good, you hear?" There was a sniff and Maddie wasn't sure which one of them it came from.

With a final nod, Troy turned to go. He did not walk into the house to say good-bye or anything else to Kyra, but headed past the garage to the driveway. Moments later his car engine revved and Troy Matthews was gone.

Maddie spent the rest of the morning watching Dustin and trying to keep Nicole entertained. She made "handwitches" for lunch, then waved good-bye to Kyra, who hadn't so much as mentioned Troy's name as she wheeled the jogging stroller that held the now-drowsy Dustin down the bricked drive. Maddie was tidying the kitchen when Gabriella Giraldi arrived bearing a pan of manicotti and a loaf of Italian bread that was still warm from the bakery oven. Joe Senior carried a trifle bowl of tiramisu and a disposable pan of eggplant parmesan.

"I don't know how you create all this fabulous food in that motel kitchen," Maddie said as she made room for the Giraldis' offerings in the refrigerator. "But we are all extremely grateful. Would you like to come over for dinner tonight and share some of it with us?"

"No, thank you," Gabriella said. "We're heading over to Disney World for a couple of days. I've been feeling that our presence is not altogether relaxing for Nicole, and we'll only be an hour-and-a-half away if you need our help or she should go into labor. Although I have a feeling she's going to make it at least another two to three weeks, which is good for the babies, if not her patience."

"I think she feels Joe has deserted her, and he tells me that when he is able to call, she's always sleeping. And that she hasn't yet called him back."

Maddie squirmed slightly under Gabriella's regard. She had tried more than once to convince Nikki to speak with Joe, but Nikki had so far resisted. "I'm sure they'll work things out when Joe gets back," she said. "Any idea when that will be?"

Gabriella shook her head. "I know he's frustrated by how this case has drawn out, and of course, he's hurt that Nikki doesn't seem to understand, but . . ." She shrugged. "It's not really my place to instruct either of them on their relationship." She looked to her husband. "Or so Joe here keeps telling me. We're going to give her a little breathing room." She turned her back on Joe Senior and lowered her voice. "But we would all appreciate it if you would encourage her to pick up and speak to him next time. In my experience, it's better to have an argument, and get things out in the open, than not to speak."

At Maddie's nod, Gabriella gave Maddie a hug then took her husband by the arm. "We'll just go in and have a quick visit with Nicole and then we'll be off." She mouthed a last "thank you" before heading into the salon.

Maddie whirled through the kitchen, wiping and straightening. And thinking about the advice she'd given Troy as well as her collaboration with Gabriella on Joe and Nikki's relationship. Listening to others and offering advice was so much easier than examining your own feelings and issues, especially when they were as muddled as hers seemed to be.

She opened the refrigerator and began to toss items that had passed their expiration dates while rearranging the things that remained. Was it enough to play housemother at Bella Flora, to spend time with her grandson, fuss over Nikki, cook meals, do laundry, serve as her ex-husband's unpaid advisor/therapist? How much had her life really changed? She yanked the now bulging trash bag out of its container and dragged it outside. And how did you go after something when you didn't actually know what you wanted?

She and Will hadn't spoken since the call in which he'd pointed out far too truthfully that she was not, in fact, working on her own life but still living for others. Was she going to let their relationship die because she lacked the courage to initiate a conversation with him? Wasn't it better to argue and get things out in the open as Gabriella had suggested than to let them fester?

Her subconscious reared its ugly, negative head as she stuffed the bag into the outside trash can. She shouted it down, too worked up to listen.

Was "being there" for William any different than taking care of everyone else? And what was wrong with taking care of others, if it gave you pleasure? Did it give her pleasure? Or had she just gotten used to her role as caregiver?

She stomped out to the seawall and stared out over the pass. Was going on the road the only way she could have William? It would probably be more fun than what her life had boiled down to at the moment. But why did it have to be one or the other? Wasn't there some middle ground? And why was she waiting to hear from him when she missed him so much?

A boat went by and then another. All of them were filled with people out having a good time. Her subconscious raised its hand, but she did not call on it. She was tired of thinking and debating. She hit speed dial and lifted the phone to her ear. She would discuss this with William. They were both adults. Adults who wanted to spend time together. They could figure it out. His voice sounded in her ear and she took a deep breath, finally prepared to tell him exactly how she felt. Which was when she realized that it was not Will, but a recording. Asking her very politely to leave a message at the sound of the tone.

Nineteen

"Thanks for coming by." Nikki managed to push herself up against the pillows so that she was closer to sitting than lying.

"It's good to see you." Bitsy smiled politely, if tentatively. "How are you feeling?"

"I'm okay. At least for someone doing such a convincing impersonation of a beached whale."

"It must be hard lying there twenty-four/seven," Bitsy said. But she did not come closer nor did she contradict the whale comparison.

"Yeah. I mean, there are those scintillating visits to the bathroom and the brief moments of ecstasy breathing fresh air out on the loggia." She looked out the window with real longing, unable to believe how cavalier she'd been about being able to walk, get out of bed, leave the house, drive a car. It was a gorgeous afternoon to be out on a boat, or walking on the beach, or even sitting in the sunshine like any other inhabitant of the state of Florida. "I'll never take being able to move or breathe fresh air for granted again." She planted her elbows in an effort to sit up straighter.

Sherlock whimpered and buried his muzzle in Bitsy's shoulder. Bitsy shifted her weight to the balls of her feet. "You look like you're ready to flee at any moment," Nikki said, noting their distance. "Have I been that awful?" She swallowed. "I seem to be driving everyone away. Joe's still in California. The Giraldis have gone to Orlando. Even Troy left, though I'm pretty sure that wasn't my fault."

"Not awful exactly. But you have been a little . . . volatile."

Nikki groaned in embarrassment. "Please sit down. I promise not to lunge at you. And I'm pretty sure I'm not going to bite."

Bitsy smiled and sat, but she still held Sherlock protectively in her arms, the better to make a strategic retreat or a hasty exit. Nikki vowed to behave like a perfectly normal human being whether she felt like one or not. "So," she said, appalled to realize how long it had been since she'd asked about anyone else. "How are things with you?"

"Well, let's see." Bitsy settled back in the chair. "I'm trying really hard to make the mental adjustment from being married to someone I loved to being abandoned by someone I'd like to hunt down and kill while adjusting from living in twenty thousand square feet to four hundred and fifty. But Avery's working on making the most of that space, so I guess it's no big deal, right?" Her smile was weary. "And I've gone from never thinking about a life plan to wishing I had a kick-ass résumé or actually any résumé that included one or two recognizable job skills."

Nikki looked carefully at Bitsy, noting the strained smile, the hollowed cheekbones, the pinpoint of panic in her eyes. Nikki knew exactly how it felt to lose everything, including life as she'd known it, and while she had built quite a lot from the poverty in which she'd begun, Bitsy had fallen much farther. And the person who'd pushed her off the ledge had been a husband rather than a brother.

"As I recall, you do have a degree from Harvard. In finance, right? It was on the questionnaire you filled out for Heart, Inc."

"Yes," Bitsy said quietly. "But I never really used it. It always felt wrong to go after a job that someone else might really need. And however horrible this is going to sound, being a Fletcher was pretty much a full-time job." She stroked Sherlock's head absently. "Honestly, I'm glad my parents aren't here to see how badly I've mucked everything up. I'm going to go down in the annals of history as the Fletcher who lost the family timber fortune."

Nikki felt a gut kick of guilt at how focused she'd been on her own fears and issues when Bitsy was dealing with such staggering realities. Or maybe it was just Little Girl 1 and Little Girl 2 battling it out for more square footage. "I'm so sorry you're dealing with all of this, Bitsy. And even sorrier that I haven't been paying attention. Have you looked into hiring a private detective to find Bertie and drag his ass back?"

"Believe me, I fantasize about it on a daily basis. But I'm going to have to find a job first. I can't believe I'm actually admitting this, but I have zero income, and what little cash I have is, well, let's just say feeding myself and Sherlock is all I can manage right now."

"We could put together a résumé highlighting your real-world skills," Nikki said.

"Which are, what? Party planning? Fund-raising?" Bitsy closed her eyes, her voice signaling defeat.

"Yes! Those are marketable skills in the corporate world. There are successful party planners who make serious money," Nikki countered. "And fund-raising? That's what companies call development."

"I have raised a lot of money for a variety of nonprofits," Bitsy said. "And I do know how to handpick committee members and get the most out of a group of volunteers. Oh, and I've handled publicity and marketing for a number of events."

"Those are executive skills and talents that could be invaluable to the right entities."

"Do you really think so?" Bitsy asked, her expression hopeful but dubious.

"I do. And maybe we could tap into some of those skills on a much smaller and more personal scale." She studied Bitsy and tried not to dwell on the fact that she and the rest of the *Do Over* team were currently more unprofitable than pretty much any nonprofit. "Would you be willing to help out with the upcoming Sand Castle Showdown?"

Bitsy's bark of laughter startled Sherlock. He lifted his head, cocking it quizzically as if to identify the unfamiliar sound. "The Sand Castle Showdown?"

"All of us put up money to help fund the renovation of the Sunshine Hotel and Beach Club because we thought that would allow us to shoot our own version of *Do Over* and fight the network's lawsuit. Kyra put in the most. She hasn't come out and said so, but I think Daniel loaned her the money. The problem is the only cottage that's sold so far is Joe's." She paused, realizing that although he'd bought it for them, she still thought of it as his. For the first time she wondered why she'd always resisted his urge to merge them into one. Was it a simple fear of being hurt? A lack of trust? Or an assumption that she was somehow not a person that anyone like Joe would ever really commit to?

"And while the number of beach club memberships has grown, it's building at a turtle's pace. We're only a few blocks from the Don. Their club membership is considerably more expensive, but it includes way more amenities and perks."

"I noticed all the empty cottage shells," Bitsy said. "And I've barely seen anyone on the property looking at them."

"The Sand Castle Showdown was meant to be a marketing event—to call attention to the hotel and beach club—and to bring people on the property. But Annelise isn't feeling well and nothing much seems to be happening. We could really use your help." Nikki's phone rang. She glanced down at the screen and saw Joe's face and number. She swallowed and looked away.

"Do you need to answer that?" Bitsy asked.

"No. I—"

"Yes, she does," Maddie said as she sailed into the room carrying a glass of juice, which she set on the bedside table. She picked up the still ringing phone and held it out to Nikki.

"No. Not . . . now. Please."

"He deserves to have his calls answered, Nikki."

"Then you answer," Nikki said. "And tell him I'm sleeping."

"Sorry. You look pretty awake to me and you can't keep avoiding him." Maddie lifted the phone to her ear. "Hi, Joe. How are you? Good." She smiled and nodded amiably. "Yes, she is awake. In fact, she's sitting right here. Hold on just a second." She extended the phone toward Nikki.

Nikki shook her head and mouthed the word "No." She felt Bitsy's eyes on her and flushed with embarrassment, but Nikki's anger at Joe's leaving had gotten all muddled with her fear and insecurity. The longer he'd been gone, the harder it had become to imagine talking on the phone and acting as if everything was fine. Admitting to herself that she bore a lot of the responsibility for the distance between them didn't mean she was ready to open herself up to the kind of conversation it might take to fix things.

She shrank back into the pillows, at least as much as someone her size could "shrink," but Maddie had that look on her face. That motherly I-know-you-better-than-you-know-yourself-now-do-what's-expected-of-you look that she couldn't imagine ever mastering.

"Come on, Bitsy. Why don't you and Sherlock come out on the loggia for a bit of fresh air while Nikki speaks to Joe?" Maddie placed the phone in Nikki's hand. "Ring the bell or text when you're finished and we'll come back."

Bitsy stood. "Don't screw this up," she said quietly to Nikki. "I've started realizing that I may have ignored warning signs that Bertie was unhappy, because I was afraid to deal with them." She turned and followed Maddie out of the salon, Sherlock in her arms.

Nikki watched them settle at the wrought iron table, their backs intentionally turned. She was definitely not ready for this conversation, but it wasn't as if it was going to be any easier tomorrow, or the day after that. Or ever. She hesitated, mentally squared her shoulders, then lifted the phone to her ear.

"Nikki?" At the sound of his voice, her pulse pounded in her ears. "Are you there? Are you all right?"

"Yes." Her voice wobbled. He had every right to be angry that she'd been dodging his calls, but the only thing she heard in his voice was concern. For her. She was an imbecile. "How's it going out there?"

"It's a mess. This witness has turned all squirrelly. One minute he's ready to testify, the next he wants nothing to do with it. And it's driving me crazy to be so far away right now." He paused. "I know you're angry and upset that I left, but I don't have a choice. I need to—"

"I know." She closed her eyes as the ugly truth hit her. She had been acting like a spoiled, silly child. Only thinking of herself and what she'd kept thinking of as her "predicament." Her poor beached whale of a self had been afraid of everything and done nothing but complain when Joe had gone to so much effort to make sure she was comfortable and surrounded by people to take care of her. It was time to grow up. Or at least pretend that she had. "I'm fine. Everything's fine. Of course, I did drive your parents and Nonna Sofia away. But other than that I'm okay. And given all the acrobatics going on, I have to assume the babies are going to be gymnasts."

"That's good." She heard the relief in his voice and knew he'd been bracing for recriminations or tears or something equally unpleasant. Shame coursed through her. "And don't feel bad about the Disney trip. I'm going to forward you the shot of Nonna Sofia on the Tower of Terror ride, Mickey ears and all."

A smile hovered on her lips. Suddenly she wanted to apologize, to tell him how sorry she was for trampling all over what should have been a joyous time and which she'd treated like an ordeal. She opened her mouth, but the words stuck in her throat. "I'll be on the lookout for it," was the best she could manage.

"Is there anything you need?" he asked. "Anything I can send or bring back?"

"No, thanks," she said. "I'm fine." And in a way she didn't understand and hadn't been before, she was.

"All I want is you," she said. But she said it very quietly and long after he'd hung up.

Posted to YouTube, 12:01 A.M.

Video: No Trespassing sign. Trash-strewn pool. Sand drifts. Tarp snapping on roof. Quick cuts of overgrown trees, shrubs, vines crawling up and over boarded-up cottages.

Audio: Music up and under.

Audio: "This is how the Sunshine Hotel and Beach Club—aka the land that time forgot—looked the first day we saw it."

Video: Dissolve to blue sky shots/seagull battalion, into renovation in progress.

Audio: "We gave the Sunshine Hotel and Beach Club a DO OVER, because whatever the network, who shall remain nameless, thinks, that's what we do."

Video: Close-ups sweating, Maddie, Avery, Nikki, and crew.

Audio: "It wasn't always pretty. In fact, it almost never was. Well, except for Ray Flamingo."

Video: Close-up Ray in pastel linen mime-whip cracking.

Sfx: Whip crack.

Audio: "While we were at it, we helped solve a mystery from the
    fifties."

Video: Shot of crime scene tape. Police and MEs on property.

Music up and under.

Audio: "And turned this fabulous mid-century hotel into a great
    place to spend the day, or to own a piece of."

Video: Dissolve to the Sunshine now—pool, lifeguard on retro
    stand, grand opening, kids running, ladies playing cards,
    close-up Ping-Pong, exteriors of cottages, landscaping.
    Rooftop deck. Hightower playing at grand opening.

Audio: "Now it's time for a SAND CASTLE SHOWDOWN!"

Video: SAND CASTLE SHOWDOWN graphic. Beach shots/view
    from rooftop.

Audio: "Come build something and enter to win one free beach
    club membership. Or come hang out on our rooftop bar and
    watch! Bring your kids, bring your family. Build on your own
    or field a team! Here's the link!"

Video: Entry link and details over sunset video shot from rooftop.
    Fade to black.

Twenty

Lori Blair did not sound like someone who dotted the *i* at the end of her name with a heart. She'd proven to be highly organized, unfailingly polite, and excruciatingly competent. But that didn't make her an acceptable stand-in for Will that day when Maddie answered her phone during a rare solo stroll on the beach. Or any day for that matter.

"Madeline?"

"Yes?"

"This is Lori Blair. William Hightower's assistant." She said this as if Maddie might have somehow forgotten.

"Yes?"

"I'm sorry to disturb you, but Will asked me to reach out to you on his behalf."

"Oh?" Even hearing the young woman refer to him as "Will" rankled. The idea that William had a "minion" calling her because he couldn't be bothered to do it himself, as her subconscious put it, rankled further.

The sun had grown weaker, causing the temperature to dip. The wet sand at the water's edge was cool on her bare feet.

"Is he all right?" Maddie asked. Because as far as she and her subconscious were concerned, the only things that would make this phone call palatable were broken fingers or a life-threatening illness.

"Yes, of course," Lori said. "He's fine."

"So he asked you to call me rather than calling me himself because . . ."

"Oh." She took a minute to consider the question. "He took a trip with Hud to the Everglades to get his head in the right place before he goes on tour. I mean, a man can only swim so many laps, right?"

Maddie thought of all the times she'd lain in Will's bed listening to him swim off the stress and the daily temptation for alcohol and drugs. She sincerely hoped that Lori was listening from a less intimate location.

"They're camping out and pretty much avoiding civilization as much as possible. So cell reception has been spotty and recharging opportunities minimal. As you might imagine, the people at Aquarian Records aren't at all happy about him being unreachable."

She listened to the smooth, confident, and undeniably efficient voice that belonged to a woman who possessed a disturbingly comprehensive knowledge of Will, his thoughts, and his feelings. It was a relief to know that Will hadn't intentionally ignored her phone message, but she absolutely hated communicating through a female interpreter who seemed to be positioned at the center of his life.

Maddie continued to walk, but the pleasure of it had begun to seep away just like the sunlight. She attempted to even out her breathing. "So what is it Will wanted you to tell me?"

"Will asked me to let you know that he'd like to attend the, I believe it's called the Sand Castle Showdown?"

"Seriously?" She didn't even know how he had heard about it.

"Yes, he said he saw the YouTube post when they stopped for fuel."

"YouTube post?" Maddie asked dubiously.

"Yes. I understand you have a full house, but if you have room for him, he'd like to build a couple of days with you onto the beginning of the tour. Or I could put him in a suite at the Don CeSar if that would be more convenient?"

Maddie picked up her pace. She didn't care one bit for how much this assistant knew about her, her family, or the current state of her relationship with William Hightower. For once she and her subconscious were totally in sync. "So he put you in charge of his sleeping situation?" She refused to believe that this young woman she'd never met was close enough to Will to be privy to that kind of information.

"I handle everything for him." Lori said this without one iota of embarrassment or doubt. "My job is to leave him free to create music and to perform at his peak."

Her subconscious snorted. Both of them wanted to know exactly what sort of performance Lori "with an *i*" was referring to.

Maddie was no longer enjoying the solitude, the sand between her toes, or anything much at all. All she could think of was getting back to Bella Flora and not losing her temper in a way she'd regret. She fixed her eyes on a kite floating high above the beach and drew a deep, though not particularly calming, breath. "So this is the thing, Lori," she finally said. "The next time you hear from your boss, you tell him he's more than welcome here. Then you be sure and tell him that he's going to have to discuss the sleeping arrangements directly with me."

• • •

"It doesn't work," Bitsy said to Avery as she motioned to the apartment-size washing machine that was stowed along with its companion dryer in a small closet near the bathroom.

"Are you sure?"

"Absolutely. I mean, I put the clothes and the detergent in like Maddie told me, and I even chose the water temperature and the kind of washing cycle I wanted." Bitsy sounded extremely pleased with herself. "But it wouldn't go on. I called maintenance, but they never sent anyone."

She checked Bitsy's face to see if she was joking. "There is no maintenance department, Bitsy. Just like there's no room service. Do you know who you spoke to?"

"No. But I waited and waited." She frowned and peered more closely at the washer. "Maybe it's broken."

"It's brand new," Avery said. "I really don't think it's broken. Why don't you show me what you did?"

The clothes still sat in the washer. Now Bitsy reset the water temperature and the wash cycle with the kind of attention that normally accompanied defusing a bomb or handling radioactive materials. Then she pushed the GE logo with her index finger.

"That's a logo," Avery said.

"I know, but I couldn't find anything that actually said 'start,' so I figured that must be it."

Avery blinked. She was fairly certain that Nikki had told them that Bitsy went to Harvard. "Did you try pulling the dial?" She pointed to the large round dial that Bitsy had used to set the wash cycle.

"Why would anyone do that?"

Avery pulled out the dial. Water began to rush into the machine.

"Wow." Bitsy's tone was practically reverent. "You really *are* handy."

Avery was careful not to laugh as she pulled the manual from the shelf above the units. "A lot of them work that way." She flipped through the booklet, folded it open to the right page, and handed it to Bitsy. "But here's the step-by-step instructions."

Bitsy smiled.

"Right, so can I show you the plans now?"

"Sure." They settled at the small dinette. Avery placed the floor plan and the pile of sketches on the table.

"Boy, it's really full," she said, looking at all the built-ins that Avery had drawn into Bitsy's one-bedroom.

"This is the kitchen/dining room L." Avery tilted the sketch so that Bitsy could see it clearly. "You see how it's all connected. This is extra storage that's been created. And here where we're sitting will be this banquette that stretches under the entire window. With this high-low table, it can be used for a lot of things and seat more people than could fit around this little table."

"Interesting."

"And over there is the built-in that will provide more storage and allow the TV to be seen from the banquette and the sofa-sitting area. We could even use furniture to create storage. For example, we could stack three to four stools on top of the end table next to the sofa. When they're in place, they turn into shelving, but you can take them apart and use them as extra seating when you have guests." She pushed the sketch that illustrated both usages in front of Bitsy.

"Cute," she said noncommittally. "It looks kind of like the inside of a mobile home. I think." She looked Avery in the eye. "I haven't ever actually been in one, but that is what they're like, right?"

"Only in the sense that we're maximizing space and making sure that everything does at least double, if not triple, duty. And I promise you that Ray Flamingo will not let this look or feel like your standard mobile home or RV."

Bitsy nodded, but she didn't look at all convinced.

"What do you think of *The Life-Changing Magic of Tidying Up*?" Avery asked. "Have you read it?"

"Part of it."

"And?" Avery prompted.

"Well, frankly, I feel bad that Marie Kondo, the author, spent most of her adolescence fixating on tidying up. I'm pretty sure she's OCD. She used to even throw away her siblings things because it felt too cluttered to her. And although I'd like to have a number one *New York Times* bestseller under my belt, it's kind of stressful reading. I mean I've already been forced to give up ninety-nine percent of my possessions and you're taking care of storage for what little I have left. I don't personally think that having less than I already do is going to magically improve my life, you know?"

"Point taken." With a wince Avery pulled out the rest of the sketches then pointed out the floor-to-ceiling drawers and cabinets that covered one bedroom wall as well as its built-in closet, and the platform bed that rested on and was surrounded by even more built-in storage. The outside storage she'd designed into the unit's private walled garden barely elicited a glimmer in Bitsy's eye. She felt a keen stab of disappointment as she realized that the design she'd been so proud of and excited about was yet another slap in Bitsy's face.

"I'm sure it will be very nice," Bitsy said diplomatically but her lip had begun to quiver. "I may just not be visualizing it in a way that would show it to its best advantage. Bertie was the one who could look at a plan or sketch and see what a space could be." Her eyes glistened with what looked like tears.

Sherlock sat up, shook his head, and looked up at Bitsy. She lifted him into her lap and buried her face in his fur.

"How are the entries for the Sand Castle Showdown coming?" Avery asked, eager to change the subject.

Bitsy raised her face and smiled, though her eyes still glistened with unshed tears. "They've definitely picked up since Kyra posted and shared her YouTube video. Have you seen it?"

"No."

"Well, you might want to. It's a fun piece, but it does tweak the network's nose." She ran a hand over Sherlock's head then down his back. "You know, when the lack of space here starts getting to me, I've been taking Sherlock for lots of long walks and I noticed the Gulf Beaches Historical Museum. It's housed in what used to be a small church and they've got a ton of great information and photos documenting Pass-a-Grille." She scratched Sherlock behind the ear. "I was thinking . . . The Sunshine Hotel is a local midcentury treasure. Maybe they'd like to participate in some way in the sand castle build."

"That's a good idea," Avery said, relieved to see Bitsy perking up.

"Thanks." Bitsy scratched Sherlock behind his other ear. The dog's eyes fluttered shut. He appeared to be smiling. "Hey, you know what else might be cool?" Bitsy sat up. "Why don't you build this unit with all the storage in sand at the Showdown?"

"Oh, but, I don't . . ." Avery stopped, thought. "That's actually a really great idea."

"Yes." Bitsy brightened. "I mean, they could see it in sand and then tour the shells and see the plans. All you'd need is sand and water and a team to build it. Maybe Hardin Morgan Construction could construct it."

Avery smiled as she began to seriously consider it. "That could be really cool. All the subcontractors could come work on the build and promote their companies at the same time."

"Yes," Bitsy said with increasing enthusiasm. "It would accomplish a lot of things. It would call attention to the hotel and the idea of these special units. Maybe Franklin Realty could hang a tiny For Sale sign outside the sand reproduction."

"You're a genius!" Avery said. "Participating in the Sand Castle Showdown will allow us to present everything we want in a really public and novel way."

"My dog, my brain, and I thank you," Bitsy said more cheerfully than Avery had seen her. As Bitsy escorted her to the door, Avery thought about all that building the model out of sand would accomplish. Now all she had to do was convince Chase, Jeff, and all their subcontractors that spending an entire day building a sand castle was actually a good use of their time.

• • •

The speedboat idled just off Bella Flora's seawall, its engine loud and throaty. Its sleek hull was painted fire engine red. White pinstripes ran down its sides.

Dustin froze on the pool step like a hunting dog on point when he spotted it.

"Who is it?" Maddie asked.

"It's Dandiel!" Dustin jumped out of the pool and ran toward the seawall, waving excitedly, his bright green puddle jumper swim aid/life vest flashing.

Kyra sat up, jolted to her feet. "Dustin! Stop! Don't get too close to the seawall." She raced across the pool deck and snatched him up, lifting him to her hip, as Daniel flashed a white-toothed smile in their direction. His dark curls were wind-tossed, his bare chest gleamed smooth and golden. He tilted his head up and called out to them. "I came to take you both for a ride!" He motioned to the Cottage Inn next door. "Meet me at the dock?"

"Boat!" Dustin shouted with excitement. Kyra tried to tamp down her own excitement. She wanted to replace it with irritation that he assumed he could simply show up without warning and whisk Dustin, and her, off anytime he felt like it. But the day was spectacular—a brilliant yellow sun hung in a bright blue sky over sparkling green water—and Dustin's face glowed with happiness, his small body practically vibrated with it. She was glad he had not yet begun to question where his daddy went when he wasn't with them or even how long he'd stay once he appeared. A smile claimed her lips without permission. "Be there in a sec!"

"Going on Dandiel's red boat!" Dustin proclaimed happily as Kyra stuffed T-shirts, flip-flops, towels, and sunscreen into a straw beach bag. Feeling her mother's eyes on her, she invited her along.

Maddie smiled back. "You two go have fun. You can tell me all about it when you get back."

On the dock Kyra handed the bag and then Dustin down to Daniel. It was hard not to grin back at him, even harder not to act like a silly schoolgirl as he reached a hand up to help her step down into the boat. She was grateful he wore sunglasses so she didn't have to look into the too-beautiful brown eyes that were so hard to say no to. But it was the warmth of his smile and the protective arms that wrapped so securely around Dustin that made him so hard to resist.

"Where are we heading?"

"I was thinking maybe Fort De Soto if you're up for it. I brought lunch." Daniel indicated a large picnic basket and small cooler near the bench seat.

"Wanna pignik!" Dustin announced with a smile that matched his father's. "And see the fort!"

"Done!" Daniel said. "Do you want to help me drive?"

At Dustin's squeal of excitement, Daniel sat back in the driver's seat and settled Dustin into his lap. "I'll get us out into the channel and then you can help me steer."

Kyra took the passenger seat, braced her feet on the dashboard, and closed her eyes, letting the salt breeze and happy chatter flow over her. Her awareness of Daniel made it impossible to doze, but she kept her eyes closed, feigning sleep, partly to let Dustin keep his father to himself and partly so that she could avoid temptation as long as possible.

The boat picked up speed. When she opened her eyes, they were running along the massive Skyway Bridge, skimming in and out of its shadow. Just past a large island teeming with birds, Daniel made a right turn and slowed slightly.

"Lookit the fort!" Dustin shouted as the remains of the Spanish outpost appeared at the end of a long sliver of white beach. Daniel eased off the throttle and angled in toward the beach, not far from where Chase had once brought them in the *Hard Case* back when she was pregnant with Dustin. He shut off the engine, and the bow of the boat slipped gently up onto the sand. Moments later she and Dustin had been handed down onto the beach and the anchor set.

She spread the blanket and set out their lunch, which consisted of gourmet sandwiches, two of which turned out to be PB&J. The cooler contained chilled juice boxes for Dustin, soft drinks, and several miniature bottles of wine.

"What's happening with the network?" He'd removed his sunglasses and she saw real interest in his eyes.

She filled him in, trying to make light of the dire circumstances they now found themselves in, but she was nowhere near the actor he was. "Our focus right now is doing whatever we can to help the Franklins sell the Sunshine cottages and beach club memberships so that everyone can at least get back what they put in."

"You know that if you need money or anything else that will make Dustin or your life better, I'm here, right?"

She nodded numbly as guilt at having risked the home he'd given them rushed through her.

"Maybe this is all a sign that the time has come to try something new," he continued. "You're incredibly talented, Kyra. I have a lot of respect for what you can capture through a lens."

After all the turmoil, the jabs from Troy, the pressure of trying to work within the network's viselike grip, his words were a balm to her soul. "That means a lot coming from you," she said. "Especially now that you've added 'director' to your résumé."

"Yes, well, we'll see how I fare on the other end of the camera soon enough." His tone was suitably self-deprecating. He had never inserted a movie star–size ego into their personal relationship. The look he gave her now was irresistibly intimate. "And have I mentioned lately what an incredible mother I think you are?" He ran a hand over Dustin's curls. "Our son is proof of that. I hope you know how much you both mean to me and how much I'd like you to be a more intrinsic part of my life."

Her heart leapt in a way it shouldn't at the look in his eyes and the sincerity in his voice. She was as susceptible as the next woman to his movie star looks and Hollywood allure, but it was his personal warmth, his obvious feelings and devotion to their child, and the ways in which he seemed to see through to the real her, that pulled at her.

She turned his words over in her mind as they ate. Was it possible he was actually considering leaving Tonja? Could he finally have had enough of what he'd described as more of a business merger than a true marriage?

As she sipped her glass of wine and watched Dustin sprawl lazily across his father's lap, her shoulders relaxed along with her guard. She breathed in the salt-tinged air, listened to Dustin's happy chatter, and sighed with pleasure. When Daniel's warm brown eyes sought hers, she did not try to evade them. The eyes that could mesmerize from the screen lulled her. Made her feel beautiful. Desired. Special.

If they'd been alone, and he were single, that look would have her twining her arms around his neck, pressing her body against his, losing herself in his kiss. He reached for her hand. Her imagination filled with hopes and dreams she'd thought she'd discarded long ago. When he ran a thumb across her skin and said, "There's something important I want to ask you," her heart thudded painfully in her chest. She half expected him to go down on one knee and beg her to marry him.

Twenty-one

"You want what?"

The question did not involve protestations of love, a rethinking of his commitment to Tonja Kay, or a proposal of marriage. It involved the absolutely unthinkable. The one thing she'd told him she would not consider. "Have you lost your mind?" She peered into Daniel's too handsome face and met the brown eyes that had turned so earnest. She could not allow herself to ever forget that he was first and foremost an actor and knew exactly, and instinctually, how to play a scene. He'd made a living off earnest coupled with sexy. "No, I take that question back. You know exactly what you want. You know your mind. You're just hoping I've lost mine."

"Dustin wanna hact with Dandiel!"

He'd asked for Dustin to play his son in the movie he was directing. Make that his and Tonja Kay's son. And he'd asked in front of Dustin without giving her the slightest warning. She turned, hoping that Dustin would forget what had been said and lose himself in the sand castle he'd started clearing a patch of sand for. But he was looking straight at his father and he was smiling.

"Wanna be movie tsar like Dandiel."

She gave Daniel a look of condemnation laced with venom. It did not require acting skill of any kind. It was a "you've crossed the line" look, a "you've got to be shitting me" look, an "et tu Brute" look. She held his eyes long enough to be sure he'd understood her. "This is something I will never agree to. I've told you that. And if for some perverse reason you had to bring it up in order for me to say no, you could have done it at a different place and time." And he could have done it without making her imagine all kinds of ridiculous things. "And you should have done it in private."

She began to shove the containers and wrappers back into the picnic basket.

"Wanna hact! Direktor tole me I'm a natchrul!" This had been when Daniel had allowed him to appear in a brief cameo with him without even asking.

"You're good at lots of things," she said to Dustin. "But acting is for grown-ups, not for small children."

"Curly Sue is a children."

Kyra swallowed and did not say that the actor who had played Curly Sue as a child had recently admitted to having overcome an addiction to alcohol while auditioning for *The Voice*—an issue that plagued so many child stars as to be considered a cliché.

"And Dora Explora . . . and the Bakyardinins are childrrens," Dustin continued.

"Those are cartoon characters, sweetheart, not real children." And to her knowledge were therefore not subject to the perils of childhood stardom. Being the son of a celebrity was tricky enough without becoming one.

Dustin stuck out his chin. He had a sweet, easygoing nature, but every once in a while he dug in. At which point he became an immovable object. She shot Daniel another look. "I think we should be getting back now."

Dustin watched her as if uncertain what to lobby for, ultimately choosing the most immediate and concrete. "Wanna bid catsel!" Dustin said. "You promised!"

"Let me get him started so you and I can discuss this." Daniel stood and pulled Dustin to his feet before she could answer. He dug through the picnic basket and cooler, coming up with a large plastic tumbler, two small plastic spoons, and a Tupperware container.

"There's no need to discuss this. Because there is nothing to discuss."

"Actually there are a few things you should know." He handed some of the makeshift sand tools to Dustin and carried the rest toward the wet sand. "Be right back."

"What part of 'no' don't you understand?" she mumbled to herself as they began to scoop out the sand that would serve as the castle's foundation. "No is no. It's not a conversation opener."

Once Dustin was happily at work, Daniel returned and dropped down on the blanket next to Kyra. If it wouldn't have been so pathetic, she would have scooted the extra six inches to the edge of the blanket in an attempt to escape his magnetic pull.

"So this is the thing," he said as if she had, in fact, agreed to discuss the situation. "The script specifically calls for a four-year-old boy to play my son."

"Yours and Tonja's."

"Well, yes."

"And whose idea was that?"

He shrugged as if he had no idea, though she'd read that he had collaborated on the screenplay.

"Why don't you pick a little blond boy that looks like Tonja?" She tried not to think too much about his "real" family, but she knew he and Tonja had several adopted children who bore more than a passing resemblance to their mother.

"That's not what the script calls for," he said as if physical characteristics were ever written in stone into a screenplay. "It's based on *The Exchange*." He named a recent bestseller about a family whose young son disappears while they're vacationing at a theme park.

"You can stop right there. I don't want my child acting out a kidnapping and fight for survival."

"You've been on film sets, Kyra. It's not like he'd actually be kidnapped or put in harm's way."

She did not remind him that she'd been on exactly one film set and that she'd been fired from it the moment Tonja Kay had gotten wind of Daniel's interest in her.

"Obviously, he'd be in no physical danger. And there's no reason it would need to be traumatic. He knows what pretending is and he loves to do it."

Kyra knew a thing or two about pretending herself. Wasn't that how she'd gotten pregnant in the first place? Wasn't that what their whole relationship had consisted of? Her pretending that Daniel loved and wanted to marry her? Her childish belief in fairy tales and happily ever afters?

"And I'll be there with him," Daniel continued. "I am the director. I control what happens. And I'll also be acting alongside him."

But so would his jealous, vindictive, foul-mouthed wife, who hated Kyra for giving him a biological child. And so would their children and each of their children's nannies. Tonja had already attempted to take Dustin away from Kyra in order to add him to the Deranian-Kay family unit, so often featured in the tabloids. That unit would be there in force, while Dustin would have only his father, who would have a movie balanced on his shoulders both as actor and first-time director. It was an impossible scenario. One that even if she'd wanted to, she could never put Dustin into.

She watched Dustin building so happily. She hadn't been able to keep him as out of the public eye as she would have liked, nor could she change his parentage and all that it entailed, but she'd done her best to give him as "normal" a childhood as possible. "Daniel, this is just not okay. I can't put him in this situation."

"Before you tell me all the reasons why not, let me tell you the reasons why. First of all, he's perfect for the role. He's my son and he not only looks like me, he has my mannerisms." He said this with pride. "We understand each other. And he really is a natural, Kyra. Not studied and faux childlike. And he loves to do this. He thinks it's fun." His voice and eyes beseeched her.

"And how unstudied do you think he would be once he had to perform this large a role in this big a film?" She shook her head. "I've told you no and I mean it. Maybe someday when he's older, if he chooses this path, but not now."

His jaw hardened. "I understand your concerns, but I don't see why you should have all the say in what Dustin does and doesn't do. I am his father, and frankly I think that gives me some say in this situation. You seem to think that just because I haven't exercised my parental rights, that means I've waived them."

His eyes were nowhere near as warm as they had been. His voice had gone several shades cooler. As she watched, she saw him intentionally dial it back. Like an actor calibrating his performance. "I think this could be good for Dustin and my relationship."

"You'll be too busy and under too much pressure to look after him and I don't want him anywhere near Tonja ever again. I certainly don't want him to be calling her "mother," even if he's acting when he does it. He's only three."

"Then come and be there with him," Daniel said in a reasonable tone that infuriated her even more. "I'll build you into the budget. *Do Over* seems to be stalled out. You could get some more film work under your belt and make money doing it."

"Listen to what you're suggesting. You're talking about igniting a potential world war on that set. That's ridiculous."

"Then send your mother with him," he said. It was much closer to a command than a request.

"Good God." She hated that he'd so clearly thought all this out. That he so obviously knew what he wanted and had no problem using her and his son to get it. She'd never seen this side of Daniel before and was not enjoying it one bit. "No," she said. "Just no. End of conversation."

"This conversation is far from over," he said. "I don't want to have to play hardball here, Kyra. But I am entitled to parental rights. And I want Dustin in my movie."

"We should be getting back." She began to get to her feet.

"Hold on." He put out a hand to stop her. She shrugged it off and stood, but she didn't storm off because where would she go? He stood and faced her. "I don't want to turn this into a serious problem or some kind of legal battle . . ."

Her heart and jaw dropped at the threat he tossed so cavalierly. Her hands fisted at her sides to keep herself from using them to pound on his chest. Despite the calm reasonable tone, he was in a position of strength and he knew it. He was nothing but a well-mannered bully.

His eyes examined her like lasers, cutting through her skin as if to get to her thoughts and motivations.

"As you think this over, bear in mind that I could go up to a million dollars for Dustin to play the role." He paused but held her eyes with his. "And possibly another quarter mill for whoever comes with him." He nodded in an oddly gentle way for someone who had just struck such a potent blow. "That's how important this is." Dustin had clearly gotten his ability to dig in and become an immovable object from both of his parents.

Kyra tried not to react as horror flooded through her. Horror that he'd named the one thing it would be almost impossible to say no to. She'd been so sure that she'd be able to make the payments on the loan she'd taken out against Bella Flora, but the 120-day grace period had passed and she'd missed the first interest payment. And she still hadn't found the guts to tell her mother and the others, who had invested most of what they'd had left and had also not been paid back, that if she didn't keep up with the payments, she could lose Bella Flora. A fact that struck terror into her heart and wouldn't sit at all well with the man in front of her, either.

. . .

Despite repeated vows not to do so, Bitsy once again Googled the name "Bertrand Baynard" on her phone. Once again, a host of photos appeared. The two of them at last year's Children's Hospital Ball, posing at the top of a Vail ski slope, sitting at a favorite outdoor café in Florence, aboard a friend's yacht off Crete. She enlarged each shot and peered closely at their faces, especially the smiles that lit them. She arranged the photos in a rough chronological order as best she could remember, trying to assess their moods and feelings. In each photo, her smile had reflected genuine happiness, and she lingered over them, treating herself to the memory of what had been happening when each had been taken. Then she repeated the exercise, focusing on Bertie's face, his smile, his body language, hunting for some clue as to when things had begun to change. Trying to determine if there had been a progression she'd been too preoccupied to notice.

Had he pulled away slowly? So subtly that she might be excused for missing the signs? Or had there been a sudden, cataclysmic rupture? But no matter how hard she scrutinized the photos, she saw nothing other than a happy, satisfied couple. She'd never before understood how the wife could possibly be the last to know, had always been certain that the wife had in some way been responsible for losing her spouse so blindly.

Because she couldn't quite help herself, she clicked through the online photos and reports of Palm Beach charity events and parties. Because she was apparently a glutton for punishment, she went to Beryl Merman's nasty-spirited gossip column, "Believe It or Not," where she saw a picture of her former home and an account of its sale by the bank, which had been written in a regretful tone that was in reality unrestrained glee.

Without thinking, she punched in her former neighbor Eleanor Wyndham's phone number. The four of them had barbecued together on occasion and sometimes met for pre-event cocktails. She and Eleanor had chaired the Make a Wish Foundation Ball together.

"Bitsy! How are you?" There was surprise, but no censure in Eleanor's voice.

"Fine." Bitsy had told herself she would not complain or whine and so she asked brightly, "How about you?"

"I'm so sorry we didn't really get to say good-bye," Eleanor said diplomatically, given that Bitsy had actually left town like a thief in the night. As if she had done something wrong and not just fallen in love with the wrong man. "I miss having you next door."

"Same here," Bitsy replied. This, at least, was the truth.

"And I cannot believe that Alex Binder is living there."

"Yes." Bitsy actually felt a perverse satisfaction that the house Bertie had insisted they buy and had loved so much now belonged to a man Bertie detested.

"You know that Sandra got their house in their divorce and so when yours became available . . ." Eleanor's voice trailed off as she realized whom she was gossiping with and about. "Sorry. But it's too terrible. And he's living there with this . . . well, let's just say no one knows where he found her or how long he'll keep her."

Bertie had referred to Alex as the preening peacock and a testament to the fact that money and class did not automatically go together. She fervently hoped that Bertie knew his beloved home was now in the peacock's hands. Hoped that he was suffering from erectile dysfunction. That he was already growing bored with the exotic dancer.

For the millionth time she wondered why, if he'd been unhappy, he hadn't simply asked for a divorce. Because of her stupidity, he would have still gotten half of her money, which was far more than many millionaires saw in a lifetime. He hadn't even cared enough about her to divorce her. As if he could put her on a shelf just in case he one day wanted to waltz back into her life and reclaim her.

"Has John heard from Bertie?" she asked, irritated with herself before she'd finished the question.

"No. And I'm so sorry. I never would have imagined Bertie behaving this way. Never."

Bitsy looked down at a photo of Bertie toasting her with a glass of champagne, his face wreathed in smiles.

"Where are you living?" Eleanor asked.

"I'm on the west coast of Florida with some friends." She would not tell even Eleanor that she and Sherlock were now living in a 450-square-foot "cottage." Shame and anger clogged her throat. Her old life had been stolen from her. She was married but had no husband. Her prospects were—no, if she thought about that, she'd start blubbering. "Now that I'm settled, I plan to make it my mission to hunt him down and make him pay." The words were out of her mouth before she could stop them. As if she had any idea how to actually do this.

"Good for you," Eleanor said. "I'll keep my ears open. Stay in touch, okay?"

"Sure." Bitsy swallowed hard and said good-bye.

She took Sherlock out to his favorite palm tree and stood thinking while he left his mark in as many places as possible. Life as she'd known it was over. Somehow she had to create a new one. She would start by doing what she could to help make the Sand Castle Showdown a success and she'd allow Avery to turn her cottage into some ode to the Tiny House. Then she'd find a way to turn her boast into reality. She didn't have the money to hire a detective or even a good attorney.

But she knew people. Lots of them. And there had to be decent attorneys who would work in exchange for a piece of her fortune once it was found and returned.

She needed to stop licking her wounds and hiding in her tiny cave so that she could figure out how to find Bertie and drag his ass—and her money—back. So that she could divorce him and see him put behind bars, where cheating, thieving, fleeing husbands belonged.

Twenty-two

"How can she not know when I'm going to deliver? Isn't that her job?" Nikki's voice rose with each syllable as Maddie led her out of Dr. Payne's office and into the elevator.

"It's not an exact science," Maddie said in a tone meant to soothe. "And it's huge that you've made it this long." It was the end of February, and Dr. Payne had congratulated Nikki on making it to thirty-eight weeks, a full week past the point at which fifty-seven percent of twins and most multiples were born. But Nikki had been in no mood to celebrate the milestone.

"The only thing that's huge is me! I'm so big, I deserve my own zip code!"

Maddie tried not to smile. "This is a really good thing for the babies. You heard what the doctor said. If your blood pressure was a little more consistent she'd be taking you off bed rest. And she wants to give little girl number two a little more time to develop before scheduling a C-section."

Nikki groaned. "I know and I swore I wouldn't complain again, or get worked up. But at this point, that's kind of like saying I'm not going to breathe. I have absolutely no control over anything. And as scared as I am, I just want this to be over.

"I feel like I'm in this constant state of alert," she continued as they stepped into the elevator. "Everyone keeps telling me it could happen any minute. Only it never does. And I want Joe here when it happens. Why hasn't Joe come back?" Tears began to spill from her eyes. Nikki pointed to them helplessly. "Oh, my God, I don't know where all these tears come from. I've cried more in the last thirty-eight weeks than I have in my entire life. My whole body is soggy."

Maddie had been relieved when Nikki began talking to Joe again on a daily basis and glad when she'd begun to pay attention to others, but the emotional roller coaster ride had not abated. Even witnessing it had proved exhausting. Nikki wasn't the only one eager for Joe's return.

"You told him to stay and finish up," Maddie pointed out as she helped Nikki into the car.

"But I didn't mean it!" Nikki wailed. "He should have known I wanted him here without me having to beg him to come."

Maddie slid into the driver's seat, started the minivan, then turned to the crying woman next to her. "I will tell you one thing I've learned about men from living with a husband and a son. Even the most tuned-in males—and they're not in the majority—are not mind readers. Ultimately, you have to be honest if you want a chance of things happening the way you want them to. You have to tell them, sometimes very specifically, exactly what you want."

Maddie winced at the certainty in her tone. Where did she get off giving advice that she herself couldn't follow? She was, after all, still feeding Steve, doing his laundry, and offering encouragement in the same way she had when they were married. And how honest had she been with Will when they'd spoken a few days ago?

The call had begun with a decidedly awkward, "Hi, Maddie. If I understood Lori correctly, I think I'm supposed to let you know that I'd like to sleep with you while I'm in St. Pete next week."

Maddie had sputtered in surprise and was still formulating a response when he'd apparently realized what he'd said. "Sorry. But it is kind of weird having a middleman, isn't it? Or is she a middle girl? Or hell, I don't know, there's probably some PC version of that. Should we make her a middle person?"

Maddie had wanted to say that she didn't really care what Lori Blair was called, but that she did care, and absolutely hated, having anyone inserted into the middle of their relationship. Wuss that she was, she'd kept that thought to herself.

"Speaking of political correctness," Will had continued, "did I tell you we've finally agreed on a new name for the band?"

"No, but I'm glad to hear it," she'd said. "No one would argue that the name 'Wasted Indian' belonged anywhere but in the seventies." Especially when Will had always insisted he had about two drops of Seminole blood for every gallon of Florida Cracker in his veins.

"What did you decide on?" she'd asked, trying for a light tone. "Sober Slightly Native American?"

He snorted. "Good thing you weren't in on that discussion. We're going to be just *Hightower*. I kind of like it—it's a testament to my family such as it was. And I feel like it includes and honors Tommy." Thomas Hightower had been Will's younger brother and bandmate who'd been a casualty of the excessive life they'd lived. Will had named his son after him.

"I like it," she'd said truthfully. "It's you, but more than you." Just as his life was now that his days of hiding out on Mermaid Point had ended. The upcoming tour would hurl him back to megastardom. She hoped his hard-won sobriety and iron determination would see him through.

"I've been missing you, Maddie-fan," he'd said in the husky

murmur that had always turned her insides to mush. Even across a phone line the words had filled her with joy and reminded her of what they'd been to each other. Absence had not made her heart grow fonder; it had allowed her heart to forget just how strong their connection was.

She'd begun to relax as he shared stories about his time out on the flats with Hudson, shared his excitement, which came laced with trepidation, about the upcoming tour. "They're sending a personal chef and a trainer out on the road with me. I guess I won't have any excuse for falling into bad habits."

"No, you won't," she'd said. Though he'd have lots of opportunity to do just that.

You should have agreed to go with him when you had the chance, her subconscious pointed out now as she parked the minivan in the driveway at Bella Flora and helped Nikki out.

Neither she nor Will had mentioned her refusal to go with him on tour. Nor had he asked her again. As she slowed her pace to Nikki's, she tried to feel good about the fact that he'd stopped pressing her, but this was a little like trying to find a silver lining in someone punching you in the stomach.

They entered through the kitchen and she reminded herself that she and Will spent time together because they enjoyed it, not because they had to. She should make the most of his upcoming visit, make it one they'd both remember.

Just in case it's your last? Her subconscious taunted while Maddie helped Nikki into the salon.

No, she admonished her subconscious as she tucked Nikki into bed. *Because we have every right to.*

. . .

A few nights later, Bella Flora filled with people, all of them intent on getting ready for the event they hoped would help set them back on track, or at least in the right direction, financially and professionally. Avery, who'd taken over the formal dining room, surfed the Web for sand-sculpting instructions as she worked out "construction" of the tiny house version of the one-bedroom cottage, stopping on occasion to pace. Nikki, ensconced in her bed, alternately ate, slept, complained, and cried for no specific reasons that Maddie could determine.

Kyra wandered from room to room, a vaguer, paler version of Avery's pacing. Worry lines creased her forehead and arrowed between her eyebrows. Her video camera rode one shoulder, but she shot little. She was hovering in the hallway when the doorbell rang.

"Kyra?" Maddie, who'd just set Dustin at his play table with a coloring book, raised her voice and waved one hand in an attempt to get her attention.

Kyra startled, looked her way.

"Are you all right?" Maddie asked.

"Hmmm?" Kyra blinked rapidly. "Sure. Of course." She hesitated. "Did you need something?"

"It's the doorbell. It rang. Can you answer it?"

Kyra returned with Bitsy, who set Sherlock on the floor next to Dustin, pulled up another chair near Nikki, and whipped open a binder filled with pages punctuated by colored sticky notes. Ray Flamingo arrived a short time later bearing gourmet cupcakes and his most winning smile. He placed the bakery box on Nikki's table then pulled up a chair next to Bitsy. After offering the box around, he chose a cupcake the same pastel blue as his shirt and began to peel off the paper. Maddie placed a cupcake in front of Dustin and another in Kyra's hand. She gently removed the video camera from Kyra's shoulder and set it out of the way.

"So," Bitsy said. "Are you guys up for a quick rundown?"

"Go for it," Ray said.

"Okay. First off, we have thirty official teams entered at one hundred dollars a pop, which more than covers our expenses for the day. Randy from the restaurant group will be selling the beach club memberships at twenty-five hundred a pop, which is half the Don CeSar price. And while we have fewer amenities, I honestly think we're a better, more casual choice for families with small children. As you know, John has invited Realtors from all over St. Pete. He and Steve will be giving tours of the property."

"Plus the bar and grille will be open, so the bigger the audience, the more food and drink will be sold," Ray pointed out. "I also heard from the president of the Deirdre Morgan Fan Club. They're going to be building a sand version of Deirdre."

Avery, who'd paced in and helped herself to a cupcake, grimaced. "You don't think they'll all come dressed up like her again, do you?"

"I know it freaks you out," Bitsy said. "But the media will eat it up. Between Will agreeing to perform and a few other surprises I'm working on, I think we're going to get a lot of coverage. We'll do our best to sell units and memberships, but it's also important for long-term success that we raise awareness of the property."

"Chase has subs coming all day to work on the sand cottage," Avery said. "And Renée Franklin and her garden club are going to create a garden made of sand around it. She said the women's sailing group from the St. Pete Yacht Club at Pass-a-Grille are planning to build some sort of sailing vessel."

"Remember, all these sand castle building teams will have friends and family coming to watch. I've already talked with Randy about making sure he has plenty of waitstaff and provisions." Bitsy smiled with satisfaction. Sherlock walked over, stood at Bitsy's feet, and nudged her leg with his muzzle.

"You've done a great job organizing things, Bitsy," Maddie said as Bitsy bent to gather Sherlock into her arms. "We really appreciate it."

Bitsy's smile grew larger. Sherlock woofed happily. Beside her, Nikki began to blubber.

"What's wrong now?" Ray asked as tears once again began to spill down Nikki's cheeks.

She shrugged, shook her head. The tears continued unchecked. "I have no earthly idea."

"Will a cupcake help?" Ray picked up a chocolate cupcake with bright pink icing and held it out to her.

"I don't know," Nikki cried. "But I don't see how it can hurt."

They munched to the sound of Nikki's sobs for a few moments. Kyra reached for her video camera and resolutely hefted it to her shoulder, but she didn't crack a smile as the rest of them teased Nikki for crying even as she ate every bite of the cupcake.

"Will you be able to shoot everything yourself?" Bitsy asked Kyra. "Because I know we're going to want plenty of video."

"Absolutely," Kyra said as she zoomed in on Nikki's tear- and icing-streaked face.

"Would you like me to reach out to Troy?" Maddie asked, uncomfortable with the troubled look still etched across her daughter's face. "He did leave a number."

"Thanks," Kyra said as she moved to shoot the group from a different angle, "but I'll be calling Troy Matthews for help right about the time that Hell finally freezes over."

Maddie stood and began to straighten the things on Nikki's bedside table. A week from tomorrow, Will would arrive. The day after that, they'd see just how many people showed up for the Sand Castle Showdown. She didn't want to believe that weekend with Will could be her last, or that the event they were all counting on would be a bust. But her glass just didn't feel anywhere near half full at the moment. She seemed to have about as much control over her thoughts as Nikki had over her moods and Kyra had over whatever was worrying her that she had not yet seen fit to share.

Posted to YouTube, 8:00 A.M.

Audio: "Can a human-size three-dimensional cottage be
reproduced in sand?"

Video: Shots of Avery sketching sped up to cartoon speed.
Exterior cottage renovation footage.

Audio: "We sure hope so! 'Cuz that's what we're going to attempt next Saturday at the Sand Castle Showdown!"

Video: Tractor pulling rake over sand. Shot of beach from rooftop.

Audio: "Come join us out behind the Sunshine Hotel and Beach Club Saturday, March fifth. We're on Pass-a-Grille Way between Thirty-first and Thirty-second just a hop, skip, and a jump from the Don CeSar."

Video: Pan across beach, zoom in on Don CeSar in distance. Animated sunset. Freeze sun just above Gulf. Entry link and graphics superimposed over freeze frame.

Audio: "There's still time to enter. Click here for an entry form. The winner will receive a free beach club membership valued at twenty-five hundred dollars! Don't want to get sandy? Come watch from the rooftop grille, where we'll have special showdown prices on food and drink, plus free ice cream sandwiches for the kids."

Video: Rooftop shots—all 360 degrees.

Audio: "Rumor has it there will be a few famous faces in the crowd and one of them will be performing."

Video: Will Hightower at microphone during grand opening. Arrow pointing at him.

Audio: "Come on out and share in the Sunshine at the Sunshine. We've got a few surprises in store!"

Kyra hit the key and posted the video to YouTube.

Twenty-three

Bella Flora pulsed with energy and excitement the night before the Sand Castle Showdown. Nikki was aware of that excitement and the conversations that swirled around her, but she was even more aware of the life inside her. She could feel the whoosh of blood through her veins and the babies', the rapid tattoo of her pulse that seemed to keep pace with their heartbeats. Her stomach rippled with their movements, and though her internal organs and lower back groaned each time a head or limb lodged against them, something had changed. The fear and worry were still there, but there was hope, too, a yearning as she let herself imagine her daughters' safe arrival. Allowed herself to wonder whether they'd have Joe's dark hair and eyes or her lighter coloring. What it would feel like to hold them, feed them.

In a chair beside Nikki's bed, Bitsy consulted her notes and went over the timetable for tomorrow's event with Maddie, like a general preparing for battle. Avery huddled with Chase and Jeff working out the steps of tomorrow's build and how best to deploy the subs who'd be there. A bowl of Cheez Doodles sat within reach. Nikki tuned in and out of the conversations taking place around her as if she were a very large fly on the wall.

"Thanks for delivering the plywood forms to the Sunshine," Avery said to Chase.

"No problem. All we have to do is assemble them and nail them together on-site—it's like framing a house. Then they get filled with compacted sand—I've got our subs assigned to shovel and bucket brigades."

"Yeah." Avery reached for a Cheez Doodle. "It looks good on paper. I sure hope it actually works in the real world. Because we have to pry off the nails and lift off the forms so that Ray has time to add the decorative details and textures."

"We have forms for these built-ins, too." Chase pointed to one of Ray's drawings. "There are going to be a lot of layers to this build." He smiled. "I think putting real accessories on the shelves and flat surfaces will add a whole other dimension. I can't wait to see the wall-hung big-screen 'sand TV.'"

"Yeah," Jeff said drily. "Maybe we can watch The Magic play while we're working."

"Ha!" Chase laughed. "We'll have to have a sand cable box or satellite dish for that."

They chuckled as Avery licked the cheese dust from her fingers.

"Won't doing all that be as much work as actually building out the model would have been?" Nikki asked.

"In a way," Avery said. "It's not like any of us have experience in sand sculpting. But a real build-out couldn't happen in one day and the only materials we'll need are plywood, nails, and sand and water."

Nikki grasped her stomach in both hands and repositioned herself against the pillows as best she could. Her eyes settled on her swollen ankles and feet, which despite all the lying around, resembled rubber gloves filled with air and then tied off. For the first time she noticed not only how fat her toes looked, but how badly she needed a pedicure. Her gaze shifted to her hands resting on top of her stomach and she winced at the sight of her chipped, jagged fingernails. She couldn't remember the last time she'd put on makeup.

At the game table Renée went over drawings with one of her garden club friends. "First a group works on the cottage garden— they'll construct the partial wall around it after we finish. Then our sand gardeners start here"—she placed a finger at the upper edge of the drawing—"and work toward the structure." Renée took a sip of a cold drink. "Thank goodness Annelise feels well enough to sit and sell beach club memberships with Randy."

They discussed the setup of the sales tables in the shade beneath the overhang just near the roof deck stairs. Nikki's eyes fluttered sleepily as Renée talked about the cooler of complimentary ice cream sandwiches and bottled waters that Nonna Sofia would hand out, which would sit next to the check-in table that Gabriella and Joe Senior had volunteered to man.

For a time she hovered between sleep and wakefulness, listening and watching while floating above it all like a near-death patient hovering over the operating table observing resuscitation attempts. The rise and fall of Steve Singer and John Franklin's voices floated through the open window from the loggia, where they were strategizing how to deal with the Realtors that had RSVPd. She was aware of Kyra moving among them shooting video. For a moment Nikki considered telling her no close-ups, but even that seemed vaguely unimportant as she floated above it all, only loosely tethered to the activity around her.

She awoke to the smell of cheese and opened her eyes to find Avery holding a slice of pizza under her nose. The smell was lovely but not at all tempting. Who ate on a cloud? She closed her eyes once again and floated higher. There but not.

"Nikki?" This time she opened her eyes to Maddie leaning over her. "Would you rather have something besides pizza? Or make a trip to the bathroom?"

Caught somewhere between the cloud she'd been resting on and the bed she seemed to be lying in, Nikki grasped Maddie's hand and squeezed it with an urgency that surprised them both. Words she'd never allowed herself to think, let alone utter, rushed out in a hoarse whisper. "If anything happens to me, you'll keep an eye out for my babies, won't you?"

Maddie straightened sharply. "Nothing's going to happen to you, Nikki. If you don't go into labor this weekend, we'll report to the hospital first thing Monday morning for your C-section. Dr. Payne said that all systems are go."

As if she were a space shuttle or a rocket about to be launched. Sometimes even when all systems were go, they didn't achieve liftoff. Sometimes they made it off the launch pad only to explode and incinerate in the atmosphere. "Promise me."

"It's normal to be apprehensive, but I'm sure everything will go just fine." Maddie's tone was soothing.

"If a choice has to be made, I want the babies to be saved. Not me." Her eyes were open now but it was a chaotic operating room she was seeing, not the salon at Bella Flora. Or even Maddie's face. "For Joe."

"Nikki, you need to stop this right now. You don't want to put those kinds of thoughts in your head."

But she hadn't put them there, she was just communicating them. Making sure her bases were covered.

"Are you all right?" Maddie's eyes ranged over her. "Does something feel off? Should I call the—"

"Just promise me."

"Of course I promise." Maddie swallowed as Nikki's eyes focused on her face. "I understand what you're saying, but Joe will be there. The paperwork will reflect your preferences and you and he will make these kinds of decisions should they ever become necessary."

"But he's not my husband," Nikki whispered. "He's not legally responsible for decisions about me."

Her cell phone rang. When she made no move, Maddie picked it up. Nikki saw the relief on her face and knew it was Joe. "Here." She handed Nikki the phone. "And please. Stop worrying."

Nikki nodded because there was no real alternative. But her thoughts began to clear. As she raised the phone to her ear, the fear began to recede. She'd never given birth before, had ceased to imagine that it could happen long ago, but her body pulsed with readiness. It was too late for worry or fear. There were no clouds to hide behind. Whatever came next, she would fight her hardest, but the outcome was out of her control.

"What's going on there? It sounds like a party." Joe's voice was crisp and clear.

"I'm lying in the middle of . . . command central . . ." she said, searching for a light tone. "Too bad Bitsy wasn't available to help plan the Normandy invasion. I've never seen such highly developed organizational skills."

"How are you feeling?" The concern in his voice was like a caress.

"Exhausted. Huge. Ready. I can practically feel your children trying to kick the door open. Or maybe they think they can punch their way out." She tried to keep the neediness out of her voice when she asked, "You are going to be back before Monday morning?"

"Absolutely. I've turned the witness over, and all I have to do now is finish up the paperwork. I managed to get a seat on a red-eye tonight. It's not direct, but I should be in Tampa just before ten A.M. tomorrow morning."

The air left Nikki's lungs in a rush of relief. "Thank God. Because I'm ready as I'm ever going to be, but I . . . I don't want to do this without you." A smile tugged at her lips. "After all, this is all your doing."

"I do believe we both had a hand in it," he teased. "And other body parts, too."

She wanted to tease him back, but her longing for him was too great. She couldn't remember why she hadn't told him more often how much she loved him or why she'd refused to marry him when she'd had the chance. She only knew that she was a more complete and better person when she was with him. And that she wanted desperately to give him the family he deserved. "Just hurry up and get home," she said. "Because I have no intention of going to that hospital without you."

. . .

Despite all there was to do and discuss, Maddie couldn't stop checking the time on her phone. Or walking down the central hallway to the foyer and then into the living room to stare out the front windows.

A text dinged in when Will's plane landed. Another arrived when he was in the car. Each message, each mile closer, lightened her mood until she was practically levitating with anticipation.

She felt Steve's eyes on her and saw his frowns, but couldn't have stopped even if she'd wanted to. She went through the motions, confirmed and double-checked every detail Bitsy brought up, held Nikki's hand, wiped pizza sauce off Dustin's face, and welcomed the Giraldis when they stopped by, but the whole time her brain kept repeating, *Will's coming. Will's on his way. He'll be here any minute.*

The doorbell had barely begun ringing before she was speed walking toward the door as if someone else might race her for the privilege of opening it.

It should have been awkward after their time apart, the insertion of Lori with an *i*, the fact that he'd soon be leaving on tour, but Maddie was too busy throwing her arms around his neck and being pulled into his arms, to think about it. His lips on hers said all the things she needed to hear and more.

"I saw all the cars," he said, still holding her tightly. "Would it be too obvious if we just went upstairs first and then said hello later?"

Her laughter was muffled against his lips and she felt deliciously wicked as she imagined stealing upstairs together. "It's tempting," she admitted. "But I doubt I could relax with everyone sitting wide awake just one floor below us." Or face them afterward.

"Good point," he murmured against her ear. "Would it be rude to ask them to leave?"

She laughed again, dizzy as a teenager just from having him there. "Given that this is not my house and there's an extremely pregnant woman currently living in the salon, I'm thinking that's out," she whispered. "But it's already nine o'clock. Dustin's in bed, the Giraldis were just leaving, and Avery, Chase, and his dad are headed back to Tampa soon. Tomorrow's a huge day for everyone. I'm thinking thirty to forty-five minutes tops."

"All right, Maddie-fan." His large hands held her close. "I think I can make that, but after forty-five minutes, all bets are off. I've been thinking about getting you in bed since I left Mermaid Point." He kissed her again, and the press of his lips and body made every nerve ending tingle. Heat rose in her cheeks. Her lips felt tender as they lifted into what she suspected was a goofy smile.

"Come on." She took him by the hand and led him into the salon, where she spent the next forty-three point two minutes watching his face as he made conversation while she flitted about seeing to Nikki, walking the Giraldis to the door, hugging Avery and the Hardins good night. The loopy smile remained plastered to her face.

Nikki was tucked in for the night, and Kyra had begun packing up her video gear for the morning. Only Steve remained in the salon when Will rose and said, "I think I'm ready to turn in. Maddie?"

She was careful not to look at Steve's face as she nodded and allowed Will to take her hand and pull her to her feet. "G'night," she said in Steve's general direction and loudly enough for Kyra to hear her in the kitchen. "See you all in the morning."

"Singer." Will nodded to Steve, slid his arm around Maddie's shoulders, and led her out of the salon, up the stairs, and into her bedroom, where he closed the door behind them with a soft click.

"Thank God." He turned her so that her back pressed against the hard surface of the door. His kiss was hot and searing. His fingers moved to the buttons of her blouse with intent. The touch of his hands on her skin as it was bared caused a fierce tug of desire deep within her. His lips moved down her neck to the hollow of her shoulder. The warmth of his breath made her shiver as he said, "I don't think I could have gone even another thirty seconds without having you."

• • •

Kyra turned off the kitchen light then walked quietly through the salon to check the back doors. The moon glowed high over the dark water of the pass and sent pinpricks of light shimmering across it. The pool house was dark, but she could make out her father's form on one of the chaises. With a sigh, she let herself out and walked slowly toward him.

"Are you all right?" she asked, lowering herself onto the edge of the chaise next to his.

"Yes. I just . . . I just can't stand seeing her with him." His eyes remained on the water. "I hate knowing they're in bed together." He took a deep breath before continuing. "I know I screwed everything up. I know she's a grown woman. I know she has every right to sleep with anyone she wants to." He turned to face her and she saw the glisten of tears in his eyes. Her father, whom she'd once idolized, had lost pretty much everything. Then he'd underestimated, and ultimately driven away, her mother. "Intellectually, I know that we're not getting back together. But . . . knowing and seeing? Those are completely different things."

She heard the unhappiness and regret ring in her father's voice, saw it carved into his face by the moonlight. This, she reminded herself, was what happened when you behaved stupidly and let the best thing that had ever happened to you get away. "You seem to be liking real estate and working with John Franklin. Maybe it's time to move out on your own and, I don't know, try to meet other women."

Her father looked almost as startled by her suggestion as she was. "I'd have to actually sell something to afford my own place. I really thought I had that house in Belle Vista sold. But honestly, kitten, I planned to put that commission toward your interest payment on the loan." He hesitated before asking, "You weren't able to make the first one, were you?"

"No." The knot of panic tightened in her chest. "I have part of it set aside from my share from the sale of Joe's cottage, and I've been careful about what I spend from Daniel's child support. But I really thought more units would have sold by now, and I was sure we'd be able to find a buyer for the documentary." She sighed. "You were dead-on about the difference between knowing and seeing. I knew I was putting Bella Flora at risk, but I didn't seriously let myself envision losing her."

"I'm sorry, Kyra. I feel terrible. It's really all my fault."

"No. I'm the one who made the decision," she said. "This is on me, not you."

"But you'd never even heard of a hard money loan before I told you."

"You explained it and you warned me," Kyra said. "You are not to blame." No, that "honor" belonged to her.

They sat in silence for a long moment, watching the spill of moonlight dapple the dark.

"Let's hope tomorrow goes well," her father said gently. "For everyone's sake." He sat up, swung his legs over the side of the chaise, and clasped one of her hands in his.

"Believe me, I'm way past hoping and on my way to praying," she said, looking up at the fortress-like walls of the only home her son had really known. "I don't ever want to have to tell Dustin or my mother that it's time to pack our bags and move because Bella Flora doesn't belong to us anymore." She couldn't even bear to imagine Daniel's anger if he ever heard that she'd pledged and lost the home he'd given them.

Twenty-four

Bitsy spent Friday night tossing and turning, her mind crammed with details, her nerve endings jangling as she scrolled through her mental checklist for the next day, an exercise that didn't come close to counting sheep. Or puffy white clouds. Or any of the other kinder, gentler things she'd attempted to turn her thoughts to during the long hours before dawn. Like the money she'd raised for charity, the scholarships she'd created and funded, the good she'd done. She'd been taught that a great fortune carried great responsibility and she'd tried to abide by that precept. Right up until she'd managed to lose it.

She dressed in the weak predawn light then did a final sweep of the cottage. Anything that didn't fit into a drawer or a closed cupboard had been removed so that Steve and John Franklin could show the cottage. Packets including floor plans and renderings of the "tiny house" built-in version were stacked on the dinette table. She pulled out the chocolate chip cookie–scented spray she'd bought and spritzed it into the air.

Outside, as she waited for Sherlock to anoint his favorite palm tree, she contemplated the silent property of which she'd been the sole occupant since Nikki had moved to Bella Flora.

The chaises surrounding the swimming pool were still coated with dew. The breeze off the Gulf was light and tangy. It whipped the tarps that covered the mounds of extra sand that had been delivered the day before. The sky grew lighter, the beach and Gulf more defined, as Sherlock sniffed and then lifted a leg on his second favorite palm tree. When he whimpered up at her, she lifted him in one arm then carried him up to the rooftop deck. Leaning over the eastern railing, she looked past the Sunshine cottages and over the condo building across Pass-a-Grille Way to watch the sun begin its ascent. Birds rose from the dark green mass of the Bird Island Preserve in the small bayou and a fishing boat angled past it and out into the bay. The houses that rimmed the water began to stand out in stark relief.

"So what do you think, Sherlock?" she asked quietly, reluctant to disturb the tranquil beauty that surrounded them. "Are we ready?"

He gave her a snuffling woof. His long, rough tongue lapped her cheek in a warmer, truer sign of affection than any she could remember. Her nerves tingled with an unfamiliar excitement. She'd chaired and hosted much larger events than the Sand Castle Showdown, but while many had been for very worthy causes, few had felt quite so personal. What happened today would impact the people who had given her a home, small though it might be, and help determine all of their futures.

From her vantage point, she saw Avery's Mini Cooper pull into a parking spot on the street. Avery emerged with a Styrofoam cup of coffee in one hand and a chunk of what looked like coffee cake in the other. Chase's pickup pulled in a few minutes later. Josh and Jason climbed out of the truck bed, and even from this distance the difference in their body language and attitudes was apparent. Josh pulled a wheelchair out of the truck bed and positioned it near the passenger side then helped Chase get Jeff settled in it while Jason slumped against the side of the truck and only began unloading it after sharp words from his father.

Kyra, Dustin, and Steve arrived in the minivan with the Giraldis, Annelise, and the Franklins just behind them. She heard sounds in the building beneath her. The Giraldi women moved slowly, helping Nikki into Joe's cottage to await his return. The rest of the crew resembled ants on their way to a picnic as they transported balloons, helium tanks, decorations, and signs to the pool area. A few minutes later Randy, who managed the dining room and rooftop grille, emerged to set up coffee and donuts on a tabletop that he fit over the vintage ice cream cooler from which ice cream sandwiches and waters would be dispensed later in the day.

Bitsy hurried down the stairs in time to see Maddie arrive with Will. Her smile was blinding and her eyes were concealed behind dark glasses even though the sun was not yet a factor. Will kissed her with a smoldering slowness that had Steve clenching his jaw. She looked, Bitsy thought, like a woman who hadn't gotten much sleep but for the best possible reasons.

After that it was semi-controlled chaos as Will, Chase, and his boys trooped out to remove the tarps from the mounded sand and cordon off and label the patches of sand that would belong to each team. Jason pushed his grandfather in the beach wheelchair that the Sunshine now owned.

Though check-in wasn't for another thirty minutes, the entrants had already begun to arrive bearing shovels, buckets, and all manner of forms and carving tools. It was a fascinating mix of people who mingled around the pool sipping coffee. The women's sailing group, The Broad Reachers, looked shipshape and nautical in navy shorts and yacht club T-shirts while the Deirdre Morgan Fan Club, led by the Amazonian Deirdre who had applied for Deirdre's position that had gone to Ray Flamingo, were dressed in flowing pant outfits and cover-ups that resembled ones Deirdre had worn. They all had blond hair in shades close to Deirdre's, which they'd tied with chiffon scarves or covered with sophisticated straw hats. Those who wore butterfly-colored shorts and bathing suits displayed legs and figures that Bitsy and pretty much every other woman present envied. Renée's gardeners were sturdier and wore long shorts paired with T-shirts that extolled the virtues of "playing in the dirt." Their head coverings tended toward pith helmets and broad-brimmed straw hats designed to keep off the sun.

Bitsy smiled with satisfaction at the buzz of excited chatter that filled the air. The day was postcard perfect, the crowd far larger than she'd dare hope for, and several local TV vans had just arrived. She poured herself one last cup of coffee, snatched a donut from the tray, and carried both to her command post near the check-in table. It felt wonderful to have a purpose and some modicum of control. For the moment at least, things were moving smoothly and all was right with her world.

. . .

"Has Jason been by here?" Chase asked Avery shortly before the official start time.

"I've been too busy going over my notes and making sure everyone knows what we're doing to notice," she said. "I thought he was with you all."

"So did I." Chase cursed under his breath. "I swear I'm going to kill that boy before this is over."

"What happened?"

"One minute he was there. Angry and pissed off to be up this early on a Saturday and beyond irritated at having to participate in something 'this lame,' but there. The next he'd parked his grandfather under a palm tree and taken off."

Avery was far too worried about how the plywood forms were going to work to get upset about Jason's defection. They'd gone round and round about Chase forcing him to come today. She'd been worried that he'd turn out to be more of a distraction than a help, but Chase had been afraid of leaving him to his own devices in Tampa all day and into the evening. Avery had finally stopped arguing when Chase reminded her, yet again, that Jason was not her problem.

She swallowed back the "I told you so" that sprang to her lips and said only, "Maybe he just went inside to use the bathroom? Or into the kitchen to bring out more donuts?"

"Nope, I looked. I even popped my head into the women's bathroom just in case."

"And?"

"And I think I scared one of the Broad Reachers half to death. In the men's room, one of the Deirdres asked me to help her retie her halter top, but there was no sign of Jason. The only good thing is he didn't manage to take the truck. So wherever he's gone, he's gone on foot."

"He'll be back," Avery said. "And I think we need to focus here. The turnout's great. And there are reporters from the *Tampa Bay Times* and a couple of the weeklies. This will help put the Sunshine in front of everyone and be good exposure for Hardin Morgan Construction—assuming the sand cottage turns out like it's supposed to and doesn't end up in a big heap."

"True," Chase agreed. "But I heard a rumor they were serving mimosas up on the rooftop. What do you say we skip the build and go up and sip a couple? We could maybe supervise from up there."

"That sounds far more attractive than it should," she conceded as worry gnawed a bigger hole in her confidence. "Unfortunately, we're not here in a supervisory capacity. Enrico and his roofing guys just arrived. And your crew has all the plywood forms stacked over there against the building. It's going to take all of us to get the structure nailed together and the sand mixed and compacted inside them in time for the walled garden to be completed and for Ray to get his end done."

"Right." Around them the teams were gathering as close to the beach as possible. Everyone clutched tools and buckets. She waved to Maddie, who'd been helping man the check-in table. Will stood nearby, smiling and signing autographs while they waited for the official start, which was now only fifteen minutes away.

Maddie gave Avery a thumbs-up, stole a glance at her watch, then stood. "Do you mind taking over here for a few minutes?" she asked Will. "All the teams are checked in and I promised Bitsy I'd take Sherlock over to Nikki's before John and Steve start showing her cottage."

"Sure."

She hid a smile as a small and extremely curvy Deirdre look-alike with a slight five o'clock shadow strutted up to Will and batted her fake eyelashes at him. Not wanting to miss the start, Maddie retrieved Sherlock from Bitsy, escorted him to a nearby palm tree, then race-walked him to Joe and Nikki's cottage.

"It's me!" Maddie called as she let herself in. The only answer was the sound of crying. "What's wrong?" she called in a panic as she rushed into the bedroom with Sherlock at her heels. "Are you okay?"

Nikki's face was tear-streaked. Her cell phone was clutched tightly in one hand.

"Are you in labor?"

Nikki shook her head sadly. "Joe called. I've been so relieved that he was finally coming back. But he was delayed getting out of San Francisco. There was some kind of mechanical failure and they had to wait for another plane."

"It'll be okay," Maddie soothed. "The main thing is that he's on his way."

"Right." Nikki swiped at the tears cascading down her cheeks then nodded without conviction. "How are things going out there? You know, in the real world. Where there's fresh air. And a sky. And people."

Sherlock whimpered as if in sympathy before settling on the floor next to Nikki's bed.

"Actually, things are looking really good," Maddie replied. "The teams are all pretty pumped up and they all brought cheering sections with them, so I think we'll be making a profit on food and drink. The Realtors will be coming through starting at ten A.M. And then there are all the Deirdres." Hoping to cheer Nikki up, she pulled some of her favorite shots up on her phone to show her. "One Deirdre was flirting with Will when I left to come here."

Nikki took the phone and examined the photo. "Yeah," she said drily even as tears continued to spill down her cheeks. "I'd hurry back if I were you. Most of the Deirdres are kind of cute."

"Very funny." Gently, she helped Nikki to the bathroom then brought her a fresh drink and her prenatal vitamins. "Is there anything else I can get you?"

Nikki sniffed. "No. Sorry for whining. I keep swearing I won't and then I do. I don't know, I'm just so tired of lying like a heap in bed. I'd love to at least come out and watch."

"It's a zoo out there and everybody's going to be working. I think you're better off in here. But I will have my phone in my pocket in case you need anything and we'll be checking on you regularly. Maybe Joe will bring you out to see the finished sculptures when he gets here." She pocketed her phone. "If you need anything, just text or call, okay?"

"Sure." Nikki nodded. "If you have a spare minute out there, maybe you should get in touch with Guinness. You know, in case they want to snap a picture of the oldest, largest, least attractive pregnant woman carrying twins for this year's book of world records." She sighed as Maddie laughed.

Maddie made it back just in time to watch the teams race to their assigned patches of sand carting their tools and supplies with them. She spotted Kyra shooting video as she moved through the herd of people. When she stopped at Hardin Morgan's build, Maddie walked out to join her.

"This is wild, isn't it?" Kyra said as she framed up a wide shot of Avery and her team scratching wall placement into the sand then digging narrow trenches to sink the plywood forms into. Avery's face was creased in concentration as she directed her crew and conferred with Jeff, who sat in his beach wheelchair holding the plans. Kyra panned the camera across to Chase, who looked a bit distracted.

"Oh, look! There's Dustin!" Maddie pointed and Kyra walked with her to the children's build, where Dustin and a crowd of kids were happily digging under a beach club counselor's direction. Kyra realized as she watched him just how seldom he was with other children. In that moment she vowed to sign him up for Mommy and me and Gymboree and all the other things that ended in "ee" that had been a part of her childhood in a two-parent suburban family. She'd been so busy struggling to make a go of *Do Over* that she hadn't thought about providing social interaction for Dustin or looking for other mothers her age. Seeing the happiness on Dustin's face, she vowed to do better.

She spent the next hour moving from spot to spot to document the day. She shot footage of her father and John Franklin as they spoke to and escorted Realtors to see the sand structure under construction and then to Bitsy's unit and the two-bedroom model. From the rooftop deck she shot down over the Plexiglas railing to provide wide shots for cover and also a bird's-eye view of the sand sculpting. Periodically she posted video to all of their social media and responded to comments about them. It was the kind of day that postcards were made to capture and that were almost impossible to do justice to. The sun was a brilliant yellow and the sky a pale, clear blue. The Gulf sparkled blue-green where it edged against the clean white sand. The breeze stirred the palms that rose like sentinels around the property. The swish of the tide and the caw of the gulls provided the perfect soundtrack. She breathed it all in and felt her nerves calm. Accepting a glass of orange juice, she drank it slowly. From here she could see not only the building in progress, but the growing number of people who'd chosen to tour the models. Today would not solve her financial problems or resolve their dilemma about what they could and couldn't do professionally, but if they sold two units and a handful or two of beach memberships, she'd be able to make that first loan payment.

She handed her empty juice glass to the waiter and refocused on the sand sculpting going on below. The crowd around the children's sand castle had grown. She narrowed her gaze to search for Dustin and found him in the center of the crowd next to a man who looked like . . . her eyes narrowed further . . . *What the hell?* . . . who *was* his father. Kyra leaned over the railing and squinted at the pack of photographers surrounding them. The tallest was Nigel Bracken. The potato-faced pap named Bill stood next to him.

Taking the stairs two at a time, she reached the registration table just as Daniel lifted Dustin up into his arms and planted a kiss on his sandy cheek for the cameras.

"What are you doing here, Daniel?" Bracken's British accent rang out practically delirious with glee.

Kyra thought this was a very good question. One that should be followed by, "And how had the paparazzi known he was coming?" "Did you know Daniel was coming?" she asked her mother.

"No."

"How about you, Dad? Will? Was this another collaborative tabloid photo op like your fake fight at the grand opening?" She studied their faces carefully, but they looked as surprised as she was.

"No, kitten," her father said. "While I can't say I'm sorry he's here getting the Sunshine more attention, he came on his own. And I'm pretty sure he brought the paparazzi with him."

The photographers shouted happily as they jockeyed for position and shot picture after picture of her child and his famous father. "Are you going to help build a castle, Daniel? How often do you see your son? Does Tonja know you're here?"

The real reporters joined the tabloid photographers. She cringed as she recognized someone she thought worked for *People* Magazine and another she'd seen on *Entertainment This Week*. This was not an unexpected celebrity spotting; this was a carefully set up scenario. One that either Daniel or someone who worked for him had orchestrated.

"What are you doing here?" the *People* magazine reporter called out. "Aren't you supposed to be prepping for *The Exchange?*"

Understanding blossomed at the mention of his movie. He was not here just to draw attention to them. He was here for a very specific reason. She raced toward the spectacle that Daniel had created, thinking only of plucking Dustin out of Daniel's arms before Daniel did what he'd come to do. She was still pushing her way through the photographers and reporters, catching only glimpses of Dustin and his dad, when Daniel put on his movie star smile and removed his sunglasses so that he could make eye contact with as many camera lenses as possible. As she neared, he made room for her at his side as if he was expecting her and said, "Kyra's the reason I'm here. I've come to try to convince Dustin's mother to let him play my son on the big screen."

Furious, she watched Dustin remove his sunglasses just like Daniel had. At his father's nod, he smiled a smile that was a smaller, sweeter version of his father's and proclaimed, "Dustin wanna hact with Dandiel!"

Twenty-five

Avery stood barefoot in what had to be her hundredth bucket of sand and water tromping it into a solid building material. She and Enrico Dante were the only members of the crew with feet small enough to fit inside the cut-open bucket to create the necessary "surface tension." And while Enrico continued to smile and make jokes about treading on grapes versus sand and water, Avery had been reduced to gritted teeth and swallowed oaths.

Squishiness aside, she and Enrico were the bottleneck—or more accurately, the bucket-neck. A factor she had not anticipated in her enthusiasm to sculpt the tiny house version of the one-bedroom cottage in sand.

Despite the thundercloud that was Chase's face and the way his eyes repeatedly scanned the beach and pool area for some sign of Jason, a distinct carnival atmosphere prevailed. Pockets of people stood watching and commenting on the sand sculptors' progress. The Deirdres were for the most part entertainers and their build was a high-energy performance that drew decidedly raucous laughter. Renée's garden club, who were busy creating gorgeous flower beds and hedges in sand, drew the most oohs and ahhs, while the kids' build had drawn the largest and most vocal audience.

Beachgoers wandered up and lingered, and an encouraging number of people seemed to be taking the tour of the property and model cottages. Conversation and the clink of glasses and silverware wafted down from the rooftop grille.

"We've got to step this up if we're going to finish in time for anyone to walk through it."

"No doubt about it," Chase agreed.

"Any ideas?" She leaned on his shoulder for support as she climbed out of the bucket.

"We go out and find more people with freakishly small feet?"

"Hey!" She punched the shoulder she'd just finished leaning on. "My feet are in total proportion to my height." Unlike other parts of her. "And so are Enrico's."

"Fine. Then we go out and look for extremely short strangers willing to stomp up and down in bucket after bucket of sand and water."

Another bucket had been filled long before she was ready to step back in and commence stomping. "I don't know. Seems like a pretty hard sell." She blew a bang off her forehead and looked for the will to continue. "Is there a plan B?"

"Our only other choice is to scale back. Like we did when we didn't have enough money to do a complete reno of the Sunshine Hotel and its beach club."

She wanted to argue. She'd spent so much time thinking about the structure, debating how detailed to make it, then collaborating with Ray Flamingo about the decorative details. Now it all seemed wasted effort on an impossible task.

"Look, why don't we just complete the walls and the built-ins and forget about the sand furniture?"

"But the whole idea was to give them a taste of the spaciousness of the design and how much could be fit inside it."

"I know what the idea was. But we achieve nothing if we're still building when the showdown's over. This way we have a chance of completing something that is at least a conversation starter and then we funnel anyone interested over to Steve and John."

"But we brought all our guys in," she argued. After all, more was, well, more. "They gave up a whole day."

"And they're having a blast," Chase pointed out. "The weather's gorgeous and they're on a beach. We've drawn a serious crowd. Will's going to perform. I'm sure they don't care exactly how much of this we build."

As he spoke, his eyes strayed and searched.

"Anything from Jason?" she asked.

His jaw hardened into a fair impression of a slab of granite.

"I'll take that as a no," she said quietly.

"Sorry." Chase ran a sandy hand through his hair in exasperation. "He knows exactly how to yank my chain and exactly how hard." He paused. Drew a deep breath. "Are you okay with stepping it down?"

When you had a Kewpie doll face and a body too small for your Dolly Parton bust, you didn't get far if you gave up every time things didn't go according to plan. But even she didn't see another choice. "I guess building less is preferable than not finishing more."

"I'll take that as a yes." He helped her into the waiting bucket. "And I'll let Ray know. When we're finished, I'm going to go find Jason if I have to look under every sea oat and palm tree on Pass-a-Grille."

"And I'll help." As she tried to resign herself to the compromises that were being made, she began to tramp the water and sand together, creating the surface tension that would make the sand molecules cling to one another. She felt a kinship with the contents currently squishing between her toes and wished her own tension had remained on the surface and hadn't burrowed so deep inside.

...

Nikki stared up at the ceiling and breathed deeply, which brought her far closer to hyperventilating than relaxing. "Okay, whoever is lying on my bladder needs to move right now." There was a sharp kick to what she thought was her kidney. One or both of them pushed off her lower back as if it were a trampoline.

She groaned and tried to reposition herself, but there were only so many positions that were still possible and none of them were comfortable. Her cell phone rang and she snatched it up. "Joe?"

"Yeah. It's me." She could tell from the way he said it that things had not improved and that he probably wasn't sitting on a plane about to barrel down a runway. First they'd waited for a new plane. Then there'd been a problem with the second plane's landing gear. When that had been fixed, a crew member had fallen ill and they'd had to wait for a replacement to arrive. Joe had finally made it out of San Francisco just ahead of a severe weather front, but he'd arrived in Denver long after the midnight flight for Tampa had left. He'd managed to talk himself onto a 6:45 A.M. flight that would have arrived at 8:30. *If* the front hadn't caught up with him. "I can't actually believe I'm saying this, but the heavy winds and snow have arrived. Every flight that hasn't been canceled has been delayed."

"For how long?" Her voice broke but there was nothing she could do about it. It was two P.M. and she'd been lying here alone all morning praying that Joe was actually in the air. Maddie, Bitsy, and Kyra had each checked in on her, bringing food she couldn't eat, escorting her to the bathroom, taking Sherlock out. But everyone had rushed in with their minds on what was going on at the showdown, and all of them had had to hurry back to their responsibilities. Which had left her lying here staring up at the ceiling. Wanting Joe. Attempting to will herself into labor. Desperate to get to the part where it was all over and everything—and everyone—was okay.

"I don't know. I don't think anyone does," he said. "But it's not looking good."

She commanded herself not to cry and was very glad they were not FaceTiming, where the sheen of tears that were welling might be visible. "So what happens now?"

"I checked in with some friends here, but even the FBI transports are grounded. There's not a ton I can do until the weather clears. But if I can't get on a plane in the next couple of hours, I'll rent a car and start driving. Or I'll stick out my thumb and start walking."

"You can't drive in that kind of weather," she said. "And assuming you could, what's driving time from Denver to Tampa?"

There was a brief silence. "Twenty-eight hours and fifty-eight minutes. Then another thirty to forty-five minutes from Tampa to St. Pete Beach."

She didn't trust herself to speak.

"Of course, walking would take a little longer," he added drily.

"Oh, Joe."

"I know. But I wouldn't have to actually drive all the way. I'd just need to get outside of the front. It seems to be moving west to east. I could head south and—"

"No," she said. "I don't want to worry about you on the road exhausted and trying to outrun that kind of weather." The tears fell then, but at least they were silent ones.

"I promised I'd be there and I will," he said. "In the meantime maybe you could have a word with the girls and ask them to stay put a little longer."

She heard the smile in his voice and pictured the quirk of his lips that had probably accompanied it. She felt a stab of love and longing when he said "the girls" as if they were already real to him and he'd already fallen in love with them.

"Yeah, I'll be sure and do that," she said. "Because they've been so obedient when I've asked them to stop kicking and tromping on my vital organs."

He chuckled and she felt as if she'd scored some important point. "I want you here more than anything," she said, swallowing in a vain effort to dislodge the emotion that jammed her throat. "And I know you'll do everything you can. But please don't do anything stupid."

While she might be able to deal with him arriving late, she could not allow herself to imagine that he might not make it at all.

. . .

Dustin's head rested on Kyra's shoulder. His sun-warmed, sand-coated body hung limp against hers, supported by her interlaced hands beneath his bottom. The kids had finished their sand castle earlier, swum in the pool like maniacs, then chowed down on hamburgers and hot dogs. Nonna Sofia had passed out ice cream sandwiches for dessert. Relay races farther down the beach had followed.

It was just past three o'clock in the afternoon and the simpler sand sculptures were finished. The Deirdres were posing for pictures beside the sand version of their idol, who lay on her side, her head propped on one hand. She was clothed in white linen, her neck was wrapped in a blue silk scarf, and her blond wig had been tucked beneath a stylish straw hat.

Renée and her garden club had finished their "landscape," which culminated in the walled garden of Hardin Morgan's tiny house sand cottage. The final structure lacked furniture and the fourth wall had been left out so that it resembled a soundstage or TV set. But the cottage footprint and square footage had been faithfully reproduced and its walls displayed an impressive array of built-ins.

Kyra had been shooting still frames of it all day so that she could put together a stop-frame version of its construction. When the real cottage was fully built-in, she planned to produce a video that melded the real and the sand versions. She could see it in her mind's eye as Ray Flamingo stepped into the sand structure and began to decorate it with the style of a magician and the patter of a master showman.

Much of her day had been spent avoiding the conversation Daniel had so clearly come here to have. Every photographer and tabloid reporter had asked her whether Dustin would appear in *The Exchange*. Her answer to each had been "No comment." But she wouldn't be able to avoid Daniel indefinitely. Somehow she was going to have to find the strength to look him in the eye and say no with enough conviction to make him understand she meant it.

On a makeshift stage beneath the stand of palm trees where he'd performed for the Sunshine Hotel and Beach Club's grand opening, William Hightower did a microphone check. Above on the roof deck people crowded the Plexiglas railing so they could see as well as hear. Those no longer sculpting sand gathered around him.

"It's a real pleasure to be here today," Will said. "And I appreciate the opportunity to practice before Hightower heads out on tour." His left hand moved up and down the neck of his guitar while his fingers began to pick out an instantly recognizable tune. There was a groundswell of applause as people recognized the opening strains of William Hightower's seminal hit, "Mermaid in You."

Maddie leaned against the main building just beyond the audience. Will shot her a wink above the heads of the crowd and her face split into a silly smile. Kyra's father stopped leafing through paperwork to seek out her mother, and Kyra saw him note the exchange. There was no smile, silly or otherwise, on his face. But as Kyra watched, she saw him shake it off and go back to what he was doing. How long did it take to get over a quarter of a century marriage? And how much worse did it feel knowing that if you'd only had the strength, you might have saved it? She'd been so certain her parents' marriage was built for the long haul, but if they couldn't make it, who could? And what if she'd married Daniel as she'd once hoped? Would it have been the happily ever after she'd imagined or just the beginning of a long and rocky road?

She felt someone step up beside her and caught the scent of Daniel's spicy cologne.

"Here." He reached for Dustin. "Let me take him. He's heavy."

"I'm fine."

He dropped his hands but he didn't step back. "You're going to have to talk to me, Kyra."

"No, I'm not. I have no intention of talking to you."

"You are, actually."

"Only to tell you I'm not talking to you." She shifted slightly and kept her eyes on William, determined not to let Daniel know how completely aware of him she was.

"I'm sorry. I probably shouldn't have ambushed you like that," he said.

"I made my position clear. I didn't say I'd think about it. I said no." She shifted Dustin in her arms to get a better grip.

This time Daniel didn't ask, but simply reached out and took him, resettling him on his own shoulder. "I just thought putting it out in the open might help you come to your senses."

"My senses? There's nothing wrong with my senses." She continued to speak quietly so as not to wake Dustin, who would no doubt once again lobby to "hact" with "Dandiel." "You had no right to put me on the spot like that, and you certainly had no right to use your son that way—as if he were a trained seal performing the way you told him."

He stepped around her so that they were face-to-face. He held Dustin gently and with experience. He and Tonja had children, and despite the one nanny per child scenario that Tonja had instituted, Kyra knew that Daniel did diapers, baths, playtime, and all kinds of other fatherly things that she did not want to think about. Because Daniel Deranian the loving, hands-on parent was even more devastatingly sexy to her than Daniel Deranian the movie star. And so much harder to resist.

"Look," he said. "I need him. *We* need him."

"Meaning you and Tonja." She stiffened at the thought. Hated imagining the conversations they must have had about her and her son.

"We've both put money of our own into this film. And it's clear that having Dustin play my son would—"

"Provide a huge amount of publicity," she finished.

"Yes."

"And bring people out to theaters just to see you and your son together."

"Yes."

"And to watch just how good an actress Tonja Kay really is. Because they'll be trying to tell how much it's eating her up for the world to see the child you created with another woman. When she couldn't give birth to one."

He closed his eyes and she thought about what Troy had said. That the studio hadn't wanted to let Daniel direct. That he needed more than just his and Tonja's names to make the film succeed. Their son, Daniel's and hers, would spark off a media frenzy that could translate into huge box office.

"Tonja asked me to tell you that you would be welcome on set. You could come and be there with Dustin and she would personally make sure you were comfortable and treated well."

"By her?" She thought of the ugly phone calls Tonja had placed, the obscenity-laced threats she'd made and meant, her attempts to take Dustin away from her and to get the network to dump them and *Do Over*. "No."

"I can pay the million dollars up front." He watched her face and she wished she was as good an actor as he was because all she could think was how that would solve so many of their problems. How it would allow her to pay back enough of the loan to hold on to Bella Flora. But then she would be doing exactly what Daniel was trying to do. Using their son for monetary gain.

"I can't," she finally said. "It's not right. He's too young. I won't do it."

She looked up then and saw all the cameras aimed at them. Realized that anyone who could had gone in for a close-up. Remembered that these people were undoubtedly world-class lip readers. She saw the surprise on their faces. No doubt they had thought they were in on a carefully choreographed announcement and not an actual disagreement. A few of them looked panicked and she imagined they might have already called in the story that Dustin's participation was a done deal. She turned her back.

"Come on, Kyra. A million dollars is a lot of money. And he wants to do this."

"He wants to please you. That's not the same thing at all. And even in today's world, three-year-olds don't make these decisions—parents who are supposed to have their best interests at heart do. And if this wasn't something you personally needed, you would agree that this would be a very bad idea."

"Don't be crazy. I can't believe you could possibly say no. I do have rights here. I didn't want to force you to do this."

"No, you thought you'd embarrass me into saying yes. Or, I don't know, blind me with the excitement and money of it all? You've called me crazy and senseless today, but I'm not. I'm just not going to allow it."

"Fine." Although his voice communicated his anger, his smile never faltered. "We'll do it the hard way. Tonja thought it would come to this, but I really thought you'd see the sense of it."

She took Dustin from Daniel. Dustin's arms went reflexively around her neck and he snuffled slightly in his sleep. He was what mattered. Not her needs and certainly not Daniel's.

Daniel had come here after discussing strategy with Tonja. Because Tonja was his wife, costar, and partner in every sense of the word. Which made Kyra the fool.

"I tried to find the kinder way," he said quite earnestly. "But unless you change your mind over the weekend, you'll be hearing from my attorney on Monday. I do have parental rights that I haven't exercised. I'm afraid I'm going to have to exercise them now."

Twenty-six

Bitsy collapsed into a chaise shortly after sunset. She had no intention of moving. Ever.

The participants and their audiences had gone. The paparazzi had followed Daniel Deranian to his limo and, she assumed, on to wherever he'd been headed. The Giraldis had left to see Nikki then gone on to their apartment. As soon as the sand cottage had been completed, Chase and Josh had helped Jeff into the truck and taken off to drive the area one last time. So far, Jason had not responded to any of their calls or texts.

Randy and his group had begun cleaning up. Bitsy considered asking for a drink but that would have required moving. And possibly speaking.

Steve Singer walked in her direction with a drowsing Dustin in his arms. Maddie and Will came with John and Renée Franklin, Annelise, and Ray.

"Thank you for everything, Bitsy," Renée said. "You did an incredible job. The day ran like clockwork."

Annelise smiled her agreement. "We're all so grateful to you for stepping in."

"My pleasure," Bitsy said, a bit surprised at just how true this was.

"Thanks to everyone's efforts, we sold a two-bedroom unit, and have a verbal commitment on a one-bedroom built-in to Avery's specifications, not to mention several other parties who expressed real interest," John said. "We took in three thousand dollars in entry fees and also sold fifteen family memberships and got a ton of exposure."

Kyra watched her father's face. Hers was harder to read as he said, "It won't take care of everything, but it does put us in a somewhat better position." He shifted Dustin in his arms. "John and Renée offered to drop Dustin and me back at Bella Flora. I'll put him to bed so you all can do your toasts and celebrate."

"Thanks, Dad," Kyra said in a voice that didn't sound at all celebratory. "Let me grab his things."

Steve nodded good night to the group in general without looking directly at Maddie, who stood with Will's arm around her.

"Don't move," Maddie said a few minutes later. "I'll be back. Will's car is here. I'm going to walk him to it and check on Nikki on the way back."

"I'll go ask Randy to make some celebratory drinks," Ray offered.

"That is a great idea," Bitsy said gratefully. "Moving's out of the question. Drinking is not."

"I'd offer to help, but I'm not sure I have the strength," Avery said from a nearby chaise. A yawn followed.

"Stay put," Ray said. "I'll be right back with liquid nourishment."

He and Kyra returned together. Ray carried a tray of very pink and very frozen strawberry margaritas elegantly balanced on one raised palm. Kyra carried a second pitcher. Ray presented the tray with a flourish. "I didn't just park cars in LA when I was getting started. I served at more than a few A-list parties." He lowered the tray, positioning it between Bitsy and Avery. Avery helped herself.

Bitsy sighed. "I don't think I have the strength to pick it up or get it to my lips."

"No problem. Allow me." Ray set the tray on a side table then brought the glass, knelt next to Bitsy's chaise, and positioned the rim between Bitsy's lips. "You've earned it." He tipped it gently so that all Bitsy had to do was swallow. She felt a glow of satisfaction and a new, unfamiliar cache of confidence that came not from what she possessed but what she was capable of. She had led an easy life, but she was not a quitter. She was strong. Resilient. She could move forward and forge a life for herself. Her first step would be finding Bertie and making him sorry he'd ever been born.

"Oh. My. God." The drink was thick and cold and tart. "This is the best margarita. Maybe the best drink I've ever had."

"I think you're right," Avery said, licking her lips but not the frothy pink mustache that remained. "It is absolutely frickin' lovely."

Ray smiled. "Randy does know his way around a blender."

"If Maddie doesn't come back soon, I may have to drink hers for her," Avery said.

"If I had an ounce of strength left, I'd fight you for it," Bitsy replied even as the sip she'd taken slid down her throat.

"No need, ladies," Ray said, holding the glass so that Bitsy could drain the last drops. "Randy promised to keep blending as long as you need him."

"Bless you both," Avery said.

"I'd have a brain freeze right now if I actually had anything left to freeze," Bitsy said as the cold stabbed at her.

Kyra drank silently and with determination.

Maddie returned, pushing Nikki in the beach wheelchair Jeff had vacated. Sherlock padded behind them.

"Goodness," Ray said with a droll smile. "There's been a jailbreak. And Maddie is an accessory." Without asking, he placed a margarita in Maddie's hand.

"She told me that if I didn't bring her, she was going for a power walk until she went into labor and didn't care if she gave birth behind a sand dune," Maddie said.

"And I'm still considering it. Oh, God, just smell that fresh air." Nikki inhaled deeply and dramatically. "I'm never going back inside. Never." She leaned as close as she could get to Maddie's margarita and inhaled that, too. "The only thing that would make this moment better would be if I was allowed to drink one or two of those. Or stand up. Or if Joe was here and I'd already given birth."

"Boy, you have a lot of conditions for making things better," Avery said between sips. "Where is Joe? Wasn't he supposed to be here this morning?"

"He's in Denver. Snowed in. He's been attempting to get here for something like thirty hours now."

"Neither rain, nor sleet, nor . . . Oh, wait, I think that's the US Mail, not the FBI," Ray teased.

"They apparently got a foot and a half or some ungodly amount. He told me he was looking for a pair of cross-country skis even if he had to steal them. I'm not entirely sure he was kidding."

"But you seem . . . okay?" Bitsy asked. Nikki had been an emotional basket case for weeks, but something had definitely changed.

"I'm all cried out. Honestly. I don't think it's possible to maintain that level of anxiety indefinitely. I'm not even afraid anymore. Well, not very. All I want is for this to be over. Any ideas other than power walking? I'm not sure I could actually get far enough to make anything happen."

"Well, I did see a few episodes of *Call the Midwife*," Avery said. "But it was kind of gory and I had to cover my eyes. I only caught glimpses between my fingers."

"Never mind that," Maddie said. "The babies are viable. They'll come in their own good time. Or Dr. Payne will deliver them Monday morning as scheduled."

"Dr. Payne?" Ray shuddered theatrically. "Every time I hear her name, I think someone really should talk to her about changing it." He stood. "I'm going to leave you to it, ladies. Oh, and I forgot to mention that the head Deirdre offered to put on a fund-raiser performance at the In & Out Club. They have several numbers featuring the Dancing Deirdres."

"Ugh. No. I know we all appreciate their participation today. But it kills me every time I have to see them dressed up like my mother. Not to mention the huge sand version lying out there right now. I don't want to watch a batch of men dressed up like her sing and dance. Not even when it's because they love her."

Randy appeared with a small tray, which he set down next to Nikki. "Wasn't sure whether you'd prefer a strawberry milkshake or an ice cream sandwich, so I brought both."

"Bless you," Nikki said gratefully. "You are a gentleman and a scholar." She took a long sip of the milkshake then eagerly unwrapped the ice cream. "Oh, God," she said after her first lick. "If we were doing 'one good thing' right now, this ice cream sandwich would be it."

"Mine would be the sand cottage not collapsing. I hated having to scale back but it didn't really seem to matter," Avery said.

"From the way Maddie's smiling, I'm guessing hers would be Will Hightower." Nikki stopped licking long enough to add, "*If* we were doing 'one good thing.'"

"Being with Will again was pretty good. In fact, we might have to upgrade our tradition to 'one great thing.'" Maddie grinned. "He invited me to come on tour again."

Nikki stopped chewing. And smiling. "You're not going, are you?" She made a face. "Sorry. That was completely selfish. Let me rephrase that. Are you going?" she asked in a faux cheerful voice.

"No. At least not right away. I told him I wanted to be here for the twins' birth and for as long as you need me afterward, but that I'd come meet him after that."

"You mean like in seventeen or eighteen years after they leave for college?" Nikki asked. "Assuming he's still touring?"

Maddie smiled. "I'm sure it won't be quite that long."

"And he's okay with that?" Bitsy asked, impressed with Maddie for standing her ground and trying to facilitate a compromise. Had she been too rigid in her relationship with Bertie? Had Bertie needed more of her in ways she hadn't seen or understood? There was no excuse for what he'd done, but was she completely blameless in the failure of their relationship?

"Well, I know it's not exactly what he wants," Maddie admitted. "But he does have Lori Blair going along to hold his hand. And I feel pretty confident that's all she's going to be holding. He seems determined to deal with the temptations on the road, and I think he's strong enough to pull it off. Besides, who really ever gets exactly what they want?"

"Rock icons and movie stars," Kyra said glumly. It was the first time she'd spoken. She hadn't touched her video camera, either. Most of her attention seemed focused on her margarita, which she finished quickly.

"What's going on, Kyra?" Nikki asked. "I've been out of the loop."

Kyra took another drink.

"Daniel was here today," Bitsy said. "Which was great in that he brought a whole pack of paparazzi with him and really perked up the crowd and the local media."

"But it was a bad thing because?" Nikki had finished the ice cream sandwich and was now licking her fingers as she aimed this question at Kyra.

"Daniel wants Dustin to costar in his new movie," Maddie said when Kyra once again chose to drink rather than speak.

"With him and Tonja?" Nikki asked.

"That's the one," Kyra finally said. "*The Exchange!*" She managed to pack the word with an odd mixture of venom and despair. "Ha!"

"Would that really be so bad?" Bitsy asked, wondering about the bond of parenting. Would her life have been different, their marriage stronger, if she and Bertie had had a child to focus on instead of only their own desires?

"Not monetarily," Kyra said. "In fact, he's throwing a lot of money at me to make me say yes." She looked down into her empty glass then back at them. "And we need money. Our share from today will allow me to pay off some of the interest on the money I borrowed. But we have to come up with a lot more than that."

"Daniel's charging you interest?" Shock vibrated in Maddie's voice. "He gave you a mansion, but he's charging you interest on a loan?"

"Not exactly." Kyra shifted uncomfortably in her seat.

Bitsy's eyes went to Kyra's face. Something was going on here. Bitsy opened her mouth, instinctively prepared to offer money. She closed it, remembering with a nasty shock that she no longer possessed unlimited funds with which to fix things.

"But you are saying that he loaned you the money for the reno and now he's trying to force you to put Dustin in the movie because you can't pay him back?" Nikki asked.

"Not exactly." Kyra looked away quickly but not before Bitsy saw the panic in her eyes. It was mixed with something that Bitsy didn't know her well enough to identify, but there was no doubt she was hiding something.

"I'm going to have to have a serious talk with Daniel." Maddie, sweet, careful, and always determined to consider all sides of a matter Maddie, was as close to rage as Bitsy had ever seen her. "And so should your father. I don't like the sound of any of this. How dare he try to force you to let Dustin be in his movie just because he loaned you money?" In full lioness-protecting-her-cubs mode, she jumped up as if she was going to see to it right that minute. "He has no right! No right at all!"

Kyra's shoulders slumped as if under the weight of the world, but she met her mother's gaze. "He does have rights, Mom. As he reminded me yet again, he is Daniel's father and therefore is entitled to parental rights." Her face reflected abject misery. "And . . ." She straightened and swallowed hard. "And the loan didn't come from Daniel. I . . . I took out a hard money loan against Bella Flora."

Maddie, Avery, and Nikki gasped. Even Bitsy felt slightly breathless as the words poured out of Kyra's mouth. "And if we don't find a way to make the payments, we're going to lose her."

. . .

Avery wasn't sure exactly how many margaritas she drank after Kyra dropped her bombshell and fled. Maddie had switched to water early on, but for Avery, the frothy concoctions became less celebratory and more necessary. They'd sat around the pool in stunned disbelief long after Randy locked up the main building. Chase had called to see if she'd seen or heard anything from Jason, and hearing the slight slur to her words, he'd made her promise she'd spend the night at Bella Flora. *Bella Flora.* Which Kyra had put at risk in an effort to reclaim *Do Over* and fight the network. *Bella Flora.* The home that they'd brought back from the brink of ruin twice and that had done the same for them.

"I will," she agreed, unable to tell Chase what had happened when he was already so upset about Jason. Her head swam in a murky soup of alcohol and Kyra's news. "Tex-it me if he shows up, ho-kay?"

"Ho-kay," Chase replied grimly. "Right after I finish strangling him for scaring the shit out of all of us."

Avery followed Maddie and Bitsy back to the cottages and waited with Bitsy while Maddie wheeled Nikki inside and tucked her back into bed. Bitsy stood under the streetlamp waiting for Sherlock to saturate his favorite palm tree. Avery's head spun, jumbling her thoughts further. She'd passed exhaustion long ago and couldn't even begin to process Kyra's news or the challenges that lay ahead. She wasn't sure how much longer she could remain upright.

Sherlock was still snuffling around tree trunks when Maddie returned looking every bit as miserable as Avery felt. "Okay," she said to Bitsy. "I'm just confirming that you're spending the night at Nikki's."

"Aye, aye." Bitsy attempted a salute but her hand didn't quite make contact with her forehead.

Maddie frowned. "If you've had too much to drink, maybe I should stay."

"Spoken like a true lightweight," Bitsy replied. "I'm not drunk, just tired."

Avery felt as if she might crumble at Maddie's feet. "All of us are exhausted, Maddie." Her yawn was large and unintended. "Including you."

"Too true," Bitsy agreed with a yawn of her own.

"All she has to do is go in Nikki and Joe's cottage and find the couch." Avery swayed slightly.

"Right," Bitsy said with another yawn. "Piece of cake." She lifted Sherlock into her arms and turned to go.

"C'mon, Maddie. Les go." The mixture of sand and grass beneath Avery's feet seemed to be crooking a finger at her. The need to be horizontal was no longer optional.

"All right," Maddie called after Bitsy. "But let me know if anything happens."

"Absolutely," Bitsy called back.

They watched Bitsy set Sherlock inside Joe and Nikki's cottage then disappear into her own.

"I hope I'm not going to regret this," Maddie said as she took Avery's keys and climbed into the driver's seat of the Mini Cooper.

"No regrets," Avery murmured as her head came to rest against the passenger window. Her head filled with disjointed images of her confrontation with Jason at the marina. Her failure to follow up on her threat. The chances she'd had to tell Chase that his son had skipped school and taken the boat without permission. That he'd been with a girl with whom he'd clearly been intimate. Her eyes closed. "And I'm pretty sure love means never having to say you're sorry . . ."

Twenty-seven

At Bella Flora, Avery took one look at the stairs and turned toward the central hallway instead.

"Aren't you coming up to bed?" Maddie had been silent on the ride back. Her tone now was hushed, her face wretched.

"I don't think I can make it," Avery said. "If I don't lie down, I'm going to fall down." She focused as best she could on Maddie's face, which was pale and troubled. "Unless you wanna, needa talk?"

"It's a little late for that, isn't it?" Maddie sighed. "God, I wish Kyra had said something before she . . ." Her voice trailed off as she turned to the stairs. "See you in the morning."

"G'night." Avery shuffled into the salon and fell onto Nikki's bed, which was the first horizontal and cushioned option she came to. Pulling the pillow beneath her head, she had the idle thought that it was a good thing pregnancy wasn't contagious. Then she wondered how long the sand sculptures would last and whether she should have stopped in the bathroom on her way to bed. The stray thoughts grew even more random and troubling as she hovered on the brink of sleep. Jason in some den of iniquity or out in the *Hard Case* intoxicated, dangerous to himself and others. All of them treading water, unable to stay afloat after losing both *Do Over* and Bella Flora.

The closer to sleep she came, the quicker the thoughts and images moved. Memories of Bella Flora zoomed by like a video on fast forward. Their first sight of Bella Flora neglected and moldy. Encased in scaffolding, her insides laid bare as they worked so frantically to save her. She saw Deirdre the day she'd arrived, claimed the master bedroom, and refused to leave. She and Chase locked in argument after argument during the renovation. The shock of their first kiss. Cheez Doodles and sunset toasts around the pool. The struggle to come up with the one good thing Maddie insisted on each night.

Her last semi-coherent image was of Bella Flora pulsing in and out, beating like some cartoon heart. Finally, mercifully, the images disappeared and there was only nothingness, blissful and dark.

. . .

Maddie walked slowly up the stairs, her hand on the banister they'd spent so many painful hours restoring. She looked in on Dustin, who slept peacefully in his big boy bed, flat on his back, his arms flung wide in abandon. Outside Kyra's closed bedroom door, she debated whether or not to knock and had finally decided to leave it for the morning when she heard the muffled sound of her daughter crying. Pushing open the door, she stepped inside.

Kyra looked up at her through tear-filled eyes. "Oh, Mom. I can't believe I've made such a total mess of everything."

Maddie moved to the bed and sat on its edge. She didn't contradict Kyra. It was a mess. A dreadful and frightening one. Bella Flora was their home, the only one they had. It had become their sanctuary, the one place where the chaos and uncertainty that plagued them was not supposed to be able to reach them. As always, her urge was to fix things, to find some way to "make it all better." But this was not a cut that needed a Band-Aid. Or a boo-boo that would feel better if only she kissed it.

"I know you meant well, but oh, Kyra, how could you? And how could your father ever have let you?"

"It wasn't his fault, Mom," Kyra said through her tears. "He explained it all to me. He tried to talk me out of it. So did John Franklin. He's the guarantor." She held a sodden tissue to her eyes in a futile effort to staunch the flow. "I was just so sure that we'd sell enough units and that we could convince the network to let us go to do our version of *Do Over*. At the very least I thought we'd be able to sell the documentary on the Sunshine Hotel." Fresh tears gushed from her eyes and spilled down her face. "Daniel offered a ridiculous amount of money for Dustin to be in his movie. It's enough to pay off most of the loan. But I just don't see how I can do it. He's way too young. And I'd have to go with him." Her lip quivered like it had as a child. "And that would mean dealing with Tonja, and being forced to watch Daniel with his *real* family." She expelled a heavy breath. "If we weren't so in need of money, I'd never even consider it." There were more tears. "And if I let Dustin do the movie because of the mess I made, then I'm no different from Daniel using our son to get what he wants." She swiped at her nose with the tissue. "I've been so incredibly stupid."

Maddie watched her daughter cry and felt her own heart ache. But there was no silver bullet, no perfect solution. "You're not stupid, Kyra. You're human. And you've made the mistake of letting wishful thinking get in the way of reality. I've been guilty of the exact same thing myself." She held the nearby trash can up and waited for Kyra to release the now useless Kleenex. "But this is something that should have been thought out thoroughly and then discussed. Technically Bella Flora belongs to you and Dustin. But this decision impacts all of us."

"I thought you of all people would understand," Kyra said through a fresh cascade of tears. "You're the one who talked about how important it is to never give up and to go down fighting."

"I meant what I said, honey. But you have to seriously consider what's at stake before the fight begins."

Kyra shuddered as she struggled to regain control. "Oh, God, Mom. What in the world am I going to do?"

"I don't know," Maddie said as Kyra sniffed and dabbed at her eyes until the tears finally stopped. Standing, she lifted the comforter so that Kyra could slip underneath it. "In the morning we'll sit down and talk this through and see if we can come up with some kind of plan." She watched Kyra pull the covers up to her chin just as she had as a child. "In the meantime, we all need to try to get some sleep."

She pulled the door closed behind her and felt the fury that had been building course through her. Sleep? She couldn't imagine it. The idea that Steve might be sleeping peacefully right now infuriated her. She took the back stairs and walked quietly past the salon, where Avery was currently snoring, and out the back door. Moments later she was throwing open the pool house door, flipping on the light, and watching her ex-husband sputter awake. When the sputtering stopped, she sat down and commanded him to explain how in the hell he could have let their daughter put Bella Flora at risk. Then she demanded to know exactly what he planned to do about it.

• • •

The sound that pierced the quiet was not immediately identifiable. It separated itself from Avery's dreams, growing louder and closer, pulling her awake. A curse brought her eyes open and shoved her into consciousness. Peering through the window into the darkness, she saw a large shape detach itself from the blackness and lurch toward Bella Flora. She shot bolt upright in bed. When a large fleshy object pressed up against the window, she jumped out of bed, a scream forming in her throat.

"Avuhreee? Issyou in there?"

She shut her mouth so that she could listen then crept toward the window. The fleshy object was a distorted face. The area around it turned foggy.

"Iss mee. Yason." The face retreated. A chair scraped across the concrete. "Kin I come in? I need a . . ." The sound of urgent and heavy urination followed. A hiccup and an exaggerated male groan of relief followed. "Ohhhh, mannn."

She crossed to the French door and yanked it open. In the spill of moonlight she saw Jason Hardin leaning against the back wall attempting to zip his pants. Behind him the wall was damp. A puddle of runoff had not yet seeped into the concrete. "You pissed on Bella Flora?" she whispered harshly, taking in his gnarled hair and rumpled clothes. "What's wrong with you?"

"Nothing. Just tired. I had to . . ." He stopped midsentence to yawn and stretch. One hand idly scratched his crotch.

Angry, she moved toward him, but stopped when his scent hit her nostrils. He reeked of alcohol and weed, and although she didn't want to acknowledge it, he also smelled of sex. Wherever he'd been, he hadn't been alone. And he definitely hadn't been sober. "Jesus, Jason. Where in the hell have you been? Do you know how worried your father is? Do you know . . ."

"Jus' need to lie down. Jus . . . just for a little."

He didn't give her a chance to debate whether to bring him inside or try to shove him in her car to drive him home, before he staggered the few steps to the nearest chaise and collapsed onto it. She was still trying to figure out her next move when his eyes shut, his head lolled to the side, and the first snore erupted from his open mouth. She looked from his inert bulk to the open

French door and back. She didn't have the strength to move him inside on her own and she wasn't sure if she would have bothered even if she could have.

Bella Flora remained dark around them. No lights came on inside. No one called out to see what was going on.

"Fine." She went inside, pulled the afghan off the couch, and threw it on top of him. Inside she picked up her phone, saw that it was three A.M. and sent a terse text to Chase saying that Jason was safe at Bella Flora and that she'd bring him to Tampa tomorrow, or rather later today. Then she climbed back into Nikki's bed, burrowed back beneath the covers, and closed her eyes. Her last thought as she let go and began to fall asleep was that she was not looking forward to reuniting Chase and Jason. And that before she did, she'd better make sure Jason showered and put on clothes that didn't bear testament to what he'd been up to.

. . .

Nikki's eyes flew open. The bedside clock read four A.M. The room was dark and close. Although the window had been left open, the air was still. A faint odor reached her nostrils. Her hand pressed into the mattress as she tried to move and she realized that the sheets were wet. No, not wet. They were soaked. *The babies.*

She heard a whimpering sound and thought it had come from her. But then a cold nose pushed against her hip. A rough tongue scraped against her bare arm. *Sherlock.*

She lay completely still, listening. Bitsy must be asleep on the couch. She needed to wake her. "Bitsy?" There was no answer. Sherlock whimpered again. "Go wake up Bitsy, Sherlock. Hurry." She managed to reach the bedside lamp. Strained farther to turn it on even though she was afraid of what she might see. Please God, she prayed as she pulled off her covers. Don't let me be lying in . . . She forced herself to look down. She and her sheets were streaked with a blood-tinged liquid. A stringy clump of blood clung to the inside of her thigh.

"Bitsy!" she shouted louder as she tried to remember if she had seen or heard Bitsy during the night. She remembered Maddie bringing her back and tucking her in. She'd heard Sherlock snuffle during the night, the shake of his tags on his collar. But had she heard Bitsy? "Bitsy?"

Sherlock remained next to the bed. He made a tight circle and woofed but he didn't leave.

"Go wake Bitsy, Sherlock!" She struggled to sit up, but tried to move carefully, not sure if she was supposed to move at all. Her nightgown was heavy, wet, and clinging as she levered to a standing position. It took time to pull it off, and even longer to find her robe. Despite the cramp she felt in the pit of her stomach, she managed to get it on and zip it up. It strained against her stomach and she thanked God for its stretchiness.

Sherlock continued to whimper, but he didn't leave her side. She found the cell phone she'd fallen asleep clutching trapped between the wet sheets and winced as she wiped it against her sleeve, praying fervently that it hadn't gotten wet enough to stop working. The screen lit up but it didn't want to take her password. The battery indicator glowed red, not even at five percent. *Shit.*

Don't panic. Just find your charger. She tried to calm herself, but she had no idea where she'd put her charger. And even less idea what had happened to Bitsy.

She staggered out to the living room but Bitsy wasn't there. There was no sign that she had been. She was almost to the door when the dull cramp she'd been feeling turned into a sharp pain that sliced through her. She doubled over and clutched her stomach. "Where is she, Sherlock? Where the hell is Bitsy?"

Sherlock raced to the front door and woofed again. He went up on his hind legs and scratched on the door. She didn't know dog talk, but clearly he was trying to tell her something. Did he know where Bitsy was or did he just need to go to the bathroom? She straightened slowly and used her hands to steady herself against the wall. Another sharp pain assaulted her before she made it to the door and fumbled the lock open. Oh, God. Were these just labor pains or had something terrible happened?

Sherlock looked at her. Barked again. She got the front door open and Sherlock bounded out. For a moment she was afraid he was going to bolt and leave her completely alone. But he turned and barked directly at her, raced in a circle as if expecting her to follow, then came back and nudged the beach wheelchair, which sat in front of the cottage.

Sherlock looked at her and woofed.

"Right, and if I get into it, are you going to push me to the hospital?" Another pain sliced through her and she clung to the porch support. When she was able to straighten, she got hold of the back of the chair and used it to steady herself as she stepped down onto the walkway. Carefully she lowered herself down into the seat. Out of breath and frightened, she looked down at her phone. The battery glared an accusing red. It registered 4%. She hit speed dial for Bitsy's phone and heard it ring in the distance. *Shit.* "What's she doing in her cottage?"

Sherlock woofed at her, turned, and took a few steps toward Bitsy's cottage, then came back and woofed again.

She punched and prodded and swiped at the screen, realizing her mistake. Faced with so little battery, she should have punched in 911. Sherlock cocked his head at her and whimpered.

"I know, I know," she said as the tears gathered, blurring his face. "I'm an idiot. I deserve to go into hard labor all alone and in the dark!"

Sherlock shook his head and barked as if giving her directions. The wheelchair's tires were designed for sand and built to be pushed, not propelled by hand. She lifted the footrests so that she could use her feet. Another pain rippled through her. Bitsy's cottage looked impossibly far.

Sherlock cocked his head and whimpered.

"Okay, Sherlock." Unable to bend over, Nikki used her feet to lift the footrests so that she could try to walk the wheelchair. "You go wake Bitsy. I'll be right behind you."

When he didn't move, she lifted her arm and pointed. "Go get Bitsy! Now!"

Her bare feet on the ground, she started trying to walk the chair, which was far more difficult than she'd imagined. Sherlock barked and circled once around her. Another pain rippled through her and she knew if she'd still been standing, she would be on the ground.

"You go ahead, Sherlock!" she begged when she was able to catch her breath. "Please! Wake Bitsy!"

Sherlock took off. Mercifully, he headed in the right direction. As she lifted her phone for a last attempt, she prayed fervently that he'd seen Rin Tin Tin or Lassie in action. And that he understood that she was depending on him to save the day.

She managed to hit speed dial for Maddie's phone, held her breath while it rang. Maddie's sleepy, wonderful voice said, "Hello?"

Relief coursed through her along with another rolling pain. She gasped for breath and had just begun to answer when the battery died completely. The screen went black.

Twenty-eight

"Where is he?"

Avery bolted out of sleep at the sound of Chase's voice. "What? Who?"

"Where's Jason? You said he was here last night and that you were bringing him to Tampa this morning. It's ten A.M., and I'm pretty sure he doesn't deserve to sleep in." His tone indicated that she didn't, either. She blinked rapidly but her eyelids clearly weren't connected to her brain, because she couldn't seem to get it started. "I . . . he . . . ten A.M.?"

She leapt out of bed, which was when she noticed that she was still wearing her clothes and that those clothes were a shambles. A hand went to her hair and she felt just how many directions it stuck out in. Her tongue ran over her teeth and she stopped taking stock.

"Be right back!" She sprinted to the guest bath to relieve herself then splashed water on her face and finger-brushed her teeth. Her face in the mirror was sunburnt from yesterday's showdown. The dark circles under her eyes were from exhaustion and from . . . Jason's raucous arrival at three A.M. She caught her breath and raced down the hallway to throw open the French door with Chase on her heels.

The pool deck was empty.

"I . . . when I went back to sleep, he was already asleep on the chaise. I . . ."

Still trying to gather her thoughts, she crossed to the pool house and pushed open the door. It was empty. There was no sign that Jason had ever been inside. She walked back to the chaise and retrieved the afghan she'd thrown over him, trying to order her thoughts.

"Where is he?" He asked this quietly but there was nothing calm about the stiffness of his body or the look in his eyes. "You told me he was here and that you were bringing him home. I assumed that meant you had an eye on him and that you intended to do what you promised."

"I didn't realize . . . He fell asleep out here and I . . ." She raised the afghan. "I put this over him and went back to bed. I guess I was more tired than I realized and . . . I'm sorry."

She went back into the house, trying to think. Chase followed.

"Sorry," she said again. "It's taking me longer than usual to get my brain in gear. I need . . ." This was when she realized there was no warm or wondrous coffee smell wafting from the kitchen. No scent or sign of Maddie, who'd earned the title "patron saint of mornings" for good reason. Bella Flora was empty. She nonetheless ran up the stairs to be sure. Bedroom and bathroom doors were open, the rooms were vacant.

Back in the salon Chase picked up a note from the bedside table and handed it to her. *At the hospital. Nikki in labor. Kyra and Dustin feeding and walking Sherlock. Maddie.* There was no mention of Jason.

"Nikki's in labor," she said dully. "And Jason . . ."

"Is clearly not here! This is serious, Avery. My son ran off to do who knows what and you tucked him in for the night. I'm curious. Did you send him off with a picnic basket?"

She saw the panic in his eyes and chose her words carefully. "I know you're upset, but that's not fair. I assumed he'd wait here or wake me up or . . . something."

"Spoken like a woman who's never had a child and who still seems to identify more with him than with the adults in this equation."

Her eyes narrowed. "You can't be seriously attacking me over this? I let you know he was safe and I would have brought him back."

"If he'd actually been here when you got around to waking up." It wasn't a question, but it was definitely a taunt. "And just so you don't think I'm overreacting here, I went through his room last night trying to figure out where he might have gone and I found a few interesting things." He pulled a sheet of paper from his pocket and unfolded it. "This is a letter notifying me that Jason was suspended for skipping the detention he got for skipping school." He pinned her with an icy blue gaze. "And I had a call from the marina to let me know that there was a balance due for gas that Jason charged the day he took the *Hard Case* out. Which coincidentally happened to be the day he skipped school."

Avery resisted the urge to step back.

"When I called the marina this morning, Chuck told me he'd seen Jason talking with a small, curvy blond woman when he and the 'hot girl' he'd taken out in the boat returned. Sound familiar?"

"Chase, I—"

"Then I found the condoms—well, that wasn't a complete shock and I guess I should be grateful he's using them. They were next to his stash of pot and these." He held up several photographs of the girl Jason had taken out on the boat. Minus the bikini and cover-up. "You met her, right?"

Avery swallowed and forced herself to look him in the eye. She could not believe how badly she'd screwed this up.

"She's underage, Avery. Which means he could actually end up labeled a sex offender or have some other tag applied to his name. And based on the gas bill, this wasn't the only time he took the boat without permission."

"I'm sorry, Chase. I told him he had to tell you what he'd done and that if he didn't, I would."

"But he didn't." His stare was merciless. "And neither did you. You knew these things were going on and you didn't tell me. I'm his father. And I am responsible for him and his well-being. Period."

She felt herself shrink under his withering stare.

"I've asked you to stay out of this, but you keep inserting yourself. Which wouldn't be quite so bad if you were clear about whose side you're on."

"Why do there have to be sides, Chase? I'm not against you. I care about all of you and I'm just trying to help. I think . . ."

"What do you think, Avery?" His tone was deadly serious.

"I think if you weren't all over him like you are, he might not need to rebel the way he does." She said this in a rush, hating how he loomed over her.

"And you picked this knowledge up, where? Oprah? Dr. Phil? It's my job to protect him even if I'm protecting him from himself."

"I hear you. But when you go on the attack like this, all the other person wants to do is run away." Lord knew, she did.

"Like my son. Who you were supposed to be watching and then bringing back to me."

"I told you I'm sorry, and I am," Avery said. "I didn't know I was supposed to keep him under house arrest." Though perhaps she might have if she'd had her wits about her. Guilt and worry and anger formed a knot in her stomach.

"We're done here," he said stiffly. "Because I need to go find my child."

He didn't ask her to come with him. She nodded a sad, miserable nod. Her gut told her that Chase was going about this all wrong, but he was right about the fact that she had never been a parent. Which meant it might be her gut that had it wrong and she had no right to argue. Silent, she watched him leave without a backward glance.

· · ·

The ride to the hospital passed in a blur of pain and a kaleidoscope of color that kept time to the wail of the siren. Things had slowed down considerably once the ambulance delivered Nikki to Bayfront Medical Center and even more so after Dr. Payne arrived and finally made sure Nikki got the epidural she'd begged the EMTs for during the ride and then again as they'd wheeled her inside. It was only as the pain faded that Nikki remembered that she owed Sherlock some very juicy bones for waking up Bitsy, who summoned the cavalry. It also allowed her to understand that the epidural would not only make her comfortable, but allow a C-section to take place quickly should it become necessary.

Maddie's arrival had been almost as comforting as the numbing medication and she'd floated peacefully for a time. Nikki was sucking on ice chips Bitsy had commandeered for her and telling herself this wasn't so bad after all now that the pain had disappeared, when one of the monitors she was attached to began to beep. A nurse hurried in and pushed some buttons. Dr. Payne arrived shortly after. Nikki's sense of well-being evaporated just as the pain had earlier.

"What's wrong? What's going on?" She clamped down hard on Maddie's hand.

"Baby B is in some distress," Dr. Payne said calmly. "We're going to go ahead and do a C-section to get them out quickly."

"Distress? What kind of distress?" Nikki stopped crunching ice. She stared into the doctor's eyes, trying to gauge the degree of urgency, but Dr. Payne's expression seemed as unruffled as her voice.

"There's no need to panic. We're all set up. It's time to get them out of there." She turned her back to Nikki. "Let's get her to the OR. I'm going to go suit up now."

Nikki attempted to swallow back the panic. "But . . . I'm waiting for Joe. I don't want to have them until Joe gets here."

Dr. Payne was already halfway out the door and did not turn back.

"Oh, God. I knew I shouldn't have relaxed. Why isn't Joe here?" Nikki squeezed Maddie's hand harder, only stopping when Maddie grimaced.

"Shhh," Maddie soothed. "You know the Giraldis went to meet his plane in Orlando a good while ago. The man has gone through hell and back to get here."

"But . . ." Nikki said as they raised the rails on each side of her bed and began to wheel her out of the room. "I'm not ready. I don't want to do this yet." This thing that she'd been waiting for so long was now moving far too quickly.

Maddie walked along beside her shushing and soothing for all she was worth. But Nikki couldn't think of anything that could calm her now.

"It's all right, Nikki," Maddie said again. "It'll all be over soon. And then you'll have those two little ones in your arms."

The hallway rushed by. She tried to quash the panic and the tears that threatened. She was a grown woman, not a child. And she was about to be a mother. Still, her heart beat too wildly. The absence of pain felt oddly disturbing as if she were coming un-tethered to what was happening.

A man in scrubs and mask was waiting just outside the op-erating room. Only his eyes and a small patch of forehead were visible. "I'll take her from here," he said to Maddie in a muffled voice. Maddie smiled, gave Nikki's hand a final squeeze, and leaned over to kiss her forehead.

"No, don't go. I don't want to be alone. I've been waiting for . . ." Tears welled again, this time at Joe's absence. She took a deep breath to banish them, but they blurred her vision.

"You'll be fine," Maddie said as she stepped back. "You're in good hands. The best." She looked up at the nameless, faceless doctor. "We'll be in the waiting room."

Then they were through the doors and inside the operating room. The medical staff stepped into place around her, Dr. Payne at her feet, the new doctor at her head. A drape was placed over her stomach. She swallowed and reminded herself that women did this every day. "Ready?" Dr. Payne smiled and stepped closer. She wasn't, not really. But she nodded. Moments later she felt movement, a slight tugging on her stomach. Her head lolled to the side. The new doctor leaned over her and she looked into the eyes above the mask. They were dark and intelligent. They glinted with an odd mixture of warmth and . . . amusement?

Her heart beat now with gladness and relief. She reached out. Joe took her hand in his. "Relax, Nik," Joe said. "It's showtime. I can hardly wait to meet our daughters."

• • •

They'd arrived in the family lounge at various times and now took turns pacing and fretting as they waited for news of Nikki's delivery.

"What's taking so long?" Bitsy had lost track of how many

times she'd asked this question. Having never given birth, she had no yardstick for comparison.

"It's barely been thirty minutes," Maddie replied though she, too, sounded somewhat on edge. "I'm sure we'll hear any minute."

Joe Senior and Gabriella held hands. Nonna Sofia's knitting needles clicked rhythmically, producing something long and neon pink. Avery had arrived a short time ago with a pained expression on her face and joined in the pacing.

Bitsy paced halfheartedly, unable to shake the guilt she felt for falling asleep in her cottage and for leaving Nikki alone. "Joe is going to go ballistic all over me when this is over," she fretted. "And I wouldn't blame him. I was just so exhausted, I pretty much passed out. God, if it weren't for Sherlock's impressive Lassie imitation, she might be giving birth on the lawn at the Sunshine right now."

"Yeah, well, Chase went ballistic on me just a few hours ago and it definitely sucks," Avery said. "It sucks even more when you know you screwed up."

"Yeah." Bitsy nodded glumly. "It would almost be a relief if Joe did yell at me."

"Chase will calm down once he finds Jason. There's nothing worse than the fear of something happening to your child," Maddie said. "And I don't believe Joe's going to be angry with you, Bitsy," Maddie said. "It was a bit of a perfect storm with him stranded, the showdown zapping everybody, and Nikki's cell phone battery giving up at the worst possible moment. Fortunately, you got her here with no harm done to her or the babies. It's a miracle Joe made it back in time."

Joe Senior smiled and patted his wife's hand. Nonna Sofia nodded and knitted. Joe had, in fact, skied cross-country to a specified spot where an agent friend had gotten him onto a private plane that had been routed to Orlando.

"I daresay this is a birthday story that will be told in the family for a long time," Joe's mother said. "We may have to give Sherlock a Giraldi family medal."

Bitsy laughed. "I still don't understand how he managed to nudge the door open and get inside. Or how he knew to take my clothes between his teeth and keep tugging and growling until I finally woke up. That dog has determination. I'm ashamed that I never saw him as anything but Bertie's until we were abandoned together."

"Well, I plan to make him his very own plate of osso buco," Sofia said. "Once the meat is gone, he'll have the bones to gnaw on."

"I hope he shares some with me," Bitsy said at a small growl from her stomach. "Whether I deserve it or not."

"It's nice to be in a hospital for a happy occasion," Avery said a short time later, no doubt thinking of Deirdre, who hadn't even made it to the hospital.

"That's for sure," Maddie agreed. "I remember sitting with Max Golden in Miami. I was glad we were with him. But it is lovely to be here to celebrate new life."

"Yeah," Avery said, cheering. "And it's practically a miracle that Joe got here just in the nick of time."

"She really didn't want to have them until he got there," Maddie said. "I think she was already attempting to talk them into staying put when they wheeled her into the operating room."

Bitsy was on her third cup of coffee and eyeing the nearby vending machine when Joe came into the room in the scrubs he'd worn. The mask hung down on his neck. His face bore the hallmarks of exhaustion as he ran a large hand through his dark hair, but a huge smile of unadulterated joy creased his face. He gave them a thumbs-up, handed his father a cigar, and hugged his mother and grandmother.

"Nikki's resting right now. Come see the girls. They are absolutely gorgeous." He led them into the nursery and up to the plate glass. A nurse carried two babies to the glass window, each swaddled in a pink baby blanket, one cradled in each arm. "That's Sofia, Nonna." He motioned to the baby on the left with the thatch of black hair. "Nikki wanted her to have your name." The other baby was auburn-haired like Nicole. Her face was scrunched up and she was crying. "That's Baby Girl Number Two," he said with a grin. "Nicole conked out right in the middle of the negotiation."

Twenty-nine

"I'm so sorry."

Nikki had lost track of the number of times Bitsy had apologized over the last two days. She'd apologized to Nikki and to Joe and pretty much anyone who stood still long enough to listen. She might have even whispered her mea culpa into the twins' tiny shell-shaped ears.

"I really am so sorry. I just can't believe I conked out like that." Bitsy stood at the foot of Nikki's hospital bed wringing her hands.

"It is kind of hard to believe you outdrank all of us without any noticeable effect and then just fell asleep on the job," Avery said without her usual heat or her signature eye roll.

"It was unfortunate, but it's not all on you," Maddie said firmly. "I knew how exhausted you were. We were all dead on our feet. I could have waited for you to get back to Nikki's before we left. Or stayed with her myself. Or at least made sure her cell phone was charged."

Bitsy turned her eyes on Nikki, but Nikki didn't have the

strength or the brain cells required to give her the shit she seemed to think she deserved. "Everything worked out," she said. "You need to get over it." Just as she needed to get with the program, get comfortable with the realities of motherhood.

Joe arrived smiling the smile that had been permanently affixed to his face since the twins had been delivered. His eyes shone with happiness as he leaned over to kiss Nikki. "It did more than work out."

"But I'd like to do something to make it up to both of you," Bitsy insisted.

"There's no need and nothing for you to do," Joe said.

"Unless you have a lead on the Mack truck that snuck into the delivery room and ran over me. Like a license plate number or identifying marker," Nikki said, catching a glimpse of her face in the mirror behind Bitsy. "Or the name of the tattoo artist who must have jumped out of that truck to ink these dark circles under my eyes."

Joe laughed easily and shot her a wink she was unable to return. When he excused himself to go check on the twins, she knew she would have given anything to feel the unadulterated joy that she saw reflected so clearly on his face.

Maddie poured a glass of water and placed it on the bedside tray. "Clearly Bitsy feels she deserves to be punished. But I think we need to make sure the punishment fits the crime."

"This should be interesting," Avery said. "I vote for permanent diaper duty. Or full-time baby nurse while Joe's at work or has to travel."

"I'm totally prepared to be on call twenty-four/seven," Bitsy said. "Or I could sleep on the couch. Just to be safe."

Nikki swallowed hard. Even the idea of being left alone with the babies filled her with terror.

"You should be an old hand at parenting," Avery said. "After taking care of Malcolm."

Nikki shuddered slightly at the mention of her felonious brother. "I'd just turned six when he was born, so I didn't handle him that much when he was an infant." She remembered the day he'd been brought home from the hospital and her mother had settled Nikki just so in a chair and then placed him briefly and reverently in her arms as if he were a great and miraculous gift. It was only years later, when their father had died and their mother had been frantically working multiple jobs, that Nikki had mothered Malcolm. And somehow created a self-absorbed, conscienceless monster. "I . . . I'm amazed and relieved that everything went okay. That both of the babies are healthy. I just . . . I don't know. I feel so . . . overwhelmed." She managed not to mention the deep-seated panic that had burrowed its way inside her.

Maddie resettled the pillow behind Nikki's head. "You're tired and you've had surgery. You need to cut yourself some slack."

Nikki dug her elbows into the mattress and attempted to reposition herself, but had to bite back a groan. Moving hurt. Holding the babies up against her stomach hurt. Walking, which they kept making her do, hurt even more. Laughing was the worst, so maybe it was a good thing she had no inclination to emit so much as a giggle.

"It'll take some time to recuperate physically. Then it's just a matter of figuring out what they want and giving it to them," Maddie said.

"I don't know if you noticed, but they don't talk," Nikki said. "And it's hard to think clearly when their faces are all scrunched up so pitifully and they're screaming." She closed her eyes for a moment, intent on beating back the panic.

Avery nodded. "Sofia and Number Two have some serious lung power."

"True," Maddie agreed. "But that's their only real means of communication right now. And you've got lots of people here eager to help you interpret what they're saying, including Joe."

"Yeah," Avery said, her tone wistful. "He doesn't seem the least bit upset or intimidated. And I'm pretty sure that smile on his face is permanent."

Maddie smiled at that.

"Maybe if I'd had FBI training, I'd be better at all this," Nikki said, ashamed that she was not only frightened of her own children, but jealous of Joe's uncomplicated happiness.

"No, you and the girls just have to get used to each other. And you have to realize that they're not going to break." Maddie stood and laid a reassuring hand on Nikki's. "The time will come when you wondered what you were ever worried about. And you'll be the only thing they need."

There were footsteps. She looked up to see Joe walking back into the room with one baby cradled gently in each arm, the nurse beaming at him in approval. Her eyes were drawn to the pink swaddled three-day-olds, who looked so tiny and fragile in their father's muscled arms.

"But I just fed them." The words were out before she could stop them. The chasm of panic opened inside her. "I don't . . . I can't . . ."

"We're going to do skin-to-skin contact," Joe said, clearly thrilled that the daily ritual in which each of them sat with an upright and largely naked baby against their own naked chest was about to begin.

Nikki looked up at the wall clock, back down at her hands. She'd lost track of time, had thought she'd have more time to prepare herself for the bonding exercise that was supposed to promote feelings of closeness between parent and child, increase breast milk supply and confidence in their ability to care for their babies. Joe had bonded with both girls at first sight and they had seemed to do the same the moment they were placed in his arms while Nikki grew alarmed at each snuffle, felt her pulse and heart race at each movement, and couldn't seem to catch her breath while their warm little bodies were pressed so tightly to hers. Kangaroo Care, as the nurses liked to call it, only made the panic spread inside her.

Maddie, Avery, and Bitsy were already excusing themselves as the nurse took the babies. Nikki sat up and managed to lever her legs over the side of the bed as Joe eagerly unbuttoned his shirt.

"I, um, I . . ." She managed to get out of bed then stood for a brief moment clinging to the bed rail as Joe took Sofia from the nurse, unwrapped the pink baby blanket, and pressed the diapered baby against his broad chest before pulling the side of his shirt over her. "My stomach is . . . something's not right. I . . . do you mind taking them both while I . . . I need to go into the bathroom."

The nurse shot her a small frown, but Joe's eyes were on the still unnamed "Number Two." "No problem. Take your time," he said as the nurse unwrapped the baby and settled her in Joe's lap, her head up against the other side of his chest.

She watched them in the mirror as she made her way to the bathroom on unsteady legs. He looked completely calm and at peace. The twins' eyes were closed, their breathing soft and easy. Neither moved a muscle or emitted a sound as Nikki closed the bathroom door behind her then lowered herself onto the closed toilet seat. Where she cried as quietly as she could so as not to disturb them.

• • •

Avery drove to Tampa the next day to pick up more clothes, check on Jeff, and possibly, if the opportunity arose, apologize once more to Chase. She was angry and hurt at the way he'd shut her out and then been so cold and merciless, but she also knew just how badly she'd handled Jason and how wrong she'd been to keep his behavior secret. As it turned out, Bitsy wasn't the only one who needed to be forgiven.

She drove slowly, barely resisting the urge to turn around. When she arrived at the Hardins' house and spotted Chase's truck in the driveway, she forced herself out of the car and up to the front door. Instead of reaching for the key in her pocket, she rang the doorbell and waited for someone to answer it.

Chase stood in the doorway with a scowl twisting his handsome face.

"May I come in?"

He stepped aside and motioned her in with a wave of his hand. The scowl remained.

"I came to apologize."

He stared at her mutely, the anger evident in his eyes.

"Because I am sorry, Chase. Truly sorry."

Still he made no comment.

"But if you really can't forgive me and move on, then I guess I'm here to get the rest of my things." She made herself look up into his eyes, which were dark and glittery and as hard as his jaw.

There was a sound. Jeff wheeled into the foyer, his back straight. "Don't be a fool, Chase."

"Don't stick your nose in this, Dad."

"Well, somebody has to. Avery made a mistake not telling you what she should have soon enough and she's said so."

"Right, so we should just pretend nothing ever happened," Chase snapped.

"Is Jason here now?" she asked. "Is he all right?"

Chase looked down at Avery. "Did you know he went on his last escapade with money he stole from Dad's wallet and mine? Or that it was only after we promised to send him away for the summer and that he would never contact her or come within a hundred yards of her that that girl's parents agreed not to swear out a complaint?"

She shook her head and her own jaw hardened. "How could I possibly know when you refuse to talk to me?"

"None of that is Avery's fault and you know it," Jeff said to his son. He moved closer. "Jason is a handful and it's going to take more than the Outward Bound program he's been accepted into for the summer to straighten him out. It's going to take all of us. This is not the time to shove away someone we have always considered family. Certainly not someone that you love and who I think, if you're lucky, still loves you."

Jeff looked now to Avery, but she stood mute, her eyes locked on Chase's. The seconds ticked out in rhythm with the dull thud of her heart.

"Got it. I'll just grab the rest of my things and get going." She brushed by him, offered Jeff a tremulous smile on her way to Chase's bedroom, where she pulled her suitcase out of the closet and began to shove her things into it. When she lugged it back out to the entry, Chase had disappeared.

"He's lost his head," Jeff said. "I know this isn't what he wants. He's just too damned proud to back off and too hurt right now to see reason."

"He's not the only one. But I don't really see what I can do about it." She had no projects waiting, no *Do Over*, and no family except for this man and the women with whom she'd thrown in her lot. If she thought about that now, she'd be blubbering all over the place. "I hope you know how much you mean to me." She wrapped her arms around Jeff's frail shoulders and hugged him as tightly as she dared. "Promise me you'll take care of yourself. And that you'll call if you need anything at all."

He hugged her back and placed a fatherly kiss on the top of her head. "Ditto."

With a last wobbly smile she turned and left, pulling the front door shut behind her.

. . .

He appeared so out of context that at first Kyra didn't understand what she was seeing. Then she thought she must be imagining him. That he was a figment of her imagination. Or a human mirage. But no, Daniel Deranian was sitting across a picnic table from her father at the Paradise Grille while Nigel and several other paparazzi snapped photographs.

"Dandiel!" Dustin sat up straight in the jogging stroller and pointed. "Dandiel and Geedad. Go there!"

Kyra wheeled the stroller toward their table, doing her best not to give the photographers a close-up of her son's angelic face or her own angry, sweat-stained one. She'd run two miles down the beach and two miles back up and she was a sodden mess, her T-shirt and running shorts clinging to her body, her high pony-tail held up in a scrunchy. She wasn't particularly vain and had never sought attention, but she flinched at the thought of her current self splashed across tabloid covers undoubtedly positioned next to an angelically beautiful and professionally airbrushed Tonja Kay. She could imagine the tagline under her photo—*Who would you choose?* Or, *So not worth it?* Or maybe even, *What was Daniel thinking?*

She reined in those pointless worries. Any possible future humiliation was nothing compared to the more important questions like, What was Daniel still doing here? Why had he brought photographers again? And what was her father, who'd never had any use for the man he'd referred to as an overrated, overpaid prick of a movie star, saying to him so earnestly?

Dustin unbuckled the seat belt, climbed out of the stroller, and went straight to Daniel, who lifted him into his lap. Her father's face flushed guiltily. "Kyra. I thought you were taking Dustin to see the babies at the hospital?"

"Nope. Nikki and Joe are bringing the babies home in a couple of hours." She advanced on the two of them, slid onto the bench beside her father. "So what's going on here?"

"Your father was just filling me in on your financial situation."

Kyra froze at the steely look in Daniel's eyes, which bore no resemblance to the conversational tone of his voice, or the amiable expression on his face. Once again, she was reminded of what he did for a living and how good he was at it.

"I'm having a hard time understanding how you could put the home I purchased for you two at risk."

She turned to her father. "I can't believe you ran and told him."

"I didn't run anywhere. Your mother made me see things in a somewhat different light, and I decided he had a right to know that you might lose Bella Flora."

"Because you think he's the only person who would put more money in to keep us from losing her."

"Isn't he?"

"All we need to meet the payments is to realize some profit from the documentary and for you to sell some cottages," she snapped. "Which would be a way better use of your time than carrying tales to Daniel."

"But they're not tales, are they?" Daniel said. "Did you or did you not take out a loan against Bella Flora that you can't pay back?"

She closed her eyes. Warned herself not to react. She did not want to upset Dustin or tip off the paparazzi to drama of any kind. "There have been setbacks I wasn't expecting," she said stiffly. "But I have every intention of paying off the loan."

"So in essence, you would risk losing the only home our son has really known rather than let him act in a movie with me?" Again there was no venom. His words were almost gentle. Only the brown eyes, which had turned darker than she'd ever seen them, gave him away.

"Wanna hact with Dandiel!" Dustin chimed in happily.

"I don't want him acting at all. And certainly not with you and Tonja," she whispered. She tried to build her own anger at her father's betrayal. Wanted to tell herself that Daniel was out of line in pressing her on this, but she had given him the ammunition. She shouldn't be surprised that he was using it.

"You would turn down the million dollars that would make this mess you've made go away?"

Her father's eyes widened in surprise. Kyra said nothing. When put that way, it sounded ridiculous. As did her actions.

"Well, I'm not going to let that happen." Daniel slid an envelope across the table. "This is a complaint of fiscal irresponsibility filed on Dustin's behalf. If you agree to let him do *The Exchange*, his salary will be used to pay off the loan. Then Bella Flora will be put in his name only, and the asset will be placed in trust for him. That trust will be overseen by a trustee of my choosing until he becomes an adult. You would also receive a salary for being on set with him."

"And if I'm able to pay off the loan? Or continue to make the payments without being late?"

"That seems unlikely, doesn't it, princess?" her father said.

"Unlikely is not the same thing as impossible." She said this through clenched lips, her eyes on Daniel's face.

"Casting will be finalized this summer. Preproduction takes place this fall. I expect to start shooting mid-January. I guess if you were able to pay off the loan in its entirety or make, say, six months' worth of payments in advance, you might look slightly less fiscally irresponsible. But I wouldn't need Dustin on set for more than six weeks. I think it would take you a lot longer than that to defend your actions or come up with that kind of money. And Dustin does have two parents."

"Kyra, turn around, luv!" Nigel's voice rang out. "Let me get a shot of the family!"

"Any announcements coming?" the photographer named Bill called.

Daniel raised an eyebrow at Kyra. She ignored him and the

photographers as she snatched up the envelope. "Come on, Dustin. Say good-bye to Daniel and Gee-dad." She stood and wheeled the stroller to the other side of the table, where she lifted Dustin off Daniel's lap and placed him back in the stroller. She did not speak or so much as glance at her father as she wheeled her son out of camera range and down the sidewalk toward the house she'd risked and, for all intents and purposes, lost.

Thirty

The cottage smelled of tomato sauce and melted cheese when Nikki and Joe brought the twins home from the hospital. All three Giraldis were there to welcome and feed them while Kyra shot video to document the occasion, undeterred by Nikki's un-made-up face, unbrushed hair, and vomit-stained shirt. Baby Sofia, who had slept all the way home in the car, still slept peacefully on her father's shoulder, her dark hair awry, one tiny fist pressed to her cheek. Their red-haired daughter, who had screamed through the entire twenty-five-minute car ride despite Nikki's best and increasingly frantic efforts to soothe her, cried on.

"I cannot believe you brought her home with only the name 'Numero Due,'" Nonna Sofia said, reaching for the squalling twin. The moment Joe's grandmother cradled her to her chest, the crying stopped. "How will she know who she is without a name?"

Savoring the quiet, Nikki lowered herself into a dinette chair and tried to shrug off the criticism along with the fact that everyone but her seemed to know where to find her daughter's "off" switch.

"Names are important, Nonna," Gabriella chided softly as she removed a large baking dish from the oven. "There's nothing wrong with taking time to think the decision through."

Nikki drew in a deep breath, but her heart continued to beat wildly and her head still rang with the screams that had reverberated through the car.

"Mother's right," Joe said easily. "Especially when you already have your namesake sewn up." He glanced down at baby Sofia, who still slept soundly on his shoulder. "I doubt Sofia's sister will be starting school with only a number for a name."

Nikki looked at Joe. He remained calm and unruffled no matter what the babies did, when the first hint of a cry made her want to flee.

Kyra lowered the camera. "Theo James plays a character called Four in the *Divergent* series. An Italian number could sound exotic and make her stand out from all the Emmas and Bellas."

"They're only four days old," Gabriella said, gently cupping her granddaughter's head of red hair. "This one has a strong personality."

"She has good lungs, that's all," Joe Senior offered. "My cousin Magdelena trained as an opera singer. Maybe this is an early form of singing."

Maddie emerged from the nursery to join them. Relief coursed through Nikki as she met Maddie's calm, reassuring gaze and warm smile. She tried to return that smile with trembling lips.

"Will you have something to eat?" Gabriella asked Nikki.

"It smells wonderful." Nikki tried the smile again. "But I don't think I could eat anything right now."

"You must keep up your strength for the babies," Nonna Sofia said, quietly glancing down at the sleeping child in her arms. "How else can you produce the milk they need?"

Nikki dropped her gaze as her eyes blurred with tears. So far nursing had been a nightmare, one more thing she'd been spectacularly inept at and couldn't imagine mastering.

"How about a slice of bread and butter? Or perhaps a small bowl of applesauce?" Gabriella asked.

"No, but thank you." Nikki blinked back the tears.

"Are you all right?" Joe asked, rising and handing Sofia to his father. His eyes plumbed hers.

"I'm just tired," Nikki said carefully. "If it's all right, I'd like to lie down for a little while." She kept her voice even and her eyes on his in an effort to hide her fear and uncertainty.

"Of course," Gabriella said. "We have lots of available arms that want to hold these two."

And all of them, including Joe Senior, could comfort her babies better than she could. *Her babies.*

"That's right," Maddie said. "And we can bring them in when they get hungry. It's best to feed them at the same time, get them on the same schedule if you can. Otherwise you'll never get any sleep." It was a testament to Maddie's diplomacy that she managed to avoid the use of names or numerals of any kind.

"Thank you," Nikki said as Joe helped her to her feet. "I appreciate it. And I appreciate you all being here. I just—"

"No need for apologies," Gabriella said. "We understand completely. We're here to make things easier. You rest, Nikki. Joe, let me dish you up a plate so you can eat while Maddie helps Nicole get settled."

Nonna Sofia and Joe Senior settled on the couch, each with a baby sleeping peacefully in their arms. Joe kissed Nikki on the cheek then sat as instructed while his mother went back to the stove and began dishing up heaping bowls of manicotti, but Nikki felt their eyes follow her as she moved slowly down the small hall with Maddie's arm wrapped gently around her shoulders.

...

Kyra sat in front of the computer monitor in her bedroom late the next afternoon as she reran the segment she'd just pulled from the original Sunshine Hotel documentary. Her worktable, which sat in front of the second-floor window, afforded a bird's-eye view over the back deck, the pass, and Shell Island beyond it. For the last hour and a half, that view had included Avery, who'd spent that time pacing a crooked loop of the deck, the pool, and the seawall, only disappearing from sight briefly when she passed behind the reclinata palm.

There was a light knock on the open bedroom door before Maddie walked in and came to stand behind Kyra's chair. "She's going to wear a hole in the concrete if she doesn't stop soon."

"Feel free to go tell her that," Kyra said, raising her eyes from the monitor to follow Avery's progress. "I said something earlier, you know, about how she might want to have it out with Chase, and she told me to mind my own business and started pacing faster. She's all yours."

"I think we need to let her wear herself out a little first," Maddie said. "In fact, I thought maybe we could leave it until we do our sunset toasts."

Kyra raised her eyes to the pale blue sky and the still-bright sun that filled it. "I don't care how long we wait, I don't think you're going to get even one small good thing out of her tonight. But I guess it's worth a try. Dad said he'd take Dustin to Gigi's for pizza and then to the playground." She hesitated. "I think it's his way of apologizing for telling Daniel about the loan."

Her mother sighed. Placing her hands on the back of Kyra's chair, she turned it so that they faced each other. "Your father should never have suggested that kind of loan, and you shouldn't have taken that kind of risk with Bella Flora—certainly not without discussing it. But Daniel was entitled to know, and I can understand why he was upset."

Her mother's eyes held hers. Kyra fought the urge to squirm.

"Dad only told him because he thought Daniel would offer to help. But I wouldn't have taken the money even if he had. And of course, that's not what happened."

"No, it's not."

Kyra watched her mother's face, noted its disapproval, and felt it keenly. Her mother could be almost relentlessly positive and liked to insist that the glass was, in fact, half full. But she was not one to sidestep what she saw as an important, if painful, conversation. In this case it was fortunate that she wasn't an "I told you so" sort of person and that she was able to move on once she'd made her point.

Kyra breathed a small sigh of relief when Maddie motioned to the computer screen and said, "So what are you working on?"

Kyra turned and moved her mouse to rouse the video. "I just finished re-editing the first third of the Sunshine Hotel documentary."

"Why? I thought you and Troy finished it some time ago."

"We finished an hour-long documentary, produced by the crew who were still under contract to *Do Over*."

"Which means?"

"Which means that the network can tie us up and prevent us from trying to sell the television rights. But our contract doesn't prevent us from streaming video and/or making that video available for free." Kyra cued up the first of ten short segments she'd created. Below, Avery continued to pace.

"But why would you want to give away something you worked so hard on?" her mother asked.

Kyra's hand hovered near the mouse. "Because I can't stand letting them lock us up the way they have or wasting this fabulous story," Kyra said.

"But what does giving it away in bits and pieces accomplish?"

"Well, it makes me feel better for one thing and makes the

footage virtually worthless to the network. And I think it could help keep the Sunshine Hotel and Beach Club in front of people. Which might help sell more memberships and cottages, which would help Renée and Annelise and maybe help us get back some of the money we all invested in the renovation." She rewound the segment and saved it, then cued up the next. Swiveling her desk chair, she looked up at her mother. "And if you subtract the financial pressure and desperation that prompted the project, I actually loved making the documentary. It's a great format, Mom. And I think these segments will make perfect demo material. Besides, I don't like people telling me what I can and can't do. Or forcing me to do or agree to something I think is wrong." Kyra winced as soon as the words left her mouth. Had she really just reintroduced the topic she'd been so relieved to leave?

Maddie did not come out and shout, "Gotcha!" She did fold her arms across her chest and look Kyra in the eye.

"No, I didn't mean to bring it up." Kyra stood, shook her head. There was no room to fall back with the desk already pressing into the backs of her thighs. "I don't want to talk about it."

"I know you don't. But you have to think this all the way through."

"Mom . . ." Standing, she could look down at her mother rather than up, but it didn't seem to matter.

"Sweetheart. Daniel *is* Dustin's father," her mother said in that quiet, reasonable tone that was so hard to argue with and pretty much impossible to ignore. "He makes movies for a living and now he's going to direct one. Would it really be so bad to let Dustin do this one film with him?"

Kyra's chin jutted out just as it always did when she was digging in for an argument. She began to fold her arms across her chest and only stopped when she noticed she was mirroring her mother.

"All I'm saying is try to open your mind and give this real thought," Maddie said. "Dustin didn't even go through the terrible twos—he skipped right over them. He's extremely mature for a child his age and shockingly easygoing. He loves spending time with his father. And it's obvious Daniel is crazy in love with him and would watch out for him. Plus you would be there to guide and protect him."

"But Tonja Kay and their children will be there, too. And you know how much she hates me and how jealous she is of Dustin." So angry that Kyra had been the one to give Daniel a biological child that she'd tried to take Dustin away from her.

"I understand that it would be uncomfortable for you," her mother said gently. "But I don't believe that Daniel would allow her to threaten or harm Dustin in any way, and given her role as costar and investor in the film, she has every reason to treat Dustin and his mother with kid gloves. It would put you back on your feet financially and lighten some of the load you're carrying."

"But he threatened me!" Kyra protested, ashamed of the tears she could feel gathering behind her lids. "And treated me like a child." She stopped just short of stomping her foot.

"I understand, Kyra." Her mother lifted a hand to cup her cheek. "It's a difficult decision. But you need to give Daniel's request serious consideration. Being a mother isn't always easy and neither is being an adult." Her smile and the softness of her touch took the sting out of her words. "But both of those positions require you to fully understand and consider your options and all their ramifications."

. . .

Avery was still pacing and Kyra was still avoiding Maddie when Bitsy arrived for sunset with Sherlock trotting at her heels. Maddie sent Bitsy after Kyra, brought the pitcher of margaritas and snacks she'd prepared out to the wrought iron table on the loggia, then walked out to the seawall, where she took Avery by the shoulders, led her into the shade, and pressed her gently into a chair. Maddie slid the bowl of Cheez Doodles in front of Avery before taking a seat.

Sherlock stretched out on the concrete while Bitsy poured the icy red concoctions and passed them around.

Maddie waited for Avery to take a Cheez Doodle. When that didn't happen, she raised her drink and waited for the others to raise theirs in toast.

"It feels weird without Nikki," Kyra said. "Especially when we know she's just down the beach."

"If I'd thought she'd have the energy, we could have done it at the Sunshine," Maddie said.

"I stopped by their cottage on my way to the car," Bitsy said. "And I don't know. I haven't really been around many new mothers or newborns, but she seems pretty overwhelmed."

"Overwhelmed goes with the territory even when you only have one baby. Twins at forty-seven?" Maddie fingered the stem of her goblet. "I can't even imagine what that feels like."

"Well, I say we make a toast to getting through the sleepless nights and the constant feedings and diaper changes," Kyra said.

"Wow, I'm getting overwhelmed just thinking about those things," Bitsy said.

"Yeah." Maddie had recognized the panic that Nikki had tried to hide but been powerless to alleviate it.

"Am I allowed to say that I hate that Bertie is having a baby with someone else?" Bitsy said. "For all I know, Delilah may have already given birth." She seemed to gag on the exotic dancer's name. "I mean Bertie never even seemed interested in having children. He used to say that I was his baby and he didn't need anything or anyone else. What a crock of shit." Her eyes glistened with unshed tears. She covered what sounded like a small sob by taking a long pull on her drink. "I used to fantasize that I'd hear from him. You know, that he'd call to tell me how unhappy he was, how much he wanted to come home, what a mistake he'd made." She raised her glass again, swallowed deeply, set it down. "If he'd just told me he wanted a divorce, he would have had half of almost everything and I'd be free to go about my life. Instead he took everything and left me here in no-man's-land."

She pulled a stack of paper out of her purse. "These are responses from all the attorneys I approached, all of whom have made large sums of money from me and my family over the years. Every one of them said no when I asked them to try to find Bertie and my money and help me divorce him on a contingency basis." Sherlock sat up and placed his chin on her lap. She stroked his head absently. "I can't let him get away with this. Losing half in a divorce would have been one thing. Having everything stolen? No!"

Sherlock woofed as if in agreement.

"What will you try next?" Kyra asked.

"I don't know. But there must be someone out there who's willing to go balls to the wall, you know? Someone who'll help bring him back and put him in jail, so that I can divorce him."

"Maybe you need to look for a smaller firm that deals with extradition? Or specializes in missing persons?" Maddie suggested. She'd barely looked at the sky as Bitsy had shared her distress.

Kyra raised her glass to Bitsy. Maddie and Avery followed suit. "Here's to finding Bertie and hauling his ass back," Kyra said.

"His skinny ass," Bitsy corrected.

"To bringing Bertie's skinny ass back!" they proclaimed.

"Balls to the wall!" Bitsy said.

"What do you think, Mom? Does Bitsy need to turn that into a good thing?" Kyra asked.

She was about to remind them all that she was not the "good enough" police, when Bitsy raised her glass once more. "I think it would be a very good thing to find a 'balls to the wall' attorney who will find Bertie and drag his skinny, cheating ass back. At this point I don't much care whether they bring him back dead or alive."

They clinked and drank. Maddie poured them another round. "Kyra?"

"What?"

"Do you have a good thing to share?" Maddie prompted.

Avery eyed the Cheez Doodles for the first time, but made no move on them.

"Well," Kyra said. "I think I've figured out a way to share the Sunshine Hotel documentary with an audience."

Avery seemed to rouse. "How?"

"I'm cutting it into short video segments for streaming."

"Interesting." Avery drained the final sip from her glass.

"What are you going to do about Daniel's movie?" Bitsy asked.

Maddie held her breath as the sun slipped in the pinkening sky. A lone pelican spread his prehistoric wings.

"I don't know," Kyra said. "I'm mulling with a mind my mother thinks I need to open."

Maddie forced herself to stay silent as the pelican left its perch on the pier to fly low over the still surface of the water.

Bitsy continued to contemplate Kyra. "If the money weren't a factor, would you consider letting Dustin be in a movie with his father?"

Maddie held her breath when Kyra tilted her head in thought.

"Maybe," Kyra said. "I don't know."

"If you were married to Daniel and he wanted your child to be in his movie, would you say yes?" Bitsy asked.

Kyra opened her mouth, closed it.

Once again, Maddie was careful not to speak. But she did fill Bitsy's empty glass to the brim then did the same for Avery.

Above them the sky went from pink to purple and the golden red sun hovered over the Gulf.

"What's happening with you and Chase?" Maddie asked Avery.

"Nothing. Nothing's happening because he's not speaking to me."

"Really?" Bitsy asked.

"Really." Avery looked as if she might jump up and start pacing again at any moment. "I've apologized repeatedly but he won't forgive me. So we seem to be finished."

"Surely that's not what he wants," Maddie said. Her heart twisted for Avery, but her thoughts turned to Will. Whom she'd texted about the twins' arrival the night he'd left and had made no time to speak with since.

"Jeff doesn't think so," Avery said. "He thinks Chase is just being stubborn. But it hurts, you know. To be ignored by someone who used to love you."

"Tell me about it." Bitsy raised her glass to her lips and drank half of it in a few gulps.

"Anyway, Jeff invited me to come see Jason off—he's going to be in the Blue Ridge Mountains for an Outward Bound program that's helped other kids turn their lives around. But I don't know. I don't think Jason wants to see me any more than Chase does. It's such a mess." Avery lifted her glass to her lips but took only a few tentative sips. She hadn't touched a single Cheez Doodle.

"You should go," Maddie said. "And at least tell them how you feel about them."

"Do you really think so?" Avery set down her glass and wiped the red froth from her upper lip.

"I do," Bitsy said firmly. "That's one of the worst things about what happened with Bertie. I never got to beg him to stay, or yell at him to leave, or even understand why he did what he did." Her voice dropped. "I didn't get to ask him why he stopped loving me. Or if he really ever had."

Kyra's eyes were pinned to Bitsy's face. Maddie hoped her words had gotten through.

"I think it's way better to say what you think, and how you feel," Maddie found herself agreeing. "It's better to know and face the truth than to run from it."

A car pulled into the drive. A car door slammed, another opened. Sherlock's ears perked up at the sound of Dustin's piping voice.

Avery raised her glass. Maddie and the others raised theirs.

"To telling and hearing the truth," Avery said.

"And to facing that truth head-on," Bitsy said.

"No matter how unpleasant that truth turns out to be," Kyra said.

They clinked glasses and downed the rest of their drinks. As dusk gathered around them, Maddie felt a bit like Custer might have felt as he rallied his troops at Little Big Horn. With Bella Flora hunkered behind them, she offered a silent prayer to the darkening sky that none of the people she cared about would be faced with truths they couldn't handle.

Thirty-one

Avery arrived at the Hardins' that Friday minutes before Jeff had said they were due to leave for the airport, and she parked the Mini Cooper in the driveway behind the boys' Explorer. Although she'd raced to get there in time, she didn't get out of her car or even turn off the engine. She sat with her eyes pinned to the front door as she tried to work up the courage to walk right up to it and knock so that she could do what she'd come to do.

She was still sitting there when the garage door rumbled up. A shimmer of anxiety snaked up her spine, turning her mouth dry and setting her nerves jangling. She'd never wanted to turn and run this much.

Now or never. She was actually leaning toward never when Josh Hardin emerged from the garage and tossed a large duffle bag in the back of the pickup. She lowered her window as he walked down to her. Surprise showed on his face.

"Hi." Avery couldn't tell whether he was glad to see her or not. Her palms turned sweaty and she debated her next move.

Stay and do what she'd come for? Or spend a few minutes with Josh and ask him to tell his dad and Jason that she'd stopped by?

When he opened her door, she got out. "Granddad and I were afraid Dad drove you away for good."

"Well, it wasn't for lack of trying. But you guys are the only family I've got. Whatever happens with your dad and me, you're not going to get rid of me so easily."

His lips turned up at the corners as she cricked her neck to look up at him. "Since I don't see a stepladder anywhere . . ." She crooked a finger and watched the smile widen as he bent down so she could hug him. She clung for a while, still contemplating flight but reluctant to let go of him. When she did, he straightened.

"How's everything going?"

He shrugged. "Jason's pissed at having to go forth into the wilderness, but he's been pissed about pretty much everything for a while. And I guess this is better than what could have happened." His voice had grown even deeper since she'd last seen him and his face bore the stubble of a full-grown man, but she could still see signs of the gangly, uncertain boy, who'd lost his mother too early and been forced to watch his little brother go off the rails.

"From what I saw online, the program's a good one," she said. "And I don't see how spending time in the Blue Ridge Mountains could hurt."

"Yeah. Leave it to Jace to get an expensive vacation out of all the shit he's pulled."

"Feel free to take my place, bro." Jason swaggered down the drive with a backpack dangling from one hand. "Looks like hard labor to me. Dad's just paying out so he doesn't have to deal with me anymore."

"Asshole. You're lucky he didn't have you locked up," Josh said to his younger brother. "Try not to fall off a mountain or anything before you get rehabilitated, okay?"

"Yeah. Whatever." Jason's tone and words were tough, but Avery had the sense the swagger was mostly for show. He dropped the backpack into the bed of the truck then watched Josh until he disappeared into the house.

"Did you come to gloat?"

"No, I came to say good-bye. And to tell you that I'm here if you ever need me."

Jason snorted. "Yeah, well, maybe you can send me a cake with a saw in it or something in case I decide to make a break for it."

She had to look up at him, too. She wished she could reach his face so she could wipe the smirk off it. "I thought you had to agree to go. And I don't exactly see you in handcuffs."

"It's not like I had a choice or anything."

"You always have a choice, Jason. And this is the perfect time to start making some good ones." She thought about their last sunset. "Try to keep an open mind and take advantage of the opportunity. And maybe you could think about someone besides yourself occasionally while you're gone."

"Like you?" he taunted.

"No. Like your father and your grandfather and your brother. They love you, Jason, and you've got this chance now to turn things around. I hope you'll take advantage of it."

He nodded but made no reply. She crooked her finger at him. He resisted at first, and for a long moment, she thought he was going to say something nasty. Reluctantly he bent over. When she wrapped her arms around him, she felt the air whoosh out of him. He didn't hug her back, but he didn't shake her off, either.

When he straightened and stepped aside, she saw Chase standing next to the truck. Jeff sat beside him in his wheelchair. She went to Jeff. As she hugged him, he whispered in her ear, "Don't let my boy intimidate you. You are the best thing that ever happened to him. He's just too damned angry and stubborn to say so."

"Well, I'm feeling a little angry myself," she said. "Can you give me a minute?"

"I can give you five." He straightened and motioned to Jason. "I need you to help me with something inside."

Jason muttered briefly, but went to his grandfather, turned the wheelchair, and pushed it toward the garage. As they disappeared, Avery moved toward Chase, replaying Maddie's words of advice. When she reached him, she went on tiptoe and grasped his sunglasses.

"Hey. I need those."

"Well, I need to see your eyes more." She slid them off, her hands no more gentle than her voice. "Because I need to be sure you're paying attention."

His jaw stiffened along with his body. But it was his eyes that almost made her turn and run. The twinkle that had always resided in them was gone. They were filled with worry, their brilliant blue faded. The new lines cut into their corners had not been caused by smiling. In fact, she couldn't remember the last time she'd seen his lips turn up in anything that resembled humor. Nonetheless she squared off in front of him and cricked her neck back to meet those eyes. God, she wished they weren't all so tall. But she didn't crook her finger.

"There are a few things I want to tell you."

He stood as still as a statue, neither nodding or moving. The urge to turn and run back to her car was almost irresistible. *If Maddie were here, she would say what she'd come to say and live with the consequences.* She drew a deep breath and forced herself to begin.

"First of all, I want to apologize one more time for not sharing what I knew as soon as I knew it. You should know me well enough to know that I would never harm you or your children intentionally, but I was wrong and I regret the harm it caused." She paused but didn't look away. "That's the last time I'm going to apologize. You can accept or not. That's up to you."

One dark eyebrow sketched upward but he didn't speak.

"I also think the Outward Bound intervention program is a great idea. Not that you asked my opinion or even told me."

He watched her through an unblinking gaze, stiff and silent. It took everything she had not to look away or flee.

"Which brings me to how much it hurts that you push me away and cut me out instead of sharing your hurt and letting me try to help." She drew one last breath. "I love you. My life would probably be a whole lot easier if I didn't, but I do."

Still he said nothing.

Her neck had begun to ache and the slow, painful thud of her heart was almost unbearable. Dread, cold and heavy, began to seep through her. "I'm not sure if anyone mentioned this to you before, but love is supposed to be a two-way thing. You know, reciprocal." She watched his face for some sign of his feelings for her, but he might have been chiseled in granite. "So this would be a good time for you to say, 'I love you, too.' Or even 'I'm sorry, Avery, but I no longer have feelings for you.'"

She waited, barely able to breathe, for him to tell her he'd chosen option two. At which point she would run back to her car and peel off before the tears came. A shadow of what looked like regret clouded his eyes, but still he said nothing. Was he really going to let her walk away without so much as a response? Was his hurt and pride that much more important to him than she was? A tiny spark of anger flickered to life at the thought. She fanned it.

"Okay," she said without so much as a waver in her voice. "That's it. I know you've got a ton of shit going on, but I can't be in a relationship with someone whose first move when things go wrong is to cut me out. I don't think that's what love, real love, is about. So once Jason's settled in the program, I suggest you find some time to think about your feelings and whether you want our relationship to continue." Her step back was intentional and measured. "Because I'm not going to wait forever. If I have to learn how to stop loving you, I will."

Surprise flickered in his eyes but still he said nothing.

"Got it. Message received." With her head up and her shoulders back, she turned and strode back to her car, careful not to run. She fired up the engine, looked back over her shoulder, and reversed down the driveway, relieved to have something other than Chase to look at. As she threw the car into drive and mashed her foot down on the gas pedal, she told herself the squeal of tires didn't mean she was fleeing. It meant she was making an exit.

• • •

Bitsy wasn't sure she actually wanted to leave her car at all. She'd followed the GPS across the Gandy Bridge to Tampa and from there to a small green clapboard house on MacDill Avenue not far from the Air Force base of the same name. It was obvious that this portion of the street had originally been residential but was now an uneasy mix of commercial and retail enterprises. It wasn't the kind of street any of the white shoe law firms she was used to would have chosen, but then those firms had already turned her down when they'd discovered she could no longer scrape up the money to pay for even an hour or two of their time. She drove past a nail salon, a Laundromat, and a combination kosher deli/Chinese restaurant before finally spotting the law office.

According to their website, Steding & Steding specialized in divorces, missing persons, and skip tracing, the very legal services she required. Best of all, it provided a free thirty-minute consultation with one of the name partners to determine whether the firm could be of help.

She found a parking space near a Goodwill resale store, climbed out of the Land Rover, and walked across the cracked sidewalk. The law firm's front window was coated with a dark film on which *Steding & Steding* had been stenciled in what had once been gold paint.

A bell tinkled cheerily as she entered the former living room, but there was no one in the reception area to hear it. The space was small and the wood floors were scuffed, but the walls had been painted a butterscotch yellow trimmed in white. She moved into a sitting area that took up most of the space and sat on one of the faux leather chairs. The magazine-strewn coffee table held a clipboarded sign-in sheet. She'd barely finished writing her name when an unmarked door on the far wall opened.

"Ms. Baynard?"

Bitsy nodded.

The middle-aged woman who walked toward her had surprisingly white skin splattered with freckles, a somewhat barrel-shaped body, and wash-and-wear red-gold hair. Her turquoise skirt fell in soft folds just below her knees. A multi-angled tunic top in white, black, and turquoise skimmed down one hip. Her black sandals were sensible, but her costume jewelry was color-fully tasteful, her smile appeared genuine, and her hazel green eyes intelligent. "I'm June Steding." She stuck out her hand and looked into Bitsy's eyes. "I'm gathering I'm not what you were hoping for."

The woman's gaze was steady, her handshake firm. But could it make a fist that would deliver a knockout punch? "I'm sorry," Bitsy said. "I hope you won't take this personally, but I need a pit bull. Someone relentless. And . . . ballsy." Not this woman who looked like a cross between June Cleaver and Margaret Thatcher.

"I've been called all of those things at one time or another." June Steding smiled. "Though I don't think it was ever a compli-ment. Why don't you come sit down and tell me why you're here?"

Steding motioned Bitsy to a chair then settled behind the antique partner's desk. The only other furnishings in the room were the file cabinets and bookcases that took up the back wall. Muted daylight shone through the tinted window that overlooked the sidewalk. A diploma from Stetson Law School and a smattering of family photos were the only decorations.

"How many other lawyers are with the firm?"

"None."

"What happened to the other Steding?"

"The other Steding was my father. He's retired. People feel better going to what looks like a two-man firm than to a lone female attorney. He does consult on cases from time to time." She studied Bitsy for a long moment. "I actually started in social work, but I found it frustrating. No real power or teeth behind your efforts, and I saw a lot of people, especially women and children, get trampled. I went back to school and got a law degree so that I could fight harder and more successfully for my clients." The attorney sat back and steepled her hands on her desk. "Why don't you go ahead and tell me what brought you here. Then we'll decide together whether I can help."

Bitsy looked the woman in the eye. "My husband ran away with an exotic dancer named Delilah and took my family's fortune with him. They're having a baby." She was ashamed to feel her eyes go damp, but she saw no judgment in June's eyes. "I want him found and brought back so that I can divorce him and the money he stole can be recovered. And then I want him put in jail for stealing everything I had and for being so crushingly disappointing."

June pulled a box of Kleenex from a drawer and pushed it toward Bitsy. "Any idea where he might have headed?"

"No. I didn't even have enough money left to hire a PI." Bitsy looked down at her hands, which were clenched in her lap. "I feel like an imbecile for being caught so unprepared, but I honestly thought he loved me. I mean, I know my money was part of the attraction but we were married for fifteen years, and he had full access to everything."

"No prenup?"

"No. That's how sure I was that we were in it for the long haul."

June Steding leaned back in her chair and shook her head. "Don't beat yourself up. You'd be shocked at how many women are taken by surprise."

Bitsy hesitated, embarrassed to ask the question she couldn't quite let go of. "I keep wondering if there might be some reason, some threat he was facing, some explanation—other than him being a greedy, selfish cheater—that might explain why he did this."

Steding's smile was kind. "I know what you want to hear. But I deal with men who leave and take everything with them all the time—though they don't usually have access to fortunes. It's pretty much never motivated by more than selfishness and greed.

"That's why I do what I do—drag back deadbeat dads and skip-out husbands then do my best to force them to take care of their children or do right by the women they made a legal promise to love, honor, and cherish. I don't do this because I can't get better-paying cases. I do this because I hate people who don't keep their word and especially those who lie to take advantage of others. It's personal for me every time."

Bitsy watched June Steding's face harden. Her hazel green eyes glittered like ice chips. She might not have the inbred viciousness of a pit bull or the shark's taste for blood, but she had a strong streak of fair play and a palpable determination and will. In every sense but the physical, this woman had what appeared to be some very large *cojones*. "I'm not sure if you know this or not, but according to Florida law in order to prove abandonment, you must be abandoned for twelve *uninterrupted months*. If your husband returns before those twelve months are over and you refuse to take him back, he could actually sue you for desertion."

"That is so wrong on every level," Bitsy said. Not that she had anything left that was worth suing for.

"Yes, it is," Steding agreed. "But Florida law can be quite twisted to my way of thinking."

"So what happens now?" Bitsy asked tentatively.

"I'll give you a standard contract to look over. If you choose to proceed, we'll begin the search online. In fact, you can save money by doing some of the legwork yourself at my direction." The attorney pulled the paperwork from a drawer and placed it on the center of her desk in front of Bitsy. "But first you need to give some serious thought to just how quickly you want to find him."

Thirty-two

Maddie tiptoed out of Nikki's bedroom and past the nursery, where both babies had somehow fallen asleep at the same time. She found Joe on the couch, head thrown back, eyes closed. His parents had gone back to the motel after dinner claiming that Nonna Sofia needed an early night, but Maddie had no doubt they were all probably down for the count by now despite the fact that the sun had not yet set.

Joe opened his eyes as she entered the living room. There were dark smudges beneath them. Even darker stubble shadowed his face. "Thanks for your help," he said groggily.

"My pleasure. It can be a little overwhelming at first."

"Tell me about it," he said, scrubbing at his eyes with the back of one hand. "I've always loved being with my sister's kids, but it seems I may have underestimated what dealing with two newborns would be like."

Maddie smiled. "It can be a bit of a shock to the system. Kyra and Andrew were four years apart, so I wasn't dealing with two newborns. From everything I've heard, twins are way more than twice as challenging."

"They are a force." Joe sat up with a yawn. "But we do have a platoon of people helping, which helps keep the panic at bay." He winced. "I'm not completely awake here. Did I just say that out loud?"

She nodded, doing her best not to smile.

"Yeah, well, this is harder than I expected. And somehow the stakes feel . . . so high."

"Higher than a hostage negotiation? Or dodging bullets?" Maddie asked. "You've been the picture of calm since you arrived at the hospital after pulling a James Bond to get there in time."

Joe ran a hand through his hair. "I'm trained to appear calm and to solve problems no matter how dire the circumstances. You can't let a person who's holding a gun on you see how nervous you are. But the girls?" He shook his head slowly. "They're so tiny and helpless. Half the time I'm afraid if I make the wrong move, I might break one of them. And . . ." He hesitated, but Maddie waited him out.

"And I'm worried about Nikki." That worry filled his eyes and voice. It was the first time he'd alluded to what she knew all of them were sensing. "I know exhaustion's part of the job description, but she seems so fragile—which is not an adjective I ever thought I'd use to describe Nikki. I feel like I need to jump in at the first cry and act like none of this is a big deal, because I'm afraid . . ." Once again he hesitated.

"Of what?" she asked softly, her eyes holding his.

"That if it gets too hard, she'll . . . I'm not sure exactly what I'm afraid of, but I don't want to find out." He expelled a breath of air as she took a seat across from him. "Any suggestions?"

"Well, for one thing, you might stop acting so competent."

He looked at her in surprise. "You don't think it makes her feel more comfortable?"

"I think it makes her feel incompetent, which is entirely normal at this stage of the game. But she's comparing herself to you and feels like she's falling short. It's important for her to handle things she's nervous about. If you're always jumping in before she can or she's always handing the babies off, it could take a lot longer for her to gain confidence."

"So you think I should fumble around? Let her see how often I seem to put those blasted diapers on backward on my first attempt? Or admit that I once fed the same baby twice instead of each of them once?"

Maddie smiled. "I wouldn't go all Three Stooges or anything, but it might help her to know she's not the only one who's nervous. I'm guessing it's the fear and stress that are causing her headaches, but it's been two weeks now. I know your folks will be heading home soon, and at some point you're going to have to go back to work. We need to find ways to help her get more comfortable."

"Thanks."

"My pleasure." Maddie stood to retrieve her purse from the counter. As Joe walked her to the door, she thought of the advice she'd handed out so freely during the last sunset. She turned to face him. "So this is none of my business," she said, speaking quickly before she could lose her nerve. "But I don't think it would hurt to remind Nikki that you, um, still want to marry her." She shifted uncomfortably. "Assuming, you know, that you still do."

"I'm not the one who said no three times." Joe looked every bit as uncomfortable as she felt. "I just figured if I stopped asking, the idea might become more appealing. You know, because sometimes what we want most are the things we think we can't have." His last statement sounded suspiciously like a direct quote.

Maddie had never been quite so tempted to roll her eyes. "No woman came up with that idea," she said firmly. "And whatever man suggested it should probably be shot."

"Yeah." He swallowed. "Sometimes when you're flying blind, you grab the first parachute you come across."

Maddie managed not to laugh. "Look, Joe, the woman is overwhelmed and seriously sleep-deprived. If you think she's going to just wake up one day and say she'd like to get married when you haven't mentioned the idea in . . . how long has it been?"

He grimaced. "A while."

"Right. Well, as they say, if you don't ask, you don't get. And of course, there's also, 'Nothing ventured, nothing gained.'" Maddie settled her purse on her shoulder. "So since you asked for suggestions, here goes. Number one—stop pretending you're Super Dad. Number two—please, before it's too late, tell her how very much you still want to marry her." She reached for the doorknob then realized there was a number three. "And no matter what she says, don't take no for an answer."

. . .

Maddie was in the minivan on the way back to Bella Flora and still smiling over Joe's confession of parental cowardice when her cell phone rang.

"Maddie?" Lori Blair sounded as perkily efficient as ever. "I've got Will on the line."

Maddie was still processing when William's voice filled her ear. "Hey there, Maddie-fan. How are things going?" The warmth in that voice reminded her just how long it had been since they'd spoken.

"Good," she said. "Unless you count Kyra's loan against Bella Flora, the number of Sunshine cottages still unsold, the loss of *Do Over*, and our lack of anything to replace it."

"Ahhh," he said. "I'm sorry to hear you're dealing with all that. Maybe we should downgrade to what Lori likes to refer to as 'Good-ish,' at least temporarily."

"I'm a little reluctant to borrow vocabulary from someone

who dots her *i* with a heart, but I may have to make an exception this time," she said. "Speaking of Lori, when did she start placing your personal calls?"

"When she started worrying that Aaron was going to let her go if she didn't look busier. I'm apparently lower maintenance than the label was expecting."

Maddie turned west then took a left onto the aptly named Gulf Way. "Maybe it's time to get more demanding. It would probably take her a couple hours to remove all the blue M&M's from the bowls backstage before each show or, I don't know, maybe you could ask her to iron your T-shirts or organize your fishing lures by size and color and insect resembled."

He snorted. "She actually suggested I trash my hotel room in Phoenix. Apparently, Aaron thinks I've lost my edge, that I'm too boring. Just because I'm eating a macrobiotic diet and don't actually want any of the women who come on to me."

The beach flew by on her right, mom-and-pop hotels and new multimillion-dollar homes passed on her left, but most of her attention was focused on not thinking about how many women he might be fending off. A handful? Two dozen? "Well, that's something I can't feel too bad about." She remembered her shock the first time she'd seen the naked photos and lacy thongs women had pressed on him when he first started performing again. A nationwide tour meant a whole country full of willing, aggressive women. All of whom were probably younger and more attractive than she was.

"Aaron wants me to at least pretend to be interested, or be seen out with someone on occasion for the press."

Unable to come up with a response that didn't sound too needy, she drove in silence.

"I told him I'm holding out for the real thing," Will said. "How long do you think it will be until you can get away?"

Even now she found it hard to believe that she was the real

thing he was referring to. "I don't know," she said truthfully, filling him in on her conversation with Joe and their concerns about Nikki as she continued south past the Hurricane Restaurant and the Paradise Grille. A few short blocks later, she pulled into Bella Flora's bricked drive. Phone still pressed to her ear, she entered through the kitchen, saw Kyra and Dustin in the pool, and went up the back stairs to her bedroom. "I wish you were here."

"Me, too." Will's voice was husky as she put the phone on speaker, set it on the bed, and began to remove her T-shirt.

"What are you doing right now?"

"I'm um . . ." She pulled the shirt over her head and reached somewhat frantically for the phone to make sure she wasn't accidentally FaceTiming. "I'm getting undressed."

"Hmmmm." His voice went even huskier and she could almost see the smile undoubtedly hovering on his lips. "I definitely wish I was there to help."

She felt a prickle of awareness as she moved into the bathroom and turned on the tub faucets.

"What are you doing now?" he asked in what she'd always thought of as his bedroom voice.

"Running a bath." She placed the phone on the rim of the tub and twisted her hair into a knot.

"I'm almost afraid to ask, seeing as how I'm a thousand miles away and all alone here. But . . . what are you wearing now?"

She felt a flush of heat spread across her chest and up her neck as she lowered herself into the bath and knew it had nothing to do with the water temperature. Warm water swirled around her naked body like a caress. "Nothing. Nothing at all." And then, "Is this an obscene phone call?"

"It could be," he said. "In fact, if your texting skills were a little more advanced, we could be sexting right now."

She smiled. "My hands are wet and way too slippery for that," she said, going for a sultry tone. "Because I'm . . . soaping my body." Her thoughts went back to the first time she'd been naked with him in the hot tub on Mermaid Point over the Fourth of July weekend when they'd had the entire island to themselves. "I wish you were here to wash my back for me."

"I'm not sure that's exactly where I'd choose to start," he teased, his voice low in his throat.

"No?" She slipped farther under the water and rested her neck against the rim of the tub.

"No." His voice was almost a growl.

Her eyes fluttered shut as she let herself remember the feel of his lips and hands skimming over her naked skin, the way his eyes darkened when he made love to her.

"God, Maddie. It's been way too long since I've had you in my arms."

"Ummm-hmmm." Her eyes grew heavier as Will's voice grew softer, his words blending together in an intimate yet soothing stream. The water lapped and caressed her as he talked. And then somehow she was just floating in its warmth, buoyed by Will's voice, adrift in darkness scattered with stars.

"Maddie? Are you there?" Will listened closely, but heard only silence on the other end of the line. "If I just put you to sleep, I'm definitely going to have to work on my technique." Torn between laughter and frustration, he sighed. "I promise to do better in person."

· · ·

Loud cries jolted Nikki awake. She lay in bed listening to the sharp, angry shrieks, willing them to stop. She reached out, but knew before she did that Joe's side of the bed was empty. She felt a flash of guilt for lying here, eyes closed against reality, when he was no doubt already in the nursery. When the crying didn't stop, she opened her eyes and focused them on the bedside clock. It was three A.M. The last thing she remembered was feeding one of the babies at what she thought was midnight.

She levered herself to a sitting position, moving carefully so as not to feel the pain that seemed lodged beneath her rib cage. Her head throbbed in time to the cries, a metronome of pain that occasionally receded, but never seemed to go away completely. Not yet ready to face the screams, she went first to the living room, where she found Joe sound asleep on the couch, an empty bottle lying on the floor nearby, Sofia sprawled across his chest. A burping diaper clutched in her tiny fist covered the lower half of his face. His dark hair stood on end. She'd never seen him quite so unkempt as he'd been in the weeks since they'd brought the babies home from the hospital or the living room and kitchen so trashed.

She lifted Sofia off his chest, drew the throw over him, then carried the sleeping baby into the nursery and laid her in her crib.

"Shhh," she whispered to her auburn-haired daughter, who lay kicking, crying, and waving her arms as if to emphasize her displeasure. Undoubtedly at Nikki for being so inept and for leaving her nameless. "Shhhhh." She bent to pick her up. "I'm sorry. If you'd just stop crying, I know I could think more clearly." But who was she kidding? Before the girls had been born, naming the babies had seemed like tempting fate. When she'd finally agreed to name Sofia Gabriella after Joe's mother and grandmother, she'd promised herself that she'd come up with the perfect name for their other daughter. But between Nikki's fear and exhaustion and her daughter's near constant crying, nothing seemed to fit. When Joe brought it up, she'd told him it was her choice and not to rush her even though she'd all but given up trying. "I'm so sorry," she said again, remorse forming a pit in her stomach. "How could I leave you without a name for two whole weeks? Will you forgive me?" The baby's eyes blinked open, and one small hand reached upward. Her cries didn't cease, but they became less frantic. Nikki drew a deep breath, exhaled, and laid her gently, if tentatively, on the changing table.

"That's a good girl," she cooed. "That's my quiet girl." Commanding her hands to stop shaking, she undid the fastenings on the diaper, remembering Joe's chagrin when she'd noticed him putting Sofia's diaper on backward just that morning. "You don't seem wet." She dropped the used diaper in the pail and fastened on a new one with surprisingly little fumbling. Not totally sure what should happen next, she debated whether to feed her or attempt to put her back to sleep. "I wish you could tell me what you want. You know, instead of crying."

The baby's cries hiccuped to a stop. Nikki drew a deep, sweet breath of relief. "Okay," she said, her voice shaky. "This is good. We can do this."

The fog of exhaustion and fear began to dissipate as she stared down into her daughter's face, which was miraculously not red or scrunched up and which, she noticed, was dominated by eyes that were shaped just like the eyes of Nikki's mother, Grace. "Okay." She swallowed. "Let's feed you and then get you back to sleep." Nikki yawned and the baby did the same. The tears on her daughter's cheeks glittered like tiny jewels. Gently, she wiped those jewels away with the pad of her thumb. "Yes, you are a gem." She smiled down at her daughter. A smile flickered on her daughter's lips and Nikki's heart swelled with love. "I don't care if the books say that's just a reflex smile," she whispered, bringing her nose down to brush against her daughter's. "Are you Mommy's little gem?"

Nikki reached down and lifted the baby gently, not out of fear that she'd cry if she wasn't held "just right," but because she wanted to feel the weight of her in her arms. "Yes," she soothed, "you are my gem, my little . . ." She cradled her daughter in one arm, looked down into her face, and *knew*. "Gemma," she breathed. The eyes that were shaped like her mother's fluttered briefly as if in acknowledgment of the name. Nikki smiled and traced one finger lightly over her daughter's eyebrow. "What do you say, Gemma Grace? Are you hungry, Gemma Grace?" The more she said the name, the more she loved it. It tripped off her tongue as if it was always meant to be. She was grinning as she slid into bed, rearranged the pillows, and propped herself against them. With her free hand, she undid the cup of her nursing bra and guided Gemma's mouth toward her nipple. It took more than a few tries to get that mouth to open. In fact, she was about to give up and go warm a bottle—something Joe would have normally already done by now—when Gemma latched on and began to suck. Nikki felt her milk release and held her breath as Gemma began to nurse more and more greedily, her tiny fist pressing gently against the heavily veined skin of Nikki's breast.

For possibly the first time since the babies' birth, she did not dwell on the fact that her breasts resembled udders or feel alarmed by her role as a brood mare, but marveled at how perfectly her body had been designed to provide sustenance.

Gemma drank hungrily—and quietly—until she went limp and the tiny fist fell away. An almost overwhelming geyser of love welled up inside Nikki. "Let's give you a good burp, shall we?" she said as she laid a cloth diaper on her shoulder then gently positioned the baby on it. She'd barely begun rubbing the tiny back when the belch came. "Well done," she said. "Not exactly graceful, but very efficient."

Gemma slept quietly on Nikki's shoulder. She didn't open her eyes, or cry. Nikki yawned and so did Gemma, expelling a warm, milky sigh.

"Sleep tight, you little jewel, you," Nikki murmured softly as she repositioned herself on her back. "In the morning I'll introduce you to your father and your sister."

Then she laid the baby on her chest, skin to skin, one tiny perfectly formed ear pressed close to Nikki's heart.

Thirty-three

Kyra lifted Dustin out of the jogging stroller and parked it near the front steps of the bungalow that housed Franklin Realty.

Dustin's face broke into a smile when he saw Renée Franklin at the front desk. Without hesitation, he ran into her open arms and looked up into her face. "Cut-cakes, Neh Nay?"

"I may have one or two here somewhere," she teased. "Your dad's in the conference room, Kyra. We'll be back in the kitchen having a late morning snack if you need us."

Her father rose and gave her a hug. A collection of photos Kyra had taken of Bella Flora, her grounds, and her incomparable view were laid out on the table. "I know you shot the photos and video yourself to save money, but you did a great job," he said. "I bet you could make a living doing beauty shots of properties if you wanted."

"I actually kind of enjoyed it," she said. "And it was really great to shoot and edit without a smart-ass looking over my shoulder." She did not mention Troy Matthews by name, but her father had shared the pool house with the network cameraman long enough that she didn't need to.

"I was thinking we'd use these photos for a printed and down-loadable trifold brochure." He handed her a mock-up he'd done. "But I just want to be sure that you want to do this. I mean, letting a stranger live in Bella Flora? That's a big thing. And, of course, we'll all have to find somewhere else to live."

Her eyes narrowed. "Is that your biggest concern, Dad? That if I rent Bella Flora, you'll have to move out?"

He flushed with guilt and, she thought, shame. "I guess I deserve that. I have been living off your good graces for far longer than I should have. But no, I've booked a few rentals and I have a closing this week on a small condo at Isla del Sol. I just want to make sure you really want to do this. Because you do have another option. Even your mother thinks that Dustin acting in Daniel's movie would be okay."

"I don't like being forced," she said for what felt like the hundredth time. "Or feeling like I'm using Dustin to make up for my mistake." And then there was the question of whether she had the strength to spend six weeks on Daniel and Tonja's set.

"All right," he said. "I'll go ahead and get the listing posted. But you can always change your mind. And you don't have to accept the first potential tenant that expresses interest." He placed a hand on her arm as she rose. "I've rented a small two-bedroom house in Belle Vista so that Andrew can come stay with me any-time he wants. And there'll always be room for you and Dustin." He gave her a lopsided smile. "I hate seeing you in this position. I can't tell you how much I wish I'd never suggested that loan."

"It's not your fault, Dad. And I'm glad you're ready to be on your own." She only wished her own future were as clear.

She found Renée and Dustin in the kitchen, where Renée was wiping the last smears of chocolate icing off Dustin's smil-ing face.

"Come on, little man." She lifted her son into her arms. "Are you ready to rock and roll?"

"Rock and roll!" He did the fist pound that William Hightower had taught him then reached out to fist bump Renée.

At the beach access, she pushed the stroller through the soft sand. When she reached the harder-packed sand at the water's edge, she turned south and broke into a slow jog. She ran easily for a time, enjoying the warm salt breeze that slid over her. The cries of swooping gulls, the hum of boat engines offshore, and the wash of the tide blended into the perfect soundtrack. When her cell phone rang, she reluctantly pulled it from the stroller pocket. When she saw the name "Deranian," she declined the call and stuffed the phone back in the canvas pocket. Her breathing had just begun to even out when it rang again. "Jeez." With one hand on the stroller, she swiped the screen open with her thumb. "What?"

"No need to bite my head off." It was Tonja Kay. The voice was instantly recognizable even with the lack of four-letter words.

Kyra didn't speak. She could count the number of phone calls she'd received from Daniel's wife on one hand, and none of them had been pleasant.

"Are you still there?"

She had a somewhat childish urge to simply hang up and pretend she'd never answered. Or maybe she could use an accent that would convince Tonja Kay that she'd gotten a wrong number. She slowed to a walk, her thumb hovering over the "disconnect" button.

"If you hang up, I'll just call back, you know." She sounded almost like a normal person and not the crazy psycho witch she had generally proven herself to be.

"Fine. What do you want?"

"I want Dustin in *The Exchange*."

"Or?" Kyra waited for the tirade couched in obscenities that were in stark contrast to Tonja's angelic face.

"Or you'll be hurting Daniel and pretty much cutting off your nose to spite your face."

Kyra slowed to a stop then walked around the stroller. One-handed, she fumbled with the clasp on Dustin's seat belt, then helped him out of his seat. "So you're worried about me, my son, and my son's father?" Kyra asked, almost, but not quite, ashamed of rubbing Tonja's nose in Dustin's parentage. She'd been wrong to sleep with someone else's husband, not that she had been Daniel's first or final extramarital fling. She'd compounded that bad behavior by falling in love with him and somehow convincing herself that he loved her.

"No. I'm worried about Daniel. And the movie we're making." There was a silence and then a grudging, "There are people who want to sabotage the film and criticize his directing no matter how good a job he does. This film can't just be a credible first effort. It needs to be huge. And that means we need every scrap of prerelease publicity we can get. If you allow Dustin to do the film, rather than forcing Daniel to win that right in court, I promise he'll be treated as if he's one of our own."

She watched Dustin pull the string bag of sand toys from the stroller and empty them onto the sand. When he picked up his favorite shovel and started digging, Kyra walked a few steps away so that she could keep an eye on him without him overhearing.

"You already tried to make him one of your own, Tonja," Kyra said. She'd also gone ape shit crazy in front of the then-six-month-old Dustin. Which had ended any possibility of Dustin being with his father if his wife was around.

"We'll get him his own nanny," Tonja continued. "I'll personally make sure he's comfortable on set. Whatever you want him to have, he'll have."

"He won't be within a hundred miles of you without me there to protect him."

"Yes." The word was tight as if pushed through clenched

teeth. "That's why you've been offered two hundred and fifty thousand dollars to be on location with Dustin. In addition to the million Dustin receives."

Not coincidentally, the amount was almost exactly what she needed to pay off the loan she'd taken out on Bella Flora.

"I'll make certain you're well treated on set."

She imagined she heard the gnashing of Tonja's perfectly capped teeth at the concession. "And the press and paparazzi?" Kyra prompted.

"We need them. That's the whole point."

"I won't allow a feeding frenzy," Kyra said firmly. "That would be a deal breaker."

"Are you actually negotiating?" Tonja asked incredulously.

Kyra watched Dustin fill his favorite pail with water and sand.

"We can control their access and keep security tight," Tonja finally said. "In fact, that could work in our favor. The harder it is to get to someone, the more interesting their story becomes."

"Are you going to be able to live with our story being rehashed in the tabloids another thousand times?" Kyra asked. She herself was sick to death of reading about how she'd been nothing but a lowly production assistant who'd been thrown off her first—and as a result last—feature film for engaging in an affair with its star. The press—legitimate and tabloid—had had a field day when it became known that she was pregnant. The furor had only grown louder when she'd given birth to the star's first, and so far only, biological son.

"I've lived with it for the last four years," Tonja said. "I can certainly handle it long enough to get this film made."

Kyra stared out over the Gulf, where a windsurfer skimmed over the surface.

"I am an actress," Tonja said. "A good one. If I had to, I could convince my own parents that I don't think you're a star stalker who chased after my husband until you caught him."

The last line was delivered in the frighteningly sweet tone of a patient, if injured, wife. "The press and the public will believe whatever I want them to believe. Only you and I will know just how much I loathe you."

Kyra closed her eyes against the sugarcoated venom. "Tell me again why I should put my son or myself anywhere near you?"

Tonja laughed so sweetly that Kyra almost missed the startling truth that followed. "Because while Daniel may not be a perfect or faithful husband, he is a great father. And I can only imagine how Dustin will feel when he's old enough to understand that he might have done something important for his father only his mother wouldn't allow it."

...

Nikki sat across from Joe at the cottage dinette in a rare moment of quiet. Gemma and Sofia were sleeping in their car seats on the floor. All four of them were still wearing pajamas even though it was going on two P.M. The living area was a shambles. Fresh stacks of Pampers teetered on the coffee table within easy reach. Discarded baby clothing littered the couch. A section of the area rug had been turned into the designated changing area and was dribbled with stains that Nikki did not want to identify. Despite the Giraldi women's best efforts, the sink once again overflowed with dirty dishes and baby bottles.

Ray Flamingo had been close to tears when he saw what had become of the space he created. Even Sherlock had whimpered in dismay thirty minutes ago when Bitsy had stopped by to deliver pressed Cuban sandwiches. Maddie came and went with a cheerful smile and words of encouragement, but there was no question who was running things and it wasn't anyone over the age of three weeks.

"I liked it better when you were pretending to be Super Dad," Nikki said as she picked at the Cuban, her stomach too unsettled to actually eat it. "You know before I caught you sound asleep with your face in the Cheerios bowl."

"Well, at least I hadn't put milk in yet," Joe replied somewhat grimly. "My mother tells me it'll get easier."

Nikki looked at him doubtfully. "She probably only said that because she's afraid we won't let them leave town if she tells us the truth."

"Gemma's not screaming quite so much," Joe said, pitching his voice close to a whisper.

Nikki nodded. It was true that once Nikki had started doing more and feeling less fearful, the newly named Gemma Grace had taken it down a notch. But Nikki had discovered that even though the screaming had lessened, her headaches had not.

"And I'm extremely grateful that you were only teasing when you told me you'd decided to name her Crysalata." Joe took a spoonful of black beans and rice that made her stomach turn. "Even if that was only because there is no actual Italian name that means 'cries a lot.'"

"Well, I like that Gemma translates to 'jewel,' and I'm glad you liked my mother's name for her middle name," Nikki said. "Gemma Grace sounds so peaceful and elegant." Which was, of course, a bit of wishful thinking.

"I'm sorry I never got to meet your mother," Joe said quietly as they cleared the table and settled together on the couch, which was about as far as either of them could make it. Nikki leaned back against him and put her feet up on the coffee table. She narrowed her gaze. She'd barely been out of the cottage for weeks and spent very little time on her feet, but her ankles looked swollen and her toes—she attempted to focus more sharply—her toes looked like stuffed sausages. She lifted her head to try to catch a glimpse of her face in a nearby mirror. Her hair hung limp around her shoulders. She couldn't remember the last time she'd taken a shower. "Do my cheeks look big to you?"

Joe's dark hair stood on end. He scrubbed a hand over his stubbled cheeks and looked at her more closely. "Maybe a little. But you're always beautiful to me."

She looked in the mirror again. She resembled a squirrel with a mouth full of acorns. She scooted back and felt the pain beneath her ribs again. She had no idea how long it was supposed to take to get back to normal. Or if she ever would. "We look like shit," she observed.

"We do," Joe agreed.

"When do you have to go back to work?"

"Not yet. That's why I was gone so long before the babies were born—so I could take a full month. You know, to enjoy every minute of my paternity leave."

Nikki snorted, but she did it quietly. She had learned the importance of letting sleeping babies sleep.

"They are incredible," Joe said. "But I've never worked this hard in my life."

"I know," Nikki said. "I'm so ashamed of myself for thinking stay-at-home mothers weren't actually working." She shifted and felt the pain again. Bile rose in her throat. Her vision blurred. She turned to look at Joe's face, but his features had gone soft and somehow out of position. She could tell that he was speaking, but the pounding in her ears made it difficult to make out the words.

"You do know that . . . love . . . right? And that I want . . ."

She blinked rapidly in an attempt to bring him back into focus. Light streaming through the blinds sliced like shards of glass and then began to strobe.

"I . . ." She used his body to lever upright. "I have to . . ." She swallowed and began to move toward the bathroom, desperate to get there before she threw up.

"Nik? What's wrong?" His voice was low but urgent. "What's happened?"

She wiped her mouth and splashed water on her face, which looked overlarge and distorted in the bathroom mirror. She blinked in fear, trying to see more clearly.

Joe came into the bathroom and put his arms around her, turning her. "Nikki? Can you hear me? What's the . . ."

His face wavered in and out in an amoeba-like blur, the words coming at her in slow motion, and still she couldn't make sense of them. She reached for him blindly, clinging with her last bit of energy as everything went dark.

Thirty-four

"I think hospital waiting rooms need to be redesigned so that there's more room for pacing," Avery said, threading past Maddie, Kyra, and Bitsy as they awaited word on Nikki.

"Sounds interesting." Maddie sat in a molded plastic chair, which could also use some redesigning, and watched Avery pace. They'd been there for over two hours and Joe had not yet emerged from ICU. Had it only been three weeks ago that they'd sat in this same hospital anticipating the twins' birth?

"Well, I hate hospitals," Kyra said. "They always make me think about Max," she said, referring to Max Golden, whose South Beach home they had renovated and who had thrown himself in front of a bullet to save Dustin. They'd been at the hospital with him when he'd died. But Max Golden had been ninety.

Avery stopped and dropped heavily into a chair. From the look on her face, Maddie guessed she was thinking about her mother, who had been felled by an aneurysm on Mermaid Point and never made it to the hospital at all.

"While you're at it, maybe you should get Ray in here to do something about all these green walls," Bitsy said. "Green is not a healing color, unless you're a plant."

They were all desperately trying to keep things light, but their eyes kept straining to the ICU entrance.

"Sure, then we can call one of the networks and pitch a new makeover show called *Doctor Décor* or *Emergency Rehab*," Kyra said.

"Nikki has to be okay, doesn't she?" Avery asked Maddie. "I mean, I don't understand what could have happened."

Maddie automatically turned to reassure Avery, but the words didn't come. Because the longer they sat with no word, the less okay things seemed. Her usual calm deserted her. For the first time she realized that she was worn out, tired of everyone looking to her for reassurance when she never seemed to be able to ask for it herself. At the moment she could use someone telling her that everything would be okay.

Bitsy left and returned with coffees and candy bars. Bathroom runs followed. Unable to sit a moment longer, Maddie stood and fled the waiting room, pulling her phone out of her purse as she went. Before she could think it through, she had hit speed dial.

William picked up on the second ring. "Maddie?"

The sound of his voice brought tears to her eyes. She couldn't seem to find her own voice to answer.

"Are you all right?" Concern for her rang in every word.

She tried to blink back the tears so that she could respond, but emotion clogged her throat even as relief that he'd answered and was just at the end of the line washed over her. She sagged against the hallway wall.

"Tell me what's wrong."

In a tear-choked voice, she told him what had happened and where they were.

"Everything will be all right," he said gently. "Joe's with her and the fact that it's taking time doesn't mean the news will be bad. He's probably just waiting until he has something solid to share."

She held the phone against her ear and moved to stand just outside the waiting room, as Will's soothing words washed over her.

"Tell me what I can do," he said. "I can get there if—"

"Oh, God, there's Joe," she said, cutting Will off. "I'll . . . Can I call you back?"

Pocketing her phone, Maddie hurried into the waiting room. Joe's dark eyes were sunken; exhaustion was written on his face. One large hand ran through his unkempt dark hair then kneaded what must have been a crick in his neck.

"Is Nikki okay?" Maddie asked in a rush.

"She will be. But if we hadn't gotten here when we did . . ." Joe's voice trailed off. He shook his head as if still trying to come to terms with reality.

"What happened? What does she have?" Kyra asked.

"She has postpartum preeclampsia." He swallowed. "If we hadn't gotten here when we did, she could have started having seizures or even a stroke."

"But her pressure stayed down once she was put on bed rest and she was fine when she was released," Maddie said in surprise.

Joe nodded. "It's apparently rare—the doctor said only about five percent of women get it postpartum. But it can happen up to six weeks after giving birth. And the symptoms can be missed because a lot of them are typical in a woman who's gone through childbirth." He dropped down into a vacant chair and expelled a harsh breath of air. "Jesus. She was completely blind for almost two hours. She could have died."

Maddie watched his face as he fought to regain control.

"What happens now?" Bitsy asked.

"They've started her on blood pressure medication and an anticonvulsive to help prevent seizures." He grimaced at the word. "She'll spend tonight in ICU then move to a regular room in the morning. They want to keep her for a few days to make sure there are no complications."

"Do you want to go back to the cottage and get cleaned up? Or maybe go have a bite?" Maddie asked.

He shook his head. "She's allowed to nurse and I think she needs . . . My parents are going to bring the girls. My mother's bringing me a change of clothes."

"We're going to head back then," Avery said. She, Kyra, and Bitsy hugged Joe. "But let us know if you or Nikki or the girls need anything."

"Thanks."

"Mom?" Kyra asked.

"I'm taking Joe down to the cafeteria for a drink and something to eat."

"No, I want to . . ." Joe began.

"I know," Maddie said, getting to her feet. "But you'll be here in the building if Nikki needs you. You need some nourishment." And the kind of comfort Will had just offered her. "You can come right back up."

In the end he followed her like Dustin might have and made no comment when she filled a tray and carried it to a small table near a window.

"I could have lost her," he said. "Forever." He swallowed and looked away. As she placed a sandwich and soft drink in front of him, she had to resist the urge to pull him into her arms and comfort him as she would have comforted Dustin.

"I've lost people I've cared about in the field," he said softly. "It's part of the job. But I was not prepared for this."

"I know," Maddie said. "It's shocking how things can change

in a heartbeat." As she'd discovered when Steve had lost everything including his job and his self-esteem in Malcolm Dyer's Ponzi scheme. When Deirdre had died between one breath and the next. Bitsy had lost her husband and her fortune in one day. "It's easy to forget when the days are full and rushing by, but there are no guarantees. And it's better not to put things off because we never really know what might happen next." She reminded herself to heed her own advice as she gave Joe her most compelling "I know what I'm talking about because I'm a mother" look. "So, if there's anything you've been meaning to take care of, Joe, there's absolutely no time like the present."

. . .

The one-bedroom, one-bath cottage Avery stood in was almost too small to pace. At 450 square feet, it was at the middle end of the tiny house spectrum. Empty as it was, with only walls, windows, and doors, it was a blank slate with almost unlimited possibilities. She liked its location at the northeast edge of the Sunshine Hotel property, bounded on two sides by a wall of interlaced hedges and trees that muffled the sounds from the street and offered the illusion of privacy. It was hers, in exchange for the money she'd invested in the Sunshine Hotel, if she wanted it.

She taped photos and magazine pages to the walls. Then she took her time measuring each room carefully, sketching her ideas on a pad as she envisioned the space, enjoying the challenge of making the most of every inch. Once the central air was installed, she could move in and live here while she finished out the space. For Bitsy's cottage, a big part of the goal had been finding room for her possessions. But Avery had perched first at Bella Flora and then on locations for *Do Over*. When she'd moved into Chase's after Deirdre's death, she'd had little more than her clothes and her father's tool belt.

She paused, waiting for the pain that always accompanied thoughts of her parents. But her father hadn't chosen to leave her and neither had Deirdre—at least not the second time. Nikki's rush to the hospital and the frantic efforts to save her were one more reminder of how unexpectedly life could change. Or end.

Chase had intentionally pushed her away. She would be a fool to waste whatever time she had left waiting for him to come to his senses and see her worth. It was time to have a home of her own, no matter how small, and a life, which could be as large as she was able to make it.

There was a knock on the open door and Ray Flamingo stepped inside. He looked fresh in his melon-colored linen shirt and billowy white pants. She knew from experience that he would look just as good when August arrived and the rest of them wilted. He looked at her sketchpad then turned slowly to take in the space.

"I'm going to build in here and create extra storage there," she said, gesturing. "I want to keep it clean lined and simple. In fact, I'm thinking of just finishing the concrete floors instead of covering them."

"I love it," Ray said. "And maybe a few bright jute rugs and bamboo shades. This place is perfect for you. You are asking me to help, right?"

"I'm counting on it," she said.

"Good. Because I need your help with something right now," Ray said with a quick, if vague, smile. "Bitsy and Maddie are up at the main building. Can you come powwow with us?"

Her nod was automatic.

"Come along then," he said with a wink and an exaggerated sway of his lean hips. "*Walk* this way."

Avery smiled at the old joke and fell in line behind him knowing that she'd never manage to walk anywhere near as gracefully as the sandy-haired linen-clad man in front of her.

...

Nikki was more than ready to leave the hospital three days later, and she didn't really care what she was wearing when she left. Or so she thought until she opened the hanging bag Joe had brought and pulled out the vintage Emilio Pucci slip dress inside. She held the sleeveless V-backed 1960s-era maxi to her chest. With wide straps, an empire waist, and abstract stripes in turquoise, blue, green, and white, it had been one of her very favorite pieces of clothing. Right up until the moment she'd been forced to sell it after her felonious brother had bankrupted her.

"Where did you find this?" she asked, running a hand over the silky fabric.

"Bitsy sent it."

"Bitsy?"

Joe smiled. "Yes, she said she'd been holding on to it for you." He reached into the bag and pulled out an adorable pair of turquoise flip-flops with sparkling stars and seahorses that dangled from the toe strap. "These are from Maddie."

"Here, can you help me slip on the dress?" She pulled off the hospital gown and raised her arms. The lightweight nylon slid down over her body like a caress. It had no zipper or closure and easily adjusted to her fuller shape. "God, I always loved this dress," she said, turning to face Joe.

His eyes darkened as he looked at her. She followed his gaze down to her swelling breasts. "Is it too low cut?" She had definitely not been a nursing mother the last time she'd worn this dress.

"Absolutely not." He leaned down and kissed her, was still kissing her when the nurse arrived with the wheelchair. "It's perfect."

She drowsed a bit on the drive home and awoke several times to feel Joe's eyes on her face. As they waited at a stoplight, she touched her cheek with the tips of her fingers. "Is my face still swollen?" She had been amazed how large her face had actually gotten, almost like a balloon that someone had blown too much air into. Thank God she hadn't burst.

"The swelling's gone down. And the doctor said your blood pressure's under control," Joe replied. "But are you sure you're okay?"

"I still feel like I was run over by a freight train, but whoever was playing Ping-Pong in my head has stopped and that pain under my ribs—the one the doctor said was my liver—is gone." She smiled up at him. "And I will be eternally grateful that my vision is back." She swallowed as she remembered the terror of being blind. "Those two hours when I couldn't see at all? That was the most frightening thing I've ever experienced."

Joe nodded. "You shaved a whole lot of years off my life, Nik. And you forced me to face what I now know is *my* biggest fear."

"You? Afraid?" she asked, surprised. "Of what?"

"Of even the idea of having to live without you." He spoke softly, his voice thick with emotion.

"Oh." She felt a rush of love and wonder.

The light changed and he turned his eyes to the road. As the car accelerated, she cocked her head and shot him a teasing smile, trying to lighten the mood. "You're not just saying that because you're afraid of being left alone to change Sofia and Gemma's diapers?"

Joe laughed. "Well, there is that. But no." He had to keep his eyes on the road, but his free hand grasped hers. "I love you, Nikki." He squeezed her hand and lifted it to his lips. "I love you totally and completely."

He looked as if he was about to say more, and happiness flooded through her. She waited, barely breathing, for what she imagined would come next. When he remained silent, she turned her gaze out the window and attempted to banish her disappointment. She didn't need a piece of paper, or a ring, or a formal promise of forever. It was a beautiful March afternoon. She was healthy and going home with a man who loved her. Home to their children and to whatever life they would carve out together. It was time to appreciate what she had and not dwell on what she might have had if only she'd said yes when she'd had the chance.

On the Bayway, she lowered her window so that she could breathe in the sweet scent of blooming gardenias that hung on the breeze. When they reached the cottage, Joe's parents had just finished feeding the girls.

"Do you feel up to going out to the pool?" Joe asked. "I'm pretty sure there's a chaise out there with your name on it."

"Sounds heavenly," she said, meaning it.

"You two go ahead," Gabriella said. "Maybe we'll bring the girls out in a little bit."

The cottage grounds seemed deserted, but as they followed the concrete pathway toward the pool, Nikki heard guitar music, the clink of glasses, and the murmur of voices. At the main building she noticed that the double doors had been thrown open. Cloth-covered tables dotted the area under the overhang. Waiters arranged trays of food on top of them. A bar had been set up at the edge of the pool deck. Beyond it, on the beach, a brightly colored strip of silk was held aloft by four poles anchored in the sand. Several rows of chairs had been set up in a horseshoe facing the tented space. The chairs were filled with people who seemed to be staring out at the blue sky and sparkling water that lay ahead.

"Oh," she said as she realized what she was watching. The Sunshine Hotel and Beach Club, with its long stretch of white sand beach and stellar sunset view, had proven a popular wedding venue. "Maybe we shouldn't intrude," she said as she turned away, unable to watch a moment longer. She tried to keep any sign of regret or envy off her face, but even she could hear the wistfulness in her voice when she said, "I wonder whose wedding it is?"

Joe took her hand and gently turned her back around. His face was wreathed in smiles. "Unless we got our signals crossed, I'm pretty sure it's ours."

Thirty-five

Joe took her arm and led her toward the beach. William Hightower stepped out of the shadow of the overhang and began to
play the opening notes of his mega-hit "Mermaid in You" on his
guitar. As they drew closer to the low wall that separated the
pool area from the beach, the guests—their guests—stood and
turned. Maddie, Kyra, and Steve Singer were in the front row
with Dustin. Avery and Bitsy and Ray Flamingo stood on the
opposite side of the aisle. Jeff and Chase Hardin had taken seats
toward the back. John and Renée Franklin sat with her sister
Annelise. Nonna Sofia was at her side.

"Ready?" Joe asked.

"Not so fast."

Surprise lit his eyes. Which was fine with Nikki.

"I think you may have skipped something."

"Is that right? And what might that be?"

"The part where you actually ask me if I'll marry you. Pref-
erably while on one knee and looking up adoringly."

"I did that before and you said no. It seemed another plan of action was necessary," he said. "And after coming so close to losing you, I wouldn't take no for an answer anyway. So . . ." He took a step. She didn't follow.

"That's not how it works. You ask. I answer. You're not allowed to skip the question."

"I hope I'm not going to need backup. I didn't bring my firearm." A smile flickered on his lips. "Although Nonna Sofia might be packing." He raised one arm as if to summon her.

She took his arm and gently lowered it. "We have two daughters now. And I refuse to have to tell them that their father never really gave me a choice. What kind of example would we be setting?"

"Nikki . . ."

"You need to ask me. For the record. And posterity and all that."

"You're serious."

Before she'd finished nodding, he dropped to one knee. There was a wince as it hit the concrete pool deck and he reached for her hand. Will Hightower stopped singing, but continued to play his guitar, picking out the melody that would serve as background for what was to come.

"Thanks, Will." Nikki nodded down at Joe. "You may proceed."

She sensed their guests crowding toward the low wall, and she thought she heard the whir of a motor drive, but Joe looked up into her eyes and spoke softly, as if they were alone. "I love you, Nicole. And I can't think of anything I want more than to marry you and spend the rest of our lives together." Love shone in his dark eyes. "Will you do me the honor of becoming my wife?"

Tears filled her eyes and she imagined she could feel her heart filling with happiness. The kind of happiness she'd never thought would be hers. She nodded.

The dark eyes twinkled. "I'm sorry, I didn't hear an answer. What did you say?"

"Yes," she whispered. "Yes."

He cocked his head and put his free hand up to one ear. "I'm having trouble hearing you. And I just want to be sure I'm not misunderstanding. You know, for posterity. In case the girls ask."

"Yes!" She knew she was smiling like a crazy woman. "Yes, I'll marry you!"

"Good." He smiled up at her as her eyes filled with tears. "Can I get up now?"

She nodded, not even trying to check the tears that slipped down her cheeks.

"Let me rephrase that," Joe said. "Will you help me up?"

She helped tug him to his feet and laughed with joy as he threw his arms around her and twirled her around. "She finally said yes!" he called out.

There were cheers from the beach.

"Never doubted it for a minute!" Ray Flamingo called back. "Let's get this show on the road. Some of us are in serious need of food and drink!"

Joe's parents stepped up on either side of them, each with one of the girls, dressed in frilly white dresses with tiny matching hair bows, in their arms. Gabriella kissed Nikki on the cheek. "I'm very glad you're going to be a part of our family, Nicole. And very grateful for these gorgeous granddaughters."

Joe Senior, who held Sofia, shot Nikki a wink and threw his arm around Joe's shoulders. "Well done, son," he said in a teasing tone and a twinkle in his dark eyes. "I was starting to worry about your powers of persuasion."

"You're not the only one," Joe said, lacing his hand through Nikki's. "I think we better go ahead and make it official before she has a chance to reconsider."

"Ha! There's no going back now." Nikki's smile grew wider

and the tears slid faster as they made their way up the sandy aisle to the justice of the peace who waited for them. There, surrounded by family and friends, they looked into each other's eyes and repeated their vows as the sun painted the sky in brilliant strokes of red and gold then disappeared beneath the still surface of the water.

• • •

Maddie stood in the shelter of Will's arm, her eyes on Nikki's face. "I've never seen her so happy. I guess sometimes it takes almost losing someone to face up to how much they mean to you," she said.

"Sometimes it just takes being on the road," Will said. "There's a reason musicians and performers end up addicted and doing things they never thought they would. It's lonely out there and it's not even close to real life. Numbing up can seem the only way to survive."

Her eyes sought his. "Are you okay?"

"I'm hanging in there," he said. "I'm too grateful for the opportunity to perform in front of people who care about my music again to screw it up. But I won't lie. It's hard work pretty much every day. And the nights, well, I'm glad there's only a few weeks left on the tour."

"It's great that you were able to take the weekend off."

An odd look passed across his face. "I miss you, Maddie, and after your call from the hospital, I needed to see for myself that you were all right." He tightened his arms around her. "I know you're pulled in a lot of directions right now, but I'm headed home after the concert in Los Angeles. Can you get away and spend some time with me at Mermaid Point? I keep hearing this melody in my head and I need to see where it goes. Plus, I'm dying to sleep in my own bed and to get out on the flats. I heard from Hud yesterday." His eyes crinkled in amusement. "He says the fish have been asking about you."

"Yeah, they're probably looking for some entertainment."

He grinned. "You do have a unique fly casting style all your own."

She felt almost giddy as he pulled her closer. Steve was moving out next week. Kyra seemed to have reached some decisions though she hadn't yet shared them. And Nikki was settling into motherhood, plus Avery and Bitsy would be living in cottages just yards away. Her cell phone vibrated in her dress pocket.

"Don't answer it," he said, his lips hovering over hers.

But Andrew wasn't there and a mother always worried that the one call she didn't answer would be the one that she'd regret. Still in Will's embrace, she looked down at the screen. "It's Lori Blair."

"Definitely don't answer it, then." He moved to hit the decline, but she'd already answered.

"Maddie!" The young woman's frantic voice reached their ears. "Thank God! I need your help. Will has gone AWOL. As in he's missing. Not on the plane! Not even in the airport!"

Maddie looked up into Will's eyes. They didn't look the least bit worried or apologetic.

"He's supposed to do an interview tomorrow afternoon in Houston. And he has a concert there the next day." The panic in Will's assistant's voice was real.

William put his finger to his lips, shook his head gently, and whispered. "I'm doing the interview tomorrow by phone. I'll be in Houston in plenty of time for the concert. I'll text her and let her know a little later." He placed a kiss on her forehead, another on the tip of her nose. "Right after I make love to you."

Maddie held the phone with a shaky hand. "I'm sorry, Lori. I, um, haven't seen him."

"But I don't know where he is! I'm pretty sure I could get fired if Aaron finds out I lost him!"

Will's lips brushed down her neck to the sensitive spot just above her collarbone as his hands cupped her buttocks.

"If I hear from him, I'll let you know," she said weakly. She ended the call as Will pulled her into an unlit corner and covered her mouth with his.

• • •

Avery had spent the last twenty-five minutes looking busy and trying not to meet Chase's eyes. She'd hugged Jeff while Chase was congratulating Nikki and Joe, fetched drinks for all three of the older Giraldis, then initiated a lengthy conversation with Ray about absolutely nothing until Ray finally leaned over and told her to get a grip before waving to Chase and inviting him over. As soon as he'd shaken Chase's hand and told her under his breath that it was time to "put on her big girl panties," Ray had excused himself, leaving her exactly where she'd tried so hard not to be.

Now she looked directly into Chase's eyes, which were far bluer than she'd remembered, and reminded herself that nothing had changed. She was preparing to leave when he said, "Jason's doing really well. He sent Josh this picture of him during a rock climb." He held up his phone so that she could see Jason grinning down from what looked like a surprisingly steep rock face.

"That's great," she said, meaning it even as she tried to steel herself against the warm blue eyes and the familiar scent of his cologne. She was not going to throw her arms around him because he'd offered a scrap of information. Chase put the phone in his breast pocket and said nothing. He seemed to be either memorizing her features or debating his next move.

"Well, nice seeing you." She turned.

His arm shot out before she could take a step away. He turned her back to face him, dropped his hand. "I . . . you never set an actual time limit. So I . . . I'm hoping I'm not too late."

She blinked in surprise.

"Do you still love me, Avery?" he asked, watching her.

She didn't speak. She would not make it easy for him. It was his turn to dangle up on the high wire. To declare himself without the safety net of knowing how she felt.

"Because I've been a moron." He said this almost conversationally.

Avery remained mute, not at all tempted to argue with his assessment of his behavior.

"I love you. And I want you to be a part of my life, of our lives. Will you move back and give it another try?"

The words he said were the ones she'd hoped to hear. For a moment, relief coursed through her. But as she studied his face, she couldn't help wondering—had those words come from his heart? Or had he said them only because she'd demanded them? What if she moved back in, and when Jason came home and things weren't perfect, as was likely the case, Chase pushed her away again? How would she survive that?

He must have seen her answer in her eyes even before she'd processed it. "It's no, isn't it? I'm too late."

"I love you, Chase. That part hasn't changed. I'm good with us spending time together. But I think we need to wait and see how everything feels when Jason comes home. I can't be in a relationship where I'm kept at arm's length. I want to be sure that I fit into your life in a way that works for all of us."

"But . . ." He reached for her hand. She didn't pull away, but for all that she hadn't known her own mind when the conversation began, she knew it now.

"I'm taking a cottage in lieu of payment. I'm going to finish it out and live here while I explore the idea of designing and building tiny houses. I'm thirty-seven-and-a-half years old and

I think it's about time I figure out exactly who I am and what I want to be when I grow up."

• • •

Nikki had slipped back to the cottage to feed the twins and managed to express enough milk for the three A.M. feedings, which Joe's parents would be handling. The Giraldis were spending the night at the cottage with the babies—so that Nikki and Joe could have the night to themselves. Sofia was already fast asleep in her crib. Gemma lay in Nikki's arms sucking quietly, one small hand curled just beneath Nikki's chin. As she lifted her to her shoulder and began to rub the small back, her wedding ring shone in the lamplight. Somehow the day that had begun in the hospital had turned into her wedding day and was about to end in the Don CeSar Hotel honeymoon suite. Because Joe was now her husband. She lifted her left hand to steal another look at the ring he had slid on her finger, and she sighed with happiness.

She laid Gemma in her crib and stood for a long moment watching the girls' small chests rise and fall, their rosebud mouths pursed in sleep.

Joe stepped up behind her and she leaned back into him. "It's almost frightening how much the three of you mean to me," he whispered, wrapping his arms around her and resting his chin on the top of her head.

"I never knew it was possible to love this deeply," she said as his arms tightened protectively. "It's, I don't know, the only word I can think of is bottomless."

"Yes." He turned her to face him. "I think that's the perfect word. I've never felt this way before, either." He kissed her and she melted into his arms, savoring his kiss and his love.

They exited the cottage to a shower of rose petals. With Joe's arm wrapped firmly around her, they hugged their way through the group and into the Jag, which had been decorated with a tail of tin cans and ribbon. Joe put the car into gear and tapped the horn in a final good-bye.

"It was so sweet of your parents to give us a night in the honeymoon suite," Nikki said with a huge yawn. "But I can barely keep my eyes open." She yawned again as the day and those before it caught up with her. Her eyelids grew heavy. "I feel like we're going to be wasting it."

"Are you kidding?" Joe asked with a yawn of his own. "Right now a whole night of uninterrupted sleep feels like a pot of gold at the end of the rainbow. Especially since I'm going to be sleeping with my *wife*."

She smiled at the word, and the relish with which he pronounced it even as her eyes fluttered shut. "I just hope I can stay awake until we get there."

Those were the last words she spoke. Joe's smile was the last thing she saw. Even though it was only a block away, she missed their arrival at the hotel's grand entrance and the expression on the face of the valet who opened the car door so that Joe could lift her into his arms. She also missed the smiles that accompanied their progress through the formal lobby, the guest on the elevator who shot Joe a wink as he pressed their floor number for them, and the bellman who opened the suite door and left without waiting for a tip as Joe carried her to the king-size bed.

She was sound asleep and snoring lightly by the time Joe managed to pull the vintage Emilio Pucci up over her head, shuck his own clothes, and slip into bed beside her. There he pulled her tight against him, closed his eyes, and promptly went to sleep.

Epilogue

Two weeks later, Bella Flora hunkered protectively around Maddie, Kyra, Avery, Bitsy, and Nikki as they gathered on the loggia to toast one another and the sunset. Although she couldn't drink them, Nikki had blended two pitchers of strawberry margaritas then made a half pitcher that was alcohol free. Bagel bites, Ted Peters smoked fish spread with crackers, and an industrial-size bag of Cheez Doodles sat on the wrought iron table. Avery had brought a small plate of pâté and crostini in memory of Deirdre, who had never met an expensive gourmet food she didn't like.

The sun still hung in the pale blue spring sky and shone through the wisps of white clouds that floated above the turquoise waters of the Gulf.

Maddie studied the women who'd come to mean so much to her and thought of all that they'd been through together, how many things had changed. Steve had actually moved out as promised and was currently babysitting his grandson in the small house that he'd rented. Nikki was now a wife and mother. All of them stood on the precipice of change. "Does anyone have a good thing to share?"

Bitsy raised her margarita. Sherlock, who had stretched out across her feet, raised his head. "I have a job," she announced. "My very first. The Franklins have hired me to help manage the Sunshine and coordinate parties and events for the beach club members." She smiled broadly. "I think it'll be a blast. It'll also fund my search for Bertie. My goal is to put him behind bars—and recover everything I possibly can."

"To gainful employment!" Nikki held her drink aloft. "And revenge!"

"I'll drink to that," Avery said as they clinked glasses and took long sips of the blended drinks. "As a soon-to-be resident of a Sunshine cottage, I'm glad you'll be running things, Bitsy. When I finish my unit, I'm going to design and build tiny homes. I think they're going to be the next big thing," she quipped. "And I like that they're efficient and compact. Just like me." She made no mention of Chase, and Maddie didn't press her as they tipped their glasses and drank under the pinkening sky.

Without planning it, Maddie's gaze moved to her daughter, who had spent the last weeks in a beehive of unexplained activity. "Kyra?" she asked now. "Anything you'd like to share?"

For a moment Maddie thought she was going to pass, but Kyra sat up and said, "So—good thing/bad thing. Someone's interested in renting Bella Flora."

A silence fell as they all imagined a stranger sitting where they were sitting, sleeping in what they'd come to think of as "their" beds. Maddie felt an odd kinship with the three bears. "Who is it?"

Kyra shook her head. "I don't know. John Franklin said the potential tenant is insisting on anonymity, but is willing to pay the majority of the rental fee up front."

"That's so weird," Avery said. "Kind of like when Daniel bought Bella Flora."

"Yeah." Kyra's eyes narrowed. "I'll have to think about it. But renting out Bella Flora for the right price will catch me up on the loan payments I wasn't able to make and give me breathing room. It'll also allow me to decide whether Dustin and I should do Daniel's film without it being about the money."

"But where will you live while Bella Flora is rented?" Nikki asked, eyeing the real margaritas with longing.

"Dustin and I could stay with Dad for a while. Or we could maybe take a two-bedroom at the Sunshine with Mom. If she wanted to." She looked at Maddie and smiled. "If we moved back into Bella Flora after the tenant leaves, we could rent out the cottage. Or Mom could keep it. We'd have options."

"And *Do Over*?" Maddie asked, remembering the night they'd sat in this very spot and believed the show would be their salvation.

"Legally, we're never going to get the chance to turn it into what we envisioned," Avery said. "I think it's time to let go."

"Yeah," Kyra said. "There's really no point. That boat has sailed."

"But what will you do?" Maddie asked her daughter.

"I loved making the documentary about the Sunshine Hotel. And there's been a great response to the video segments I've been streaming. I think I'd like to make documentaries about strong, impressive women. The kind that rise to the occasion and do what needs to be done. Like my mother," she said. "And the rest of you." Kyra raised her glass. "Every one of you inspires me."

They toasted themselves, the sun, which had grown brighter as it slid toward the water's surface, and one another.

"God, I'd give anything for a margarita with actual alcohol in it," Nikki said.

"Is there a good thing in there somewhere?" Avery asked.

"No," Nikki said. "But my whole life feels like such a good thing that I'm almost afraid to believe it. And I never would have had Joe or Sofia and Gemma or any of the incredible things in my life if it weren't for Bella Flora and all of you and even Malcolm. If he hadn't bankrupted everyone, I never would have met you." Tears spilled from her eyes and dampened her cheeks. "Oh, God. I'm sorry." She fanned her face as if that might somehow dry up or stop her tears. "It's these post-pregnancy hormones and lack of sleep," she sobbed. "The last full night's sleep I had was my wedding night."

"That sounds so wrong for so many reasons." Avery refilled her glass and topped off the others.

"Yesterday, I cried all the way through *The Parent Trap*, you know the remake with Lindsey Lohan. And then I cried all over again when the original one with Hayley Mills came on." Nikki smiled crookedly through the tears that continued to fall. "Joe threatened to cancel Turner Classic Movies."

"Jeez." Avery refilled everyone's glasses. "Remind me not to ever get pregnant." She sighed. "Though I guess I'd have to actually sleep with someone for that to happen."

Nikki cried harder. "Please don't use the word 'sleep' around me."

"How about you, Maddie?" Bitsy asked, lifting Sherlock onto her lap and scratching him gently behind the ear. "Do you have any plans?"

"I do," Maddie said with a far larger smile than she'd intended. "I'm going to spend a few weeks with Will on Mermaid Point."

"Well, at least someone will be having sex," Avery said.

"Some of us will have to live vicariously through her," Bitsy added.

Nikki sighed. "Some of us will be nursing babies and trying to remember when we used to have the energy to have sex."

Maddie laughed. "I'm pretty sure you'll have sex again someday, Nikki."

"Do you really think so?" she asked as if Maddie had just said she might one day live on the moon.

"I do," Maddie replied. "And while I'm down there, I'm going to think about what I want to do next." She looked at the women who had become such an integral part of her life. "These last years have been about survival, but I believe the future can be whatever we decide to make of it. Kyra's right, we can be strong and even impressive on our own. Together we're pretty close to invincible."

"Great," Nikki groaned. "You're making me cry again."

"Sorry," Maddie said, but she wasn't. In fact, she could feel her lips twisting into a grin.

"To friendship!" Bitsy drained her glass and slammed it on the table.

"To Bella Flora!" Kyra did the same.

"To us!" Nikki said through her tears.

Maddie raised her glass and blinked back tears of her own. "To always being able to come up with at least one good thing."

ONE GOOD THING

WENDY WAX

Discussion Questions

1. When the book opens, Bitsy Baynard is dealing with the fact that her husband stole all of her money and ran away with another woman. Do you think Bitsy should have made Bertrand sign a prenup? Do you believe in prenups?

2. Bitsy and Bertrand were initially introduced by Nicole Grant of Heart Inc., who worked as a matchmaker. Do you think matchmakers can be a successful way to find love? Would you ever hire a matchmaker?

3. William Hightower could have any woman he wants. Why do you think he is attracted to Madeline Singer? Will asks Maddie to go on tour with him, and Maddie is reluctant to do so. Do you understand her reluctance? Why do you think women often have such a hard time putting their needs first?

4. Nicole is terrified that Joe is going to change his mind and leave her and the babies. She doesn't believe she can have a happy family of her own. Why do you think Nikki feels this

way? Have you ever been in a situation where you knew your fear wasn't warranted, but you were terrified anyway? How did you handle it?

5. Avery Lawford is an architect and licensed contractor who finds the aromas surrounding construction relaxing. She attributes this to spending time on her father's construction sites as a child. What is your stress buster? When and how did you discover it?

6. Chase and his son Jason are at odds for most of the book, and Avery finds herself caught between them. Do you think she handles the situation well? How do you feel about Chase's behavior? Why is he so tough on Avery?

7. What do you think Bella Flora symbolizes for Maddie, Nicole, Avery, and Kyra? Is there a family home or a place like Mermaid Point that holds particular significance for you? Why? Would you risk losing it for the chance to achieve a lifelong dream or goal?

8. Kyra has to decide whether or not to let her son, Dustin, star in a move with his father. What do you think she should do? Would you let your child star in a movie? Is that kind of pressure and attention good or bad for a child?

9. What do you think of the tiny house movement? Would you want to live in a tiny house? How many square feet would you need to feel comfortable?

10. At the end of each day, Maddie, Nicole, Avery, and Kyra share one good thing to toast to at sunset. What—or who—is your one good thing today? Wendy Wax would love to know, so feel free to record it on your camera phone and share it on Wendy's website at authorwendywax.com.

Photo by Beth Kelly

Wendy Wax, a former broadcaster, is the author of thirteen novels, including *Sunshine Beach*, *A Week at the Lake*, *While We Were Watching Downton Abbey*, *The House on Mermaid Point*, *Ocean Beach*, and *Ten Beach Road*. The mother of two grown sons, she lives in Atlanta with her husband and is doing her best to adjust to the quiet of her recently emptied nest.

Visit her online at authorwendywax.com and on Facebook at facebook.com/AuthorWendyWax, and follow her on Twitter @Wendy_Wax.